Zygmunt Miłoszewski, born in Warsaw in 1976, is a journalist and a rising star of Polish fiction. His first novel, *The Intercom*, was published in 2005 to high acclaim. In 2006 he published a novel for young readers, *The Adder Mountains*, and in 2007 the crime novel *Entanglement*. The author is working on screenplays based on *The Intercom* and *Entanglement* and is writing a sequel to the latter, also featuring Public Prosecutor Teodor Szacki.

ENTANGLEMENT

Zygmunt Miłoszewski

Translated from the Polish
by Antonia Lloyd-Jones

BITTER LEMON PRESS
LONDON

BITTER LEMON PRESS

First published in the United Kingdom in 2010 by
Bitter Lemon Press, 37 Arundel Gardens, London W11 2LW
www.bitterlemonpress.com

First published in Polish as *Uwiklanie*
by Wydawnictwo W.A.B., 2007

This edition has been published with the financial support of
The Book Institute – the © POLAND Translation Programme

Bitter Lemon Press gratefully acknowledges the financial assistance
of the Arts Council of England

A CIP record for this book is available from the British Library

ISBN 978–1–904738–44–2

Typeset by Alma Books Ltd
Printed and bound in UK by CPI Cox and Wyman

For Monika, times a thousand

"No one is evil, just entangled."
– Bert Hellinger

Entanglement

1

Sunday, 5th June 2005

The revived Jarocin festival is a big success, with ten thousand people listening to rock bands Dżem, Armia and TSA. The JP2 generation takes part in the annual prayer meeting at Lednica. Zbigniew Religa, cardiac surgeon and politician, has announced that he will run for President and that he wants to be the "candidate for national reconciliation". At the tenth anniversary "Aviation Picnic" air show held in Góraszka, two F-16 fighters are on display, prompting an enthusiastic response from the crowd. In Baku the Polish team thrash Azerbaijan 3—0, despite a poor display, and the Azerbaijani trainer beats up the referee. In Warsaw, police distribute grisly photos of car-crash victims to drivers as a warning. In the suburb of Mokotów a number 122 bus catches fire, and on Kinowa Street an ambulance overturns while carrying a liver for transplant. The driver, a nurse and a doctor are taken to hospital with bruising, the liver is unharmed and is transplanted that same day into a patient at the hospital on Stefan Banach Street. Maximum temperature in the capital — twenty degrees, with showers.

I

"Let me tell you a fairy tale. Long, long ago in a small provincial town there lived a carpenter. The people in the town were poor, they couldn't afford new tables and chairs, so the carpenter was penniless too. He had a hard time making ends meet, and the older he got, the less he believed his fate could ever change, although he longed for it more than anyone else on earth, because he had a beautiful daughter and he wanted her to do better in life than he had. One summer's day a wealthy gentleman called at the carpenter's home. 'Carpenter,' he said, 'my long lost brother is coming to see me. I want to give him a dazzling present, and as he is coming from a land that is rich in gold, silver and precious stones, I have decided to give him a jewellery box of extraordinary beauty. If you succeed in making it by the Sunday after the next full moon, you will never complain of poverty again.' Naturally the carpenter agreed, and got down to the job straight away. It was unusually painstaking and difficult work, because he wanted to combine many different kinds of wood, and to decorate the box with miniature carvings of legendary creatures. He ate little, and hardly slept at all – he just worked. Meanwhile, news of the wealthy gentleman's visit and his unusual commission soon spread about the town. Its citizens were very fond of the humble carpenter, and every day someone came by with a kind word and tried to help him with his woodcarving. The baker, the merchant, the fisherman, even the innkeeper – each one of them grabbed a chisel, hammers and files, wanting the carpenter to finish his work on time. Unfortunately, none of them was capable of doing his job, and the carpenter's daughter watched sorrowfully as, instead of concentrating on carving the jewellery box, her father corrected all the things his friends had spoiled. One morning, when there were only four days left until the deadline, and the craftsman was tearing his hair out in desperation, his daughter stood outside the door of their cottage and drove away everyone who came by to help. The whole town took offence, and now no one ever spoke of the carpenter except as a boor and an ingrate, and of his daughter as an ill-mannered old maid. I'd like to tell you that although he lost his friends, the carpenter did in fact enchant the wealthy gentleman with his intricate work, but that wouldn't be the truth. Because when, on the Sunday after the full moon, the wealthy gentleman called at his house, he drove off at once in a rage, empty-handed. Only many days later did the carpenter finish the jewellery box, and then he gave it to his daughter."

Cezary Rudzki finished his story, cleared his throat and poured himself a cup of coffee from the thermos. His three patients, two women and a man, were sitting on the other side of the table – only Henryk was missing.

"So what's the moral of the story?" asked Euzebiusz Kaim, the man sitting on the left.

"Whatever moral you choose to find in it," replied Rudzki. "I know what I wanted to say, but you know better than I do what you want to understand by it and what meaning you need right now. We don't comment on fairy tales."

Kaim said nothing. Rudzki was silent too, stroking his white beard, which some people thought made him look like Hemingway. He was wondering if he should refer in some way to the previous day's events. According to the rules, he shouldn't. But nevertheless...

"To take advantage of the fact that Henryk isn't here," he said, "I'd like to remind you all that it's not just fairy tales that we don't comment on. We don't comment on the course of the therapy either. That is one of the basic rules. Even if a session is as intense as yesterday's. We should keep quiet all the more."

"Why?" asked Euzebiusz Kaim, without looking up from his plate.

"Because then we use words and attempts at interpretation to cover up what we have discovered. Meantime the truth must start to take effect. Find a way through to our souls. It would be dishonest towards all of us to kill the truth through academic debate. Please believe me, it's better this way."

They went on eating in silence. The June sunshine was pouring in through the narrow windows that looked like arrow slits, painting the dark hall in bright stripes. The room was very modest. There was a long wooden table with no tablecloth, a few chairs, a crucifix above the door, a small cupboard, an electric kettle and a tiny fridge. Nothing else. When Rudzki found this place – a quiet refuge in the very heart of the city – he was thrilled. He reckoned the church rooms would be more favourable for therapy than the agro-tourism farms he had previously hired. He was right. Even though there were a church, a school, a doctor's surgery and several private businesses located in the building, and the Łazienkowska Highway ran past it, there was a great sense of peace here. And that was what his patients needed most of all.

Peace had its price. There was no kitchen, and he had had to buy the fridge, kettle, thermos and cutlery set himself. He ordered the meals from outside. They stayed in single cells, and also had at their disposal the refectory, where they were sitting now, and another small classroom where the sessions were held. It had cross-vaulting, supported on three thick columns. It wasn't exactly St Leonard's Crypt in the Wawel Cathedral, but compared with the tiny room in which he usually received his patients, it almost was.

Now, however, he was wondering if he hadn't chosen too gloomy and enclosed a location. He felt as if the emotions released during the sessions remained between the walls, bouncing off them like rubber balls, and hitting anyone who had the misfortune to be there on the rebound. He was barely alive after yesterday's events, and he was glad it would soon be over. He wanted to get out of here as soon as possible.

He drank a sip of coffee.

Hanna Kwiatkowska, the thirty-five-year-old woman sitting opposite Rudzki, was turning a teaspoon in her fingers, without taking her eyes off him.

"Yes?" he asked.

"I'm worried," she replied in a wooden tone of voice. "It's a quarter past nine already, but Henryk's not here. Perhaps you should go and check if everything's all right, Doctor."

He stood up.

"I will," he said. "I think Henryk is just sleeping off yesterday's emotions."

He went down a narrow corridor – everything in this building was narrow – to Henryk's room. He knocked. No reply. He knocked again, more firmly.

"Henryk, time to wake up!" he called through the door.

He waited a second longer, then pressed the handle and went inside. The room was empty. The bed had been made and there were no personal belongings. Rudzki went back to the refectory. Three heads turned in his direction simultaneously, as if belonging to a single body. It reminded him of the dragons in children's book illustrations.

"Henryk has left us. Please don't take it personally. It's not the first or the last time a patient has given up the therapy rather abruptly. Especially after such an intensive session as yesterday's. I hope what he experienced will start to work and he'll feel better."

Hanna Kwiatkowska didn't even shudder. Kaim shrugged. Barbara Jarczyk, the last of his three – until recently four – patients, glanced at Rudzki and asked:

"Is that the end? In that case can we go home now?"

The therapist shook his head.

"Please go to your rooms for half an hour to rest and calm down. At ten on the dot we'll meet in the classroom."

All three – Euzebiusz, Barbara and Hanna – nodded and left. Rudzki walked around the table, checked to see if there was still some coffee in the thermos and poured himself a full cup. He cursed, because he'd forgotten to leave room for the milk. Now he had the choice between pouring some away or drinking it. He couldn't stand the taste of black coffee. He tipped a little into the waste bin. He added some milk and stood by the window. He gazed at the cars going down the street and the Legia soccer stadium on the other side. How could those bunglers lose the league again, he thought. They won't even be the runners-up – slaughtering Wisła and the 5-0 win two weeks ago were all for nothing. But maybe they'd at least manage to win the cup – tomorrow was the first semifinal against Groclin. Against Groclin, whom Legia had never once beaten in the past four years. It's like another bloody curse.

He began to laugh quietly. Incredible how the human brain works – able to think about the soccer league at a time like this. He glanced at his watch. Half an hour to go.

Just before ten he left the refectory and went to the bathroom to brush his teeth. On the way he passed Barbara Jarczyk. Seeing him go in the opposite direction, away from the classroom, she gave him a questioning look.

"I'm just coming," he said.

He hadn't had time to put the toothpaste on his brush when he heard a scream.

II

Teodor Szacki was woken up by what usually woke him on a Sunday. No, it wasn't a hangover, thirst, or the need to pee, the bright sunlight that was coming through the straw blinds, or the rain drumming on the balcony roof. It was Helka, his seven-year-old daughter, who jumped onto Szacki with such force that the Ikea sofa bed creaked beneath him.

He opened one eye, and a chestnut curl fell into it.

"Do you see? Granny put curls in my hair."

"I see," he said, pulling the hair from his eye. "Pity she didn't tie you up with them."

He kissed his daughter on the brow, pushed her off and got up to go to the toilet. He was in the doorway when something moved on the other side of the bed.

"Put the water on for my coffee," he heard a mumble from under the duvet.

Housewives' Choice, like every weekend. At once he felt irritated. He had slept ten hours, but he was incredibly tired. He couldn't remember when this had started. He could lie in bed half the day, but even so he got up with a bad taste in his mouth, sand in his eyes and a pain flickering between his temples. It made no sense.

"Why don't you just ask me to make you coffee?" he said grudgingly to his wife.

"Because I'll do it myself," she said, though he could hardly distinguish the words. "I don't want to bother you."

Szacki rolled his eyes upwards in a theatrical way. Helka laughed.

"You always say that, but I always make it for you anyway!"

"You don't have to. I'm only asking you to put on the water."

He peed and then made his wife some coffee, trying not to look at the pile of dirty pots in the sink. A quarter of an hour washing-up, if he wanted to make the promised breakfast. God, how tired he was. Instead of sleeping until noon and then watching television, like all the other guys in this patriarchal country, he was trying to be a super-husband and super-dad.

Weronika dragged herself out of bed and stood in the hall, examining herself critically in the mirror. He gave her a critical look too. She'd always been sexy, but she'd never looked like a model. However, it was hard to find an excuse for the double chin and the spare tyre. And that T-shirt. He didn't insist on her sleeping in ribbons and lace every night, but bloody hell, why did she keep wearing that T-shirt with the faded message "Disco fun" that must have dated back to the days of food parcels?

He handed her a cup. She glanced at him with puffy eyes and scratched herself under her breast. She said thank you, gave him an automatic peck on the nose and went to take a shower.

Szacki sighed, passed a hand through his milk-white hair and went into the kitchen.

"So what's really the matter with me?" he thought, as he tried to unearth a washing-up sponge from under the dirty plates. Making the coffee took a moment, the washing-up a second moment, breakfast a third. Just one stupid half-hour and everyone would be happy. He felt even more tired at the thought of all the time that went trickling through his fingers. Hours stuck in traffic jams, thousands of hours wasted in court, pointless gaps at work when the most he could do was play Patience while waiting for something, waiting for someone, waiting for waiting. Waiting as an excuse for doing nothing whatsoever. Waiting as the most tiring profession in the world. A coalface miner feels more rested than I do, he mentally pitied himself, as he tried to put a glass on the drying rack although there wasn't any room for it. Why hadn't he taken the dry things off at the start? Damn it all. Does everyone find life so tiresome?

The phone rang. Helka picked it up. He heard the conversation as he went into the sitting room, wiping his hands on a tea towel.

"Daddy's here, but he can't come to the phone because he's doing the washing-up and making us scrambled eggs…"

He took the receiver from his daughter's hand.

"Hello, Szacki here."

"Good morning, Prosecutor. I don't want to worry you, but you're not going to fix scrambled eggs for anyone today. For supper maybe." He heard the familiar voice and sing-song eastern accent of Oleg Kuzniecow from the police station on Wilcza Street.

"Oleg, please, don't do this to me."

"It's not me, Prosecutor, it's the city that's calling you."

III

The large old Citroën sailed under the central support of Świętokrzyski Bridge with a grace that many of the cars appearing there as pushy product placement in Polish romantic comedies would have envied. "Maybe that Piskorski is a scammer," thought Szacki, remembering the scandal about the financing of this and a second new bridge that had lost the former mayor of Warsaw his job, "but the bridges are standing." Under Mayor Kaczyński it was unthinkable that anyone would dare to make a decision about an investment on that scale. Especially before the elections. Weronika was a lawyer at the City Council, and more than once she had told him how the decisions were made nowadays – to be on the safe side, they weren't made at all.

He drove down into the Powiśle district and, as usual, breathed a sigh of relief. He was on home ground. He had lived in the Praga district across the river for ten years now, but he still couldn't get used to it. He had tried, but his new mini-homeland had only one virtue to his mind – it was close to central Warsaw. He passed the Ateneum Theatre, where he had once fallen in love with *Antigone in New York*, the hospital where he was born, the sports centre where he learned to play tennis, the park that stretched below the Parliament buildings, where he and his brother used to fool around on sledges, and the swimming pool where he had learned to swim and caught athlete's foot. Here he was in the City Centre. At the centre of his city, the centre of his country, the centre of his life. The ugliest *axis mundi* imaginable.

He drove under a crumbling viaduct, turned into Łazienkowska Street and parked outside the arts centre, after a fond thought about the soccer stadium that stood two hundred yards further down, where the capital's warriors had only just made mincemeat of Wisła, the Kraków team. He wasn't interested in sport, but Weronika was such an ardent fan that, like it or not, he could recite by heart the results of all the Legia matches for the past two years. Tomorrow his wife was sure to head off to the match in her tricolour scarf. The semi-final of the cup, wasn't it?

He locked the car and glanced at the building on the other side of the street, one of the weirdest constructions in the capital, next to which the Palace of Culture and the Żelazna Brama estate seemed like examples of far less invasive architecture, quite discreet really. There used to be a parish church here, the Virgin Mary of Częstochowa, but it was destroyed during the war, when this was one of the points of resistance during the Warsaw Uprising. Left unreconstructed for decades, it had been a creepy place full of gloomy ruins, the stumps of columns and open cellars. When it was finally resurrected, it became the epitome of the city's chaotic style. Anyone who drove down the Łazienkowska Highway got a view of this redbrick chimera, a cross between a church, a monastery, a fortress and Gargamel's palace. And now a corpse had been found here.

Szacki adjusted the knot in his tie and crossed to the other side of the road. It began to spit with rain. A patrol car and an unmarked police car were standing by the gate. A few rubbernecks emerged from the morning mist. Oleg Kuzniecow was talking to a technician from the Warsaw Police Forensic Laboratory. He broke off the conversation and came up to Szacki. They shook hands.

"Off to Party headquarters on Rozbrat Street for cocktails afterwards, eh?" quipped the policeman, straightening the facings of his jacket for him.

"The rumours about the politicization of the Public Prosecution Service are just as exaggerated as the gossip about extra sources of funding for Warsaw's police," retorted Szacki. He didn't like people making fun of his clothes. Whatever the weather, he always wore a suit and tie, because he was a public prosecutor, not a greengrocer.

"What have we got?" he asked, taking out a cigarette – the first of the three he allowed himself daily.

"One body, four suspects."

"Christ, not more alcohol-induced slaughter. Even in this bloody city, I didn't think you could find a drinking den in a church. And to cap it all they've done it on a Sunday – there's no respect." Szacki was genuinely disgusted, and still furious that his family Sunday had fallen victim to the killing too.

"You're not entirely right, Teo," muttered Kuzniecow, turning in every direction to try and find a spot where the wind wouldn't blow out his lighter flame. "As well as the church there are all sorts of businesses in this building. They've sub-let space to a school, a health centre, various Catholic organizations, and there's also a place for religious retreats. Different groups of people come here for the weekend to pray, talk, listen to sermons and so on. Right now a psychotherapist has hired the rooms for three days with four of his patients. They worked on Friday, worked on Saturday and parted ways after supper. This morning the doctor and three of the patients came to breakfast. They found the fourth one a little later. You'll see what state he's in. The rooms are in a separate wing; it's impossible to get there without going past the porter's lodge. There are bars on the windows. No one saw anything, no one heard anything. And so far no one's confessed either. One body, four suspects – all sober and well-to-do. What do you say to that?"

Szacki stubbed out his cigarette and took a few steps over to a dustbin in order to dispose of it. Kuzniecow flicked his own dog-end into the road, straight under the wheels of a number 171 bus.

"I don't believe in stories like that, Oleg. It'll soon turn out the porter slept half the night, some yob went in to steal some money for booze, bumped into the poor neurotic on the way, got even more scared than he was and stuck a knife into him.

He'll crow about it to one of your narks, and that'll be the end of it."

Kuzniecow shrugged.

Szacki believed in what he'd said to Oleg, but he felt rising curiosity as they entered through the main door and headed down a narrow corridor to the small classroom where the corpse was lying. He took a deep breath to control his nervous excitement and also his fear of coming into contact with a body. By the time he saw it, his face was the picture of professional indifference. Teodor Szacki could hide behind the mask of an official, a guardian of law and order in the Polish Republic.

IV

A man in a pale-grey suit, aged about fifty, a bit stout, with lots of grey hair but no bald patch, was lying on his back on the floor, which was covered in a greenish lino that didn't go with the low cross-vaulting at all. Next to him stood a grey old-fashioned suitcase that didn't have a zip to close it, but two metal locks, and was also secured by some short straps done up with buckles.

There wasn't much blood, almost none at all, but Szacki didn't feel any the better for that. It cost him a lot to take a firm step towards the victim and squat down next to his head. He let out a bilious belch and swallowed his saliva.

"Fingerprints?" he asked nonchalantly.

"None on the murder weapon, Sir," replied the chief technician, kneeling on the other side of the body. "We collected some in other places, and some trace evidence too. Should we take some odour samples?"

Szacki shook his head. If the deceased had spent the past two days with one of the people who had killed him, his odour wouldn't help at all. They'd refuted that sort of circumstantial evidence so many times when he'd tried it in court that it wasn't worth bothering the technicians for nothing.

"What exactly is this?" he said, addressing Kuzniecow and pointing at the spike with a black-plastic handle that was sticking out of the victim's right eye. It was a relief that thanks to the question he could turn his gaze on the policeman, instead of looking at the dark-red-and-grey matter that must once have been the man's eye, but now had congealed on his cheek in a shape that stubbornly made Szacki think of a Formula One racing car.

"A meat skewer," said Oleg. "Or something of the kind. There's a whole set in the same style in the dining room. Knives, a cleaver, forks and spoons."

Szacki nodded. The murder weapon came from in here. So what were the chances that the murderer came from the outside? Practically none; theoretically the court might think there was as big a crowd in here as on busy Marszałkowska Street, which no one had noticed. But all possible doubts… etc.

He was wondering how to play things with the witnesses, or, in fact, suspects, when one of the uniformed policemen looked in the hall.

"Superintendent, his wife's here. Would you?"

Szacki went outside with Oleg.

"What was his name?" he whispered to Kuzniecow.

"Henryk Telak. The wife's called Jadwiga."

By the patrol car stood a woman of the kind men describe as handsome. Quite tall, slender, wearing glasses, with slightly greying dark hair and distinct facial features, she was dressed in a bright-green dress and sandals. She must have been a beauty once, and now proudly carried her fading charm.

Kuzniecow went up to her and bowed.

"Good morning, I am Oleg Kuzniecow, I'm the Police Superintendent. This is the Public Prosecutor, Teodor Szacki, who'll be conducting the investigation. Please accept our deepest condolences. We promise to do everything in our power to find and convict your husband's murderer."

The woman nodded. She looked absent, and must already have taken something to sedate herself. Perhaps she wasn't yet fully conscious of what had happened. Szacki knew that the first reaction to the death of a loved one is disbelief. The pain comes later.

"How did it happen?" she asked.

"Assault and robbery," lied Szacki with the self-confident glibness that had sometimes led people to advise him to take up advocacy. "So far it looks as if a burglar broke in at night and ran into your husband by accident – he may even have tried to stop the man. The thief killed him."

"How?" she asked.

The two men swapped glances.

"Your husband was struck in the head by a sharp object." Szacki couldn't stand crime-related Newspeak, but it was the best language for depriving death of its drama. It sounded milder than "Someone stuck a meat skewer into his brain through his eye". "He died instantly. The doctor says it happened so quickly he can't have had time to feel any pain."

"That's something at least," she said after a moment's silence, and looked up for the first time. "Can I see him?" she asked, gazing at Szacki, who immediately remembered the grey stain, the shape of a racing car.

"There's no need."

"I'd like to say goodbye to him."

"They're still collecting evidence," added Kuzniecow. "It's not very private in there, and besides, please believe me, it's not a pleasant sight."

"As you wish," she agreed resignedly, and Szacki held back a sigh of relief. "Can I go now?"

"Of course. Please just leave your details. I will have to talk to you some more."

The woman dictated her address and phone number to Kuzniecow.

"What about the body?" she asked.

"Unfortunately we'll have to do an autopsy. But on Friday at the latest the undertaker will be able to collect it."

"That's good. Maybe it'll be possible to arrange the funeral for Saturday. A man's got to be buried before Sunday, otherwise another family member will die the same year."

"That's just superstition," replied Szacki. He took two business cards from his pocket and handed them to the widow. "One has my phone number, the other has the number of a centre that offers support to the families of crime victims. I advise you to call them. It might help."

"Are they any good at resurrecting husbands?"

Szacki didn't want the conversation to continue in this direction. Bizarre remarks such as these were usually a prelude to hysteria.

"No, they resurrect the living. Bring them back to life, to which they often don't want to return. Of course you'll do whatever you feel appropriate. I just believe that they are people who can help."

She nodded and put both cards away in her handbag. The cop and the prosecutor said goodbye to her and went back into the building.

Oleg asked Szacki if he wanted to question the people from the therapy group now. Szacki was in two minds how to play it, and although as a first reaction he had decided to talk to them as soon as possible, right here even, now he thought it would be better to put it off for a while, to let them sweat for a bit – the good old Lieutenant Columbo method. He wondered what they were thinking about in their cells. *Cells* – how apt. They must all be mulling over every single word and gesture from the past two days, looking for signs that show which of them might be the murderer. Except for the actual murderer – he (or she) must be wondering whether he has betrayed himself by word or gesture over the past two days. But all this makes the sensational assumption that one of them really did do the killing. Could the idea that the murderer came from the outside be excluded? No, it couldn't. As usual at this stage nothing could be excluded. Yes, it might be an interesting case, a nice change after all those run-of-the-mill city murders. A nasty stench, some empty bottles, gore on the walls, a woman who looked thirty years older than the age on her ID sobbing on the floor, the surprised dopey pals, unable to believe one of them had knifed a mate in a drunken daze – how many times had he seen that?

"No," he replied. "I'll tell you what we'll do. Question them now – after all, that's the usual procedure. But you do it, not some constable who was still living with mummy and daddy in the suburbs of Siedlce a fortnight ago – calmly and casually, treating each one as a witness. When did they last see Telak? When did they meet? What did they do last night? Don't ask about what connects them, about the therapy – let them feel safe, and I'll have a reason to call them back again a few times."

"You're full of ideas," said Oleg huffily. "You're telling me to play with them to prepare the ground for you. Make transcripts, write clearly, have it read through..."

"Get some lady constable to write it out for you in nice round letters. Let's meet up in the morning at Wilcza Street; we'll exchange documents, have a chat and decide what next. I was meant to be going to the sentencing for the Pieszczoch case, but I'll ask Ewa to go for me."

"You're buying the coffee."

"For pity's sake. I'm an underpaid civil servant, not a corrupt traffic cop. My wife is a civil servant too. We make ourselves instant coffee at work, we don't buy it for anyone."

Oleg took out a cigarette. Szacki only just stopped himself from doing the same. He didn't want to have just one left for the rest of the day.

"You're buying the coffee, there's no argument."

"You're a filthy Russki."

"So they're always telling me. See you in Gorączka at nine?"

"I hate that flatfoot's dive."

"At Brama then?"

Szacki nodded. Oleg saw him to his car.

"I'm afraid this might be a tough one," said the policeman. "If the murderer didn't make any mistakes, and the rest of them didn't see anything, it's pretty hopeless."

Szacki couldn't resist smiling.

"They always make mistakes," he said.

V

He couldn't remember when the weather in the Tatra mountains had ever been so kind to him. From the summit of Kopa Kondracka he had a perfect view in all directions; only far above the Slovak part of the High Tatras could he see some tiny clouds. Ever since he had parked early that morning in Kiry, taken a short walk in the Kościeliska Valley and started to climb up the Czerwone Wierchy – the four "Red Peaks" – the sun had been with him the whole time. From halfway up, where the path began to climb more and more steeply, the dwarf mountain pines gave no chance of shade, and there were no streams nearby, the hike had turned into a route march across a red-hot frying pan. It reminded him of stories he'd heard about American soldiers in Vietnam, whose brain fluid got cooked during the day under their sun-baked helmets. He had always thought it must be nonsense, but now that was how he felt, except that his head was protected not by a helmet, but a beige hat, a souvenir brought back from a trip to Australia long ago.

As he neared the ridge, black spots started dancing before his eyes, and his legs went weak. He cursed his own stupidity – that of a seventy-year-old who thinks he can still do as much of everything as before. Drink as much, make love as much, hike in the mountains as much.

On the ridge he sank to the ground, letting the wind cool him, and listened to the frantic rhythm of his heart. Tough, he thought – better to croak on Ciemniak Peak than on Marszałkowska Street in central Warsaw. Once his heart had calmed down a bit, he thought it would be better yet to die on Małołączniak Peak, across the saddle, because it sounded like the name of a bird – much better than being killed by bloody Ciemniak, meaning "ignoramus". If he died there, they'd go on telling jokes about him long after. So he dragged himself over to Małołączniak, drank a little coffee from his thermos while trying not to think about his muscle number one, and by sheer impetus reached the top of Kopa Kondracka. It was quite amazing, but it looked as if his weak heart combined with his old man's stupidity weren't going to kill him this time either. He poured himself another mug of coffee, took out a sandwich wrapped in tin foil and gazed at the pot-bellied thirty-year-olds coming up the poor old Kopa with as much effort as if it were twenty thousand feet high. He felt like advising them to bring oxygen with them.

How can they let themselves go like that? he thought, as he disdainfully watched them barely trudging along. At their age he could run the route from the shelter in Kondratowa Valley up the Kopa and back again first thing in the morning, via the dip called Piekło, meaning "hell", just to get warm and work up an appetite for breakfast. Yes, those were the days. Everything was clear, everything made sense, everything was easy.

He stretched out his tanned calves in the sunshine – covered in grey hairs, they were still muscular – and switched on his mobile to send a text message to his wife, who was waiting for him at the guesthouse near Strążyska Valley. The phone had only just found a signal when it rang. The man cursed and answered it.

"Yes?"

"Good morning, this is Igor. I've got some bad news for you."

"Yes?"

"Henryk's dead."

"How did it happen?"

"I'm afraid it was a nasty accident."

He didn't waste a moment considering what to say in reply.

"That really is sad news. I'll do my best to come back tomorrow, but you must place a condolences announcement in the newspaper as soon as possible. Got that?"

"Of course."

He switched off the phone. He no longer felt like texting his wife. He drank the rest of the coffee, put on his backpack and set off towards the pass below the Kopa. He'd have a beer at Kalatówki Clearing and think how to tell her they'd have to go back to Warsaw. Almost forty years together, and he still found that sort of conversation stressful.

VI

Prosecutor Teodor Szacki had some trouble firing up the powerful three-litre engine of his Citroën V6 – the autogas installation was playing up again – waited for the hydraulic system to lift his dragon off the ground, and set off towards the highway along the River Vistula, intending to cross over Łazienkowski Bridge. At the last moment he changed his mind, turned towards Wilanów and stopped the car at the bus stop near Gagarin Street. He switched on the hazard lights.

Long ago, ten years ago, which meant ages ago, he and Weronika had lived here, before Helka was born. It was a studio flat on the second floor, and both windows looked onto the highway. A nightmare. In the daytime one huge lorry after another came, after dark it was the night buses and little Fiat 126s going at seventy miles per hour. He had learned to distinguish makes of car by the sound of their engines. A layer of thick black dust would collect on the furniture, and the window would be dirty half an hour after cleaning it. It was worst of all in summer. They'd had to open the windows or else suffocate, but then it was impossible to talk or watch television. It was quite another matter that in those days they made love more often than they watched the news. And now? He wasn't sure they made it to the national average, which had once amused them so much. What? There really are people who only do it once a week? Ha ha ha!

Szacki snorted with laughter and rolled down the window. It was raining steadily now, and raindrops fell inside the car, leaving dark spots on the upholstery. In the windows of their old flat, a petite blonde was wandering about in a top with shoulder straps; her hair came down to her shoulders.

I wonder what it would be like, thought Szacki, if I were to park in the courtyard and go up to the flat on the second floor, and find that girl waiting for me? If I had a completely different life, different CDs, different books on the shelves, if I smelled a different body lying next to me. We could go for a walk in Łazienki Park, I'd tell her why I had to be at work today – let's say at an architectural studio; she'd say I was brave and that she'd buy me an ice cream near the Theatre on the Island. Everything would be different.

How unfair it is that we only have one life, mused Szacki, and that it so quickly bores us.

One thing's for sure, he thought, as he turned the car key. I need a change. I bloody well need a change.

2

Monday, 6th June 2005

Vatican priest Father Konrad Hejmo sends a special statement from Rome explaining at length and in a roundabout way that he did not collaborate with the Communist secret police. Also in Rome, Pope Benedict XVI re-emphasizes the Church's opposition to homosexual marriages, abortion and genetic engineering. Committed Catholic, presidential candidate and Mayor of Warsaw Lech Kaczyński bans the Equality Parade and stresses that the pig-headed attitude of "some groups" is of course to do with the elections. Former President Lech Wałęsa invites current President Aleksander Kwaśniewski and his wife to his name-day party. In central Warsaw artist Joanna Rajkowska fixes fresh leaves to her artificial-palm-tree installation on Jerozolimskie Avenue. At the jail on Rakowiecka Street the rock band that has been formed there gives its first concert, and nearby on Spacerowa Street an eighty-six-year-old woman gets stuck in the bathtub for twenty-four hours. In the evening the semi-finals of the Polish Cup are held. Legia Warsaw are playing at home against Groclin, and Wisła Kraków against Zagłębie Lubin. Maximum temperature in the capital: eighteen degrees — some rain, cloudy.

Szacki took his daughter to playschool, drove Weronika to the City Council on Miodowa Street and on the dot of nine was sitting in the Brama café on Krucza Street, waiting for Oleg. He was hungry, but thought it a pity to waste fifteen zlotys or more on breakfast. On the other hand, it was only the beginning of the month, so he still had money in his account. He hadn't slaved away studying, doing his legal training and working as an assessor just to end up denying himself breakfast. He ordered a cheese and tomato omelette.

The waitress was just serving him the food when Kuzniecow appeared.

"Well, well," he said, as he sat down on the other side of the table. "Brought a jar of your instant from the office, eh, so the lady can make you some coffee?"

Without passing comment, Szacki gave the policeman a meaningful look. Kuzniecow ordered a black coffee and took a wad of documents out of his briefcase.

"Here you have the official memo, the site inspection report and the witness interviews. And the search reports – you've got to approve them for me. I took your advice and sweet-talked a nice, lusty young trainee into helping. Look what lovely round letters. Her handwriting looks almost as fantastic as she does."

"I've never yet seen a pretty policewoman," snapped Szacki.

"Maybe you don't fancy girls in uniforms. I always imagine them in nothing but the cap and blouse with only two buttons done up…"

"Better tell me what happened yesterday."

Kuzniecow sat his angular body straight on the chair and folded his hands as if to pray.

"I'm ninety-nine per cent certain," he began in a serious, solemn tone, "the butler did it."

Szacki laid his knife and fork against the edge of his plate and sighed heavily. Communicating with policemen was sometimes like being a teacher with a class full of children suffering from ADHD: it took a lot of patience and self-control.

"Are you going to get to the point?" he asked coldly.

Kuzniecow shook his head in disbelief.

"You're such a petty bureaucrat, Teodor. Read for yourself exactly what they said. No one knows anyone, no one knows anything, no one saw anything. They're all very sorry, they're shocked. They met a week ago; only Rudzki, the psychotherapist, had known him for longer, a year or so. They all noticed that the deceased was introverted and depressed. They spoke so convincingly that I found myself wondering if he hadn't committed suicide."

"You must be joking. By sticking a skewer in his eye?" Szacki wiped his mouth on his napkin. The omelette hadn't been bad at all.

"Right, it's hardly likely. But if people are capable of shooting themselves in the head or biting off and swallowing their own tongues, you see what I mean. Anyway, ask the pathologist. And on the subject of tongues, have you heard the one about the lady speech therapist who had such a well-trained tongue that she choked on it while doing her exercises? Not bad, eh?"

"So what are your impressions?" asked Szacki, without commenting on the joke.

Kuzniecow smacked his lips and fell into thought. Szacki waited patiently. He knew that few people were as sharp or had as astute a sense of observation as this larger-than-life, far-too-jovial cop with the Russian name.

"You'll see for yourself," he said at last. "They all made a very good impression. None of them was unnaturally self-controlled, or unnaturally excited and shocked. And often that's how you can tell a murderer. Either he pretends to be cold as ice or mad with despair. Any departure from the norm is suspicious, but they're all on the level. More or less."

"Or else one of them knows how to behave himself," suggested Szacki.

"Yes, the therapist, I thought of that too. Besides, he knew the victim the longest – he might have had a motive. I was even ready to lock him up for forty-eight hours if he'd betrayed himself in any way, but nothing of the kind. He's a bit superior and arrogant, like all shrinks – bloody nutters, the lot of them. But I didn't feel he was lying."

In other words we've got a load of shit, thought Szacki, putting out a hand to stop the waitress from taking his roll and butter away with the empty plate. He'd paid enough – he was going to eat every last crumb of it.

"Maybe it really was a blunder while a burglar was on the job," he said.

"Maybe," agreed Kuzniecow. "They're all educated, intelligent people. Do you believe one of them would decide to commit murder in such a theatrical place? They don't have to read crime fiction to know we'll keep sniffing around them to the bitter end. No one in their right mind would ever kill in such an idiotic way. It's senseless."

Kuzniecow was right. It had promised to be interesting, but it looked as if they were seeking a petty thief who had accidentally become a murderer. Which meant they'd have to follow the usual routine, thought Szacki, making a mental checklist.

"Tell the press we're looking for people who were hanging about there that night and might have seen something. Interrogate all the watchmen, security guards, priests, anyone who was working there at the weekend. Find out who's king of the castle and who rented the place to Rudzki so I can talk to him. I was planning to go there in the week anyway to take a good look at it all."

Kuzniecow nodded – the prosecutor's instructions were obvious to him. "Just write it down for me when you get a moment so I've got confirmation in writing."

"Fine. And I've got one more request, without confirmation."

"Yes?"

"Keep an eye on Rudzki for the next few days. I've got absolutely nothing to charge him with, but for now he's the main suspect. I'm afraid he'll do a runner and that'll be the end of it."

"What do you mean? Don't you believe the bold Polish police force will track him down?"

"Don't make me laugh. In this country you only have to leave your registered address to disappear for ever."

Kuzniecow laughed out loud.

"You're not just a petty bureaucrat, you're a cynic too," he said, getting himself ready to go. "Give my best to your lovely sexy wife."

Szacki raised an eyebrow. He wasn't sure if Kuzniecow was talking about the same woman who trailed around the house complaining of new pains every day.

II

On the way to his room Szacki got a documents file from the office. Catalogue number ID 803/05. Unbelievable. In other words soon they'd have a thousand registered inquiries and break last year's record by miles. It looked as if a small area of central Warsaw was the blackest spot on the crime map of Poland. Admittedly, most of the inquiries conducted here were to do with economic, financial and accounting scams that were handled by a separate unit – the result of the fact that perhaps eighty per cent of all the businesses in Poland had their head offices between Unia Lubelska Square and Bankowy Square – but there was no lack of ordinary criminals either. Almost twenty prosecutors in the "First ID", or the First Investigative Department, worked on thefts, muggings, rapes and assaults – and also on plenty of cases that the guys from organized crime at the regional prosecutor's office were supposed to deal with. In practice the stars from organized crime – or "OC" as it was known – chose the more interesting incidents for themselves, and left the "everyday shootings" to the district office. As a result, the OC Prosecutor from the regional office had a few cases on his books, while the District Prosecutor had a few dozen. Or in fact a few hundred, if you included ongoing inquiries, ones that had been shelved, ones that depended on finding a particular witness and ones that were waiting to be heard in court but had been postponed for the umpteenth time. Szacki, who even so was in a fairly comfortable position for a district prosecutor because he really only dealt with murders, had tried last week to count up all his cases. It came to 111, 112 with Telak's murder – 111 if the sentence were passed today in the Pieszczoch case, and 113 if the judge decided to send the case back to the prosecutor's office. He shouldn't – it had all been prepared perfectly, and in Szacki's view Chajnert was the best judge in the Warsaw district.

Unfortunately, relations between the Prosecution Service and the courts had been getting worse from year to year. Even though the prosecutor's work was closer to a judge's job than a policeman's, and the Prosecution Service was the "armed forces" of the judiciary, the distance was increasing between officials with purple trimming on their gowns – the judges – and officials with red trimming – the prosecutors. A month ago Szacki's boss, Janina Chorko, had gone to the regional court on Leszno Street to ask for a date to be set as soon as possible for a well-publicized case concerning multiple rapes at a sports centre on Nowowiejska Street. She had been given a dressing down and told that the courts are independent and no prosecutor was going to tell them how they should do their job. It was laughable – not so bad when insults were the only result of such hostility, but worse when it was the verdicts that suffered. Sometimes Szacki got the impression that only a case where the accused confessed all on the first day of the inquiry and then repeated his confession three times in the courtroom was one you could count on winning. All the rest were a lottery.

He tossed his umbrella into a corner of the room, which for the next two weeks he didn't have to share with the usual colleague, because she had gone to a sanatorium with her sickly child, for the third time this year. In fact he had been given two of her cases, but at least he didn't have to look at the mess she made around herself. He sat at his desk, which he always tried to keep in impeccable order, and took out a sheet of paper listing the phone numbers of the people from Łazienkowska Street. He had his hand on the receiver when Maryla, his boss's secretary, put her head round the door.

"Your presence is requested in the parlour," she said.

"Be there in fifteen."

"She said, and I quote: 'When he says he'll be there in fifteen, tell him I mean right now!'"

"I'll be there in a moment."

"She said, and I quote —"

"I'll be there in a moment," he said firmly, pointing meaningfully at the receiver he was holding. Maryla rolled her eyes and left.

He quickly made appointments for the afternoon with Barbara Jarczyk and Hanna Kwiatkowska – there were just minor problems with Euzebiusz Kaim.

"I've got a meeting today outside town."

"Please postpone it."

"It's a very important meeting."

"I see. Should I write you a sick note or have you arrested at once?"

There was a long silence.

"Actually it's not that important."

"Excellent. In that case, see you at three o'clock."

The therapist wasn't answering. Szacki left him a message and felt a nasty cramp in his stomach. He hoped the guy had just unplugged the phone for a while. He preferred not to think about other eventualities. He called the mortuary on Oczko Street too, found out the autopsy was due to take place on Wednesday morning at ten and left the room.

"Our offices appear to be in different dimensions of time and space," the boss greeted him, "because my 'right now' is equivalent to exactly ten minutes later in your world, Prosecutor."

"I didn't know I'd been allocated an office," replied Szacki, sitting down.

The District Prosecutor for Warsaw City Centre, Janina Chorko, gave an acid smile. She was several years older than Szacki; her grey suit blended with her grey hair and her nicotine-grey face. Always a bit sulky, with a wrinkled brow, she gave the lie to the theory that there aren't any ugly women. Janina Chorko was ugly, was perfectly aware of the fact and did not try to cover up her defects with clothes or make-up. Quite the opposite – she consciously made herself sour, malicious and painfully businesslike, which was in perfect harmony with her appearance, turning her into the archetypal boss from hell. The new prosecutors were afraid of her, and the trainees hid in the toilet whenever she came down the corridor.

As a prosecutor she was brilliant. Szacki thought highly of her, because she was not just a mediocre official promoted for loyalty and following correct procedure, but someone from the very front line. She had served her time at the district office in the Warsaw district of Wola, then in the organized crime department at the Regional Prosecutor's office on the street called Krakowskie Przedmieście, and finally ended up here, at Krucza Street in the City Centre, where with an iron hand she ran the most complicated district in Poland. Within her office she was capable of reducing the biggest star to a heap of misery, but when dealing with outsiders she never went against her people, often taking big risks on their behalf. Szacki had heard that they'd been afraid of her at the regional office too, especially in the Preparatory Proceedings Department, where they had rarely dared to reject a decision initialled by her. However, Szacki had had more than one experience during Chorko's reign of not getting permission to call an expert witness for financial reasons (any expense above 2,500 zlotys had to be approved by the Regional Prosecutor), and in every other prosecutor's office that was daily bread.

They had worked together for seven years and had great respect for each other, though they weren't friends. They had never got onto first-name terms, which suited them both. They shared the view that cold official relationships are conducive to good professional work, especially when the plaque at the entrance features the national emblem – the crowned eagle – rather than a colourful company logo.

Szacki briefly summarized the events from Łazienkowska Street, outlined his plans for the next few days and his suspicions about Rudzki, the psychotherapist. Suspicions which, however, could not provide grounds for any sort of action against him.

"When's the autopsy?" asked Chorko.

"Wednesday morning."

"In that case please give me an inquiry plan and your hypotheses by three on Wednesday. At the latest. And don't forget that you have to write the indictment in the Nidziecka case by the end of the week. I trusted you and initialled the commutation from remand to supervision, but it doesn't make me any the calmer. I'd like that case to be in court as soon as possible."

Szacki nodded. Unable to decide on the legal classification, he had put it off from last week.

"As we're having a chat, there are two other things. Firstly, please don't exploit female colleagues who fancy you – go to your own trials. Secondly, I'd like you to help Jurek and Tadeusz with narcotics."

Szacki failed to hide a scowl.

"Yes, Prosecutor? Got a problem? Surely you don't want me to think you're incapable of teamwork? Especially in cases that demand lots of laborious, boring and unsatisfying tasks?"

Too true, thought Szacki.

"Please give me a week so I can concentrate on this murder. We'll be carrying on with narcotics for months; I'll have time to get involved in it," he said.

"A week. I'll tell Tadeusz that from Monday you're working together."

This time Szacki remained stony-faced, though it cost him a lot. The grim hope occurred to him that some more corpses would turn up during the week, which would save him from some boring work with boring colleagues.

The audience came to an end. He had his hand on the doorknob when he heard Chorko say:

"Please don't think I'm paying you a compliment, but you look great in that suit. Like a real star of the bar association."

Szacki turned and smiled. He adjusted his shirt cuffs, fastened with fashionable wooden cufflinks.

"That wasn't a compliment, Prosecutor, as you very well know."

III

The abrupt end to the trip to Zakopane meant the atmosphere in the luxury Audi A8, in which they were rapidly returning to Warsaw, was as cold as the stream of air pouring from the vents. His wife had packed up in silence, and then spent the whole night in silence, lying as far from him as possible on the spacious bed in the apartment; that morning she had got into the car in silence and travelled home in silence. Nothing helped – neither her favourite Glenn Miller, nor lunch at a fabulous Greek restaurant which by some strange twist of fate was situated in Kroczyce, less than twenty miles from the Katowice highway. He had made a detour specially, knowing how much she loved Greek food. Naturally, she had eaten it, but she hadn't said a word.

When he stopped near their villa at Leśna Polana near Magdalenka to drop her off, and watched her silently walking to the garden gate, something inside him snapped. He switched off Glenn Miller's bloody racket and opened the window.

"Just think what a squalid dump you'd be coming home to if it weren't for what I do," he screamed.

Half an hour later he was in the garage underneath the Intraco building, where his company's modest office was located. The company could have afforded rooms in the Metropolitan or one of the skyscrapers near the ONZ roundabout, but he liked this spot. It had its own style, and he could endlessly admire the panorama from the windows on the thirty-second floor. He got out of the lift, nodded to a secretary as lovely as the sunrise over a ridge in the Tatras and without knocking went into the Chairman's office. His office. Igor was already waiting for him. At the sight of the boss he got up.

"Sit down. Do you know how many times a woman goes through menopause? I must be witnessing it for the third time by now. And I was warned off taking a young wife. To hell with that."

Instead of answering, Igor poured a drink – Cutty Sark with two lumps of ice and a dash of soda. He handed it to the Chairman, who had meanwhile fetched a laptop out of the safe. They sat down on either side of the desk.

"Now tell me what happened."

"Henryk was murdered on Saturday night in the church buildings on Łazienkowska Street."

"What the bloody hell was he doing there?"

"He was taking part in group therapy. It may be that one of the other participants killed him, or maybe someone else who knew he'd be in the place and that suspicion would fall on someone there. Or maybe a burglar, so the police claim."

"A bastard, not a burglar. They always say that to get the press off their backs. Who's in charge of the investigation?"

"Kuzniecow on Wilcza Street, and Szacki on Krucza."

"Excellent," said the Chairman, laughing out loud. "To think they had to go and rub him out right in the City Centre. Couldn't they do it in Ochota? Or the Praga district? It wouldn't be any problem there."

Igor shrugged. The Chairman put down his empty glass on the desk, logged onto the system, put a special key in the USB port that enabled access to a coded folder and found the right file. Any attempt at opening the folder without the key would have ended in irreversible deletion of the data. He quickly ran through the contents, which were more or less familiar to him. He paused for thought.

"What shall we do?" asked Igor. "The first procedure is already in motion."

"We'll stick with it."

"Are you sure?"

"Yes. I don't think the person who killed Henryk wanted to go any further – if that's what it's about. I think we can feel safe."

"What about Szacki and Kuzniecow?"

"Let's wait and see how things develop."

Igor nodded. Without being asked he picked up the elegant, heavy-bottomed glass, in which the ice lumps were still rattling, and reached for the bottle.

IV

Teodor Szacki signed his name on the "Prosecution Reference File", made a note that an inquiry was being conducted "in the case of the taking of the life of Henryk Telak in the church building rooms at 14 Łazienkowska Street, Warsaw, on the night of 4th–5th June 2005, i.e. an offence covered by Article 148, paragraph 1 of the Penal Code", and stopped writing at the box marked "versus". Unfortunately he would have to leave it blank. Experience had taught him that investigations conducted "in the case of" were definitely more than likely to finish many months later with a document being sent to the Regional Prosecutor's office asking them to approve a decision "to dismiss by reason of failure to identify the offender, in accordance with Article 322, paragraph 1 of the Penal Procedure Code". There in the record you entered the words "perpetrator unknown", and took it back to the archive with a bad taste in your mouth. Better to have a suspect from the start, then you didn't have to wander about in the dark.

He carefully read through the material provided by Kuzniecow, but didn't conclude much more from it beyond what the policeman had told him. Nothing had been found during the searches; the only deviation from the norm was an empty bottle of sleeping pills left by Telak in the bathroom. Strange, thought Szacki, someone taking that sort of pills shouldn't really be getting up at night, dressing and leaving. He wrote on a sheet of paper: "medicine – prescription, fingerprints, wife". All they had found in Telak's suitcase were some clothes, toiletries and a book, a crime novel called *Headland of Pseuds*. Szacki had heard of it – apparently it was largely set in Warsaw. He was ready to bet a hundred hard-earned zlotys that the word "prosecutor" didn't appear in it once, and that meanwhile a brave lone cop did it all by himself, including establishing the time of death. In Telak's wallet there were some documents, a little cash, a video library card, some family photos and some lottery tickets.

He wrote: "wallet – examine".

Nothing to latch on to. Nothing.

There was a knock at the door.

"Come in!" said Szacki, looking at his watch in surprise. Kwiatkowska was not supposed to be there for half an hour.

In came a girl he didn't know. She was about twenty-five, neither pretty nor ugly, a brunette with curly hair cut short and rectangular glasses with opalescent frames. Quite slender; not particularly his type.

"I'm sorry I didn't call in advance, but I was just passing and I thought —"

"Yes? What brings you here?" Szacki interrupted her, praying to himself that she wasn't a lunatic coming to complain about electricity being put through her keyhole.

"My name's Monika Grzelka, I'm a journalist —"

"Oh no, Madam," he interrupted her again. "The Prosecution Press Spokesman has his office on Krakowskie Przedmieście – he's a nice fellow, I'm sure he'll be happy to answer all your questions."

That was all he needed. A young thing, only good-looking enough to work in radio, to whom he'd have to explain the difference between suspect and accused, and even so she'd screw it up in her article. Undaunted by his manner, the girl sat down and smiled radiantly. She had a nice, intelligent, impish smile. Infectious. Szacki clenched his teeth to stop himself from smiling back at her.

She reached into her handbag and gave him a business card. Monika Grzelka, journalist, *Rzeczpospolita* – one of the serious dailies.

He reached into a drawer, took out the Press Spokesman's card and handed it to her without saying a word. She stopped smiling, and he felt mean.

"I don't think your name is familiar," he said, to erase the bad impression.

She blushed, and he thought he'd done pretty well.

"I used to do local council issues, but from today I'm writing about crime."

"Is that a promotion?"

"Yes, sort of."

"It won't be easy to write a crime column in a boring enough way for it to appear in *Rzeczpospolita*," he noted.

"I actually came here to make your acquaintance and to ask you for an in-depth interview, but I can see nothing will come of it."

"I'm not a lawyer, I'm a civil servant," he said. "I don't need advertising."

She nodded and glanced around his shabby little room. He was sure she was stifling a nasty comment, such as: "Right, you can tell it's public sector in here", or "And there's no hiding it".

"If you don't wish to talk about general matters, let's talk about one in particular. I'm writing about the murder on Łazienkowska Street. You can of course tell me a lot of official lies, but then you won't have any influence on what appears in the paper. Or you can tell me the truth, but I doubt you will. Or you can at least tell me the half-truth, then I won't have to print all the rumours from police headquarters."

He cursed mentally. Sometimes he felt as if asking the police for discretion was about as effective as printing out the secrets of an inquiry on posters and sticking them up on advertising pillars.

"Surely you don't expect me to have any truths, half-truths or even quarter-truths about what happened the day after a murder?"

"So what did happen?"

"A man was murdered."

She burst out laughing.

"You're a very rude prosecutor," she said, leaning towards him.

Again, it cost him an effort not to smile, but he managed it.

"Two sentences and I'll be off."

He thought about it – it was a decent offer.

"One: a man, Henryk T., forty-six years old, was murdered on Saturday night in the church buildings on Łazienkowska Street with the use of a sharp instrument."

"What sort of instrument?"

"A very sharp one."

"A skewer?"

"Perhaps."

"And the second sentence?"

"Secondly: the police and the prosecutor are assuming that Henryk T. was the victim of a burglar whom he ran into by accident, but they are not excluding the possibility that it was a premeditated murder. Intensive operations are under way to identify the offender. For the time being no one has been charged."

She finished taking notes.

"A good-looking man, dresses beautifully, has a nice voice and talks like a fax from the neighbourhood policeman."

He allowed himself a faint smile.

"Please don't write more than that about the case. It might cause us harm."

"Now it's please, is it?" She stood up and zipped her handbag shut. She was wearing a cream skirt above the knee and black flat-heeled shoes that showed off her feet. He noticed a red mark on her leg; while they were talking she had kept this leg casually folded on her knee. "And what will I get for that?"

"You might find out a bit more, when others will get nothing but a fax from the city police."

"And might it be possible to invite you for coffee? And will you talk to me in a language generally regarded as Polish?"

"No."

She hung her bag on her shoulder and strode briskly to the door. Before closing it, she looked at him and said:

"I don't remember the last time a man treated me as badly as you have, Prosecutor. I'm sorry to have taken up your time."

And she was gone. Szacki was sorry too. Irritated, he got up from his chair to hang up his jacket, and walked into a cloud of perfume left behind by the journalist. Romance by Ralph Lauren – Weronika used to wear it. He loved that fragrance.

WITNESS INTERVIEW TRANSCRIPT. Hanna Kwiatkowska, date of birth 22nd July 1970, resident at Okrzeja Street, Warsaw, has higher education, teacher of Polish at high school No. 30 in Warsaw. Relationship to parties: none, no criminal record for bearing false witness.

Cautioned re criminal responsibility under Article 233 of the Penal Code, her statement is as follows:

"I met Henryk Telak the previous Sunday at psychotherapist Cezary Rudzki's consulting room, which was where I also met Euzebiusz Kaim and Barbara Jarczyk. The four of us were to spend two days at the retreat on Łazienkowska Street taking part in group therapy, known as 'Family Constellation Therapy'. I had never met anyone in the group before, I only knew Cezary Rudzki, to whom I had been going for six months for individual therapy, usually once a week.

"We all met on Friday, 3rd June, in the afternoon, ate supper together and went to bed early. There were no therapy sessions. We only had to get a good night's sleep. Next day after breakfast Mr Kaim's therapy session took place. In this constellation I played the role of Mr Kaim's ex-wife, and I found it sad, because I felt unloved. Mr Telak played Mr Kaim's father, and Mrs Jarczyk his mother. In this constellation Mr Telak was pushed aside, just like Mr Kaim's real father within his family. So I had no feeling with regard to him. After the lunch break we had Mr Telak's session. Mrs Jarczyk played his wife, Mr Kaim his son, and I was his daughter, who committed suicide two years ago at the age of fifteen. It was awfully sad and depressing. I felt so bad I wanted to commit suicide myself. During the constellation some very depressing things emerged, but I should stress that I don't know if they were true. They must have been most depressing for Mr Telak, because we were all telling him we didn't love him, and I even said it was because of him that I'd committed suicide. That was dreadful. We had to stop, because Mrs Jarczyk collapsed. That happened at about 8 p.m. At about 8.30 I went to my room, before that I was in the kitchen for a bite to eat and a cup of tea. I went down the corridor with Mr Telak, who had the room next to mine. I saw him go inside, and I didn't go out again after that. No one came into my room. I didn't hear anyone leaving any of the other rooms or moving about in the corridor. I was worn out by the therapy and by about 9.30 I was asleep. In the morning my alarm rang half an hour before breakfast, at 8.30. I remember being sorry there wasn't a shower in my room. At breakfast we didn't talk much. Mr Rudzki told us a fairy tale, and asked us not to discuss what had happened the day before. We were worried that Mr Telak wasn't there. Mr Rudzki went to call him, but came straight back and said Mr Telak had run away, and that this happens. At breakfast I didn't notice anyone behaving oddly or differently from before. At about 9.30 I went to my room to rest. At about 10 o'clock I

heard Mrs Jarczyk scream. I ran to the classroom and saw Mr Telak's body. I thought I was going to be sick, so I left the room, and didn't go back in there again. Mrs Jarczyk and Mr Kaim were there with the body, and as I left I passed Mr Rudzki who was running towards the classroom.

"I can confirm that both on Saturday evening and during breakfast we talked very little to each other, because that is the recommendation for the therapy. That is why I had no opportunity to get to know Mr Telak socially.

"That is all I have to say on the matter. I hereby confirm that this is an accurate transcript of my statement."

Hanna Kwiatkowska signed each page and handed the transcript to Szacki. Kuzniecow had mentioned that she was quite badly shaken, but apart from that, rather a good-looking girl. It was true. Hanna Kwiatkowska had a pretty, intelligent face and her slightly hooked nose gave her a surly appeal and a certain aristocratic charm. In twenty years she'd look like a pre-war countess. Her smooth, mousy hair came down to her shoulders, and its ends curled outwards. And although no fashion house would have offered her a job advertising underwear on the catwalk, plenty of men would have been happy to take a good look at her well-proportioned, attractive body. It was quite another matter how many of them would be scared off by the restless look in her eyes. Szacki for sure.

"Well, is that all?" she asked. "We talked for such a long time."

"I'm a prosecutor, not a writer," said Szacki. "I can't convey all the nuances of the conversation in the transcript, and besides, it's not necessary. Impressions and nuances only matter to me if they allow me to establish new facts."

"It's a bit like with my pupils at school. It's not the impression they make that counts, but the knowledge they demonstrate."

"Always?"

"I try my best," she replied. She smiled, but she was so tense the smile changed into a scowl.

Szacki looked at her and wondered if she was capable of killing someone. If she was, then maybe she'd do it in exactly that way – grab a skewer, lash out and accidentally hit the spot. Lots of hysteria, lots of panic, lots of pure accident. He could see the woman was trying to keep her chin up, but it felt as if her jittery nerves were making the air in the room quiver.

"You must be having a tough time at school right now," he said as an opener, so he'd be able to watch her a while longer during a neutral conversation.

"Well, yes, you know what it's like, the end of the school year. They all come along, wanting to improve their marks, change a C plus into a B minus, complete an overdue test, and suddenly all their essays turn up. There's really no question of teaching any classes. We've got until next Friday to give all the marks, so we've still got two more weeks of this madness."

"I live quite near the school where you work."

"Oh, really? Where's that?"

"On Burdziński Street."

"Oh yes, that's only two blocks away. Do you like it there?"

"Not particularly."

She leaned towards him, as if wanting to betray a shameful secret and said: "Neither do I. And those children, Jesus Christ, sometimes it's like being in a reformatory or a madhouse. My nerves are in tatters. Don't get me wrong, they're good kids, but why do they have to throw bangers in the corridors? I just don't get it. And all those jokes about penises – they're over twelve years old! Sometimes I'm so embarrassed. You won't believe me, but I've just had a text message from one of my pupils saying that she's fallen in love with a priest and might do something to herself. I'll show you – maybe it's a matter for the prosecutor?"

She started searching for her phone in her handbag, and

Szacki began to regret having set her off on a neutral topic. Was that how a murderess behaved? Wouldn't she be eager to get out of there as soon as possible, rather than showing him text messages? Was it really possible to act quite so well?

She handed him the phone: "IMustTellSomeoneILoveFather MarekICan'tBearToLiveHelp".

"There's no signature," he noted.

Plainly becoming increasingly relaxed, she brushed that aside, saying: "Well, yes, but I found out who it's from – her obliging friends gave her away. But I don't know. So it's not something for the prosecutor then?"

"So what do you think – did one of your group kill Mr Telak?"

She stiffened.

"Of course not. Surely you don't imagine one of us is the murderer?"

"Can you vouch for people you've only just met?"

She folded her arms across her chest. Szacki behaved like a basilisk, never letting his gaze drop from her eyes. She had a tic; her right eyelid kept steadily twitching.

"Well, no, but they're normal people – I heard about their lives. It must have been some cut-throat, some horrible criminal."

Rascal, rogue, thug, thought Szacki spitefully.

"Perhaps. But maybe it was one of you. We have to consider that scenario too. I realize it's hard for you, but please try to remember if anything happened, anything at all, some tiny thing, that made the idea pass through your head, even if it was a totally unjustified thought, 'maybe it was him' or 'maybe it was her'. Hmm?"

"I find it very awkward to cast aspersions, but, er… at the therapy it emerged that Henryk's wife hates him terribly, and Barbara enacted her anger so vividly, I don't know, it's silly to say it…"

WITNESS INTERVIEW TRANSCRIPT. Barbara Jarczyk, born 8th August 1946, resident of Bartniak Street, Grodzisk Mazowiecki, has higher education, employed as chief accountant at the Sosnex Wooden Toy Factory.

She really did look like an accountant, or a retired teacher. Plump, in a suit that must have been bought at a shop for plump ladies. With a plump face and fluffy hair. Wearing glasses. Szacki had never imagined people of her age went to therapy. He had always thought it was more the thirty- to forty-year-olds, worn out by the rat race, who went in search of a cure for their fears and depression. Though on the other hand, it was better to drain the marsh of your soul late than never. He frowned, unable to shake off his surprise at having come up with this idiotic metaphor.

She spoke in a flat monotone, her voice showing no emotion. Szacki automatically noted down almost word for word the same thing he had heard from Kwiatkowska, wondering if there were any languages in the world that entirely lacked intonation. Mrs Jarczyk could definitely have learned them in a week.

"Just before ten I came out of my room and set off towards the therapy classroom. On the way I passed Mr Rudzki, who was going in the opposite direction."

Szacki came to.

"Are you trying to say Mr Rudzki saw the corpse before you did?"

"I don't know that. I doubt it. The room where we ate our meals was next to the therapy classroom, in another part of the building from our bedrooms. He could have stayed there longer at breakfast, I have no idea. I did give him a look of surprise, because he was going the opposite way, but he said he was just coming, and I felt embarrassed, because then I realized he was simply going to the toilet. I don't think he'd have been quite so calm if he'd found Henryk's body."

He noted this down without passing comment. What do these therapists do to people to prevent any of them from coming to the most obvious conclusion: that he was the murderer?

"I went into the classroom. I remember that I was feeling very scared, because the therapy was going to be about me this time. I had a glimmer of hope that without Henryk we'd have to postpone it, because there'd be too few people, you see. So I was scared, and in the first instance I didn't notice him, I couldn't stop thinking how I should place Hanna and Euzebiusz in the role of my children."

Mrs Jarczyk fell silent. Szacki did not push her.

"I saw his legs," she said at length. "I went closer and saw the body, and that skewer in his eye, and that was all. And when I realized what I was looking at, I started to tremble."

"Who came running first?"

"Hanna."

"Are you sure?"

"Yes, I think I am. Then Mr Rudzki, and lastly Euzebiusz."

"Please tell me what happened when you were all standing over the body. Who said what, and how they behaved."

"If I'm being frank, the main thing I remember is that skewer sticking out of his eye. It was horrible. But the others? I don't remember Hanna at all – she may have left the room very quickly. I think Euzebiusz checked Henryk's pulse, and wanted to pull it out of his eye, but the doctor shouted that we mustn't touch anything and that we should call the police, and we had to get out of there as soon as possible, because we'd destroy the evidence."

"Like an ace cop from an American thriller," said Szacki, unable to deny himself a small comment.

"Did we do the wrong thing?"

"You did very well. Really."

The phone rang. He apologized to Jarczyk and picked up the receiver.

"Hi, Teo. I didn't want to come in because you've got a witness, but Pieszczoch got fifteen years."

"Excellent. How was the judgement?"

"Superb. He didn't reproach us for anything, in fact he repeated your wording from the indictment and closing speech to the cameras. You should claim royalties. There might not even be an appeal. Pieszczoch is a really horrid little shit, and in his lawyer's place I'd be afraid he'd get a few years more on appeal."

Ewa was right. Pieszczoch had killed his wife with malice aforethought, out of totally unjustified hatred. It was a nasty domestic crime of the kind that not even the gutter press are interested in. A squalid one-room flat, an unemployed couple, tears, screaming and rows, then he'd banged her head against the corner of a cupboard instead of the usual slapping about the chops. For fifteen minutes without stopping. Even the pathologist was shocked. And that, in the opinion of the defence, was supposed to be "a beating with fatal consequences". Good God, Szacki would rather sweep the streets that hire himself out as a mouthpiece in criminal cases.

"Thanks, Ewa. I owe you coffee."

"Take me to bed?"

He stifled a smile.

"I've got to go. Bye."

Jarczyk's gaze was wandering around the room. There was nothing of interest in there, apart from the view of the grey Ministry of Agriculture building outside. There were some funny children's drawings above Ala's desk, and next to Szacki's there was just a calendar with pictures of the Tatras and Sztaundynger's words in a frame: "Whether the wind blows from far or near, the breath of the Tatras is always here".

"What do you think – which of your group murdered him?" he asked.

The question surprised her.

"I don't know. I have no idea. I just found the body."

"I see. But if you had to single out one person, who would it be? Please trust your instincts. I'm asking off the record – there certainly won't be any consequences. After all, you observed those people for two days almost non-stop."

Barbara Jarczyk adjusted her glasses. She sat very still, without looking at Szacki, but at some point on the wall behind him. Finally, without turning her head, she said: "At the session Euzebiusz played the role of Henryk's son. And that son, at least in Euzebiusz's rendition, was dreadfully sad, but you could also see how much he'd been wronged by the father. And so I thought perhaps it was him, out of vengeance against his father, you see. That he had no love for him, or in general."

Only now did she look at Szacki, who couldn't understand this at all. An adult man was supposed to have killed another guy because during therapy he had pretended to be his son who wasn't loved enough? What nonsense.

"I see," he said. "Thank you very much."

She read the transcript carefully before signing it. Several times she pulled a face, but didn't say anything. They said goodbye, and Szacki warned her that he would be sure to call her back again, maybe several times. Jarczyk was standing by the door when one more question occurred to him.

"What did you feel when you found him?"

"At first I was horrified, it was a dreadful sight. But once I'd calmed down I felt a sort of relief."

"Relief?"

"Please don't get me wrong. Henryk told us a lot about himself and about his family, and I…" she said, nervously locking her fingers as she searched for the right words, "I've never met anyone so unhappy. And I thought perhaps someone did him a service, because there really can't be any worlds where Henryk could be worse off than here."

WITNESS INTERVIEW TRANSCRIPT. Euzebiusz Kaim, born 14th July 1965, resident of Mehoffer Street, Warsaw, has secondary education, employed as a unit manager at HQ Marketing Polska.

In Oleg's opinion, rich, arrogant, and hell knows what he was doing in therapy. In Szacki's opinion too. Next to this guy's suit, the prosecutor's smart outfit looked like a rag dug out of an Indian second-hand shop. Szacki could appreciate that, and he felt a stab of envy as Kaim sat down opposite him. He would never be able to afford clothes like that.

Kaim wasn't just superbly dressed. He was also muscular and tanned, as if he'd done nothing for the past three weeks but go running and play tennis on a beach in Crete. Despite his flat stomach and regular sessions at the pool, Szacki felt as pale and flabby as a worm from the nematode family. His ego was bolstered a bit by the thought that he was the representative of authority here, and this pretty boy might turn out to be a murderer.

In a nice, manly voice, matter-of-fact and specific, without going over the top or omitting any details, Kaim made his statement. He remembered the scene with the corpse the same way as Jarczyk, but Szacki was interested in something else.

"What sort of a person do you think Henryk Telak was?" he asked.

"An unhappy one," replied Kaim without a moment's hesitation. "Very unhappy. I realize not everyone's life works out, but he had exceptionally bad luck. I'm sure you know his daughter committed suicide."

Szacki confirmed that he did.

"And do you know his son has a bad heart?"

Szacki said he didn't.

"They found out about it six months after they buried Kasia, their daughter. Dreadful. I get *slivers* down the spine just thinking about it. I've got a son of a similar age, and it makes me weak at the knees to imagine us going to get the results of routine tests and having the doctor say there's something odd about them and they'll have to be done again. And then... well, you know."

"So what exactly was the psychodrama like, in which you played Mr Telak's son?"

"I wouldn't call it a psychodrama, it's something far deeper, inexplicable. Magic. Cezary is sure to explain the theory to you, I'm not capable of that. It was the first time I'd taken part in a constellation and..." – he searched for the right term – "it's an experience bordering on loss of consciousness. When Mr Telak arranged us all, I immediately felt bad. Very bad. And the longer I stood there, the worse it got and the less I felt like myself. OK, you're already looking at me like I'm round the twist, but I'll finish anyway. I didn't so much pretend to be Bartek as really become him. Please don't ask me how that can be."

Szacki thought that if an expert had to examine them all, the State Treasury would spend a fortune.

"Earlier you were the main subject of the constellation," he said.

"Right, but I didn't take it quite so badly. OK, it was a very tough experience, when I saw why my marriage had fallen apart, but those were my own emotions. Do you see? Even if they were hidden somewhere deep down, even if they were forced out of me, they were mine, my own. But later, with Bartek and Henryk... dreadful, as if I'd had my identity bulldozed. I want to forget about it as quickly as possible."

"Is it long since you divorced?"

"No, not long, a year ago. And not so much divorced, as separated. We didn't go to court. But now perhaps we'll manage to *botch* it all up again."

"Sorry?"

"Sorry what?"

"You said 'botch it all up again'."

"Oh, of course I meant *patch* it all up. Please ignore my slips of the tongue. I've got a connection missing in my brain, and all my life I've mixed up idioms and compound phrases. No one can explain why."

What a nutter, thought Szacki – he makes a good impression, but he's a nutter.

"Of course, I understand. During the therapy, when you were playing the role of Henryk's son, did you feel hatred towards your – let's call him – father?"

"I'm sorry, but what are you driving at?"

"Please answer the question."

Kaim was silent, turning his mobile phone in his hands. It must have been very expensive – the display screen alone was bigger than Szacki's entire phone.

"Yes, I did feel hatred towards him. In the first instant I wanted to deny it, but that would have been pointless. I'm sure you'll watch the recording, and you'll see that."

Szacki made a note: "therapy – video?"

"What are you going to ask me now? Did I want to kill him? Did I kill him?"

"Did you kill him?"

"No."

"Did you want to?"

"No. Really I didn't."

"So what do you think, who did kill him?"

"How should I know? In the papers they said it was a thief."

"But if it was one of you?" Szacki dug a bit deeper.

"Hanna," replied Kaim without hesitation.

"Why?"

"Simple. She was his daughter who committed suicide at the age of fifteen. I'm *dread* sure it's because her father abused her as a child. That wasn't obvious at the therapy, but they're always writing about it in the papers. Hanna sensed that, something shifted gear in her head, and she killed him."

Once Kaim had left, Szacki opened the window wide and sat on the sill to smoke his second cigarette. It was coming up to four, and there was already a line of cars on Krucza Street, heading towards the Avenue. Still high in the sky, the sun had finally pushed its way through the clouds and was warming the damp pavements; there was a smell of wet dust in the air. Perfect weather to go for a walk with a girl, thought Szacki. Sit down by the fountain in the Saxon Garden, lay your head on her knees and tell her about the books you read as a child. He couldn't remember the last time he and Weronika had simply gone for a walk like that. He couldn't remember when he'd ever told anyone about the books he read as a child. Worse than that, he couldn't remember when he'd last read anything that wasn't entitled "Prosecution Reference File". More and more often he felt empty and burned out. Was it just his age?

Perhaps I should call a therapist? he thought, and laughed out loud.

Of course he should. He sat down at his desk and dialled Rudzki's number. For a long time no one answered. He was just about to give up when he heard a click.

"Yes," said a voice that sounded as if it were coming all the way from Kamchatka.

Szacki introduced himself and told Rudzki he must come and see him as soon as possible. After today's interviews it was clear the therapist and his entire bizarre therapy could provide the key to the whole case. Rudzki apologized and said he'd been lying in bed with a high temperature all day. He realized that sounded like an idiotic excuse, but he really couldn't come. However, he'd be glad to see Szacki at his place.

Szacki thought about it. On the one hand, he'd prefer to meet on his own ground, but on the other he was eager to talk to the therapist. So he agreed. He wrote down an address in Ochota and promised to be there in an hour.

He hung up, and cursed. Hadn't he promised Weronika he'd be home at five and would stay in with the little one so she could go to the match? Of course he could try explaining, and she might even understand, but... Well, quite – but. He called Rudzki again and postponed the meeting until next day at nine a.m. The therapist was pleased and said he'd do all he could to be back on his feet and of sound mind by then. Szacki thought it odd that he'd used that expression. After all, flu is not the same as schizophrenia.

V

Helka was triumphant. She'd beaten her father three times at ludo (once when she finished he still had all his pieces in base). Now it all looked as if she'd win at lotto too. She was two pairs ahead, and there were only ten more cards lying on the floor to be picked up. Five pairs. And it was her move. If she didn't make a mistake, the evening would belong to her. She turned over a card – a pine tree covered in snow. With a confident gesture she turned over the next one – a pine tree covered in snow. She didn't say anything, just glanced at him radiantly. She put the cards on her pile and scrupulously counted the difference.

"I've got three more than you," she declared.

"It's not over yet," remarked Szacki. "Go on."

The little girl quickly turned over a card – a robin. She frowned. She reached for the card lying nearest to her and hesitated. She glanced enquiringly at her father. Szacki knew the robin was there, but he just shrugged his shoulders. He wasn't going to help today. Helka changed her mind and turned over a different card – a badger.

"Oh no!" she groaned.

"Oh yes," replied Szacki, gathering up both robins. Three more pairs to get, and only two behind. He knew what the remaining cards were. He stuck his tongue out at his daughter and turned over the same badger as she had just done.

Helka hid her face in her hands.

"I don't want to look," she announced.

Szacki pretended to be wondering.

"Now, where was that second badger? Did we ever find him?"

Helka nodded, looking at him through her fingers. Szacki suspended a hand over the badger card. His daughter squeezed her eyelids shut. He laughed to himself, reached out and turned over a card with – some raspberries.

"Oh no!" he groaned.

"Oh yes," cried Helka, quickly picking up the remaining three pairs, and threw her arms around his neck.

"So who's the Queen of the Lotto?"

"I'm the King of the Lotto," he cheekily claimed.

"No you're not!"

"Yes I am! Losing today was the exception."

The door banged shut. Weronika was home.

"Mummy, do you know how many times I beat Daddy at ludo?"

"No, I don't."

"Three times. And once at lotto."

"Wonderful, maybe you should play football for Legia Warsaw."

Szacki put the lotto away in its box, got up from the floor and went into the hall. His wife tossed her tricolour scarf on a hook. She was dressed for the match – thin polo neck, anorak, jeans, ankle-high sneakers. Contact lenses instead of glasses. The stadium on Łazienkowska Street wasn't a good place to show off your charms.

"Don't say they were beaten."

"They drew, but it was as good as being beaten. Włodarczyk missed three golden opportunities – even I'd have scored. They played the last twenty minutes with only ten men because that cretin Nowacki got two yellow cards. First for a foul, then for stupidly faking an injury. What an idiot. But even so we were in the lead the whole game…"

"Who scored?"

"Karwan headed it off a pass from Włodarczyk. Groclin equalized a few minutes before the end. What a disgrace! It's not worth talking about."

"When's the rematch in Groclin?"

"The fifteenth."

"Are you going?"

"I don't know. I don't want to hear an entire stadium full of village idiots bellowing: 'Legless Warsaw!'"

Szacki nodded sympathetically and went into the kitchen to make supper. Weronika came in for a smoke. As he made the sandwiches, he told her about the Telak case and today's interviews.

"Interesting. Babinicz once told me about a therapy like that. I remember thinking it sounded like a sect."

"Well, I never, Mr Babinicz has turned up in our house again," cut in Szacki, without looking up from the board on which he was slicing tomatoes for a salad with feta and sunflower seeds.

"Teo, please don't be a pain. Do I keep asking you which of the trainees makes you coffee?"

"I make it for myself."

"Right, like we only met yesterday, eh?"

He just shrugged. He didn't feel like bickering. Once it had just been a joke. Later on jealousy had crept into the jokes. Now all such conversations quickly turned into aggressive provocation on both sides.

He finished the salad, served himself some, chivvied his daughter into the bathroom and sat down at the computer. He needed to switch off from the rest of the world for a while; he needed to play a game. He was proud of the fact that he had gone through every evolutionary stage in this particular field, from ZX Spectrum and Atari with games recorded on cassette tapes, via C64 and Amiga with floppy discs, to the first PCs with greenish monochrome monitors, and finally today's machines, which created alternative worlds in millions of colours and real time right before your very eyes. He was sure the ever-more-perfect games with better and better storylines would soon be cultural events on a par with the novels of Dan Brown and the films of Steven Spielberg. Admittedly, the world of computer games hadn't achieved the equivalent of *The Name of the Rose* or *Amadeus* yet, but it was only a matter of time. He usually played adventure and strategy games, but today he felt like being the one just man on a tropical island, where a very evil doctor was conducting very evil genetic experiments, and benefiting from the protection of some very evil mercenaries. If only those people at the trials knew what the haughty, impeccably dressed prosecutor, whose hair was white at just thirty-six, did in the evenings… He felt like laughing every time he fired up the computer.

"You're not going to play games, are you?" asked Weronika.

"Just half an hour," he replied, angry at himself for explaining.

"I thought we were having a talk."

Of course he felt guilty.

"In half an hour. You're not going to bed yet, are you?"

"I don't know, I'm tired. I might go to bed early."

"I'll be done in a moment, honest. I'll just get to a save point," he replied automatically, already focused on a sniper lurking on the bridge of a smashed-up Japanese aircraft carrier.

"I've got a bullet here with your name on it," thundered out of the speakers, and seconds later one of the mercenaries ripped the air apart with a burst of machine-gun fire. He dodged behind the aircraft carrier's metal span, but even so the mercenary got him. Dammit.

"Sorry, but could you put on headphones?" asked Weronika coldly.

He reached for them.

"I'll make a new hole in you!" rasped the speakers hatefully, before he'd had time to plug in the jack.

3

Tuesday, 7th June 2005

Seventy per cent of Poles claim that the life and teachings of Pope John Paul II have changed their lives. The Pope is viewed negatively by zero per cent. Polish President Aleksander Kwaśniewski appeals to Marshal of the Sejm — chairman of the Polish parliament — Włodzimierz Cimoszewicz to change his mind and run in the forthcoming presidential election. A physicist at Adam Mickiewicz University in Poznań publishes a theory that ever so often a super-predator will inevitably appear on Earth, a real killing machine that tidies up the planet. Punk rock band Green Day give a concert at the Spodek stadium in Katowice. In Warsaw three trams crash outside the National Museum and thirteen people are taken to hospital. The Museum of Technology within the Palace of Culture and Science is given a defibrillator by journalist and charity promoter Jerzy Owsiak to help save the lives of visitors who suffer heart attacks. More and more people are protesting against the ban on the Equality Parade. The organizers are announcing rallies for which they do not have to have permission. Maximum temperature in the capital — fifteen degrees, despite which it is quite sunny with no rainfall.

I

Being a therapist is undoubtedly a lucrative profession, thought Teodor Szacki as he parked outside a brand-new apartment block on Pawiński Street. He sat in the car for a while longer to listen to the end of 'Original of the Species' from U2's latest album. A brilliant track, a brilliant album – the boys from Dublin had finally returned to their rock-music roots. As he reported to the doorman at a porter's lodge clad in marble and granite, and then walked across a beautifully maintained courtyard with a fountain and a children's play area, he thought being a therapist must be a bloody lucrative profession. And as he entered Rudzki's apartment on the eleventh floor he reckoned he'd give anything to be back at the start of his career again, as he'd be sure to choose psychology.

Rudzki really did seem unwell, and his age added to the impression. A sixty-year-old man can look great, but only when he takes the trouble. At Łazienkowska Street on Sunday, Rudzki had looked excellent, like a cross between Ernest Hemingway and Sean Connery. Today, with straggly greasy hair and dark rings around his eyes, and tightly wrapped in a dressing gown, he was a sickly old man.

The apartment must have been quite large, about three hundred square feet, but Szacki could only make a guess about that, and about the layout of the rooms in the private part. Rudzki showed him into the lounge, and this time Szacki simply couldn't hold back his emotions. The rectangular room, with an adjoining kitchen, was about one hundred and twenty square feet in size (his whole flat was only 170), and the walls facing north and west were entirely made of glass, consisting of nothing but windows. The view knocked him for six. To the west there wasn't all that much to see – the roofs of Ochota, the hideous dome of the Blue City shopping centre and Szczęśliwicka Hill. But to the north lay Warsaw's version of Manhattan flaunting itself. From this spot all the skyscrapers in the City Centre appeared to be standing next to each other, both the old ones – the Forum Hotel, the Marriott and Intraco II, and the new ones – the Intercontinental, Golden Terraces, Rondo 1, the Daewoo building and of course the Palace of Culture, which even provided an interesting contrast to the sea of glass surrounding it. The view was so totally of Warsaw that it even surpassed the panorama of the left bank from Gdański Bridge. Szacki decided he'd have to find an excuse to come and see Rudzki after dark. A search, perhaps?

"Impressive, isn't it?" croaked Rudzki as he handed Szacki a mug of coffee. "You must come round after dark one day. Some nights I spend a whole hour at the window without getting at all tired of it."

Szacki called himself to order.

"Yes indeed, it could be nice," he commented indifferently.

WITNESS INTERVIEW TRANSCRIPT. Cezary Rudzki, born 2nd August 1944, resident at Pawiński Street, has higher education, runs a private psychology consultancy. Relationship to parties: none, no criminal record for bearing false witness.

Cautioned re criminal responsibility under Article 233 of the Penal Code, his statement is as follows:

"I met Henryk Telak by chance in November last year. I was organizing a psychotherapy conference and was looking for a company to print invitations and posters for it. That was how I came across a firm called Polgrafex, the manager or deputy manager of which was Henryk Telak. I had no contact with him at that point, just with one of the salesmen. A week later I wanted to collect my order, but it wasn't ready. I insisted on speaking to the manager, and so I met Henryk Telak. He was very nice, he assured me they would deliver my order that very day by courier at their own cost; he apologized and offered me a cup of coffee. Over coffee he started asking about my job, because he was interested in the theme of the invitations and posters. I told him what a therapist does, that I try to help people, and that I often come across people for whom life has lost its meaning. Then he told me about his daughter's suicide

and his son's illness, and admitted that he couldn't live with it all. I asked if he'd like to come and see me. He said he wasn't sure, but a week later he called and made an appointment. We met once a week on Thursdays, here at my apartment.

"I did not tape-record the sessions, I just made notes. Mr Telak was silent a lot of the time, and often wept. He had had a difficult life. He had run away from home at the age of sixteen, and not long after his parents had been killed in a car crash. He had never had the chance to say goodbye to them and hadn't even known about the funeral. As a result, he felt very guilty, and this sense of guilt had placed a heavy burden on his later life. His marriage to Jadwiga Telak – whom in my view he loved very much, and his children too – was not a success, something he talked about with sadness and shame. During his therapy we focused on his family background, to help him to come out of the shadow of his deceased parents. I judged that to be the basis for healing the relationships within his current family. I believed it was producing results, and the Family Constellation Therapy this weekend was supposed to dot the i's and cross the t's. In this constellation Henryk Telak was actually my main concern. The other people, whom I selected from among my patients, are in a much better psychological state. They are suffering from relatively mild neuroses."

To the interrogator's question whether in the course of his therapy Henryk Telak ever mentioned any enemies or people who were ill-disposed towards him, the witness replies: "Henryk Telak appeared to be such a depressed, introverted person, that he was probably quite unnoticed by those around him. I know nothing about his enemies. I do not think he had any."

As he wrote it all down, Szacki watched Rudzki closely. The therapist spoke quietly, calmly and confidently. His voice inspired trust, and he must surely have known how to use it to put a patient into a hypnotic trance without much trouble. Szacki wondered if he could possibly have confided in Rudzki: told him how his stomach ached every time he got home; how he had to drink two beers before bed to get to sleep easily; how the chilly atmosphere between himself and Weronika was doing him in; how the air hung heavy with rancour and disappointment over the Ikea furniture in their flat in a block on Burdziński Street; how sometimes he wondered what they had in common, apart from their child and their bank account; and how sometimes he would stand outside a flower shop – he'd have liked to buy her flowers, and he knew she'd be pleased, but he never did, he always found an excuse instead. Either it was already late, and the flowers weren't very pretty by now, or he thought it a shame to give his wife flowers from the Praga district florists' – they always looked like leftovers that hadn't sold in the City Centre two days earlier. Or else he didn't want to part with his change, because he still had to go and buy food. But only fifty yards further on there was an ATM. And a rose only cost five zlotys. Sometimes he also thought: Why should I buy flowers? When was the last time I got anything from her? A CD or a book, or even a text message other than "sliced loaf and cigarettes"? So he'd walk away from the flower shop, angry at himself and ashamed, and stop at the shop for the fucking sliced loaf, which he'd bought every other day for the past eight years in the same shop from the same saleswoman. Funny how he could see that she was getting older, while feeling as if he were exactly the same person as when he'd done the shopping there for the very first time. That had been in July. Szacki had been wearing a tracksuit, covered in dust from moving house. He was happy with the flat, happy to know that soon he'd be eating rolls and drinking kefir with the most beautiful woman in the world. He was happy the saleswoman was so nice. In those days he had long dark hair tied in a short plait, not the milk-white crew cut that made him look like the infantry sergeant out of an American war film.

* * *

Cezary Rudzki politely but very firmly refused to answer any questions about Kwiatkowska's, Jarczyk's and Kaim's therapy. Szacki did not insist. He would have to charge one of them before he could get a court order forcing Rudzki to hand over the paperwork. As Rudzki described the day when the body had been found, Szacki noted with regret that none of the people interviewed so far appeared to be the murderer. Their statements were logical and seemed to be sincere; there was a clearly audible note of sadness at the death of Henryk Telak and a large dose of empathy for him. Besides, he couldn't imagine what motive any of them could have had for killing Telak.

So thought Prosecutor Teodor Szacki on Tuesday 7th of June at 10.30 a.m. Two hours later he was already convinced that one of Rudzki's three patients had to be the murderer.

"I'm quite surprised it's you that's talking to me and not the police," said the therapist suddenly.

"You mustn't believe what you see on TV. In this country it's the prosecutor who conducts the serious inquiries. The police help as much as they're told to, but all they do on their own is chase car thieves and burglars."

"Surely you're exaggerating."

"A little," smiled Szacki.

"You must feel under-appreciated."

"I'd prefer to talk about facts, not feelings."

"Yes, it's always easier. What else would you like to know?"

"I'd like to know what happened on Saturday evening. And what Family Constellation Therapy is. And why your patients' voices quiver whenever they talk about it."

"In that case we will have to talk about feelings."

"I'll manage to put up with it."

The therapist stood up, went over to the bookshelf and started rummaging in a black briefcase.

"I'm unable to explain it to you," he said. "Unfortunately it's not possible. Totally unfeasible."

Szacki gnashed his teeth. What an old fool. Now they'd got to the point, things should be moving forwards, not coming to a standstill.

"Please try. Maybe it'll work."

"No way. I won't try telling you," he said, turning round and smiling apologetically at Szacki, who was shaking with fury inside. "But I can show you," he said, holding up a small video camera.

The scene is the hall in the building on Łazienkowska Street. Telak, Kaim, Kwiatkowska and Jarczyk are sitting next to each other. Then Rudzki appears in the frame.

Rudzki: Mr Telak, please go ahead.

Telak stands up, smiling nervously. Szacki felt a shiver down his spine. *Telak is wearing the same clothes as when he was found dead.* Szacki couldn't help thinking that any minute now he'd lie down on the floor and one of the others would get up and stick a skewer in his eye. Then a mark the shape of a racing car would appear on his cheek.

Telak: Maybe someone else should have their turn now?

Rudzki: We drew lots. But please say if you're not ready.

A long silence.

Telak: All right, I'll give it a go.

Rudzki: OK. First we'll arrange the family background. Mrs Jarczyk will be your mother, and Mr Kaim your father. Please arrange them.

Telak takes Mrs Jarczyk by the hand and leads her to the far end of the room. He shows her to a spot right next to the wall, where she stands facing it. Then he positions Kaim next to her, also with his face to the wall. Telak himself stands in the middle of the room, looking at their backs.

Rudzki: All set?

Telak: Yes.

Rudzki: Mrs Jarczyk, please tell us how you're feeling.

Jarczyk: I'm sad, I wish I could see my son. I miss him.

Rudzki: And what about you?

Kaim: Not good. I can feel him staring at my back. I want to turn round. Or get away. I can feel pressure on my neck, just as if someone were holding me on a leash.

Jarczyk: Yes, I feel the same way. Or like I've been put in the corner as a punishment. I feel bad. I feel guilty.

Telak: I'd like to go up to them.

Kaim: May I turn round?

Rudzki: Not yet. (To Telak) Please go up to your parents and stand behind them.

Telak stands just behind Kaim and Jarczyk.

Rudzki (to Telak): How do you feel now?

Telak: Better, much better. This is how I wanted it.

Kaim (with an effort): But I find this unbearable. I've got the wall in front of me and my son behind me. I don't know why he came here, but I don't want him here. Christ, I can hardly keep upright. I'm suffocating. Please let me move away, or get him out of here.

Rudzki: Just a little longer.

The therapist stopped the tape. The image of Telak standing behind his "parents" froze on the screen. Szacki looked at him in amazement.

"Is it a sort of theatre?" he asked. "Have they been given a script in advance telling them how to behave?"

Rudzki shook his head.

"No, and what's more they hardly know a thing about Mr Telak. They don't know that he ran away from home, they don't know that his parents died in a tragic accident and that he never got the chance to say goodbye to them. Nothing. You see, essentially this form of therapy is extremely simple, if we compare it for example with psychoanalysis, which to my mind is usually totally ineffective in any case."

Szacki gestured to interrupt him.

"Please, one thing at a time," he said.

"All right. You apply for Family Constellation Therapy because you're having a tough time, things are really bad and difficult, but you don't know why. You tell a few facts about yourself – your parents, siblings, wife, children, first wife, father's first wife, etc. All the people in your family are important, alive or dead. And then you arrange them spatially. You take each of them by the hand, lead them to the right spot and show them which way to face. You'll be surprised to hear it, but people often see what's wrong right at that very moment, and why they feel so bad. For example, because their wife is standing where their mother ought to be. Or because their child is keeping them apart from their wife. In short, because the right order has been disturbed. You only have to arrange them correctly and the patient comes out of the therapy a different person. In just five minutes."

"Why does Kaim say he's suffocating and about to faint?"

"Because the representatives can feel the emotions of the people they're replacing."

"But Telak's parents died years ago."

"Including the dead."

"I see. And I suppose at the end you have to dance naked round a bonfire wearing a wooden mask?"

Rudzki fell silent, plainly offended by the prosecutor's comment. Szacki noticed and apologized.

"I can understand your attitude a bit – I was very sceptical at first too," said Rudzki in his defence. "I thought the patient must somehow be broadcasting his own emotions and programming them into the representatives. But very often during constellations family secrets come to light that the patient had no idea about."

"For example?"

"For example, Bert Hellinger himself, who created this method, once arranged a thirty-five-year-old Swede who was suffering from autism. The man kept stubbornly staring at his own hands, which usually means —"

"Murder."

"How did you know?"

"Lady Macbeth."

"Exactly. Staring at the ground means a grave, someone who has died, and examining your own hands or a hand-washing gesture means killing. Gestures like these are typical of people suffering from autism and people who stammer. Both conditions have lots of common features, and one of them is the fact that during constellation therapy the source of the illness often turns out to be a murder. But to go back to the Swede: Hellinger knew from an interview with the family that his grandmother had had an affair with a sailor, and that the sailor had murdered her. So Hellinger introduced the grandmother and the grandfather into the constellation. And the person representing the grandfather started staring at his hands in an identical way. What do we conclude from that?"

"He was the murderer, not the sailor."

"Exactly. Something came to light that no one in the family had a clue about. The grandfather had been dead for years, but the crime he had committed, the monstrous, unexpiated guilt, was the cause of the grandson's autism."

Szacki's head was starting to ache. He'd have to buy a book to understand it all. He'd also have to find an expert to give an opinion on the video.

"I understand," he said, rubbing his temples, "but that was an extreme case. What's going on here?" he asked, pointing at the television screen.

"Leaving the family is interpreted within the system as a serious transgression," explained Rudzki. "Henryk felt incredibly guilty as a result. He also felt guilty because he hadn't said goodbye to his parents. And if there's a sense of guilt, there's no mourning. A sense of guilt connects us very strongly with the deceased, and as a result we refuse to let them go. Are you familiar with the phases of mourning?"

Szacki searched his memory.

"Disbelief, despair, organizing, adapting?"

The therapist looked at him in amazement.

"You're right. However, in reality many people stop at the second phase – despair, which no one understands and which turns into loneliness. And this uncompleted mourning remains within the family, causing each successive generation to be connected with death. Please look at what's happening. Henryk wants to go after his parents, but they don't want that. Their place is in the world of the dead, and his is in the world of the living. Let's watch some more."

Rudzki (to Telak): I know you want to stand here, but that's not the right place for you. Please go back to the middle of the room.

Telak goes back.

Kaim: What a relief…

Telak: Please turn around now.

Kaim and Jarczyk turn round.

Jarczyk: That's much better. I'm glad I can see my son.

Kaim: So am I.

Rudzki (to Telak): What about you?

Telak: I'm glad they're looking at me, and that they're with me. But I'd like to go to them.

Rudzki: That's impossible. We'll do it another way.

Rudzki goes up to Kaim and Jarczyk, leads them over to Telak and positions them slightly to one side, behind him.

Kaim: That's perfect. I can see my son, but I'm not obstructing him. I'm not standing in his way.

Jarczyk: It warms my heart. I'd like to hug him, tell him I love him and wish him all the very best.

Rudzki: Wait a moment. (To Telak) Do you feel better too?

Telak: It's easier, but there's still something missing.

Rudzki: The resolution, but we'll do that later.

"What sort of resolution?" asked Szacki, and the therapist stopped the film. "I was wondering earlier what all this is leading to. What does it take to reach exoneration?"

Instead of answering Rudzki started to cough violently and ran to the bathroom, from where sounds of hawking and spitting were audible for quite a time until he came back, red in the face.

"I think I've got tonsillitis," he croaked. "Would you like some tea?"

Szacki said he'd love some. Neither of them broke the silence until they were sitting beside each other again with steaming mugs of tea. Rudzki squeezed the juice of an entire lemon into his mug, then stirred in a lot of honey.

"Best thing for a sore throat," he said, taking a sip. "The resolution involves uttering so-called resolving sentences that the therapist tells the patient and the people representing his family to say. In this case I think Henryk's parents would have said: 'My son, we're going away, and you're staying behind. We love you and we're happy you're here.' Whereas Henryk would have said: 'I'm letting you go. I'm staying here. Think well of me.' Perhaps. It's hard to tell – the resolving sentences usually appear in my head when the right moment comes along."

"And this wasn't the right moment?"

"No. I wanted to leave it to the end. Any more questions?"
Szacki said no.

Rudzki: Good. Now let's replace Mr Telak's family with chairs. (He moves Jarczyk and Kaim aside and puts two chairs in their place.) Now Mr Telak will arrange his current family. Mrs Jarczyk will be his wife, Mr Kaim his son and Miss Kwiatkowska his daughter.
Telak: But my daughter…
Rudzki: Please arrange them.
Telak positions his family, then goes back to his place. Now it looks like this: on the right, slightly behind Telak stand the two chairs representing his parents. On the left, a few yards in front of him, stands Jarczyk (his wife), looking at Telak. Behind her Kwiatkowska and Kaim are standing next to each other. They're looking towards the chairs. Telak isn't looking at any of them.
Rudzki: OK, so that's how it looks. Mr Telak?
Telak: I feel rotten. Guilty. I've got spots before my eyes. May I sit down?
Rudzki: Of course. Please sit on the floor and take a deep breath.
Telak sits down, puts his hands to his mouth and breathes deeply. He keeps his gaze fixed on a single point in space.
Jarczyk: I like it when he feels bad.
Rudzki: And the children?
Kaim: I'm happy to have my sister standing next to me.
Kwiatkowska: And I'd like to go and join my grandparents. I can see them best. I can't see my father at all, my mother's blocking my view of him.
Kaim: I want to go and join my grandparents too. Along with my sister.

The therapist stopped the tape again.

"Do you understand what's happening now?" he asked Szacki.

"Telak is entirely alone. His wife isn't standing beside him, or even letting the children see him. I feel sorry for him."

"Please take note of what the children are saying. They want to be together, and they want to go to the grandparents. What does that mean?"

"They want to die."

"Exactly."

"Why is that?"

"Out of love. Out of love for their father. He broke the system by leaving home without saying goodbye to his parents, and he never made up for it – he didn't pay them due respect. The rule is that someone within the system has to take penance upon himself, and it's usually the child, who comes into the system as a new element. Please understand that things that haven't been resolved don't disappear by themselves, but enter the system. Guilt and evil remain, they're present and perceptible to everyone all the time. The child entering the system takes on the burden of restoring the balance, because he inherits guilt, fear and anger. Do you see?"

"Like Luke Skywalker in *Star Wars*?"

"What?"

"I'm sorry, it's a silly joke. Yes, I think I understand."

"Then let's see what happens next."

Rudzki leads Kwiatkowska and Kaim away from behind Jarczyk. Now they're all standing next to each other, looking at Telak.

Jarczyk (trembling and speaking with difficulty): I don't want my children to stand here. I don't want them to go to my husband's parents. I felt better when they were standing behind me.

Kwiatkowska: I'm glad I can see Daddy and my grandparents. I love them very much. Especially Daddy. I can see he's sad and I'd like to help him.

Kaim: Yes, I agree with my sister, but I feel quite faint. My heart is aching and I'm shaking badly.

Kwiatkowska: May I go over to my grandparents? I feel physically drawn to them.

Rudzki: All right, but just two paces.

Beaming, Kwiatkowska walks towards the chairs. At this sight Jarczyk starts to cry. Pale as the wall, Kaim is rubbing his breastbone.

This time it was Szacki who reached for the remote and stopped the film. Kaim's grimace of pain froze on the screen, and so did Telak's vacant stare, fixed on the wall.

"How can it be possible for Kaim's heart to be aching?" he asked. "I know he's aware that Telak's son is ill, but all the same..."

"That's a tricky one. There's a certain theory, called the theory of morphogenetic fields, that's used to explain Hellinger's therapy. According to this theory, the sort of people we are does not depend on our genes alone, but also on an electromagnetic field. Hellinger says our soul resonates with everything that has happened within our family, and is connected with the living and the dead. During Family Constellation Therapy a stranger can enter into that resonance. We call it the 'knowing field'."

"Do you believe that?"

Rudzki made a vague gesture implying that he was prepared to accept the theory, but only for lack of any other.

"I don't think it matters. What's important is whether something works or not. I don't know how a computer works, but I get a great deal of use out of it."

"Did Telak's son fall ill after his sister's suicide?" asked Szacki.

"Yes, that was when Bartek's heart defect appeared. Illness is always a sign of a breach in the order. Its main dynamic is 'rather me than you'. We decide to suffer in order to relieve another family member. Only restoring the balance and order allows the illness to be cured."

"Doesn't Bartek have a better chance of recovery now that his father has gone?"

Rudzki coughed. He waved apologetically and went into the kitchen, where he blew his nose noisily.

"Mr Szacki," he called from in there, "I wouldn't be taking quite so long to consider the answer if it weren't for your profession and the purpose of your visit. Do you see?"

Szacki got up, took his mug and asked for something to drink.

"So what's the answer?" he asked, pouring into the mug some still mineral water that his host had handed to him.

"I don't know. Maybe. But only maybe. Or perhaps his condition will get even worse. You realize that Mr Telak didn't depart in peace, having settled all his affairs. I think Bartek's condition would have righted itself once the constellation was completed. A change occurs in the field, and from then on it resonates in a different way. That's why the changes are also perceptible in people who aren't taking part in the constellation – they might not even know about it."

They went back to the sofa.

Rudzki: Mr Telak, please get up now.

Telak gets up with evident effort. Jarczyk is crying even louder.

Rudzki (to Kwiatkowska): Why do you want to go to your grandparents?

Kwiatkowska: I want to relieve Daddy.

Telak (devastated): No, that's not possible, I refuse to hear of it.

Kaim: I'm longing to go to my sister and my grandparents. I'm in pain. I want it to stop hurting. And for Dad to feel better.

Jarczyk: This is unbearable. I want him to go away (she points at Telak). I don't love him, I don't even like him, he's repulsive and alien to me. I want everything to calm down. I want him to be gone, not the children.

Telak: But I haven't done anything... (His voice falters, he's incapable of carrying on.)

Jarczyk: I can feel coldness and emptiness. And hatred. It's your fault my child is dead! (She breaks into heart-rending sobs.) Do you understand? My daughter is dead, and my son's going to join her. You've murdered my child!

Kwiatkowska: Daddy, I did it for you. Why can't you understand that? Daddy! (She starts crying.)

Telak sinks to his knees. The entire time he never looks at anyone.

Telak (in a whisper): Leave me alone, it's not my fault.

Kaim (with an effort): Don't worry, Dad, we'll help you.

Kaim goes up to his sister and grabs her hand.

Kwiatkowska: Yes, Daddy, we'll both help you.

They take a step towards the chairs.

Jarczyk: No! I beg you, no! You can't leave me alone with him! You mustn't go. Please don't go, don't leave me alone. Please, please, please.

Kaim turns to face her.

Kaim: Don't be angry, Mum. We have to do it for Dad.

Jarczyk faints. Clearly alarmed, Rudzki runs up to her and kneels down.

Rudzki (to the others): OK, that's all for today, we'll finish this tomorrow morning. It's a bad thing we're stopping, but there's no alternative. Please go to your rooms, please don't talk or read any books. We'll meet up at breakfast tomorrow at nine.

Kwiatkowska and Kaim stare at each other as if shaken out of a trance. They let go of each other's hand and leave the frame. Rudzki lays Jarczyk on her side and goes up to the camera. The entire time Telak is on his knees in the background, staring into space.

The screen went fuzzy. The therapist and the prosecutor sat side by side in silence. After quite a while Szacki got up, went over to the camera and took out the tape.

"That's dreadful," he said, staring at the black plastic box. "Weren't you afraid he'd commit suicide?"

"I admit it occurred to me. But I wasn't afraid."

"How come?"

"I'll tell you something. It's a well-known story – it happened in Leipzig some time ago. Hellinger arranged a woman, and during the constellation it emerged that she was frigid, incapable of love. Her children were afraid of her and wanted to go to their father, whom she had rejected. Hellinger said: 'Here is a cold heart.' Soon after the woman left the room. The other participants in the therapy were afraid she might kill herself, but Hellinger didn't go after her."

"And then what?"

"She hanged herself a few days later, and left a letter saying that she couldn't go on living."

"Pretty effective therapy," muttered Szacki.

"You think you're joking, but in fact you're right. How can we be so sure a premature death is always a loss? That it's always the worst solution? That you have to be saved from it at any price? Perhaps something emerges from life that is greater than it. We all have a need in our souls for the end to come once life is fulfilled. In some people it appears earlier. Do you understand that?"

"I do, but I don't accept it."

"So you must be an omnipotent person if you want to stand in the way of death. I feel humble towards it. If you deprive someone of the right to die, you're actually showing that person a lack of respect. Standing in the way of death is an unreasonable belief in one's own greatness."

The therapist was standing next to Szacki by the French windows. An ambulance was driving down Grójecka Street towards the City Centre with its siren on. The piercing noise was growing more and more insistent. Rudzki closed the window and total silence reigned in the apartment.

"You see, the root of it all is love," he said. "Kasia killed herself to relieve Telak, to take part of his guilt with her. But you say we must stand in the way of death at any cost. How can we not respect such a beautiful act of love and self-sacrifice? We should accept this child's gift. Otherwise after death she will feel rejected. Love simply exists. There's no way of exerting an influence on it. It's helpless. And it's so deep that it hurts. A deep bond and pain go hand in hand."

"That sounds very nice," replied Szacki. "But maybe that's all. It's hard for me to believe someone would commit suicide because his father ran away from home. A person is responsible for his own actions."

"It's impossible not to be entangled – so says Hellinger."

"It's possible to be free, and so say I."

Rudzki started laughing, but his laughter changed into a coughing fit. He escaped to the bathroom, and when he came back, wiping his wet face with a towel, he said: "But is it possible to be free from eating? In the system no one is free."

II

Szacki had a terrible headache. He got into the car, let Pink Floyd play 'Hey You' very quietly, and swallowed some ibuprofen. He opened the window and tried to organize his thoughts. Now he realized why none of the people taking part in the therapy had mentioned the therapist during their interviews – because the therapist was really just an observer, standing in a safe spot, outside the storm of emotions raging under the cross-vaulting in the classroom on Łazienkowska Street.

What had happened on the night of Saturday to Sunday? He could imagine each scene perfectly. The classroom plunged in darkness, yellow light coming from the sodium lamps outside, and shadows moving in columns across the walls whenever a car went down the street. Henryk Telak trying his best to make as little noise as possible as he creeps out of the building. He thinks no one can see him, but that's not true.

Because Barbara Jarczyk can see him. The woman who fainted a few hours earlier, unable to bear the emotions of Telak's wife. Supposing Rudzki's right, thought Szacki reluctantly. Suppose there is a field that allows you to feel other people's emotions during Family Constellation Therapy, and Jarczyk could feel Mrs Telak's emotions. Hatred, aversion, anger, the pain caused by her child's suicide; the fear that her other child would soon be gone too. Except that Jarczyk, unlike Telak's wife, was aware that Henryk was the "culprit". That it was because of him, or for him, that the daughter had committed suicide and the son had fallen ill. Who knows, maybe the idea has sprung up in Jarczyk's head that she can save her "son" by killing Telak. She seizes the skewer and goes after him. Telak hears footsteps, turns round and sees Jarczyk. He's not afraid, he just feels silly that he's going to have to explain himself. Jarczyk strikes. "For my child," she says, but Telak can no longer hear her.

But in that case would Jarczyk have remembered to wipe off the fingerprints? Would she be able to lie so well? And would she have gone to discover the body herself, or rather wouldn't she have waited for someone else to find it?

Scene two: Telak is walking across the hall. He thinks no one can see him, but that's not true. Kaim is watching him, and for the second time that day he's feeling a sharp pain in his heart. The field is working. Kaim is thinking about his dead sister, and about how much life he's still got left. He wants to stop Telak. He wants to complete the therapy and save "himself". But Telak doesn't want to stay there. Kaim insists. Telak refuses and starts heading for the exit. Kaim blocks his way and strikes.

In this particular case, Szacki was sure Kaim would have quickly come to his senses, tidied up and wiped off the fingerprints. And he was capable of lying in a convincing way.

Scene three: Telak thinks no one can see him, but that's not true. Kwiatkowska, his dead daughter, is watching him from a corner of the room. Like a phantom. Maybe she's thinking about how much she has missed, how many years of life, how much happiness, how much travel, how many men, how many children. She has lost everything, purely to help a man who is now sneaking away. He doesn't care about her sacrifice, he's not concerned about her death. "Why are you running away, Daddy?" she asks, emerging from the shadows. "I'm not your dad, you lunatic," replies Telak, and tries to get past her. "How can you? When I've done so much for you," says Kwiatkowska reproachfully. Grief and sorrow mix with rage inside her. "What crap! You didn't do it – go and get cured, woman," says the pissed-off Telak.

Kwiatkowka strikes.

The pill was starting to work. Szacki felt a little better, and kindly allowed Roger Waters to sing 'Bring the Boys Back Home' a touch louder. He called Kuzniecow and drove to the police station. He wanted to have a chat, and to take the opportunity to examine the victim's wallet. He didn't think it had any significance, but Telak was the key to this case. The better he got to know him, the more likely he was to understand the culprit's motive. Or the motive of the virtual culprit, controlled by the ego of a stranger.

My God, isn't it all a bit too screwed up? he thought, as he waited for the light to change, allowing him turn from Pruszkowska Street into Żwirko i Wigura Avenue.

III

In the canteen at the City Centre police station on Wilcza Street Kuzniecow ordered a coffee and a chocolate cake, and Szacki ordered tomato juice. He'd already swallowed too much caffeine in all those mugs of coffee and tea at Rudzki's place. He told the policeman about yesterday's interviews and today's visit to the therapist.

"Twisted," said Kuzniecow, unsuccessfully trying to slice off a bit of cake with his fork without letting whipped cream squirt out in all directions. "So in a way Telak's wife and son are just as much suspects."

"Not suspects. It's more that if they have a convincing motive, the people involved in the therapy could have been driven by that motive. I'll interview them tomorrow – we'll see."

"If that turns out to be true, any second-rate lawyer will get them out of trouble. Just think – you see a person for the first time in your life, then a quarter of an hour later you pretend to be his son, and as a result you grab a skewer and stick it in his eye. In other words, you as yourself have absolutely no motive at all."

Szacki shook his head. He'd already thought of that too. He asked if they'd managed to establish any facts at Łazienkowska Street.

"Not a thing. There are a couple of people left to question, but I don't think we'll get a result. They arrived on Friday, sat there locked in and didn't communicate with anyone. The girl who brought them food and did the washing-up spoke to Rudzki twice. She never saw any of the patients. The priest who rented out the room had one meeting with Rudzki, and the conversation lasted five minutes. Rudzki is a member of the Christian Psychologists' Association – he was recommended, so the priest had no doubts. Now he's sorry and he hopes we catch the criminal. Very nice fellow, I talked to him myself. Looks a bit of a wanker, like all of them, but he's quite businesslike."

"Is there anything missing from the church?"

"Not a bean."

"Security guard?"

"Stop or I'll choke laughing. A sixty-eight-year-old man dozing in front of a tiny television in the porter's lodge. I could have gone in there at night with ten mates, shot the entire company with a machine gun, and he'd still have sworn it was all peace and quiet with no one hanging about. There are no signs of a break-in, but the door was probably open."

Szacki raised his hands in a gesture of impatience and brought them down on the table.

"Brilliant," he growled.

"What do you mean?" asked Kuzniecow, raising his voice.

"As usual you've established shit all."

"What do you think I'm supposed to do? Turn back time, tell them to employ an observant doorman and install cameras?"

Szacki buried his face in his hands.

"Sorry, Oleg, I'm having a rotten day. That therapist's given me a headache – for all I know he's infected me with something. What's more I've forgotten why I'm here."

"You wanted to see me because you like me," said Kuzniecow, stroking the prosecutor's white hair.

"Fuck off."

"Aaaww, what a rude prosecutor."

Szacki bust out laughing.

"Someone's said that to me every day lately. I was going to take a look at Telak's things, mainly his wallet, and I wanted to tell you to take fingerprints from the bottle of sleeping pills and question the people at Polgrafex. Any enemies, conflicts, badly placed investments, relationships at work. You should also show them pictures of Rudzki and the whole fabulous threesome. Rudzki was there once, they should recognize him, but if they recognize any of the others, that'll be something. I'll show them to Mrs Telak and her son. It might turn out they weren't strangers at all."

Kuzniecow grimaced.

"I doubt it too," replied Szacki, pulling a similar face, and he drank the dregs of his tomato juice. Only now did he remember that he liked it best with salt and pepper.

He had only seen Henryk Telak's face once and he'd done his best to do so for as short a time as possible, despite which he could be sure the daughter looked incredibly like him. The same thick eyebrows meeting gently above the nose, the same nose with a thick bridge to it. Neither the former nor the latter ever made any woman prettier, so the girl staring at him from the photo looked common. And also provincial, which she undoubtedly owed to the coarse features she had inherited from her father. Telak's son looked as if he'd been adopted. Szacki couldn't find any features to connect his boyish appearance with his father and sister. Nor was he particularly like his mother, who didn't look transparent and ethereal, which seemed from the picture to be her son's main characteristics. Surprising how very dissimilar children can be to their parents.

The girl and boy were not smiling, though these weren't passport photos, but two pieces of a family photograph taken at the seaside, with waves visible in the background. The photograph had been cut in half, and there was a black velvet ribbon running through the half showing Kasia. Szacki wondered why Telak had cut the photograph in two. He must have been afraid the mourning ribbon would imply that both his children had died.

As well as the photos, the wallet contained an identity card and a driving licence, from which it emerged that Henryk Telak was born in May 1959 in Ciechanów and that he knew how to ride a motorbike. A few credit cards, two marked "business", surely for company accounts. A prescription for Duomox – an antibiotic for tonsillitis, if Szacki remembered correctly. A speeding ticket – 200 zlotys. A postage stamp with a picture of the Olympic ski-jumper Adam Małysz – Szacki was surprised it had ever been issued. A card for the Beverly Hills video library in Powiśle. A card for collecting points from BP. A card from the Coffee Heaven chain, almost entirely filled. Just one more stamp and Telak would have got his next coffee for free. A few faded, illegible till receipts. Szacki did the same – he'd buy something, take the receipt as a guarantee, and the saleswoman would advise him in a friendly way to photocopy it, or else it'd fade, so he'd agree, stick the receipt in his wallet and forget about it. Two lottery tickets confirming that bets had been placed, and two lottery forms filled in by hand. Evidently Telak believed in the magic of figures rather than random luck. He had some lucky numbers too. On each coupon and each form one set was identical: 7, 8, 9, 17, 19, 22. Szacki wrote down these numbers, and after thinking for a while he noted down all the sets of numbers Telak had listed for Saturday's lottery. After all, no one had checked it in Monday's paper, and who knows? Maybe Telak had got all six right. Szacki felt ashamed at the thought that he could keep the coupons for himself instead of handing them over to the widow. Could he really? Of course not! Or maybe he could? A round million, maybe more – he wouldn't have to work for the rest of his life. He had often wondered if it was true that everyone had his price. How much would it take for him to drop an inquiry, for example? A hundred thousand, two hundred thousand? It'd be interesting to see at what price he'd start to wonder, instead of simply saying "no".

IV

Henryk Telak hadn't even got three numbers right. Szacki had dug out yesterday's paper at the prosecution front office and checked the numbers. Two right three times, and of the "lucky numbers" only 22 was correct. He also got a copy of *Rzeczpospolita* and read Miss Grzelka's article about the murder, confirming his opinion that this paper was capable of turning any case into a sensation on a par with a new type of margarine appearing in the shops. Boring, boring and more boring. Despite which he still felt bad at the thought of how he'd treated the journalist yesterday. He could still remember her smile as she said: "You're a very rude prosecutor." Maybe she wasn't his type, but that smile... Perhaps he should call her? All in all, why not? You only live once, and in twenty years' time no young journalist would want to go out for a coffee with him. He'd been faithful as a hound for the past ten years, yet somehow he didn't feel particularly proud of the fact. Quite the contrary – he couldn't help feeling as if life were passing him by as he gave up the best side of it.

He took Grzelka's business card out of the desk drawer, turned it in his fingers for a while, took the decision, put his hand on the receiver, and just then the phone rang.

"Good afternoon, Ireneusz Nawrocki calling."

"Good afternoon, Superintendent," replied Szacki, putting the business card aside with some sense of relief.

Nawrocki was a policeman from City Police Headquarters, perhaps the most original of all the cops in the city. Szacki thought highly of him but didn't like him. They had worked together twice, and each time trying to get information out of Nawrocki on what he was doing, what he'd done and what he was planning to do had been like an inquiry in itself. Nawrocki went his own ways, but none of them ran past the prosecutor's office, and hardly anyone was as bothered by that as Szacki, who wanted tight control over every stage of the proceedings. But both their inquiries had ended in success, so Szacki had to admit that thanks to the information gathered by the policeman he'd written an unusually powerful indictment.

"Do you remember the corpse they dug up at the play-school?"

Szacki said he did. It was a well-publicized case. They'd been renovating the play area at a nursery school on Krucza Street to replace the ancient swings with an adventure playground, a sports pitch and so on. They'd dug up the play area and found a body. An old one, so everyone had thought it might date from the war, from the Uprising. But it soon appeared that it was a thirteen-year-old schoolgirl from the school next door to the nursery who'd gone missing in 1993. They'd located all her classmates and teachers, it had been a huge job. Of course it was all a waste of time, because hardly anyone could remember what they'd been doing on one particular night ten years ago. They had some files from the inquiry into the girl's disappearance, but that sort of case is conducted in a completely different way – certain questions are never asked. Finally the inquiry was suspended because they hadn't been able to establish the addresses of several of the girl's friends. The police had tried looking for them, but not very persistently. He knew that Nawrocki was still plodding along at this case, but he had given up begging him for information. He knew that if the policeman did find anything, he'd still have to ask for the inquiry to be reinstated.

"So this man rang the police anonymously," Nawrocki told him in a monotonous tone, which reminded Szacki of an academic lecturer, "and told a very interesting story."

"Well?" Szacki didn't believe in anonymous stories.

"He said that Boniczka – that was the girl's name, Sylwia Boniczka – was raped by three boys from another class in her year, one of whom was repeating the year. You remember what happened – she left a friend's house on Poznańska Street late at night and never got home. She must have walked past the school on the way. And there are always various guys hanging around outside school, at any time of day or night, you know what I mean. Maybe not nowadays, but at one time that was the case."

Szacki started to wonder. Indeed, they hadn't questioned any pupils apart from her classmates, they'd just relied on the old inquiry files, which hadn't brought any results. The pathologist had been unable to establish whether the girl had been raped, so they'd spent the whole time conducting it as a murder case, not a rape. As far as he could remember, Boniczka hadn't been in contact with the kids from other classes. They would have checked at the time.

"Did the guy who called anonymously give any names?" asked Szacki, not even trying to hide the mockery in his voice.

"No. But he did give some extra facts. Very interesting ones and, in my humble opinion, demanding a follow-up," Nawrocki went on in his monotone. "He said it wasn't the rapists who killed her. That after the incident she went to her father, and he was the one who killed her and buried her in the playground. That he couldn't bear the shame. That he didn't want people to find out."

Teodor Szacki felt the skin on the back of his neck and shoulders go numb.

"Prosecutor, do you remember who Boniczka's father was?" asked Nawrocki.

"Yes, he was the school caretaker," replied Szacki.

"Exactly. So maybe you'll get the files out of the cupboard?"

"Of course. Please just send me a message confirming this conversation. Try to find all the pupils repeating a year from the other classes and put the necessary pressure on them, then I'll interrogate the father."

"I can interrogate him myself, Prosecutor," suggested Nawrocki.

Szacki hesitated. He had a lot to do, including a huge pile of paperwork, but he didn't want to give way to Nawrocki.

"We'll see," he said, trying to put off the decision. "First let's test the theory about the rape. And there's one more thing, Superintendent." He paused, but there wasn't the slightest cough from the other end. "I don't think you've told me everything."

Silence.

"I mean, nowadays you can quite quickly and easily trace anyone who calls the police. Are you sure you don't know who it was?"

"Do you promise it won't have any bearing on your decision?"

"Yes, I promise."

"Well, we did trace the man, and he turned out to be from Łódź. I even went there to talk to him." Nawrocki fell silent, and Szacki was just about to say "And…", but he stopped himself.

"And he turned out to be a very nice old gentleman. A clairvoyant. He'd once read about the case in the paper, then he'd had a dream about what had happened. He'd hesitated for a while, but in the end he'd called. I know what you might think, but you must admit it holds water."

Szacki agreed reluctantly. He trusted his own instincts, but not retired clairvoyants who called the police anonymously. Except that this time the old boy's visions did match one of his theories. He'd always thought it was no accident the girl had been buried in the grounds of the playschool right next to the high school where her father worked. But he'd never had even the shadow of a clue to draw on. Besides, he'd been afraid his theory might prove correct.

Nawrocki hung up, and Szacki wrote down: "Boniczka – files, father, wait for I.N." He should get on with writing the indictment in the Nidziecka case now, but he didn't feel inspired. He should draft the decisions to discontinue two other inquiries, but he didn't feel like it. He should number the documents in an armed robbery case, but he felt even less like doing that – there were four volumes of them. Hopeless paperwork. He should call Monika Grzelka, but he didn't have the courage.

He picked up the stapler, the basic tool for any prosecutor's job, and put it on the desk in front of him. He gathered the papers to one side to make a bit of space. Good, he thought, let's suppose that's me. And this is Weronika – he got an apple from his briefcase, took a bite out of it and arranged it opposite the stapler. And this is Helka – he put his mobile phone next to the stapler. And my parents – two plastic mugs landed to one side, also clearly facing towards the stapler.

What's the conclusion? Szacki asked himself. That they're all gawping at me and they all want something from me. That I've got no space in front of me. That I'm the prisoner of my own family, the hook for this entire bloody arrangement. Or rather system, as Rudzki called it.

Something was bothering him about the objects scattered on the desk. He felt as if he hadn't arranged everyone. He added his brother, in the form of a box of paper clips, but his brother was on the side and didn't really have any significance. Death, thought Szacki, look for death. Find someone who could have left a sense of mourning behind them. His grandparents? Not especially – they had all died at an advanced age and they'd had time to say goodbye to everyone. Some other relative perhaps? Szacki's mother had a sister in Wrocław, but his aunt was in good health. His father had a younger brother who lived in Żoliborz. Hold on a moment. Szacki remembered that his father had had another younger brother too, who had died at barely two years old. How old was his father then? Four, maybe five. He took a cigarette packet from his pocket, thought for a while and placed it next to his father, almost exactly opposite himself. Curiously, his deceased uncle was staring straight at him. It made Szacki feel uneasy. He'd always thought he was named after his grandfathers – Teodor after his father's father and Wiktor after his mother's. Now he realized that his father's dead brother was also called Wiktor. How strange. So had his father named him after his father and his dead brother? Maybe that was why their relationship had been and was still so complicated. And why was that bloody dead uncle gawping at him? And did it have any consequences for him? Or for his daughter? Helka was also facing towards the uncle. Szacki's mouth suddenly felt terribly dry and he took a swig of water.

"Hello, if you like we can have a whip round to buy you some building blocks," said Prosecutor Jerzy Bińczyk sticking his head round the door. For two years, which was as long as they'd known each other, Bińczyk had been a puzzle to Szacki. How can you be an idler and a careerist all at once? he wondered whenever he saw Bińczyk, with his receding hairline, his crumpled jacket and his tie made of a mysterious Chinese material. Was it possible to produce PVC so thin it could be tied in a knot?

"It must be tough in your village in winter, eh?" said Szacki sympathetically.

"What's that?" Bińczyk frowned.

"No need to knock, is there? But keeping the door propped open with a sheaf of straw must get bloody windy."

Bińczyk went purple. Furious, he thrust a hand into the room and knocked as hard as he could on Szacki's door.

"Better? I was brought up on Hoża Street, so leave it out."

"Really? So there's a Hoża Street on the Nowy Dwór housing estate as well as in the City Centre?" Szacki felt like taking it out on someone.

Bińczyk rolled his eyes.

"I heard you'll be working with us on the goods from Central Station."

"Maybe from Monday."

"Great, then perhaps you'd take a look at the files this week, find an expert witness to estimate the market value of the drugs and write a ruling on getting an expert opinion."

"We've had Monday this week already. I was talking about next Monday."

"Be human, Teo. We're buried in work, we're way behind, the remand deadline will pass soon, and the supervisory board's putting on the pressure."

So you're hurting, thought Szacki. You're afraid you won't shine at the Regional Prosecutor's office, that they won't remember you for ever as that clever guy who was really great at preparatory proceedings, but as the one who couldn't get an inquiry completed within the deadline. Oh dear, maybe you'll have to stay until five a couple of times. You'll survive, boy. Same goes for your pal. Bloody skivers, and then they complain the loudest when the Prosecution Service gets bad press.

"I won't be able to, sorry. Maybe not even next week," he said.

"Don't joke about it!" said Bińczyk, making a face like a spoiled kid. "The old witch must have told you."

"She did mention such an eventuality."

"Have I ever told you working with you is a nightmare?"

"Don't worry. They're going to transfer me. You'll have peace."

"Really? Where to?" Bińczyk became distinctly animated.

"To the supervisory board on Krakowskie Przedmieście. They say they want someone to keep an eye on the inquiries at City Centre. We've been getting worse and worse results."

Bińczyk just stuck out his middle finger and left. Szacki replied with the same gesture, but only once the door had closed. He stared at the objects arranged on his desk, removed himself – in other words the stapler – from the constellation and put it on the window sill.

"Time for some changes," he said aloud, stuck a staple in Grzelka's business card and rang the number. She recognized his voice at once, and they agreed to meet at five in Cava on the corner of Nowy Świat and Foksal Streets. As he reached for the armed robbery files, Szacki could still hear her low voice saying what a nice surprise it was. Even when he saw a card attached to the first page with the message: "Expenses sheet – don't forget!" he didn't stop smiling.

V

In theory, things were looking up. Arranging to meet a girl for coffee – guys do that sort of thing, don't they? Meanwhile Szacki felt like someone whose tooth suddenly starts hurting badly while he's travelling in the wastes of Kazakhstan and who knows the only hope for him is a trip to the local dentist. He was shivering slightly, though it wasn't all that cold, there was a buzzing noise in his left ear, and his hands were cold and damp. He felt like a clown in his suit and coat, while everyone around him was wearing at most anoraks thrown over T-shirts.

Something must have happened in the city because there was an endless chain of trams standing in Jerozolimskie Avenue, and the cars heading for the Praga district were stuck in a gigantic traffic jam. He thought Miss Grzelka would be sure to be late, because it was the exact route that she'd have to take to get to Nowy Świat Street from the newspaper office which was blocked. That was better even – it's always more comfortable to be the person waiting. He passed the old Polish Press Agency building, waited for the lights to change and crossed the avenue. He took leaflets from several students. He didn't need them, but Weronika had taught him to take them, because that way you help people whose jobs aren't easy or well paid. At the Empik bookshop there was a poster announcing the arrival of the new *Splinter Cell*, the third one now. It was one of his favourite games, and he'd be happy to reassume the role of Sam Fisher, the embittered tough guy.

He passed the legendary Amatorska Café, ran across Nowy Świat at an illegal point and reached Foksal Street. Monika Grzelka was already waiting in the café garden. She noticed him immediately and waved.

"I see you walk at the swaggering pace of a cavalryman," she said as he came up to the table.

"But I haven't got a coat with a crimson lining," he said, offering his hand in greeting.

"The cruel Fifth Procurator of the City Centre?"

"Have no fear – I think the people of Warsaw will prefer to let the beautiful woman go rather than Barabbas." He couldn't believe he was spouting such nonsense.

She burst into sincere laughter, and Szacki suppressed a smile, unable to shake off the shock. What if she'd chosen a different story? One he didn't know? He'd have made a proper fool of himself. He sat down, trying to look confident and a little blasé. He hung his coat on the back of the neighbouring chair. He looked at the journalist and wondered if he hadn't judged her too harshly yesterday. She had a freshness and energy about her, which added to her appeal. Wearing a blouse with a black gemstone decorating her neckline, she looked charming. He felt like paying her a compliment.

"Nice tie," she said.

"Thank you," he replied, and thought he'd get revenge by saying how great she looked in that blouse, but he didn't respond. He was afraid it would sound like "Hey, babe, I'd like to screw you standing up".

She ordered a latte and a piece of *kaimak* cake, he asked for a small black coffee and spent a while wondering what cake to choose. He'd have loved a meringue, but he was afraid he'd make an idiot of himself as soon as he tried cutting it and sent meringue flying in all directions, and would end up paying more attention to the food than to the conversation. He chose a cheesecake. How original you are, Teodor, he dressed himself down mentally. Go on and ask for instant coffee and a packet of Sobieskis, and you'll be a real Polish prosecutor through and through.

She didn't ask why he had called her, but even so he explained that he felt ashamed of how he'd behaved yesterday. He praised her article, at which she just made a face – she must have realized it wasn't in the world champion's league.

"I didn't know enough," she said, and shrugged.

Then she told him a little about her job. That she was worried about whether she'd manage, that she felt nervous dealing with people from the police, the Prosecution Service and the courts.

"Some of them can be brusque," she sighed in a surge of sincerity, and blushed.

Just then his mobile rang. He glanced at the display. It said "Kitten", in other words, Weronika. O God, could it be possible women were telepathic? After all, he had called her to say he'd be late. Hadn't he? He wasn't sure any more. Rather than answer it, he just turned off the phone. Tough – at worst he'd make something up later.

Miss Grzelka asked if there was any news on the murder case on Łazienkowska Street, adding at once that she wasn't asking for professional reasons, but out of personal curiosity. He wanted to tell her the truth, but he knew it would be injudicious to do so.

"Yes, there is," he said, "but I can't talk about it. Please forgive me."

She nodded.

"I do have something else for you though – let's call it a present to say sorry."

"I thought the coffee was my present."

"On the contrary, coffee in your company is a present for me." She fluttered her eyelashes comically, and Szacki found it charming. "I'm now writing the indictment for a murder case, and next week we're going to send it to court. It's a very interesting case, I think it might make a good contribution to an article on domestic violence."

"Who was the killer? He or she?"

"She was."

"Any details?"

"I'd prefer not to tell them now. Not at a café table. I'll give you a copy of the indictment – it'll all be in there. Then we can talk, if you've got any questions." He thought that sounded as indifferent as he could make it, and that she wouldn't be able to detect any hint of hope in his voice.

"Can you do that?"

"Do what?"

"Give someone a copy of an indictment?"

"Of course, it's a public document prepared by a civil servant. The trial starts from the indictment, and the entire court proceedings are open, as long as the court doesn't have some reason to decide otherwise."

They went on talking for a while about court and prosecution procedures. Szacki was surprised she was so interested. For him it was a laborious bureaucratic burden and a pointless waste of time. Every prosecutor should really have an assistant to take care of all that rubbish.

"Do you read crime novels?" she suddenly asked, just after they'd ordered a glass of wine each and requested an ashtray. It turned out the girl smoked, and Szacki was glad he still had two cigarettes left.

He did read them, yes. Some of their tastes were different – he liked the tough guys such as Lehane and Chandler, and she liked the writers who played with the genre such as Leon and Camilleri – but as for Rankin and Mankell, they were one hundred per cent in agreement. For the next half hour they talked about Inspector Rebus adventures. When Szacki glanced at his watch, mentally telling himself off for doing so, it was coming up to seven. She noticed his action.

"I don't know about you, Mr Szacki, but I've got to fly now," she said.

He nodded. He wondered who should suggest they call each other by their first names. On the one hand, she was a woman, and on the other he was about ten years older than her – traditionally either the woman or the older person should do it. What a silly situation. Maybe next time they met it would come up somehow. He reached into his jacket pocket for a business card, scrawled his mobile number on it and handed it to her.

"Please feel free to call if you have any questions, Miss Grzelka."

She smiled roguishly. "Even in the evenings?"

"If you have any questions," he repeated emphatically, thinking at the same time of his switched-off phone and how many messages Weronika would have left by now.

"In fact I have got a question, a personal one."

He made a gesture encouraging her to go ahead.

"Why do you have such white hair?" she asked.

Yes, that was a personal question. Could he tell her the truth? How when Helka was three years old she'd fallen ill with a blood infection. How she'd lain in the hospital on Niekłańska Street, barely alive, her thin little body pale to the point of transparency, hooked up to a drip. How he and Weronika had wept in the hospital corridor, huddled together, not sleeping, not eating, as they'd waited for the verdict. How the doctor hadn't promised any improvement. How they had prayed ardently for hours on end, though neither of them was a believer. How he'd fallen asleep in spite of himself and then woken up terrified that he'd slept through the moment when his daughter died and that he hadn't said goodbye to her. Barely conscious, he'd run into the ward where the little one was lying. She was alive. It was seven in the morning, December, pitch black outside. He'd seen his reflection in the mirror and given a silent scream, because in a single night his hair had gone completely white.

"Genes," he replied. "I started going grey when I was still at school. I console myself that it's better to have white hair than be bald. Do you like it?"

She laughed.

"Hmmm. It's sexy. Maybe very sexy. Goodbye, Prosecutor Szacki."

VI

You have three new voice messages: "Hi, call me"; "What's the point of having a mobile if either you switch it off or you don't take it with you? Call me as soon as you get this message"; "Hi, guess who. If you're still alive, get a loaf of bread on the way home and some cigarettes for me, because I forgot. If you're not, come and see me in a dream and tell me where your insurance policy is."

As he listened to the last one he started laughing. At moments like these he remembered why he'd fallen in love with this girl, the only one who'd been able to regard him with pity when he'd made a monkey of himself at college. God, how many years was it now? Ten years since the wedding, and how long had they known each other? Fourteen. More than a third of his life. Almost half. He could hardly believe it. At the last minute, just before nine, he'd made it to the shop and got a loaf of bread and some cigarettes. The saleswoman – the same one as eight years ago – had smiled at him. Strange, but they never exchanged a word more than what you usually say when you're shopping. Briefly he thought of saying something else – they'd known each other for so many years, but he paid without a word and left. At home he walked straight into the inner circle of hell.

"Daddy, Daddy, why can't I have my birthday at McDonald's?"

"Why haven't you gone to bed yet?" he replied smartly.

"Because Mum didn't tell me to."

"Seriously?"

An armchair creaked in the sitting room.

"That brat is as big a liar as you are," shouted Weronika from inside the flat.

Szacki looked at his daughter, who was standing in the hall with an angelic expression on her face.

"I never tell lies," he whispered.

"Neither do I," whispered Helka.

Weronika came up to them and looked helplessly at the little girl with chestnut-coloured hair.

"Do something, you're her father after all. Tell her she's got to brush her teeth and go to bed, and that she's not having her birthday at McDonald's. Over my dead body."

"Everyone has their birthday at McDonald's," said Helka.

"I don't care what everyone does," muttered Weronika. "And I'm not interested in you two either. Where have you been all this time?" she asked Szacki, kissing him on the nose by way of greeting. "Have you been drinking?" she added, frowning.

"I had to meet up with Oleg and I drank tea and apple juice," he lied glibly – he suffered from the usual prosecutor's aberration; he thought everyone told lies, and he did his best to recognize exactly when they were doing it, but he also knew that, unless you tell them straight out they're being deceived, or unless you're spouting horrendous, improbable nonsense, normal people take everything at face value.

"You should have invited them over, we haven't met up for ages. I wonder how Natalia's doing?"

Szacki hung up his coat and jacket. It was a relief to take off his tie and shoes. Maybe I should learn how to go to work in a T-shirt and sandals after all, he thought – it'd be much more comfortable. The whole time Helka went on standing in the hall with her head drooping and her arms crossed. He picked her up and cuddled her.

"And what if we find a really fabulous place?" he said. "A hundred times better than McDonald's, with a huge playground? Where you can run about and all that?"

"There aren't any places like that," replied Helka.

"But what if we find one?"

"I'll think about it."

"In that case will you go and brush your teeth now and give us some time to look?"

She nodded in silence, let him put her down and ran to the bathroom. He wondered where they were going to find a playground where they could hold her birthday party for a reasonable price.

He went into the kitchen, took a can of beer out of the fridge, opened it and stood beside Weronika. She cuddled up to him and began to purr.

"I'm hardly alive."

"Just like me," he said.

They stood without talking, until the silence was broken by a bleep announcing a text message.

"That's yours," muttered Weronika.

Szacki went into the hall and took the phone out of his jacket. "Thank you for a wonderful evening. You're a very rude prosecutor, but a very nice one too. MG."

"What is it?" asked Weronika.

"Just an advert. Send a hundred texts and you might win a mug. Something like that, I deleted it."

The final remark was actually true.

4

Wednesday, 8th June 2005

Argentina beat Brazil 3—1 in the World Cup qualifying stages. The first child is born whose mother
had part of an ovary transplanted from another
woman. Archbishop Stanisław Dziwisz visits Kraków
and announces that he will not burn any of John
Paul II's notebooks. In Popowo, the suburban site
of the women's prison, a conference is held on
"women in prison". Up to a third of those convicted are murderesses, usually victims of domestic
violence. From today anyone who identifies those
guilty of killing cormorants at the bird sanctu-
ary on Lake Jeziorak will be rewarded with a home
cinema and 10,000 zlotys. An advertising code of
conduct is established for Polish breweries: they
will not be allowed to use the images of people or
characters who have a particular influence on mi-
nors. In Warsaw a big gala is held to celebrate the
fiftieth anniversary of the Palace of Youth, within
the Palace of Culture; a twenty-foot-high monu-
ment is erected on Ujazdowskie Avenue in memory
of General Stefan "Grot" Rowecki; and at Pawiak,
the Second World War prison, the bronze sculpture
of an elm tree is unveiled, which was a symbol of
freedom for the prisoners. The police broke up a
gang of criminals making alcohol out of windscreen
washing fluid. Ten thousand litres of the drink
were seized and two people were taken into custody. Maximum temperature in the city — thirteen
degrees; no sun and a little rain.

Teodor Szacki had always been surprised by the number of corpses they crammed into the Forensic Medicine Unit on Oczko Street. Besides Telak, there were three more bodies on the other dissection tables, and four more waiting by the window on hospital stretchers. There was a smell of steak tartare in the air, seasoned with a faint odour of faeces and vomit – the result of examining the intestines and stomach. The "necrophiliacs" who were going to deal with Telak were quite young. The older one was about forty, the younger looked as if he'd only just graduated. Szacki stood by the wall. He'd never been fascinated by autopsies, though he knew a good pathologist could tell more from a corpse than the entire Forensics Laboratory (of which the City Police Headquarters were so proud) could from evidence secured at the incident site. All the same, he wanted it to be over as soon as possible.

The older doctor gave him a derisive look as he pulled on his latex gloves.

"Was it you who asked us to check if the deceased had stuck the skewer in his own eye?"

For pity's sake, thought Szacki, spare me a wisecracking pathologist. That's too much so early in the day.

"We have to know," he replied calmly.

"A very cunning theory," said the doctor, smiling mischievously, and began to give the body a thorough examination.

The assistant took notes.

"There are no signs of bruising, cuts, stab wounds or lacerations or bullet holes on the limbs and trunk," dictated the pathologist. He carefully lifted the sunken eyelid under which Telak's eye had once been. "Right eye missing, fragments of vitreous body and cornea visible on the cheek." He put a finger in the eye socket and dug out the remains of something grey; Szacki squinted to lose focus. "Skull bone behind right eye socket crushed, pushed inwards, in all likelihood by a sharp instrument." He lifted the head and examined it closely, parting the hair. "Otherwise the head shows no evidence of other injuries."

"I'm shuddering at the thought of the next instruction," the surgeon said to Szacki, as with a confident movement he made a Y-shaped incision in Telak's ribcage and belly, folded back the skin and hooked it on the chin; meanwhile his assistant "scalped" the skull. "Now let's think, maybe this'll be it: 'We want you to establish if the deceased, found with his head cut off under a tramcar, could possibly have cut it off himself with a pair of scissors, then lain down on the tracks and waited for an approaching vehicle.'"

"People do all sorts of things," said Szacki, raising his voice to shout over the noise of the electric saw the younger pathologist was using to cut the skull. As usual at this moment he wanted to leave – he couldn't bear the wet squelch that went with opening the head. He belched biliously when he heard the loathsome sound. Just like the noise when you try to clear a blocked sink.

Szacki was expecting more jokes, but the surgeons concentrated on their work. The younger one was tying something up deep inside the trunk, while with expert movements the older one was using an instrument deceptively similar to a bread knife to remove Telak's internal organs and put them on a spare table top at the corpse's feet. Then he went up to the open skull.

"Good, cutting up the offal can wait – there's nothing there anyway. Let's take a look at this head." He moved a small aluminium table up to the open skull, gently removed Telak's grey-and-red brain and put it on a tray. He peered inside the skull. Suddenly he frowned.

"He must have found it intolerable – maybe he really did kill himself," he said seriously. Szacki took two paces closer.

"What is it?" he asked.

The doctor rummaged inside Telak's head, clearly trying to

pull something out that was putting up resistance. A scene from *Alien* appeared before Szacki's eyes. The pathologist twisted his hand, as if trying to turn a key in a lock, and slowly withdrew it. There between his fingers was a rolled-up condom.

"I think he had an obsession but he couldn't live with it. Poor guy..." The doctor lowered his head pensively, while his assistant shook with suppressed laughter, and Szacki bit his lip.

"You must be aware there's a paragraph in the penal code about desecrating corpses," he said coldly.

The pathologist threw the condom in the bin and gave Szacki the sort of look children in class give the teacher's pet.

"How do you people manage to be such boring bureaucrats?" he asked. "Do you get special training?"

"We have psychological tests during our studies," replied Szacki. "Will you carry on, or do I have to call the office and ask for two days' leave?"

The doctor didn't answer. In silence he examined the inside of the skull and, very carefully, the brain, then cut the internal organs into slices. Szacki recognized the heart, lungs and stomach. He belched again. He should have drunk tea that morning, not coffee, he thought. Finally the surgeon looked inside the stomach; the air was filled with a sour odour.

"Your client was sick shortly before he died," the doctor told the prosecutor. "Pretty thoroughly."

Szacki immediately thought of the empty bottle of sleeping pills found in his room.

"Can we tell what did it?" he asked

"You mean was it the carrot or the chops?" said the pathologist, unable to resist a little irony.

"I mean toxicology."

"Of course we can, we just need instructions. Should we check everything, or for the presence of a particular substance?"

"A particular one."

"You know what? We could write out a toxicology form on the spot. It'll be quicker."

Szacki replied that he'd find out the name of the substance while they were sewing him up.

"OK," said the pathologist. "The victim was healthy, there were no pathological changes in the internal organs. Heart fine, lungs of a non-smoker, no cancer, no ulcers. I'd like to be in that sort of condition when I'm fifty. Cause of death obvious, in other words damage to the brain caused by a sharp instrument. The skewer pierced the substantia nigra and medulla oblongata, the oldest parts of the brain responsible for the basic life processes. The perfect thrust. He died instantly. Compared with this, a bullet in the temple is a long and painful death. The skewer went through the brain and stopped at the occipital bone – you can see the mark from the inside. In other words the blow was pretty hard, but not powerful enough to make a hole in the skull."

"Could a woman have delivered a blow like that?" asked Szacki.

"Easily. The skull bone in the eye socket is thin, it doesn't take much force to pierce it, and after that it's just jelly. It's hard for me to tell the height of the attacker, to forestall your next question, but I think he can't have been either very small or very tall. There's a seventy per cent chance he was the same height as the victim, but that's just for your information, I can't write that in the report."

"Could he have done it himself?"

The doctor thought for a while. Behind him the other surgeon was unceremoniously packing the organs into the dissected Telak, filling the empty spots with crumpled-up newspaper.

"I doubt it. Firstly, it'd be the first time I ever heard of someone committing suicide this way. And I don't mean the skewer, just the very idea of sticking something into one's own brain through the eye. Can you imagine anyone doing that? I can't. Secondly, it would be technically difficult. The skewer is long, it's hard to get hold of, and hard to apply force. But of course it is doable. I can't rule it out one hundred per cent."

Szacki thanked him and went outside to call Oleg and find out the name of the drug.

"Tranquiloxyl, active ingredient alphazolam, two milligram tablets," the policeman read out from his notes. "By the way, we've done the fingerprints."

"And?" asked Szacki.

"Telak's and Jarczyk's are on the bottle. No others."

II

WITNESS INTERVIEW TRANSCRIPT. Jadwiga Telak, born 20th November 1962, resident at Karłowicz Street in Warsaw, has higher education, unemployed. Relationship to parties: wife of Henryk Telak (victim), no previous convictions for bearing false witness.

Cautioned re criminal responsibility under Article 233 of the Penal Code, her statement is as follows:

"I have been married to Henryk Telak since 1988, and two children were born of this union: Katarzyna (known as Kasia), in 1988, and Bartosz (known as Bartek), in 1991. My daughter committed suicide in September 2003. Until then my relationship with my husband was good, though of course there were better and worse times. However, after our daughter's death we became very distant from each other. We tried hard to pretend everything was all right, we thought that would be better for Bartek, who was twelve at the time. But it was just a pretence. We had started talking about how to part ways in a civilized manner, and that was when Bartek fell ill. That is, he was already ill earlier, but that was when he collapsed, and after some tests it turned out he had a fatal heart defect. Unless a miracle occurs or we get an

organ for transplant, he will die within two years, that's what they told us. It was terrible news, which paradoxically brought us very close to each other. Together we fought to get the best doctors and hospitals. It cost us a fortune, but my husband ran a printing firm and we were well off. Thanks to our son's illness we didn't even have time to brood about our daughter's death, and that was a good thing. But Henryk felt crushed by it all. He couldn't sleep, he'd jolt awake with a scream, and he sometimes took a tranquillizer. He drank, but not to get drunk. In autumn last year he met Cezary Rudzki and started going to see him for therapy. I can't remember how they met, Mr Rudzki had some business at Polgrafex, as far as I remember. At first the therapy didn't lead to any improvement, but after some time, roughly three months, my husband had calmed down a bit. He was still sad, but he was no longer having panic attacks. At the same time, thanks to a stay at a hospital in Germany, my son's condition improved a bit and we were hoping he could wait longer for a new heart. That was in February. My husband was still going to therapy, so I wasn't surprised when he said he wanted to take part in a two-day group session. I was even quite pleased I'd have a couple of days on my own. I'm not sure, but on the Sunday before the therapy I think my husband had a meeting with Mr Rudzki. On Thursday he didn't have his weekly session, but on Friday he went straight from work to Łazienkowska Street. He called in the evening to say he had to switch off his phone and wouldn't be able to call me, but that we'd see each other on Sunday. I said I was keeping my fingers crossed. On Sunday morning the police called. On Saturday evening my son and I stayed at home. Bartek was going to go out to see some friends, but he had a headache and stayed in. I watched a thriller on television until late, about midnight, and Bartek played a racing-car game on the computer."

Teodor Szacki was sorry there weren't two more boxes to fill in on the interview form. The information they would contain could not constitute proof or circumstantial evidence in the case, but for those conducting or resuming an inquiry they'd be priceless. The first would be a description of the person being interviewed, and second a subjective appraisal by the interviewer.

Opposite Szacki sat a woman of forty-three, well-groomed, tall and slender, a classic beauty. And yet she gave the impression of being old and troubled. Was it because of death, which had so violently invaded her home? First her daughter, then her husband, soon her son as well, probably. How long would she hang on until she went too? She spoke about her tragedies in a tone entirely devoid of emotion, as if she were describing an episode from a television series, not her own life. Where was the hatred he had seen on the tape at Rudzki's? That the participants in the therapy had told him about? Hatred that had the magical force to push a stranger into committing murder? Could it be that pain had brought her to such a state? And could she really be feeling any pain at all, if she hated her husband so much and desired his death so strongly?

"Do you personally know Cezary Rudzki?" he asked.

She shook her head.

"Please reply in complete sentences."

"No, I don't know Mr Rudzki. I've never set eyes on him. Not counting the photo on the jacket of the psychology manual I have at home."

"And do you know Barbara Jarczyk, Hanna Kwiatkowska or Euzebiusz Kaim?"

"The names mean nothing to me," she replied.

He showed her some photos, but she didn't recognize anyone in them. A blank look, no emotion at all. Szacki tried to find a way to shake her out of it. If she were playing games it wasn't going to be easy.

"Why did your daughter commit suicide?"

"Is this necessary?"

"Forgive me, but this isn't a friendly chat, it's a witness interview in a murder case."

She nodded.

"You asked why. No one knows. Why does a fifteen-year-old girl decide to swallow some pills? I don't think God himself could tell you the answer to that question. When my son found her..." Her voice faltered and she fell silent.

"When my son found her," she said after a pause, "we thought it was an accident. It was in the morning, and she hadn't come down for breakfast. I shouted to tell her to get up now, or she'd be late for school. I was cross because I'd made an appointment with a friend who had come all the way from Poznań and I didn't want to keep her waiting. I told Bartek to hurry her up. Of course he made a face as if to say I was exploiting him. But off he went. I heard him going up the stairs, singing: 'Get up, get up, you sleepyhead, stop fooling around, get out of bed...' I was making them sandwiches and got a blob of mayonnaise on my trousers. I almost lost my temper because those were the trousers I wanted to go out in, and if I put on another pair my blouse wouldn't go with them, the usual sort of women's concerns. I tried wiping the mark off with water and drying the trousers with a hairdryer. It really was getting late. I was just wiping the stained spot with a bit of damp paper towel, when Bartek came back into the kitchen. I took one look at him and didn't ask any questions, I just ran upstairs."

She closed her eyes. Szacki's mouth felt dry, and the room had become small and dark. Helka was seven years old. Could he imagine her being fifteen and not coming down to breakfast, then himself getting cross and going to drag her out of bed because he didn't want to be late for an autopsy? Yes, he could imagine that. Just as he had often imagined her blue and lifeless, the victim of some idiot or just bad luck. Or lying on the dissecting table at Oczko Street – her skull opening with a wet squelch. "Jolly good, we'll cut up the offal later."

He felt short of breath. He stood up, poured some still mineral water into two glasses and put one in front of Mrs Telak. She glanced at him.

"I have a daughter too," he said.

"Only you have a daughter," she replied, drank some water and carried on: "I am not capable of telling you what happened later. I remember that we thought it was an accident. An illness, a heart attack, a haemorrhage – that sort of thing can happen to young people too, can't it?"

Szacki said yes. He was trying to listen, but he could still see the image of the sliced-up organs being stuffed into the belly with some newspapers as wadding.

"But the doctor told us the truth. Then we found the letter. There was nothing in it, at least not to interest you. A few vague sentences, no explanations why she'd decided to go. I can remember the shape of each letter written on that page torn from her Polish exercise book. First in large, fancy letters, 'Dearest Family', and an exclamation mark. Under that it said: 'Don't worry'. Full stop. 'I love you all, and You, Dad, the most'. Full stop. 'You' and 'Dad' with capital letters. A flourish that looked like an infinity sign drawn with a red felt-tip. And the last sentence: 'We'll meet again in Nangijala'. With no full stop. And right at the end: 'Warsaw, 17th September 2003, 22:00'. Just like in an official letter. She even put the time."

"In Nangijala?" asked the prosecutor.

"It's a fairytale land you go to after death. It's from a book by Astrid Lindgren. If you don't know it, do buy it and read it to your daughter. It's a beautiful story. Though I'm not very fond of it myself."

"How did your husband take it?"

She gave him a cold look.

"I realize I'm being interviewed as a witness in a murder case but I'd be grateful if you'd limit the number of stupid questions," she hissed. "Naturally, he took it very badly. He almost died – he spent two weeks in hospital. What would you have done? Taken your wife on holiday?"

She took out a cigarette and lit it. He offered her a cup to have somewhere to tap the ash, and thanked providence for sending his office mate on medical leave. Indeed it was a stupid question, but at least something was starting to happen.

"Did he feel guilty?" he asked.

"Of course." She shrugged. "So did I. I still do. Every day I think of all the things we must have done wrong to make it happen. I think about it many times a day."

"And did you blame your husband for your daughter's death?"

"What sort of a question is that?"

"A simple one. She wrote in her letter that she especially loved her father. Maybe their relationship was closer, perhaps you found reasons for her suicide in it?"

She stubbed out her cigarette, closed her eyes and gave a deep sigh. When she looked at Szacki again, he almost ducked in his chair to escape that gaze.

"Forgive my language, but what the fuck are you trying to insinuate? What on earth are you thinking in that bloody civil servant's, badly paid head of yours when you say 'closer relationship'? And please be sure to record what we're saying word for word. Otherwise I won't even sign the page giving my personal details."

"Absolutely." Instead of pulling away he leaned even further forwards over the desk, never letting his gaze drop from her eyes, cold as the Baltic Sea in June. "But please just answer the question instead of showering me with insults."

"My late husband and my late daughter got on perfectly. Better than anyone else in the family. Sometimes I was jealous, I felt left out. It was incredible, they could read each other's thoughts. Whenever they went sailing together they just sent a postcard. Whenever I went on holiday with the children, Kasia made me call her dad every day. You know what it's like. People always say they love all their children equally, and the children also say they love their parents the same. But it's not true. In our family Kasia loved Henryk the best, and Henryk Kasia. And when she committed suicide, half of Henryk died. The murderer didn't so much kill him as finish him off. If by some miracle you ever track him down, maybe you'll petition for a lower sentence because he didn't murder a man – it was a semi-corpse."

She spoke the final word in a tone that made shivers go down Szacki's spine. He didn't want to go on with this conversation, but he couldn't just drop it.

"I understand," he said politely. "Now please answer the question."

"What question?"

"Did you blame your husband for your daughter's death?"

She lit another cigarette.

"No one was as close to her as he was. No one knew her or understood her as well. How come he wasn't able to prevent it? I've often wondered about that as I've watched him kneeling by her grave. Does that answer your question?"

"Let's suppose so," he agreed graciously and told her briefly how the therapy had gone on Łazienkowska Street. When he finished, her face looked like a death mask. He couldn't see a trace of emotion in it.

"We weren't the perfect happy couple. And I often felt I wouldn't have had much objection if Henryk had found someone else and left me. But what you're saying... I have never heard such horrendous nonsense. To say our daughter killed herself and our son has a lethal illness because Henryk wasn't at his parents' funeral? Can you actually hear what you're saying? That it's as if I know that, and desire his death? And what happens? The woman from the therapy feels for me so strongly that she takes your 'sharp instrument' – in other words a kitchen skewer, as I had to find out from the newspaper – and sticks it in his head? Do your superiors know about these ideas of yours?"

She lit another cigarette. Szacki took one out too. His first one.

"Please understand me. Murder isn't like the theft of a car radio. We have to investigate every lead thoroughly."

"If you made as much effort as this for the theft of car radios, maybe there'd be less of it."

In his heart Szacki agreed with her. He knew it didn't make sense to continue the therapy theme. Maybe later, once he knew more. He questioned her cautiously about any potential enemies, but she denied that Telak had any.

"He was pretty colourless, if I'm being honest," she said. "People like that rarely have enemies."

Curious. It was the second time he'd heard that, and the second time he felt he was being deceived.

"May I collect my husband from the mortuary?" she asked on the way out, after closely reading and then signing the statement. Before that he had to add the usual formula at the end, "That is all I have to testify in this matter", and thought that wasn't necessarily in keeping with the truth.

"Yes, any day from eight a.m. to three p.m. You have to call in advance and make an appointment. I'd advise you to instruct your undertakers to do it. Please forgive my frankness, but after an autopsy a person is, if possible, far more dead than before it." He remembered how Kuzniecow had once told him that on Oczko Street there's no atmosphere of death at all, just the atmosphere of a mortuary. "Better have the professionals dress him, tidy him up and put him in his coffin first. Even so you'll have to identify him before the coffin is closed and removed from the forensics lab. Those are the rules."

She nodded to say goodbye and went out. And although she left his room as an exhausted woman filled with nothing but grief and pain, Szacki couldn't forget the abuse she had hurled at the ideas that had emerged from his "bloody civil servant's head". If she had started to threaten him at that point, he'd have been terrified.

III

He glanced at his watch – twelve. Telak's son was coming at one; luckily his mother hadn't insisted on being present at his interview. In theory she had that right, but in practice it was only exercised during interviews with children, not great big fifteen-year-olds. He had an hour. How ridiculous. If he had two, he could write the inquiry plan; if he had three, the indictment in the Nidziecka case. But in this situation he didn't want to get anything started. Once again he felt tired. And on top of that he still had the feeling he'd overlooked something crucial – as if he had some piece of information, maybe even already recorded in the files, that he had failed to notice. He should carefully read through all the material gathered so far. He should also ask around to see if anyone knew of a place with a ball pit where they could hold Helka's birthday party. Anyway, what a bloody stupid fashion. In his day everyone got together for birthday parties at their own homes and it was OK. Had he really thought "in my day"? Oh God, was he really that old?

He made himself coffee.

He took a look at the newspaper.

Bugger all was happening. President Kwaśniewski was appealing to Cimoszewicz to run for President. Why bother to write about such boring stuff? Szacki reckoned there should be a ban on the daily reporting of politics. A two-column article once a month would be quite enough.

Politicians lived in an isolated world, convinced they were doing something madly important all the time, which they absolutely had to describe at a press conference. Then they were given confirmation by excited political commentators, convinced of their own importance, who also believed in the significance of the events, probably just to rationalize their pointless jobs. Even so, despite the efforts of both groups and the mass attempt of the media to present unimportant information as essential, the entire nation couldn't give a shit about them. In the winter Szacki, Weronika and Helka had gone on holiday – they'd been away for two weeks. All that time he hadn't read a single newspaper. He'd come home and everything was the same as before. Absolutely nothing had happened. But when he looked at the press, it turned out the world had been collapsing on a daily basis, the government was toppling, the opposition was tearing its hair out, the Internal Security Agency had compromised itself, the polls were indicating a new line-up every hour, the parliamentary committees were talking themselves to death, etc. The effect: zero.

Just then Maryla came in.

"From the Regional Office on Krakowskie Przedmieście," she said, put a memo down in front of him and left without another word.

Szacki read it, cursed, picked up his coffee and ran out of the room. At a fast pace he walked past the secretary, who hadn't clopped her way back to her desk yet, knocked on Chorko's door and, without waiting to be invited, went inside.

"Good day, Szacki," she said, peering at him over her glasses, without removing her hands from the computer keyboard.

"Good day. They've refused the draft dismissal of the

Sienkiewicz murder case a third time," he said, putting the memo from the regional office on her desk.

"I know."

"It's nonsensical. If I write an indictment, the court won't just drop the charges against them, they'll make fun of us. And those pen-pushers are perfectly aware of it. They're only interested in statistics and nothing else: to submit an indictment and get it off their plates, then let the court worry about it." Szacki was trying to keep his cool, but the tone of resentment was all too audible in his voice.

"I know, Prosecutor," confirmed Chorko.

The Sienkiewicz murder case was a typical central-Warsaw drinking-den killing. They'd been drinking in a threesome, and woken up in a twosome, the third one having had his throat slashed, preventing him from coming round again. All three men's fingerprints were found on the knife. The two who were still alive swore in unison that they couldn't remember a thing, moreover they had called the police themselves. It was clear one of them was the murderer, but it wasn't clear which – there wasn't even a hint of circumstantial evidence to identify the culprit. And they couldn't charge both of them. It was an idiotic situation. They had the murderer, and yet they didn't.

"You are aware that if we charge them jointly, even the stupidest lawyer will get them off. If we draw straws and charge one of them, he won't even need one. They'll drop the charges at the first deadline."

Chorko took off her glasses, which she only used for writing on the computer, and tidied her fringe. Her curls looked as if they'd been transplanted from a poodle.

"Prosecutor Szacki," she said. "I am equally aware of what you are saying and of the fact that the prosecution system has a hierarchical structure. That means the higher up the hierarchy, the closer to our boss, who is usually..." She pointed at Szacki, wanting him to finish the sentence.

"A halfwit with a political title, sent here to gain points for his pals in the polls."

"Exactly. But please don't say that to the press, unless you want to spend the rest of your days in the General Correspondence Department. And that's why our officious colleagues from Krakowskie Przedmieście..." She pointed at Szacki again.

"Are already gearing up for a change of guard, and just in case are trying to be more radical, more uncompromising and tougher than the single egg the Kaczyński brothers emerged from." The twin politicians were famous for their rigid attitudes.

"So if you understand it all so well, Prosecutor Szacki, why do you come in here and make a fuss? I'm not your enemy. I simply understand that if we refuse to kowtow once in a while, we'll be put out to grass, and less reliable people will be put in our place. Do you think that'd be better for this colourful city or for the Warsaw City Centre District Prosecutor's Office?"

Szacki crossed his legs, straightened his trouser crease and gave a deep sigh.

"I'll tell you something in confidence," he said.

"Is this going to be juicy?" she asked.

He didn't smile. Janina Chorko was the last person on earth he'd want to flirt with.

"A week ago I had a call from Butkus."

"The Lithuanian gangster?"

"In person. They've set the date of his trial for two months from now. He said he isn't sorry, and that if for example I wanted to change the trimming on my gown from prosecutor's red to barrister's green, he's ready to pay twenty thousand for the mere fact of taking on the defence, ten thousand for each extended trial date and an extra fifty for an acquittal."

"Would you be capable of that?"

Chorko settled herself more comfortably in her chair and undid a button of her blouse. Szacki could feel himself sweating. Was this really happening?

"Of course. I conducted the inquiry until the big shots on Krakowskie Przedmieście took it away from me, I helped write the indictment."

"That's not what I meant. Would you be capable of crossing to the other side of the barricades so easily?"

For a while Szacki sat there in silence. Stupid question. If he were, he'd have done it ages ago. What kept him here, if not a childish belief in the sheriff's star? He was on a civil servant's wage – a prosecutor in the centre of Warsaw earned the same as one in Sleepy Hollow in the backwoods. No bonuses. A statutory ban on earning extra in any way except by giving lectures, for which he still had to have special permission – assuming anyone would ever offer him such a rare opportunity. No standard working hours, which in practice meant sixty hours a week. On top of all that he had to be present at autopsies and carry out the orders of his numerous superiors without a murmur. In the entire Prosecution Service there were more heads of department than there were directors of state enterprises. Society regarded the prosecutor as the bad guy who releases bandits caught by the good old police. Or else the bad guy who made such a cat's arse of the paperwork that the court had to let the bandit go. In their turn, the blockheads from the parliament building on Wiejska Street treated the Prosecution Service like their own private army for harassing their political opponents. Oh well, what a shit-hot job, he thought bitterly. It was worth all that grinding away at college.

"That barricade has more sides to it," he replied evasively, because he didn't want to confide in his boss.

"But of course, Prosecutor. I can see you in my mind's eye, sitting in a solicitor's office, writing out letters giving legal notice or wondering if it would still be worth chasing a debtor for the extra interest."

Chorko began toying with the collar of her blouse. Soon she'd lean forwards and he'd be forced to look at her cleavage. And that he definitely didn't fancy.

"We've all got bills to pay," he said, shrugging.

"But to get to the point, you'll write the indictment, won't you? Perhaps we can reach a compromise. Don't charge them with murder, but with failing to provide help. There's always something. We'll see what we can do with it."

He nodded reluctantly. He'd already thought of that.

"I warn you it won't be an extremely long or convincing indictment."

"I'll initial it anyway. And let me remind you about the inquiry plan for the Telak case and the indictment for the Nidziecka case."

He nodded and stood up.

"Nice having a chat with you, Prosecutor," said Chorko, smiling radiantly. Szacki was reminded of the figures in Brueghel's paintings. He responded with a faint half-smile and left.

Bartosz Telak was sitting in a chair outside his room, playing with his mobile phone.

IV

He liked going to the sauna at the Warszawianka Club in the middle of the day, when there were no hordes of savages and he could enjoy the facilities in peace. He sat on the top bench in the dry sauna until he started to see spots before his eyes and every breath made his throat burn. Finally he left, hung his towel on a peg and walked naked to a large tub full of ice-cold water standing in the middle of the room. Millions of tiny needles stuck into his body. He dived under, and only then did he cry out. How fabulous it felt. He lay for a while longer in the cold water, got out, wrapped himself in a towel and lay on a recliner in the garden. Igor handed him a bottle of cold orange juice. Yes, there are moments when all a man needs is a little warmth, a little cold and a little orange juice. The lads from the Warsaw Pact – not that he was fond of them – knew what they were doing when they built themselves such a great pool.

Next to him a twenty-something couple were lying so close to each other that if they got a quarter of an inch nearer it'd be sexual intercourse in a public place. By turns they whispered quietly or giggled aloud. He gave a hostile glance in their direction. The girl wasn't bad-looking, though it wouldn't have done her any harm to thin out the bush in her armpits and go to aerobics once or twice. The boy was weedy, like all of them in that generation. Skinny little arms, skinny little legs, facial hair like on a piece of pork crackling, ribcage like a consumptive.

"They should put up the prices," he said to Igor loud enough to be sure the young couple could hear him. "As it is, any old riff-raff can sit here for hours on end."

Igor nodded understandingly. The couple first went quiet, then the boy whispered something and the girl started giggling like a freak. He wanted to get up and smash him in the face. But he decided not to take any notice of them.

"Well, so it looks like there'll be no trouble with Henryk?" he addressed Igor.

"Yes, I don't think we've anything to worry about," he replied. "Szacki should be writing the inquiry plan today, then we'll know more."

"When will we get it?"

"This evening," replied Igor, as if it was completely natural for them to get copies of all the internal documents from all the prosecutor's offices in Poland.

"Excellent," said the Chairman, and took a large swig of juice. He liked it when everything was running predictably and perfectly.

V

Kuzniecow had a son the same age as Bartosz Telak, and lately he never described him in any other way except as an "animal". "Sometimes I feel like putting a lock on our bedroom door," he said. "He's so big and shaggy, he moves like a caged tiger. His mood changes every ten minutes, he's got more hormones in his blood than an athlete's got steroids. If we're going to have a quarrel in the evening, I think to myself: will he come with a knife, or won't he come at all? And if he does, will I cope? I'm no weakling, but there's nothing wrong with him either."

Stories like this merely testified to the fact that Kuzniecow was a jerk. A sick imagination and all those years working for the police had given him bipolar disease. That's what Szacki always thought. Now, as he sat down opposite Telak junior, it crossed his mind that there might be a grain of truth in the policeman's strange remarks. The teenager had very delicate papery looks, with black hair and black eyebrows that gave extra emphasis to his pallor. He was very thin, which neither his baggy trousers nor his loose-fitting shirt could conceal. Quite the opposite – his large clothes made him look even more fragile. Szacki knew the boy was fatally ill. And yet in his movements and his eyes there was a predatory look, aggression and desperation. Maybe it can't be otherwise when the time is approaching to fight for your place in the world? Szacki was incapable of remembering what it had been like to be that age. He'd drunk a lot, wanked a lot and discussed politics with his friends a lot. And apart from that? A black hole. He'd argued with his parents, that was for sure. But had he hated them? Were there times when he'd wished them dead? Would he have agreed to their death if it were going to guarantee him freedom and independence? He remembered the trial of a teenage matricide from Pruszków who had explained in court: "…and then the idea came into my head of my mother not being there". Had a similar idea arisen in the head of Henryk Telak's son?

WITNESS INTERVIEW TRANSCRIPT. Bartosz Telak, born 20th March 1991, resident at Karłowicz Street in Warsaw, primary education, pupil at Lycée No. 2 on Narbutt Street. Relationship to parties: son of Henryk Telak (victim), no criminal record for bearing false witness.

Cautioned re *criminal responsibility under Article 233 of the Penal Code, his statement is as follows:*

Five minutes later Szacki felt like scrawling "Bugger all to testify!" in huge letters across the form, because the young man was trying to communicate in nothing but nods and shakes of the head, monosyllables and grunts.

"What do you know about your father going to therapy?"

"He went."

"Anything else?"

Denial.

"Did you talk about it?"

Denial.

"Do you know the people he went to therapy with?"

Denial.

"Do you recognize anyone in these photos?"

Denial.

Completely pointless, thought Szacki, we'll never get anywhere like this.

"What were you doing on Saturday evening?"

"Playing."

"What?"

"*Call of Duty.*"

"One or two?"

"Two."

"Which campaign?"

The boy settled more in the chair.

"For God's sake."

"Russian, British or American?"

"Russian."

"You didn't get far."

"Right. I can't get past the bit in Stalingrad where you have to fire from the Town Hall window. I'm not able to take them all out, someone always sneaks under and creeps up on me from behind. And when I watch my back, the whole Fascist army comes from the front with their machine guns."

Szacki nodded understandingly. That mission had taken even him a good few hours of effort.

"Unfortunately there's no good way," he said. "The best is to kill off as many as you can first, then watch the rear and use the sniper rifle to pick off just the ones with machine guns. If you hold out for long enough, eventually you get a message about a new task. It's an idiotic mission, its entire difficulty depends on the fact that they've multiplied the usual number of Germans by ten. But on the whole it's OK."

"Well, it must have been like that, don't you think?"

"The war? Yes, surely. You run about blindly with your rifle jamming, it's nothing but chaos with bullets whizzing past and your friends falling all around you. And all you're interested in is getting to the nearest pit, hiding in there, throwing a grenade and rushing onwards. The sound is important."

"I've got 5.1 speakers."

"Congratulations. I've got 2.1s, my flat's too small for 5.1s. But I usually play with headphones anyway because my wife gets mad at me."

"Mum comes in and tells me she doesn't want tanks driving through her home. Interrogations are nothing like this in the movies."

Szacki was surprised by the sudden change of topic, but he replied instantly: "I can't conduct this interview this way. Why don't you answer my questions?"

The boy shrugged.

"I didn't think it would matter."

"You're father's been killed, and I want to know who did it and why. You don't think that matters?"

He shrugged again.

"No, because it won't bring him back to life again. Besides, what's the difference whether I answer in full sentences or just say yes or no? Surely the important thing is to tell the truth."

Szacki put the report aside. He didn't actually think the boy could know anything that would be evidence in the case. He was concerned about something else.

"And do you wish your father would come back to life?" he asked.

He was expecting Telak to shrug, but he sat quite still, not so much as batting an eyelid.

"Yes and no," he replied.

"Was he a bad father?"

"He never hit us and he didn't want us to scrub his back for him, if that's what you mean. He didn't shout much either. He was the average boring Polish father. I didn't hate him or love him. Maybe it's the shock, but I can't actually arouse any emotion in myself following his death. I'm telling you the truth."

Szacki wished his witnesses always gave such frank answers. He gave the boy a respectful nod.

"Did he change after your sister's death?"

"He aged. But before that only my sister could get through to him anyway, so for me it didn't matter."

"Did you blame him for your sister's death?"

He hesitated.

"No more than anyone else around."

Szacki thought about the pills found in Telak's room on Łazienkowska Street.

"Would you be surprised if he'd committed suicide?"

"No, not particularly. I'm more surprised that someone murdered him. What for?"

Good question. Once again Szacki felt very tired. And how the hell was he to know what for? He felt as if it was all falling apart. The theory that someone from the therapy group had killed Telak seemed to him either probable or fantastical by turns. But increasingly the latter. None of the interviews had brought anything new to the case. Obvious answers to obvious questions. Maybe he should give up, commission the police for the entire inquiry and calmly wait for the most probable result – a dismissal, perpetrator unknown.

"I really don't know," he replied sincerely. Well, semi-sincerely. He couldn't have explained it rationally, but he wanted to give the boy the impression that he was stuck on the spot and didn't know what to do next.

"You've got to find the motive, the opportunity and the murder weapon."

"Thanks. I read crime novels too. Do you know of anyone who would gain from your father's death?"

"Not me. I'm sure you know I'm ill and will probably die soon."

Szacki said yes.

"There are three things that can save me: a miracle, the national health service or a transplant at a private hospital abroad. What do you think, which of them is the most likely? Exactly. And what do you think, how much did my chances decrease when I lost my father, the company director? Exactly."

What could he say? Was else could he ask? He thanked the boy and wished him success with *Call of Duty*. He didn't even give him the transcript to sign – there was absolutely nothing there.

"Will you be at the funeral on Saturday?" asked Telak junior on the way out.

"Of course." Szacki scolded himself mentally for not thinking of it earlier. It would probably be the only chance to see Telak's family and the people from the therapy group all in one place.

VI

Writing out the statement of facts, his hypotheses and the inquiry plan took him less time than he had expected. Less than ninety minutes. Considering he'd spent at least half that time thinking about Monika Grzelka – not a bad result. What should he do now? The last woman he'd seduced was Weronika, and that had happened more than ten years ago. And actually it wasn't so much he that had seduced her, as she him. Memory was limited to a vague "somehow it just happened of its own accord". He liked her, they'd talked a bit, suddenly they'd started kissing – correction: suddenly she'd started kissing him – and a week later they'd ended up in bed. Two weeks later he could no longer imagine life without her.

That's all I have to give in evidence on the case, he thought. Not counting his high school and early student adventures. And two short affairs from early in his marriage that he tried to forget about. And one – unfortunately – non-consummated acquaintance with a lady prosecutor from Piaseczno. Until now he'd always consoled himself that it had worked out for the best, because he did have a wife and child, and he ought to be good, but the truth was different – he was bloody sorry. How does that saying go? Better to sin and be sorry than be sorry you didn't sin. Another stupid bit of folk wisdom that only looks good on paper. They'd met on a case involving the murder of a developer. The body was in the City Centre, but the family, friends, company and everything else was in the nearby town of Piaseczno. They had worked together. At length and intensively. They had worked and talked, talked and worked, talked and talked. One night he'd driven her home and kissed her in the car. He'd been amazed a kiss could taste so different. That it could all be so new. That lips could have such a different shape, a tongue such a different texture, breath such a different flavour.

"We can't go on kissing like this for ever," she'd said, and he knew it wasn't a simple statement of fact but a proposition. She'd done everything, she'd merely required confirmation from him. But even so he'd chickened out. He'd trembled with fear.

"We can't take this any further," he'd gasped eventually. She had just smiled, kissed him one more time and got out. She'd waved from the stairwell. Then he'd seen a light shining on the second floor. He'd sat in the car for another hour, battling with himself. Finally he'd driven away. He'd sped down Puławska Street back to Weronika, feeling glad he'd done the right thing. But at the heart of it he knew it wasn't loyalty that had stopped him – however you understood it – or love – however you understood that. He'd been held back by fear. The humiliating memory of his nervous trembling had stayed with him for a long time after he'd lain down beside his wife, feeling relief as he cuddled up to the familiar curves of her body.

That was then. What about now? He was thirty-five, soon to be thirty-six. How much longer did he have to wait to experience what it's like when every square inch of someone's body is a surprise? It's now or never, he thought.

He dialled the number.

"Good day, this is Szacki."

"Oh, hi… I mean, good day, Prosecutor."

He took a deep breath.

"Please call me Teo."

"Monika. Pity you didn't suggest it yesterday – we could have kissed to celebrate."

The familiar trembling was back. He was glad they were talking by phone.

"I hope we'll make up for it," said a strange voice, which to Szacki's mind wasn't his own at all.

"Hmm, that's just what I was thinking," she said. "So when?"

He thought frantically. Christ Almighty, he had to have an excuse, otherwise his intentions would be obvious.

"Maybe Friday?" he suggested. "I'll have that indictment for you." The final remark was so stupid that if embarrassment had a temperature Szacki would have burst into flames. What other good ideas have you got, Teodor? he asked himself. A date at the forensics lab?

"Oh, yes, the indictment." Now he could no longer be in any doubt what she thought of it. "Six p.m. at Szpilka? It's not far from your office." The way she said the word "office" it sounded as if he were a clerk of the lowliest rank at a provincial post office.

"Wonderful idea," he said, thinking at the same time he must call the bank and check his account. Did Weronika read the statements? He couldn't remember.

"Well, goodbye until Friday," she said.

"Bye," he replied, immediately feeling sure that of all the nonsense in this conversation his final "bye" deserved a gold medal.

He put down the receiver and took off his jacket. He was trembling, and sweating like a Swede on holiday in Tunisia. He drank two glasses of mineral water in two goes and thought thank God he'd written the sodding inquiry plan earlier, because now without a doubt he wouldn't be able to sit still any longer.

He got up, planning to go for a walk to the minimart next to the bookshop on the Avenue for a cola, when the phone rang. He froze at the thought that it might be Monika, and only picked it up on the third ring.

Kuzniecow.

The policeman told him the results of the interviews at Polgrafex, Telak's firm. Or rather the lack of results. A pleasant man – calm, unaggressive, ran the firm pretty well. No one had any complaints, no one said anything bad about him. In fact one of the managers let slip that now they might succeed in pushing the firm onto new tracks, but it was just the usual careerist talk.

"And you should definitely interview his secretary," said Kuzniecow.

"Why? Did they have an affair?" Szacki was sceptical.

"No, but she's really hot stuff, I could interview her any day of the week. Ideally in uniform, in the interview room at Mostowski Palace. You know, the one downstairs…"

"Oleg, for pity's sake, your fantasies make me feel sick. I'm afraid you'll start showing me pictures of Alsatian dogs in handcuffs next."

"What's your problem?" said the policeman, taking offence. "You call her in, take a look, write some crap in a report. Fifteen minutes and you're done – it'll take you more time to go and get a porn mag from the Empik shop."

"Fuck you. Did she say anything?"

"That Telak never parted with his digital Dictaphone, on which he recorded everything. Business meetings, ideas, notes, conversations, deadlines. Some people simply remember, some write things down, some make notes on their mobile. But he recorded them. I called his wife to confirm the Dictaphone is nowhere in the house."

"In other words something's gone missing," said Szacki.

"Looks like it. Strange, but it's a fact."

"Yes, it rather destroys the convenient theory about the burglar in a panic, doesn't it? Leaves behind a wallet full of credit cards but takes a Dictaphone – pretty odd."

"Do you think we should search all their flats?" asked Kuzniecow.

"I have no idea. I'm just thinking about it," replied Szacki, rubbing the bridge of his nose with his thumb. He needed that cola. "No, not yet. Let's hold off until Monday. There's something I have to check."

Kuzniecow didn't insist, but Szacki knew he had a different view. And who knows, maybe he was right. Szacki didn't want to decide right now to raid the flats of all the suspects. He felt it wouldn't be right.

Finally he gave up on the cola and devoted the next three hours to finding an expert witness who was a specialist on Family Constellation Therapy. While he was about it he noticed that the name of Cezary Rudzki featured on the list of experts. In fact he was the first person to be suggested to him. Only after a few calls to acquaintances at the psychiatry institute on Sobieski Street did he get a different name.

"A pretty eccentric guy, but once you accept that he's incredibly interesting," a familiar psychiatrist told him. Pressed by Szacki, he refused to disclose what this "eccentricity" involved, but just kept repeating that Szacki would have to see for himself.

"I'd just like to see the transcript of that meeting," he said at the end of the conversation, and started to snigger like a madman.

Doctor, heal thyself, thought Szacki. As he usually did whenever he had to deal with psychologists and psychiatrists.

The therapist was called Jeremiasz Wróbel. Szacki called, briefly described the case and made an appointment for Friday. The conversation was short, but he didn't get the impression that he was talking to a particularly nutty person.

VII

His study at home was predominantly in the office style of the 1970s, but it didn't bother him, quite the contrary. Sometimes he even sought out some gadget or other from that era on the Internet as a new exhibit for his museum. Lately he'd bought the *Great Universal Encyclopedia* published by PWN in the 1960s – thirteen volumes of it – and he was considering the original Soviet edition of *The History of the Second World War* in twelve volumes. Editions like these looked good in his glass-fronted bookcase.

As well as the bookcase, there was a large French-polished desk, a lamp with a green shade, an ebonized telephone and a black leather armchair with a chrome frame. There was oak parquet, a thick wine-red rug and dark panelling on the walls. He hadn't been able to resist hanging a rack of antlers above the door. Dreadful kitsch, but it suited this interior to perfection.

Only he was allowed in the study. He did the cleaning in here himself, dusted and washed the windows. The door was secured by one mighty lock, for which there were only two keys. One he always had on him, the other was kept in a safe at the office on Stawki Street. And the point of it all was not that he kept valuable objects or secret documents in his study, though undoubtedly a search conducted in this room would have revealed facts capable of damaging the careers of several people in the public eye. What he was concerned about was privacy; about having his own place, where no one – not his wife, or his lover, or his children, who came to visit less and less – would have access.

Now he was sitting by the window in a deep armchair upholstered in dark-green corduroy, drinking tea as he read Norman Davies's book about Wrocław and waited for the phone to ring. He was feeling calm, and yet he couldn't concentrate on his reading. For the third time he started the same paragraph, but his thoughts kept drifting away to Henryk and the man conducting the inquiry. He was keen to know what Prosecutor Teodor Szacki had come up with.

Finally the phone rang.

"It's Igor. I know everything. Shall I fax you the lot?"

"Don't go over the top, I've got more interesting things to read," he said, marking his place in Davies's book with a postcard he got from his daughter living in Santa Fe, and put it down on a coffee table next to his chair. "You can summarize."

"The statement of facts is the statement of facts. Nothing we don't know about. Henryk plus the therapist plus the three patients. The patients had never met before; the therapist had been giving Henryk individual treatment for six months. They got to the place on Friday…"

"Don't witter on. Hypotheses?"

"First one: Henryk was murdered accidentally by someone committing theft by breaking and entering."

"That doesn't concern us. Next?"

"The murderer is one of the people taking part in the therapy or the therapist. Each of them had the opportunity, but none of them – or so it appears from the evidence gathered so far – had a motive that could justify committing murder. At least not a direct one. Some of the circumstantial evidence implies that the therapy was a very painful process. Under the influence of these emotions, one of the patients could have taken Henryk's life."

"What sort of bullshit is that?" he bristled. "People kill because they're drunk or for money. And they said this Szacki wasn't bad. Oh well, yet another disappointment. So what's our white-haired prosecutor planning to do?"

He had to wait while Igor found the relevant bit.

"He's planning to ask the opinion of an expert on the therapy techniques applied in the case of the deceased and to investigate his professional and social environment, to confirm or exclude any previous contact with the witnesses. Apart from that, routine activities, blah blah blah."

He sucked in air noisily.

"Yes, that's worse."

"I wouldn't get too upset about it," said Igor.

"Why not?"

"Henryk wasn't particularly sociable or professionally active, and he only met up with us from time to time by chance. They'll question a few of his friends, maybe some of Polgrafex's clients. I don't think it can be a danger for us. We'll keep a finger on the pulse and keep getting up-to-date information from the police and the prosecutor's. Apart from anything, we've got more important, much more complicated matters to see to."

He agreed with Igor. They couldn't devote a lot of strength and resources to the Telak affair. And as it all implied that the case would fall apart at the seams and the only result would be another "perpetrator unknown" in the Ministry of Justice statistics, there was nothing to worry about.

5

Thursday, 9th June 2005

In Japan, Triumph presents the ecological bra — not only can you join the cups together to make a model of the world, but it's totally biodegradable. After a few years the shoulder straps change into compost. Research shows that thirty-seven per cent of Poles prefer plain ice cream, twenty-five per cent vanilla, and twenty-two per cent chocolate. Meanwhile in Africa 25,000 people are dying of hunger and lack of water every day, Bono tells the head of the European Commission. Polish State Railways are under threat of strikes. The unions agree to restructuring with a human face, not the kind that causes "terror and poverty". Cimoszewicz is "considering a change of mind", Kaczyński I (leader of the "Law & Justice" Party) is seeking to correct a report that said he called MP Zygmunt Wrzodak a "tramp", and now Kaczyński II (the Mayor of Warsaw) is banning the equality rallies; homosexuals are calling for civic disobedience. In the penultimate round of the First League, Legia beat GKS Katowice, who are being relegated to the Second League, and Dariusz Dziekanowski makes it into the club's Gallery of Fame for playing 101 matches and scoring forty-five goals. The city guard start patrolling the Old Town in Melex electric vehicles, prompting even more ridicule than usual, and the police catch the murderer of a twenty-eight-year-old woman. The couple met on the Internet, and after killing her the man stole a computer, which the police found at the home where he lived with his pregnant wife.

For lack of funds the hospital on Banach Street has started sending away patients with cancer untreated. Maximum temperature: sixteen degrees; cold and cloudy, but no rain.

I

Hard-boiled egg in tartare sauce, beefed up with a large portion of green peas. No lawyer in Warsaw was unfamiliar with this particular delicacy, a cult item on the menu at the Warsaw Regional Court canteen.

Teodor Szacki took two helpings, for himself and Weronika, put them on a plastic tray next to two instant coffees and took it over to their table. He missed the old court canteen – a large hall that stank of fried food and cheap cigarettes, its walls gone yellow with age, filth and grease, thirty feet high, full of small metal tables, reminiscent of a provincial station waiting room. A magical place – going up the high steps leading into the canteen had been like looking through a microscope at a section of the main artery of the judiciary. The judges – usually up in the little gallery, having a two-course lunch, on their own. The lawyers – usually having coffee together, sitting with their legs crossed, greeting each other sincerely and at the same time casually, blithely, as if they'd dropped in at the club for a cigar and a glass of whisky. Witnesses from the underworld, big shots and emaciated women in evening make-up – probably feeling just the same here as anywhere. Guys bowed over a piece of meat, women sipping mineral water from the bottle. The victims' families – grey, sad, by some miracle always finding the most wretched little tables, staring suspiciously at everyone around them. The prosecutors – eating alone, whatever and however, just to get it over and done with. Knowing they couldn't get anything done on time, that whatever they did it'd be too little, there'd always be something left for next day, which was already planned out from start to finish; infuriated by every recess the judge ordered, too short to do anything and too long to bear in peace. The court reporters – too many people at one small table, with no room for all the coffee cups, cigarette packets, ashtrays and plates of tongue. Too noisy, swapping jokes and anecdotes, now and then jumping up to greet a familiar lawyer, draw him aside and whisper questions to him. The rest would cast glances in his direction, curious whether he knew something they didn't. "Any news?" they'd ask when their colleague returned, knowing he'd reply with the invariable joke: "Oh, nothing special, you'll read about it in tomorrow's paper."

There was none of that atmosphere in the new canteen, where everything seemed kind of ordinary. Weronika had crushed him recently by claiming it felt good in here because the atmosphere was like at the City Council buffet – what could be good about that?

He sat down next to his wife and put the coffee and egg in front of her. She was looking pretty. Suit, make-up, sheer wine-red blouse with a low neckline. When they met in the evening, she'd be wearing a T-shirt, slippers from Ikea and a mask of all-day tiredness.

"Christ, what a dreadful case," she said, adding cream to her coffee from a plastic container.

"Bierut again?" he asked. Most of the cases Weronika conducted concerned property that people had been deprived of after the war by force of a decree issued by the Communist president, Bolesław Bierut. Now they were reclaiming their tenement houses, but if in the meantime several of the communal flats had been sold to the tenants, the owner de facto regained only part of the building. So then he sued the city for compensation. Each case of this kind was a boring lottery; sometimes by using legal loopholes you could shift the obligation to the state's cost, rather than the city's, sometimes you could postpone it, but you could hardly ever win.

"No, unfortunately not." She took off her jacket and hung it on the back of the chair. Her blouse had very short sleeves, he could see the scar from her TB inoculation, and suddenly he felt a massive urge for sex. "The city awards special grants to hundreds of organizations of various kinds, which they have to account for later on. A year ago we awarded a small sum to a youth club in the Praga district that takes care of children with ADHD and various other conditions. Mainly children from Praga families, as you can imagine. So we got their report, where it says as plain as day that they used the money to pay the electricity bill, or else they'd have been cut off, although they got the funding for therapeutic activities."

"It's hard to conduct therapeutic activities without electricity," he commented.

"Jesus, Teo, you don't have to explain that to me. But rules are rules. As they used the grant wrongly, I have to write and tell them to return the money..."

"Which of course they won't, because they haven't got any."

"So then we have to sue them. Obviously, we'll win, we'll send round a bailiff, the bailiff won't get anywhere; it's all a complete sham. Of course the teachers from the place have already been to see me, they begged and pleaded, and soon I'll be doing the same in the courtroom. But I really can't do a thing." She buried her face in her hands. "Rules are rules."

He leaned forward, took her hand and kissed her on the palm.

"But you do look very sexy," he said.

"What a perv you are. Give me a rest," she said, laughing, and wound her legs round his. "Best time for sex, isn't it?" she murmured. "This evening we won't feel like it any more."

"We'll make ourselves some coffee and we'll see. Maybe it'll work."

"I'll make a big jug of it," she said, running a finger along the edge of her blouse, revealing more cleavage.

"Just stay in that blouse."

"Don't you like my teddy-bear T-shirt?"

He couldn't help laughing. She was the person closest to him, and he was sorry he couldn't tell her about all his dilemmas, fears and hopes to do with Monika. He'd like to open a bottle of Carmenère or Primitivo, sit down next to her in bed and tell her some funny stories, how he'd been afraid to order a meringue so he wouldn't have to battle with it in front of the girl. Funny? Funny. Would she have laughed? Absolutely. They did almost everything together, but he could only cheat on her separately.

They bantered for a while, then Weronika quickly ran upstairs, while he stayed put for a bit longer to look at the paper. For once there was something interesting: an interview with the female head of a prison in Puławy. She talked about the women convicts, mostly victims of domestic violence who one fine day had finally taken a swing at their husbands – often with a decisive result. This was exactly the case with Mariola Nidziecka. He had to charge her. And he didn't know what with. That is, he knew, but he also knew his classification would cause the officious old bag in charge to have palpitations. Providing Chorko would accept it at all.

Apart from that it was the usual stuff: an interview with Cimoszewicz, who "in the face of such great pressure" was having to give serious consideration to changing his mind and running for President. Szacki hoped that Communist-Party wonderboy would read the entire paper today, because several pages further on there was an article about some American research which proved irrefutably that voters are guided at the ballot box by the candidate's looks, not his abilities. Or maybe I'm wrong? thought Szacki, stuffing the newspaper into his briefcase. Maybe his foxy face will win him the election?

He left the court catacombs and went out into the atrium, which was big enough to house several railway depots. The sun was shining in through the enormous windows, carving corridors in the dust, like in a Gothic church. At one time you could smoke in here, but now Szacki had to go outside for the first of his three cigarettes.

"Good morning, Prosecutor, would you like a cigarette?" he heard as soon as he passed through the heavy revolving doors.

Bogdan Nebb from *Gazeta Wyborcza* newspaper. The only journalist he could talk to without feeling sick. Not counting Monika. He glanced at the packet of RI Lights being held out towards him.

"No, thank you, I prefer my own," he replied and reached into his jacket pocket for the silver packet of Benson & Hedges, which had finally become available in Poland recently. He thought they tasted worse than when he used to buy them abroad. They lit up.

"The Gliński trial's starting next week. Are you prosecuting?" the journalist asked.

"I've just come to look through the files before the trial."

"Curious case. Not very obvious."

"To whom?" replied Szacki laconically, unable to admit that Nebb was right. But he was. The body of evidence was so-so and a good lawyer should win it. He would have known how to undermine the circumstantial evidence he himself had gathered. The question was whether Gliński's lawyer would know too.

"Are you going to insist on that classification?"

Szacki smiled.

"You'll discover all in the courtroom."

"Mr Prosecutor, after all these years…"

"Mr Nebb, after all these years you're trying to get something out of me."

The journalist tapped ash into the brimfull ashtray.

"I heard you're conducting the inquiry into the murder on Łazienkowska Street."

"I was on duty that day. I thought you weren't working on the current crime columns any more."

"My friends told me it's an interesting case."

"I thought you were taking a cautious approach to your police sources these days," said Szacki, alluding to the recent well-publicized affair when on Monday *Gazeta Wyborcza* had written about a criminal gang at National Police Headquarters, on Tuesday and Wednesday had insisted on their story despite a series of denials, and on Friday had grassed on their informers, claiming they'd deliberately misled them. For Szacki it proved the rightness of the basic principle that he followed in his contacts with the media: never say anything they wouldn't know anyway.

"The press makes mistakes too, Mr Prosecutor. Like any authority."

"The difference is we don't choose the press in general elections," Szacki retorted. "History teaches us that self-proclaimed authority makes the most mistakes. And is the best at covering them up."

The journalist smiled weakly and stubbed out his cigarette.

"But somehow it works, doesn't it? See you in court, Mr Prosecutor."

Szacki nodded to him, went back inside and glanced up at the historic clock hanging in the atrium above the cloakrooms. It was late. And he still had so much to do. Once again he felt tired.

II

Teodor Szacki sat on the bed where Henryk Telak had spent almost two nights. He took the site inspection report out of his briefcase, and looked through it again, although he had already done that earlier. There was nothing in it, just the obvious. Yet again. Discouraged, he put down the report and looked around the dark room. A bed, a small table next to it, a lamp, an Ikea rug, a shallow wardrobe, a mirror on the wall, a cross above the door. There wasn't even a chair. There was one small window with two handles; the paint was coming off the frame, and the glass was begging to be cleaned from both sides.

Earlier on Szacki had looked around the other bedrooms – they all looked the same. On the way to Łazienkowska Street he thought maybe something would inspire him, he'd see some detail, or his instinct would tell him who the murderer was. None of it. From the courtyard – theoretically locked at night, but Szacki didn't believe anyone kept an eye on it – you entered via an ugly brown door into a vestibule. From the vestibule you could go through to the refectory, or to the classroom where the body was found, or go on down a narrow corridor leading to the bedrooms (there were seven of them in all) and the bathroom. Further on there was another vestibule and a passage to another part of the monastery. Though Szacki wasn't sure the word "monastery" was apt. When he looked at the building from the outside it was. But inside it was more like a neglected office that hadn't been done up for years, dark and gloomy. The passage was blocked off by pinewood double doors that were never opened.

Hopeless, thought Szacki. When the police searched these rooms, and all the witnesses' personal belongings, just after the body was found, they found absolutely nothing at all that might be connected with the case. Nothing they could treat as circumstantial evidence or even a hint of it. Hopeless. If nothing came of his visit to the expert tomorrow, from Monday he'd have to go and join the narcotics squad.

He jumped up when the door opened abruptly and there stood Father Mieczysław Paczek. Kuzniecow wasn't entirely wrong in saying they all looked like fanatical wankers. The priests Szacki had met in his career always seemed a bit dull, with a misty gaze and a sort of softness, just as if they'd spent too long sitting in a bath of hot water. With his benevolently concerned smile Father Paczek was no different from the rest. Well, almost. He spoke quickly, without priestly solemnity, and as he talked he gave the impression of being bright and down-to-earth. Szacki realized the priest had nothing to say that could help. Yet another disappointment.

"Have you found anything?" asked the priest.

"Unfortunately not, Father," replied Szacki, standing up. "It looks as if only a miracle can push this inquiry forwards. If there's anything you can do about it," he pointed upwards meaningfully, "I'd be grateful."

"You're on the right side, Prosecutor," said the priest, knotting his fingers as if eager to fall to his knees at once and say prayers for the inquiry. "And that means you have some powerful allies."

"Maybe they're so powerful they don't even know that somewhere out there in the trenches a handful of soldiers from the allied army are trying to stand up to superior enemy forces. Maybe they think this bit of the front is lost already anyway, so they'd rather send their reinforcements somewhere else?"

"You're not just one of a few soldiers, Prosecutor, you're a lieutenant in a great big army – the enemy forces aren't so numerous at all, and your bit of the front will always be one of the most important."

"Could I at least have a rifle that doesn't jam?"

Father Paczek laughed.

"You'll have to ask for that yourself. But I can give you something else. I don't know if it'll be useful – we found it yesterday in the chapel. I would have called the police, but I thought that as you were going to be here, I could pass it on to you. I think it belonged to the unfortunate victim, because it has the name Henryk Telak inscribed on the back, and I recall from the papers that the poor man was called Henryk T."

As he said this, he handed Szacki a small red-and-silver digital Dictaphone.

As the prosecutor took it, he glanced spontaneously at the cross above the door.

You don't want to believe it, he thought.

III

In the interview room at the police station on Wilcza Street were: Szacki, Kuzniecow, Telak's Dictaphone and some spare batteries.

"Do you know how to work it?" asked the policeman, turning the electronic gadget in his large hand.

Szacki took the Dictaphone from him.

"Anyone does. It's a tape recorder, not a CAT scanner."

"Really?" Kuzniecow leaned back on his chair and crossed his arms over his chest. "So where do you insert the cassettes?"

Szacki gave a half-suppressed smile. Just enough to show he got the joke. The policeman rolled his eyes and reached for a sixteen-page notebook lying on the table with a dachshund on the cover. He opened it at the first page and in nice neat letters he printed: "Lesson One. Subject: Listening to the tape recorder without a cassette".

"Can we start now?" asked Szacki. "Or do we have to go to IT class first?"

"Fuck the IT class," whispered Oleg conspiratorially. "We'd be better off going to the changing rooms. The girls have got PT. Anka promised to show me her tits with no bra in exchange for a bar of chocolate."

Szacki did not respond. He raised his eyebrows questioningly. Kuzniecow just sighed and nodded.

Szacki pressed "play" with great force, as if at least a confession by the murderer were recorded on the Dictaphone. First came some rustling noises, then Telak's surprisingly high voice:

"Twenty-third of May 2005, ten o'clock. Meeting of Polgrafex representatives and printing-inks wholesaler Kannex. Present on behalf of Polgrafex: Henryk Telak…"

The recording went on for an hour, and was full of incomprehensible printing terms, such as CMYK, pantone, trapping, knockout fonts, etc. Despite Kuzniecow's prompting, Szacki was afraid to wind it on, in case of missing something. The policeman ostentatiously yawned and drew abstract patterns and naked women in his exercise book, both equally crudely. However, when the next item on the tape turned out to be a company meeting on marketing and sales, Szacki yielded and fast-forwarded, checking every three minutes to see if something was happening. He knew that even so he'd have to listen to the whole thing later on. Maybe he'd come across an argument about money, maybe he'd accidentally find out about pressures at work. That sort of motive couldn't be excluded.

However, while listening cursorily to this and several more boring business meetings he found nothing to interest him. He felt drowsy at the very idea that he'd have to play it all back again. He needed a coffee. Oleg was happy to leave the room, and came back a few minutes later with two cups of dishwater the colour of the River Vistula.

"The espresso machine's broken," he explained, presenting Szacki with a plastic cup.

The display showed there were three more files left on the tape. Szacki had already reconciled himself to the idea that there'd be nothing in them and the Dictaphone would turn out to be a dead end, just like everything else in this inquiry.

He pressed "play".

"Saturday, the fourth of June 2005, eleven a.m. Constellation therapy with the participation of…"

"Excuse me, but what are you doing?" Szacki recognized the voice of Rudzki, this time not calm and therapeutic, but aggressive and resentful.

"I'm recording on a Dictaphone," replied Telak, clearly surprised by the attack.

"Please switch it off immediately," said Rudzki firmly.

"Why? You're recording our meetings, so surely I can too."

"Out of the question. You are not alone here, your recording would infringe the privacy of the other patients. The entire therapy will be recorded on video anyway, and the only cassette will remain with me. I repeat: please put it away at once."

At that moment Telak must have switched the Dictaphone off. Kuzniecow glanced at Szacki.

"Our doctor's rather nervy," he said.

Indeed, Szacki was surprised. Also by the fact that none of the other participants in the therapy had said a word.

Two more files. He pressed "play".

Silence, just quiet rustling, as if the Dictaphone had switched itself on by accident in his pocket. Then came Telak's terrified voice:

"Saturday, the fourth of June 2005, about… eleven p.m., I'm not sure. I'm not sure of anything any more. Somehow I must check this is not a dream, not a hallucination, and I'm not going mad. Can I have lost my mind? Is this the end? Cancer? Or maybe I'm just exhausted? I must record this, after all, it's not possible… But if I'm dreaming this, and I'm dreaming that I'm recording it, and soon I'll be dreaming I'm listening to it, then… But anyway…"

There was a knock, as if Telak had put the Dictaphone on the floor. Then there was a scraping noise. Szacki turned up the volume. They could hear rustling and Telak's rapid breathing, also a strange smacking noise, as if the man were nervously licking his lips. Nothing apart from that. Maybe he really was seeing things, thought Szacki; maybe he went nuts after the therapy and tried recording his hallucinations. Suddenly the prosecutor froze, and his neck muscles tensed painfully. Out of the tiny speaker came a quiet, girlish voice.

"Daddy, Daddy…"

Szacki pressed "pause".

"Is it just me that's screwed up or can you hear that too?" asked Kuzniecow.

The prosecutor looked at him and pressed the button.

"Yes?" wheezed Telak.

"Daddy, Daddy…"

"Is that you, Princess?" The voice sounded as if Telak were dead already. Szacki felt as if he were listening to the conversation of two ghosts.

"Daddy, Daddy…"

"What is it, darling? What's happened?"

"I miss you."

"I miss you too, Princess."

A long silence. All they could hear were rustling noises and Telak smacking his lips.

"I've got to go now."

Telak started crying.

"Wait, talk to me. It's so long that you've been gone."

"I have to go now, Daddy, really."

The girl's voice was getting fainter and fainter.

"Will you come and see me again?" sobbed Telak.

"I don't know, probably not," replied the voice. "Maybe you'll come to me. One day… Bye-bye, Daddy…" The final words were inaudible.

End of recording.

"There's one more on here," said Szacki.

"Let's give ourselves a break," suggested Kuzniecow. "I'll nip out for a bottle of vodka or a sack of tranquillizers. Oh, and a saucer, a candle and a board with letters so we can summon Telak's daughter as a witness. Can you imagine the judge getting a transcript like that? Born, resident at, died, statement as follows."

"Do you think it was Jarczyk or Kwiatkowska?"

"Fuck knows, the voice isn't like either of theirs." Kuzniecow tipped the rest of the coffee down his throat and threw the cup at the waste bin, but missed. Brown stains splashed the wall.

"But it was barely audible. Send someone to both of them with some sort of tomfool questions, get them recorded and we'll have it all analysed for comparison. Your boys at the forensics lab have got some new sound-analysis toys, they'll be happy to do it."

"I'll send someone to Mrs Telak too," said Kuzniecow.

"Surely you don't think…"

"I don't think anything, I'm just a great big Russki. I check and rule out by turns."

Szacki nodded. Kuzniecow was right. He found it hard to imagine Mrs Telak crossing Warsaw at night to lurk outside her husband's door and pretend to be their dead daughter. But every day he came across facts that he couldn't have imagined only an hour before.

He pressed "play" one last time.

"Sunday, the fifth of June 2005, at… five after midnight." Telak's was the voice of an extremely weary, worn-out man. He must have been in another place, maybe in the chapel. "I'm recording this for my wife, Jadwiga. Forgive me for talking to you this way, it would be more appropriate to write a letter, but you know how much I've always hated writing. Of course I could have made an exception this time, maybe I should have, but I don't think it really matters. I mean, maybe it matters to you – it's always been hard for me to tell what's important to you and what isn't."

Telak paused abruptly, sighed, and after a while he went on: "But to get to the point. I have decided to commit suicide."

Szacki and Kuzniecow glanced at each other simultaneously, raising their eyebrows in identical expressions of surprise.

"Perhaps it's all the same to you, perhaps you'll ask: Why? It's hard for me to explain. Partly because I have nothing left to live for. You don't love me, as I've always been aware. Perhaps you even hate me. Kasia is dead. The only thing ahead of me is Bartek's death and funeral, and I don't want to wait around for that. I'm sorry to be leaving you with it, but I really am no longer capable of bearing the thought that I've got to live through another day. On top of that, today I found out I'm guilty of Kasia's death and Bartek's illness. Maybe it's true, maybe not, I don't know. But maybe my death will make Bartek feel better. It sounds absurd, but who knows – maybe it's true. Strange, I feel as if I'm repeating the same sentences and phrases over and over. In any case, I've never been particularly close to him in life, maybe my death at least will be a good thing for him. And there's another reason, perhaps the most important – I don't want to wait years and years to see my princess again in Nangijala. I know you don't like that book, and I know there probably isn't a Nangijala, or a Nangilima, or Heaven or anything else. Just emptiness. But I prefer emptiness to my life full of grief, regret and feelings of guilt. There's so much death around me – it looks as if I'm dangerous to anyone close to me. All the better for me to go. Don't worry about money. I've never told you this before, but I'm insured for a high sum, and Igor runs a trust fund for me. You're authorized to use my bank account, you just have to call him. He also knows where I'm insured. The money was meant to be for the children, maybe it'll be useful for Bartek's operation if the opportunity arises for a transplant abroad. Kiss him for me and remember I have always loved you more than you're capable of imagining. Now I should say: Don't cry, Jadzia, we'll meet again in Nangijala. But I don't think you'll despair. Nor do I think you'd want to see me after death. So I'll just say: Bye-bye, darling."

The recording broke off abruptly, as if Telak were afraid of what else he might say. The final word did not even sound like "darling", but just "darl". Kuzniecow set the Dictaphone spinning on the table. They sat in silence, considering what they'd just heard.

"I still don't want to believe he committed suicide," he said. "Can you imagine it? The guy records a farewell letter, goes and swallows some pills, but soon after he gives up and does a lot of puking. He gets dressed, packs and leaves. But on the way he changes his mind, grabs a skewer and sticks it in his eye. I don't buy that."

"Neither do I," said Szacki, spinning the Dictaphone the other way. "But I don't buy the burglar idea either. The anger at the therapy, Jarczyk and her pills, someone – maybe Kwiatkowska – pretending to be the ghost of Telak's daughter. Too many things are happening for that skewer to be accidental. The trouble is, apart from the fantastic theory of the therapeutic field that transfers hatred from one person to another, we have nothing to suggest a motive."

"Or we're unable to see it," said Kuzniecow, putting Szacki's thoughts into words, so all that remained was to nod in agreement.

"But we'll succeed in the end," Szacki soon added. "For now, tomorrow I'm meeting with the expert, you're sorting out the sound analysis, you'll find out who Igor is and interview him. It'll also be necessary to transcribe what's on the Dictaphone and give the farewell letter to the widow. Let's call each other in the evening. Or drop in at my office. I'm sure I'll be there late,

I've got two cartloads of office work to get through. I must go and get a supply of staples today."

"There's one more question I just can't answer," said Kuzniecow, tapping a fat finger on the Dictaphone.

"Well?"

"Where do you insert the cassettes?"

IV

"I remember I was terribly tired from first thing in the morning." Those were the first words Mariola Nidziecka said during her interview, seven hours after her husband's murder. It was two a.m. and Szacki felt like reacting by saying he hadn't had much rest either, but he restrained himself. Luckily. Half an hour later he knew he had never been, and never would be as tired as Mariola Nidziecka had been that morning.

The woman was thirty-five, but looked forty-five, a skinny blonde with badly cut thin hair, stuck together in strings that hung down her cheeks. She put her right hand on her knees, while her left swung, the elbow bent at a strange angle. Then he found out that five years earlier her husband Nidziecki had broken her arm by laying it on the table and hitting it with a kitchen stool. After five whacks the joint was shattered. Rehabilitation hadn't helped. Nidziecka had a slightly flattened nose, bent to the left, so she had to breathe through her mouth. Then he found out that two years earlier her husband had broken it with a chopping board. The thin hair could not hide a misshapen ear. Then he found out that a year ago her husband had flattened her ear with an iron when he discovered that she was incapable of ironing his shirts properly. She had screamed so loud that for once the neighbours had called the police. Ever since her hearing had been poor, and sometimes she seemed to hear buzzing.

"Did you ever have a forensic medical examination?" he asked.

Not always, but sometimes she had. Then he found out that her file at the regional clinic was as thick as the phone book. As he read it, he was reminded of historical documents describing the torture of prisoners in concentration camps.

"Why didn't you file a case for harassment?"

She had, five years ago. He had almost killed her when he found out. He had slashed her with a disposable razor. The sentence had been two years suspended for five. He came home from the courtroom sad, so he'd only raped her. She'd expected something worse. "Now I might go and do time, so you'd better watch out," he had warned her. "Before they shut me up you're going to bite the dust." "You'll never do that," the words had escaped her, "you'd have no one to torment." "I've still got a daughter, I'll manage," he'd replied. She believed him. Just in case, from that day on she'd given him reasons to hit her instead of the child.

"But sometimes I used to wonder what it would be like if he wasn't there. If he wasn't there at all."

"Does that mean you planned the murder?" he asked.

"No, I didn't," she replied, and he sighed with relief, because otherwise he'd have been left with no choice but to charge her with murder under Article 148, paragraph 1. Then the minimum sentence would be eight years. "I just wondered what it would be like."

The day when she'd woken up so tired, Zuzia had come home from school in tears. She'd quarrelled with a boy. He had pulled at her, she'd pulled away, and the strap on her satchel had broken. "So you've been fighting with boys," her father had said as they were eating dinner, stuffed cabbage leaves in tomato sauce and mashed potatoes. His favourite. Zuzia had vehemently denied it. She said it wasn't her who'd been fighting, but they had pulled her. "For no reason at all?" he'd asked, mashing up the potatoes and tomato sauce, turning them into pinkish goo. The girl vehemently agreed. Nidziecka knew she'd been too vehement. She was numb with terror; she had no idea what to do. She knew he would want to punish Zuzia. She'd have to come to her defence, and then he'd kill her. And no one would ever defend Zuzia again, just as no one had ever defended her.

"All right," he had said after dinner, wiping his mouth on a napkin, leaving a pink mark, like a consumptive's cough. "You've got to understand you mustn't provoke rows with boys." "I understand," replied Zuzia, who had only now realized where the conversation had been leading from the start, but by now it was too late. "You've got to understand," he explained, "that if I give you a smack now, you'll never forget you're not allowed to do that. Otherwise by tomorrow you'll already have forgotten, and the day after that the same thing will happen, and in a week you'll have a reputation as a troublemaker, and it's hard to go through life with that sort of label."

The little girl had burst into tears.

"No hysterics," he'd said, annoyed by now. "Let's get it over with. Believe me, this is harder for me than it is for you." He rose, picked up his daughter from her chair and dragged her towards her bedroom.

"I sat there as if paralysed. He had hit her sometimes before, but compared with what he did to me it was stroking. I was glad he treated her so mildly. Now I could sense he might do more, but I was still hoping he'd only hit her a few times."

"Why didn't you call the police?"

She shrugged.

"I was afraid he'd hear me. I was afraid as soon as I went out he'd do something to Zuzia. I was afraid that even if I did call they'd tell me they're not my bodyguards. That has happened before now."

"So what did you do?"

"Nothing. I waited to see what would happen. And then I saw him take a braided leather lead off the clothes rack. We used to have a dog, a sort of mongrelly Alsatian. He was hit by a bus a couple of years ago. Somehow I've never had the heart to throw away the lead. I loved that dog. I started shouting that he was to leave her alone now, otherwise I'd call the police and he'd go to prison."

"And what happened then?"

"He said I shouldn't interfere but should remember what he'd said earlier. Then I replied that he should watch out because he wasn't immortal either. Then he let the child go, came up to me and lashed me with the lead. It didn't even hurt, because the hardest blow hit my hair, but the end of the lead wound around my head and cut my lip —" she put her finger to a scab at the corner of her mouth. "Zuzia began to wail of course. Then he went mad, shouting that neither of us would ever forget this day. Then I stood up. He swung the lead, but I raised my hand and it wound around my arm. That upset him terribly. He pushed me onto the work surface, but as we were both still holding the lead, he came flying after me. I was afraid that would be the end of me. I reached out a hand, grabbed the bread knife and stuck it in his side. I wasn't trying to kill him, I just wanted him to stop. He flew at me and lost his balance."

"Why didn't you withdraw the hand holding the knife?"

She licked her lips and looked at him. For a long time. He understood, but he couldn't put it in the report. However, he had to write something down. Without dropping her gaze, she opened her mouth, then gently shook her head. She understood. And instead of what she was probably intending to say, in other words "I didn't want to", she replied:

"I wasn't quick enough. It all happened in a flash."

And that was how the earth came to carry one less son of a bitch, he felt like adding as the punchline. But instead of saying anything, he let her finish her story. The inquiry had confirmed that the woman's life was hell. Even the victim's own parents had picked him to shreds. Nidziecka's father-in-law was amazed it was him that was dead and not her. "But that's good, very good," he'd kept saying over and over.

A simple case. At least for the police. They'd arrested her, interviewed her, got a confession, the end. The rest of the job was up to the prosecutor and the court. The policeman didn't have to wonder which article in the Penal Code had been contravened, how to classify the crime and what penalty to demand. The policeman didn't have a supervisor above him in the shape of the Preparatory Proceedings Department who'd write him letters demanding that he catch criminals in a different way. Szacki often wondered if he wouldn't have been a better policeman than a prosecutor. As it was, he performed lots of tasks that his colleagues had only heard of, never done. He went to incident scenes and autopsies, and sometimes even took the trouble to go and see a witness to interview him on the spot. Rarely, but he did do it. Though on the other hand, as a policeman, often living on the fringes of the underworld, making concessions, occasionally turning a blind eye in exchange for something, he wouldn't have had the satisfaction he got from being part of the legal machine, whose aim was to administer justice – the penalty for breaking the law.

Now, as he wondered about the legal classification, he felt as if the merciless machine had got stuck. He knew what was expected of him – that he should charge Nidziecka as severely as possible under Article 148, paragraph 1: "Whoever kills a person is liable to a penalty of imprisonment for a term of no less than eight years." Would that be in accordance with the law? Surely. Szacki was convinced Nidziecka had wanted to kill her husband. And that alone should have interested him. The court would probably have given her a low sentence, a special commutation of the sentence and so on, but still: that would mean Nidziecka was a worse murderer than the merciless thugs responsible for "causing grievous bodily harm resulting in death". He could decide on Article 148, paragraph 4: "Whoever kills a person while in a state of extreme agitation justified by the circumstances is liable to a penalty of imprisonment of from one to ten years". One year was less than eight.

Szacki pushed the computer keyboard away from him. He had already written the entire indictment, he was just missing the classification and the grounds for it in a few sentences. In fact he felt like writing a draft decision to dismiss under the rule of self-defence – the right to repulse an unlawful attack. Without doubt that was what had happened here. But the supervisory board would stamp him into the ground if in such an obvious case he didn't submit an indictment that plainly improved the official statistics.

Finally he wrote down the classification from Article 155: "Whoever causes a person's death unintentionally is liable to a penalty of imprisonment for from three months to five years."

"And I'll quit this rotten job sooner than change that," he said aloud to himself.

Half an hour later the indictment was ready. He left it with Chorko's secretary, as the boss had just gone home. It was six p.m. High time to leave this charming place, he thought. He packed up quickly and switched off his computer. Just then the phone rang. He cursed out loud. For an instant he simply wanted to leave, but duty triumphed. As usual.

It was Nawrocki calling. He had located the people from the parallel class to Sylwia Boniczka's, including someone repeating the year, as the clairvoyant had said. Some of them had no idea what he was talking about, some seemed truly scared, and the one repeating the year was terrified. He'd trembled all over, and Nawrocki was convinced that if he'd put more pressure on him he'd have cracked. Szacki didn't say it aloud, but he was sorry Nawrocki had interviewed the man. Although the policeman had a brain like a computer, physically he looked like a wimp and wasn't best suited to "putting pressure" on interviewees. Kuzniecow was quite another matter – he only had to appear in the doorway and they all became very talkative in an instant.

"I don't think we could establish a rape case," said Nawrocki. "There's no injured party, no evidence, no proof, no circumstantial evidence; there's just the clairvoyant and a few potential suspects who are digging in their heels."

"What about the father?"

"Well, yes, I've had an idea that we should interview him jointly."

"How do you mean jointly?"

"I think if he's squeezed a bit he'll tell the truth. But we've only got one chance. If he doesn't admit it the first time, that'll be it. So I suggest a massed attack: policeman, prosecutor, the darkest interview room in Mostowski Palace, being brought there by the police, a two-hour wait... Do you see, Prosecutor?"

Theatre, thought Szacki, he's suggesting bloody theatre. What should I do now? Go to the costume-hire place and get a bad cop's mask?

"What time?" he asked after a short silence, regretting it before the words had reached Nawrocki.

"What about six tomorrow evening?" suggested the policeman, sounding as if they were off to a nice pub.

"The perfect time," said Szacki emphatically. "Don't forget I only drink lightly chilled red wine, best of all from the Puglia region of Italy. And the table mustn't be too near the window or by the door."

"Sorry?"

"Never mind. Tomorrow at six at your place. I'll call from downstairs."

It was approaching seven as he turned off Świętokrzyski Bridge onto Szczecińskie Embankment towards the zoo and politely joined the queue in the left lane. The right one ended just past the little bridge at Praga port – you could only turn right from it – which didn't prevent some crafty customers from driving all the way down it, then playing dumb with their indicators on. Szacki never let them in.

He glanced at the ugly river-police building, and thought it was just about the start of the season for bodies in the Vistula. Drunken bathing, rape in the bushes, bets who could swim further. Luckily they rarely found anything in the City Centre section of the brown river. He couldn't bear drowned bodies, those livid, swollen corpses that looked like seals with the fur shaved off. He hoped this season he'd be spared that nightmare. A year ago, when they'd found one right by Gdański Bridge, he had felt like moving it by hand a few yards further down – then his colleagues from the Żoliborz district would have had to deal with it. Fortunately the case was simple – the guy turned out to be a suicide who had jumped off Siekierkowski Bridge. Szacki had never understood why he had fully undressed before doing it, but didn't put that in his letter to the wife. The wife claimed he had always been very shy.

At the lanes by the main entrance to the zoo he had to stop to let a man and his daughter cross the road. The man was several years older than him, horribly emaciated, maybe sick. The girl was Helka's age. She was holding a balloon shaped like Piglet. Szacki thought how strange it was that all the cases he was involved in lately featured fathers and daughters. Boniczka, who may have murdered his daughter out of shame and buried her at night in the nursery school playground. Nidziecki, dragging his daughter into her bedroom and explaining that it was harder for him than for her. Telak wanting to commit suicide to follow his daughter into death. But also perhaps in some twisted way guilty of her death. And himself. Desperately wanting change, chasing after a young journalist. Was he prepared to sacrifice his daughter? And what exactly did it mean, "sacrifice"? It was too early for solutions of that kind. But why too early? he wondered, as he waited for the lights to change at the corner of Ratuszowa and Jagiellońska Streets. A hopeless junction. If there was traffic, at most two cars could turn left. And that only if the drivers were quick to react. Why too early? Wasn't it better to sort it out at once and have a free hand? Not have to tremble during dates in case his wife called. Not have to deceive either one or the other party.

He parked outside the house.

"What fucking bullshit," he said aloud, putting the radio-control panel in his briefcase. "You're getting worse, Szacki, worse and worse."

6

Friday, 10th June 2005

UEFA has decided that Liverpool can after all defend its title in the next season of the Champions League, though it shouldn't, because it only took fifth place in the Premiership. The Moscow Prosecutor's Office has ruled that there is nothing wrong with the expression "Jewish aggression as a form of Satanism". The centrist Polish People's Party authorities have decided that Jarosław Kalinowski will be their party's candidate for President. The candidate wants to hold a debate during the campaign on what Poland should be like. But in the polls Lech Kaczyński gains two points again, leaving independent Zbigniew Religa eight points behind. From other polls it appears that most Poles support Mayor Kaczyński's crusade against gays, but most Varsovians do not. A bomb scare in the capital. Fearing a sarin attack, for three hours in the afternoon the police block off the main junction in the city and suspend the metro. The resulting mega-jam probably exceeds the hoaxer's boldest expectations. Meanwhile at Warsaw Zoo lumps have appeared on Buba the elephant's trunk, probably caused by a virus. She is bearing her treatment bravely and doesn't have to be anaesthetized for it. Maximum temperature — 18 degrees; fairly sunny, no rain.

I

Dr Jeremiasz Wróbel resembled a cat. His face looked as if it had been drawn with a compass, pale and freckled, with short, sparse red stubble and sparse, curly red hair cut very short. On top of that, he had no profile. Although looking at him face on, you did get an impression of some depth, from the side his face was almost flat. It crossed Szacki's mind that as a child he must always have slept on his stomach, and always on the floor. His ears stuck so closely to his head that he didn't seem to have any at all. He looked peculiar, but was, as Szacki had to admit, extremely amiable. His voice was nice and warm, similar to Rudzki's therapist voice, but more velvety. If Szacki had had to choose which one to tell his problems to, he'd undoubtedly have chosen Wróbel. Maybe because he wasn't implicated in a murder.

They soon left the doctor's tiny study at the Institute of Psychiatry and Neurology on Sobieski Street and went down a corridor into a conference room, where the doctor could watch the recording of the constellation held at Łazienkowska Street. They only exchanged a few words. Szacki did most of the talking, describing the inquiry to Wróbel. He also explained why, instead of making a request for a written opinion in the usual manner, he had insisted on a meeting.

"This recording might be the key to the mystery of Telak's murder," he said. "Therefore, I'll also be ordering a written opinion from you for the files, but for now I need to know what you think of it as soon as possible."

"Prosecutor, you stand out among your kind like an erection at an OAPs' club," said the therapist as he switched on the light in the small conference room. There was a hospital odour mixed with the smell of coffee and new carpeting. Szacki was starting to understand why the idea of transcribing a conversation with Wróbel prompted mirth.

"We psychotherapists rarely host representatives of your office. I think each of you should talk to us in person before and after we give an expert opinion. But that is just my view, and I am merely a humble assistant in the Lord's garden, entrusted with caring for the vegetable bed."

Szacki had it on the tip of his tongue to say the "vegetables" should be treated individually, not as a group, but all he said was that, unless something had changed since yesterday, the Prosecution Service was simply too understaffed to meet with every expert witness.

The therapist watched the recording in silent concentration. Several times he made notes. Then he reached the bit where Kwiatkowska and Kaim went closer to the chairs representing Telak's parents, Jarczyk was in hysterics and Telak himself was staring into space, his face twisted with pain. He stopped the image.

"Ask your question," he urged, turning to face Szacki.

"Why did you stop it at that moment?"

"First the foreplay, then the climax," said the therapist, shaking his head.

Szacki almost said automatically: "You talk just like my wife", but he stopped himself at the last moment. He was at work.

"First of all, I'd like to know if this therapy was conducted according to the rules of the art."

Wróbel leaned back in his chair and locked his fingers behind his head.

"You see, the *ars therapeutica* is a bit like the *ars amandi*. There's no single perfect way to bring any woman to orgasm in three minutes, nor is there any one position that would suit everyone."

"Without wishing to adopt your poetic form of expression," said Szacki, starting to feel annoyed, "nevertheless I will ask: was it sex or was it rape?"

"Definitely not rape," replied Wróbel. "Bold sex, but the kind without any leather costumes or police caps. You see, theoretically in Family Constellation Therapy there should be more people taking part. I can lend you a DVD with a recording of constellations conducted by Hellinger himself. There's a full room, a large audience as well as the patients. There's never a shortage of people to arrange as some distant relative or wife's lover. But what Mr Rudzki did – substituting chairs for the patient's parents at a moment when they no longer had a role to play – is acceptable. Sometimes you do in fact do that when there's a lack of representatives."

"Here there were only four people from the start," noted Szacki. "Isn't that too few? Obviously everyone has parents, their own family, grandparents. Isn't it hard to work in such a small group?"

"It could be, but I can see where Rudzki's coming from. I'm not keen on those orgies either – sometimes all that's missing is animals. I like to have my fun in groups of ten best of all. Rudzki has gone even further. OK, you could even call it an interesting experiment. And from what I can see the field is working, and that's not bad at all. You can't deny it."

Szacki didn't.

"Apart from that you must realize that Dr Cezary Rudzki is no novice. He may not be as widely known as Eichelberger or He-Whose-Name-Is-No-Longer-To-Be-Uttered" – Szacki knew he must mean the therapist Andrzej Samson, exposed as a paedophile amid a great public scandal – "but in our field Rudzki's a major figure. More than once he has experimented with therapies that seemed as stable as a sixteen-year-old's sex drive, and often brought off amazing results."

"So in your view he didn't make any mistakes?"

Jeremiasz Wróbel smacked his lips, frowned and scratched behind his ear. Szacki thought that if he were to take his photo now and send it to the organizers of a cat show, he'd be sure to qualify.

"In my view he made one important error," he said at last. "That is, you see, I'd have done it differently. But it may be that friend Rudzki had some other plans. He knew he'd do it all at the end."

"More specifically?"

"Yes, sorry. When the issue with the patient's parents was explained, before bringing his current family into the constellation, in my view he should have introduced some resolving sentences. As that was left in a state of suspension, the continuation must have been incredibly hard for the patient. If order had been brought in the family of origin, if the patient had felt immediate relief thanks to reconciliation with his parents, if from then on he had ceased to feel guilty towards them, he'd have entered the next stage of the therapy feeling stronger. What's more, I'm sure the rest of the participants would have felt better, and those terrible scenes would not have taken place."

Szacki suddenly felt a complete mental blank. He sat and stared at Wróbel, and could only think about one thing: there was nothing, once again nothing, no progress. It all works, it's all in order, it all makes sense. Just the corpse with a skewer in his eye doesn't quite fit in somehow.

"Do the emotions go on working after the constellation is over?" he asked at last.

"Meaning?" Wróbel didn't understand the question.

"If during the constellation Mrs X represents Mr Y's passionate lover, and then runs into him after the session in the hotel lobby, does she go to bed with him?"

The doctor thought for a long while.

"Interesting question. I think that even if those weren't her emotions, she would experience them as if they were. The memory of being fascinated, attracted to Mr Y. Yes, of course she wouldn't start writhing at his feet moaning 'fuck me', but if they'd started flirting, it wouldn't be so hard for them to decide on sex. That's what I think."

Szacki told him about the voice of the "daughter" recorded on Telak's Dictaphone.

"And are you sure it was the woman representing his daughter?"

"Ninety per cent. We're doing sound tests to be sure."

"Interesting. Does Rudzki know about this?"

"No, he doesn't. And I wouldn't like him to find out from you."

"Yes, of course. You see, it could be significant that the constellation was so brutally interrupted. We usually try to bring it to an end ourselves; interruptions are very rare, sometimes there are breaks lasting several days for the patient to be able to gather information about his family. But it always happens gently, whereas here, at the moment when the field was working strongest, the participants suddenly parted ways. Could it be that they went back to their rooms 'possessed' by the people they were representing? I don't know. I've never come across such a case before, but, well…"

"It sounds logical?" suggested Szacki.

"Yes. I'd compare it with the situation of a patient under hypnosis. I can bring him out of it, but I can also leave him in it. Eventually the state of hypnosis passes into sleep, and after that the patient wakes up as if nothing has happened. Perhaps it was similar here. The constellation was brutally interrupted, and before they'd recovered, for some time yet, the patients were not just themselves, but also the people they represented. Perhaps."

Wróbel stared into space, exactly like Telak, frozen in the frame on the television screen.

"Are you able to say how long someone could remain in such a state of 'hypnosis'?" asked the prosecutor.

"No, I have no idea. But I can sense where you're heading, and I think it's a blind alley. Like a transvestite's sexual organs. On the surface the prospect might look promising, but take off a few layers and it's disappointing."

"Why?"

"Medical limitations, which are sure to be overcome sooner or later. It's not easy to shape a vagina and implant it inside the body. That's why transvestites limit themselves to clothing that…"

Szacki wasn't listening. He closed his eyes and took a few deep breaths in an effort to calm down.

"Why is my reasoning a blind alley?"

"Oh, sorry." Wróbel didn't look at all embarrassed. He moved his chair closer to the television. "Take a look at the way they're standing," he said, pointing at "the Telak family". "Opposite each other. And that always means disorder. Conflict, longing, unsettled issues. The outcome of a constellation is always a semicircle: the people stand next to each other, they can observe each other, but they have a space in front of them, they don't have to fight anyone for their place. Please note that here the patient's children are standing next to each other, which means they are in harmony. So too are the patient's parents, represented by the chairs. But apart from that they're all scattered about, and chaos is the dominant feature of the constellation. If the session had lasted longer, we'd have seen on the recording how more people would have been reconciled, and then they'd have taken their places next to each other in a semicircle. This whole therapy works because each of them wants to feel better, not worse. And committing a crime overloads the system in a dreadful way – the most dreadful, the worst of all possible ways. And so I doubt if representing a member of the patient's family was the motive for the murder."

"Are you sure?"

"We're talking about the human psyche, Prosecutor. I'm not sure of anything."

"What about this story that Telak's daughter committed suicide and his son fell ill in order to give him relief? To me that sounds improbable."

Wróbel stood up and started pacing the room. He stuck his hands in the pockets of his doctor's coat. His movements were catlike too. He gave the impression of being about to do something completely unexpected – to start miaowing, for example – which made Szacki feel tense. He turned his head to relax the muscles in his neck. As usual it didn't help at all – he should finally treat himself to a massage. It probably wasn't all that expensive.

"In constellations we set ourselves two basic questions. Firstly: who is missing, and who should join the constellation? It's often like an inquiry, digging about in the dirty laundry of family history. Secondly: who should depart? Who should be allowed to do that? The mechanism is always the same. If we don't allow someone to depart – in the sense of 'die' as well as 'go away' – instead of that person, the children leave. It's usually the adults who are guilty, and the children want to help them, so they take the guilt on themselves, and leave instead of the person who ought to leave. That is the order of love. That's why the therapist allies himself with the children rather than the adults."

"But suicide straight away?" Szacki was getting the same feeling he'd had during his conversation with Rudzki. He understood, but he didn't want to believe it.

"Often the cause of suicide is a wish to relieve the pain of a parent who has lost his former partner in tragic circumstances. I think Rudzki's theory concerning the unexpiated guilt about leaving home that was felt by... What was his name?"

"Telak."

"…felt by Telak holds water. But I wouldn't be at all surprised if his lover or former partner had been killed in a car crash, and he never came to terms with it, maybe in some way felt guilty. To such an extent that his daughter decided to atone for that guilt for him. You should know that if they're allowed to depart, former partners are usually represented by the children."

Jeremiasz Wróbel stopped talking, and Szacki was unable to think of any reasonable question to ask. His mind was a blank. Every day he got new information about this case and every day he failed to move forwards. It made no sense.

"And now perhaps you can tell me why you stopped the tape at that point?" he finally asked.

"Absolutely," replied the psychiatrist, smiling in a way that Szacki found quite obscene. "What do you think – why didn't Telak look at his wife or children once during the constellation, although there was so much going on between them?"

Szacki felt as if he'd been called up to the blackboard.

"I don't know, I hadn't thought about it. Is he afraid to? Does he feel guilty towards them? Is he ashamed?"

"None of those things," said Wróbel, shaking his head. "He simply can't take his eyes off the person who's standing right opposite him and who is probably the most important of all in this constellation. I don't know who it is, but that tie is terribly strong. Please note that he doesn't even blink – he's looking at that person the whole time."

"But there's no one there!" Szacki suddenly felt furious. He'd frittered away so many hours with this lunatic. He got up. Wróbel rose to his feet too.

"Of course there is," he replied calmly, moving his nose in a feline way. "There stands the person who's missing from the constellation. Do you want to make progress in your inquiry? Then go and find that missing person. Just find out who Telak is staring at with such panic and fear in his eyes."

Prosecutor Teodor Szacki nodded his head in silence, gazing at the fuzzy image of Telak's pained face, quivering slightly on the television screen. That look had worried him earlier on, but he had ignored his instinct, knowing Telak was drained by the therapy. Now he understood that his face wasn't pained. It had worried him, because he'd seen that look before, in the eyes of people he'd interrogated – a mixture of fear and hatred.

He switched off the machine and removed the tape.

"Wouldn't you like to take part in a constellation?" the therapist asked Szacki as they walked towards the main exit together. "See what it's like from the inside?"

Szacki opened his mouth to answer that he'd be very willing, but in the short while it took for the air to get from his lungs to his vocal cords, the mental image arose of himself arranging his parents, Weronika and Helka, and the therapist asking how they were feeling.

"No, thank you. That's probably not necessary."

Wróbel smiled in a feline way, but didn't pass comment. Only at the door, when he'd already said goodbye to Szacki, did he say:

"If someone in the constellation seems to be good and someone else bad, it's almost always the other way around. Please remember that."

II

Not many bits of this metropolis look like a genuine city, rather than a large area cluttered with streets and buildings. However, even in this dump there are some beautiful bits, thought Szacki, as he drove down Belwederska Street towards the city centre. This section of the Royal Way, from Gagarin Street to Triple Cross Square was one of the few that bore witness to what this city had once been and what it could be. First the modern mass of the Hyatt hotel, then the Russian embassy, the Belweder Palace, Łazienki Park, the government buildings, then Ujazdowski Park and the embassies on Ujazdowskie Avenue (with the exception of the breeze block the Americans had built themselves), and finally the big-city Triple Cross Square. Szacki didn't like Nowy Świat, and couldn't understand all the fuss about that street where the buildings looked as if they'd been transferred from Kielce. Ugly, low little tenements, one not at all suited to another. Szacki couldn't believe Nowy Świat and the squalid Chmielna Street fancied themselves as the prettiest part of town. Maybe only so visitors from the provinces could feel at home here.

But now Nowy Świat made him think of the Cava café and Miss Grzelka – that is, Monika – and it was hard for him to foster any ill feeling for the place. He wished she was waiting there, and that instead of going to work on Krucza Street he could have a cup of coffee with her, sit and chat like friends. Or like potential lovers. Was that really his intention? An affair? How could he possibly do it? To have a lover, you had to have a bachelor flat or the money for a hotel, or at least work non-standard hours that could justify your absence from home. He, meanwhile, was a poor civil servant who came home from work every day at eight at the latest.

What am I actually doing, he thought, as he went round the Prosecution Service building for the second time looking for a parking place – the only official one was taken. And what do I really imagine? Am I truly so starved of sex and love that it's enough for me to meet with a woman a couple of times and no longer be capable of thinking about anything else?

Finally he found a place on Żurawia Street, not far the Szpilka café. It was one o'clock. In five hours he'd be sitting there with Monika, having supper, stretching his budget. He wondered how she'd be dressed. He locked the car when finally it dawned on him.

Monika, Szpilka, six p.m.
Nawrocki, police headquarters, six p.m.
Fuck.

Pinned to the door of his room he found a message to come and see the boss IMMEDIATELY. Of course it was about Nidziecka. He ignored it, went inside and called Nawrocki, but the policeman had already summoned Boniczka's father to police HQ, and it was impossible to cancel. Szacki thought he could persuade Nawrocki to apply a sort of harassment – summon him, keep him in the corridor, then let him go and invite him to come back the next day (the secret police had done it to his grandfather in the 1950s) – but he dropped the idea. He preferred to get it over and done with. He called Monika.

"Hi, has something come up?" she asked before he'd had time to speak.

"I have to be at police HQ at six – I've no idea how long it'll take. Sorry."

"So maybe call me if it doesn't take long. And don't say sorry for no reason. What'll you say when you do something really naughty?"

Szacki gulped. He was sure she heard him do it. Should he tell the truth, that after the interrogation he'd have to go home? And did he really have to? Was he the father of a family, or a little kid who has to ask his mummy's permission to come home late from the playground? And in fact why couldn't he say that? After all, if she wanted to flirt with a married man, she must know what she was choosing to do. But what if she was some sort of madwoman who'd start calling Weronika and screaming "He's mine, all mine"? He panicked.

"I don't want to promise anything, because I really don't think I'll make it today," he said, trying to buy time. Why the fuck hadn't he made a plan before calling her?

"Hmm, that's a pity."

"Maybe tomorrow during the day – I'll be hanging about in town, could we make a lunch?" he stammered ungrammatically, when he finally remembered that tomorrow he'd have to be at Telak's funeral. He could always tell Weronika he had to drop in at work after the funeral. Should he take a change of clothes? Maybe he should – he couldn't go to the pub in a suit that was good for family ceremonies like weddings and funerals. Bugger it.

They agreed that he'd send a text once he knew at what time they could meet, and she'd just have a light breakfast (mango, coffee, maybe a small sandwich) and wait to hear from him. Instantly he imagined her lying in bed in the morning, with tousled hair, reading the paper and licking mango juice off her fingers. Would he ever see that for real?

Oleg Kuzniecow was not happy about having to question the people from Telak's circle again, this time about his lovers, former partners and girlfriends at school.

"Are you crazy?" he moaned. "How do you think I'm supposed to check that? His parents are dead, his wife can't possibly know a thing, and I've already asked his work colleagues about it."

Szacki was unyielding.

"Find out what high school he went to, what and where he studied, find his male and female friends, and question them. That's what the police do anyway, for fuck's sake – look for people and interview them. I just fill in forms and number the pages in files."

Oleg sent him a torrent of abuse down the phone.

"I'd understand if it would still do any good," he grumbled. "But the whole time we've just been chasing shadows, nothing solid. Say we find some bit of fluff of his who was killed in a car crash when he was driving. Say he felt terribly guilty about it and that's why his daughter killed herself. So what? Can you tell me how that moves the inquiry forwards?"

Szacki could not. He knew it would probably be just another bit of non-essential information that would take a lot of work to obtain. A solid chunk of hard work of no use to anyone. But did they have any alternative?

So he told the policeman, who growled that he was behaving like some grand company director.

"You're pissed off because we haven't got anything, and you're making some panic-stricken moves to give the impression that you're doing something. I know you – it's just that you don't want to get on with some other job. Can't you at least wait until next week for the results of the voiceprint analysis? Then you'll know for sure if it was Kwiatkowska pretending to be Telak's daughter. You know Jarczyk's fingerprints are on the bottle of pills. That's enough to search their places and check they haven't got something else to connect them with Telak. I'd give Kaim and Rudzki the once-over too. If only to stop them from feeling too secure. And as for Rudzki, can't you have a chat with him about Telak's past? He ought to know something – the guy confided in him once a week, didn't he?"

Kuzniecow was right. And at the same time he wasn't. Rudzki was a potential suspect, and as such he was hardly a reliable source of information. His revelations would have to be verified in any case.

So he didn't give in to Kuzniecow. Yet straight after finishing the conversation with the policeman, he called Cezary Rudzki and asked him to come in on Monday. In the process he discovered that the therapist would be at tomorrow's funeral too.

Janina Chorko had put on make-up. It was terrible. Without make-up she was just ugly; with it she looked like a corpse that the undertaker's children have made up with mummy's cosmetics just for fun, and that as a result of these efforts has come back to life and gone to work. She was wearing a thin polo-neck top and maybe nothing underneath. And to think only a short time ago he was sure nothing could excite him like a woman's breasts. That was the distant past, prehistory, the Silurian era, the Devonian, the Cambrian. He was afraid to look at her, which was easy because she immediately started to give him a dressing-down, so he could lower his gaze in relief and play the ticked-off prosecutor.

Murder is murder, it's not up to the prosecutor to help the defendant out, surely he hadn't forgotten what they'd talked about the other day, he could always change the classification in the courtroom without pissing off all his superiors in the process, and so on.

"No," he replied curtly, once she had finished, raising his head and looking her in the eyes. Just in the eyes. He took his cigarettes out of his jacket pocket and lit the first one that day. And it was long past noon – not bad at all.

"There's no smoking in this building," she said coldly, lighting up herself. He knew he should have offered her a light, but he was afraid she'd get the wrong idea. She took an ashtray full of dog-ends out of a drawer and put it on the desk between them.

"What do you mean, 'no'?"

"I mean I'm not going to charge Mariola Nidziecka with murder," he said very slowly and very calmly. "To tell the truth, I'm surprised I wrote an indictment at all in a case of such obvious use of self-defence. I'm ashamed I yielded to imaginary pressure. Evidently, my intuition was right. But even so there's no worse censorship than self-censorship. Please excuse me, as my boss and the person responsible for my decisions too."

Chorko blew smoke at the ceiling and leaned towards him. She sighed heavily, straight into the ashtray, raising a cloud of ash. Szacki pretended not to notice.

"Are you screwing me around, Mr Szacki?" she whispered.

"I'm saying," he replied, unable to use a verb that he associated with sex, "I've had enough of predicting what someone's going to like and what they're not. I'm saying we should work the way we regard as correct, and only start worrying when someone gives us a hard time about it. I'm saying I start worrying when I hear you telling me I should read my superiors' minds, because I've always thought you were different. I'm saying that I'm extremely sorry about it. And I'm asking: do you think that legal classification is wrong?"

The head of the City Centre District Prosecutor's Office stubbed out her dog-end with the firm gesture of an inveterate smoker and offered Szacki the ashtray. She sank back in her fake-leather armchair, and suddenly Szacki saw the old, tired woman in her.

"Prosecutor Szacki," she said resignedly. "I'm an old, tired woman, who has seen more of these stories than I should have. And I'd be the first to sign a decision to dismiss this case under the rules for self-defence. What's more, I think that son of a bitch should be dug up, resurrected and put away for years on end. And you're right that the longer I sit in a leather armchair instead of interviewing witnesses, the more I think about 'what they'll say'. It's not good, dammit. And I thought about what I told you yesterday: that sometimes you have to give way in order to survive. A lesser evil. Do you agree?"

"Partly yes, partly no," he replied diplomatically. That was a question no prosecutor in Poland could have categorically answered with a clean conscience.

"Yes, they should write that underneath the eagle above the door as our heraldic motto. Partly yes, partly no. But more of a no?"

"More of a no."

"You're right." She sighed again. "I'll sign your indictment, we'll send it to Krakowskie Przedmieście and we'll see what happens. And if things become unbearable, we'll have to think again. One of my friends from Wola qualified as a legal adviser and got a job in the legal department at a mineral water factory in Beskidy. She's got a holiday home in the mountains, works eight hours a day and earns twelve thousand a month. And no one throws acid in her face or scratches her car out of spite because she's 'that bitch from the prosecution'."

Szacki nodded in silence. She was right, but he was afraid that if he started agreeing with her too eagerly, she'd think she'd found a fraternal soul in him and would suggest he drop in at her place for a glass of wine and a nice little chat about the sad lot of the prosecutor in the Polish Republic. He waited a while out of courtesy, thanked the boss, muttered something about a huge pile of paperwork and went out, leaving Janina Chorko surrounded by unhappy thoughts, the stink of cigarettes and the smell of her imitation leather chair.

III

He went to Mostowski Palace on foot, because the entire city centre was stuck in a gigantic traffic jam. Not a single vehicle could cross the heart of the city – the roundabout by the Rotunda. Nowadays it wasn't actually "the roundabout by the Rotunda" any more, but officially "Dmowski Roundabout", in memory of the pre-war politician, who had been honoured by having this utterly charmless junction of two motorways named after him. Szacki could easily have got to Bankowy Square by metro, but the underground railway was closed too. Therefore, not without pleasure, he walked down Bracka Street towards Piłsudski Palace, hoping the city would get moving by the time the interview ended so he'd be able to go back to the office by bus.

It was a nice stroll, and Szacki thought that if he were to drive a blindfolded foreigner from Okęcie airport to the start of it, then take him for a walk along this route, cover his eyes again at the end and take him back to Okęcie, the tourist might go away with the impression that Warsaw was a very pretty city. Chaotic, but pretty. And full of cafés, pubs and clubs, as there were plenty on this route.

Especially the section along Świętokrzyska Street, Mazowiecka and Kredytowa Streets with their beautiful tenement buildings, art supply shops (as if Warsaw were a city of artists), the Protestant church on Małachowski Square, the Zachęta Gallery (as if it were a city of art) and the stunning panorama of Piłsudski Square, with the Wielki Theatre (city of theatre) and Norman Foster's Metropolitan building (city of fine architecture, ha ha ha).

And finally the walk through the Saxon Garden, with the mandatory stop to admire the Polish girls sunning themselves on the benches. For many years Szacki had been unable to bear this place, because here on one of those benches he'd been turned down by a girl he was in love with at school. Not long ago he'd seen her in a shop. Her balding husband was pushing a trolley with items spilling out of it, and she had a sulky face as she dragged a couple of children after her. Or maybe she was dragging one and carrying the other? What Szacki really remembered best from the entire scene was that she had greasy hair and her roots were showing. He had pretended not to know her.

At Bankowy Square Szacki quickened his pace; it was a few minutes after six. He ran through the underpass to the small square in front of the Muranów cinema and immediately felt guilty. He regarded himself as a member of the intelligentsia, and as such he shouldn't miss any premiere at the Muranów, where instead of Hollywood trash they showed more-or-less-ambitious European films. Meanwhile he'd only ever been there once in a blue moon. He kept promising himself he'd see them later on DVD, but he never took out any ambitious European films. Bah, he didn't even fancy watching those boring things on

TV. This time they were showing *Reconstruction*, some sort of Danish reflection on the meaning of life, apparently. He turned his gaze from the accusingly large letters of the repertoire. Half a minute later he was in the atrium of the classical Mostowski Palace, where the tsarist authorities had once been based, then the Polish army, then the Civic Militia; now it was the City Police Headquarters.

Nawrocki had made an effort. He had kept his promise, putting Olgierd Boniczka in the smallest, gloomiest interview room in the building. Szacki wasn't at all sure it really was an interview room – Nawrocki may have put a table and three chairs in some forgotten box room just to make Boniczka feel as if he was having a Gestapo-style interrogation. The room was a few square feet in size, with dirty walls, a dirty door and no windows. The only source of light was a bulb hanging on a wire from the ceiling. Luckily Nawrocki had stopped before lugging in a desk lamp on the end of an arm – a standard prop for totalitarian interrogations.

"I'm sorry you've had to wait," said Nawrocki to the man who was sitting at the small hardboard table, looking scared. The veneer, imitating a non-existent type of wood, was frayed at the edges, and in several places there were cigarette burns. "This is Prosecutor Teodor Szacki from the City Centre District Prosecutor's Office. We thought the matter so important that we're talking to you together."

Boniczka instantly stood up. Szacki indicated that he could sit down. He took a chair himself and sat by the door, leaving the policeman and the interviewee at the table. He didn't say anything, because he didn't have to. Boniczka gave him a frightened look. People often reacted to the presence of the prosecutor this way. For them a policeman was someone acceptable. He plodded around the housing estate in uniform, made a note of the yobs' IDs and took a bribe if you drove too fast after drinking. He was our lad, battling with life, who knows it's never easy and that nothing's black or white. The prosecutor was associated with the sort of officials with whom nothing could ever be sorted, who didn't understand a thing, spoke in an incomprehensible language and were always against you. So Szacki kept quiet, knowing that for now his suit and his stern expression were enough to do the job. Compared with him, Nawrocki looked like "one of us" – fat and neglected, with a puffy face and thin, greasy hair, in a yellow shirt unbuttoned at the neck with no tie and a crumpled grey-green jacket. Now and then he blew his nose, clearly suffering from some sort of allergy.

Boniczka's only similarity to the policeman was that they both looked as if they'd only ever heard of final high-school exams, not taken them (despite appearances, Nawrocki had two degrees, in law and psychology). Very thin, skinny even, with the particular leanness of a man who does physical work and already knew the taste of harmful substances in primary school. There really was something of the janitor about him, and Szacki thought he gave off a smell of sweat, cleaning fluids, cellars and rotting leaves. He had a very thick, very black moustache and very black hair with a distinct bald patch on the top of his head. He kept his hands on his knees with his fingers locked as he cast suspicious glances, now at the prosecutor, now at the policeman, who was looking through the documents in silence.

"What's this actually about?" croaked Boniczka finally, and cleared his throat. "Why do you want to talk to me?"

"Some new circumstances have come to light in the case of your daughter's murder," replied Nawrocki. He set aside the documents, switched on the tape recorder, leaned his elbows on the table and folded his hands as if to pray.

"Yes?"

Without answering, Nawrocki just looked at Boniczka reproachfully.

"Have you caught them?"

Nawrocki sighed and smacked his lips.

"Were you aware of the fact that your daughter was raped shortly before she was murdered?"

Szacki had been waiting for this question. Now he watched Boniczka closely through slightly lowered eyelids, trying to recognize the emotions in his face. The man raised his eyebrows a little, that was all.

"What do you mean? Have I misunderstood? And are you only telling me about it now?"

"We've only just found out about it ourselves," replied the policeman and gave a mighty sneeze, then spent the next few moments wiping his nose. "Sorry, I'm allergic to dust. Quite by chance, while investigating another case we picked up the trail of the rapists."

"And what then? Did they admit they killed Sylwia?"

"No."

Boniczka cast a brief glance at the policeman, then at the prosecutor.

"But maybe you don't believe them?"

"Whether we do or don't, that's our business. First we wanted to talk to you. They told us exactly what happened that evening."

And Nawrocki started telling the story. Twice Boniczka asked the policeman to stop, but in vain. The second time Szacki almost joined in with the suspect's request. The superintendent didn't spare them a single detail. Starting from the first moments, when someone shouted to the girl as she was crossing Hoża Street: "Sylwia, wait, it's me!", via the tussle in the stairwell at the apartment building when she didn't want to come in "for a while", the insistence that "it'll be cool" and the chortled remark that "everyone knows when a bird says 'no' she means 'yes' and 'yes' means 'please be my guest'", up to the scene in the flat on the first floor.

The prosecutor realized that Nawrocki had not found all this out from the rapists – if such they were – who had denied everything. If he was bluffing, it was a blind alley. Sylwia Boniczka might have told her father exactly what happened that evening, and then their suspect would quickly twig that they didn't really know anything. If he wasn't bluffing, he was probably quoting the story told him by the clairvoyant. Szacki cursed mentally. Clairvoyants and screwed-up therapies – his work was getting more and more like a bad TV series about a prosecutor who investigates paranormal phenomena. Nawrocki could have warned him.

"When she left, or rather when they'd thrown her out of the flat, threatening her as a parting shot with what would happen if she told anyone about their – as they put it – 'little knees-up', at first she didn't know where she was. All she knew was that she felt very cold. She set off, instinctively heading towards home. But as she went past the school, she thought of you. She stood at the bottom of the steps for a while, then went up to the door and rang the bell. A tearful teenage girl in a green top, a denim skirt with shiny appliqué, and her first ever pair of high-heeled shoes – one of them broken."

Nawrocki paused. Boniczka was rocking back and forth. Szacki was multiplying three-figure numbers in his head to kill the images of the rape scene that kept arising in his imagination. A crime that, in his opinion, should be punished on the same scale as murder. Rape was murder, even if the corpse went on walking about the streets for years after.

"She didn't have a broken heel, she arrived barefoot," Boniczka suddenly whispered, without interrupting his steady rocking.

"How can you know, if she never found you?"

"She did, she did find me," muttered Boniczka. "Do you know, she discarded the shoes herself on the way? Funny, but she was terribly sorry about them. She kept saying they were such wonderful shoes, she liked them so much. And that when her heel broke as she was walking down Hoża Street she thought she'd better throw them away, but at once she'd begun to regret it. She asked if I could go and get those shoes for her, because she was afraid. Finally she wouldn't talk about anything else, just those shoes. My shoes, my shoes, go and fetch them for me, Dad, my shoes, they must still be there."

Szacki was trying not to listen. All he could think was that maybe he should take his family, or at least his daughter, and get as far away from this city as possible. How he hated this place.

"Did you go and fetch them?" asked Nawrocki.

Olgierd Boniczka said he had. Plain black court shoes with a strap around the ankle. If it weren't for the broken heel, they'd have looked straight out of the box. It was the first time she'd worn them outside – before that she'd only worn them in the house, to practise walking in them.

"And what happened after that?"

"When I came back, she was trying to hang herself with the cable from the electric cooker. She didn't protest when I took it away from her. She was glad I'd brought the shoes. She put them on and started telling me again that she'd been afraid of falling over, and as a result she'd missed the tram because she couldn't run to catch it; on the way there she and her friend had walked arm in arm... And so on without a break. About nothing else. And then she asked me to kill her."

Boniczka fell silent. Szacki and Nawrocki held their breath. The whirr of the tape recorder suddenly became perfectly audible.

"It's funny how very unlike their parents children can be," said Boniczka, and Szacki involuntarily shuddered. It occurred to him that someone else had said the same thing to him recently. But who? He couldn't remember.

"Everyone always used to say how like me Sylwia was. The same eyebrows, the same eyes, the same hair. The spitting image of her dad. But she wasn't my daughter. There wasn't a drop of my blood in her veins."

"How's that?" asked Nawrocki.

"Iza, my wife, was raped a month after our wedding. One evening she was on her way back from the station to my parents' house, where we were living then. Sylwia was the rapist's child. When Iza got home, all she kept talking about was the lilac. It was the end of May, and there really was a smell of lilac everywhere, most of all near the station. Enough to make you feel sick when you walked past. And she kept going on about that lilac. Then she stopped. We never talked about it again. Not about the rape or the lilac. We pretended Sylwia was our daughter. It's a very small town, so it never even crossed our minds to go to the police about it. Except that Iza was never again the woman I'd married. She was empty. She went to work, took care of the child, cooked, cleaned, baked on Sundays. She stopped going to church, and I had a hard time persuading her that we should have Sylwia christened. She didn't come to her first communion because the entire church was decorated with lilac. She saw that from a distance and went back home. Sylwia cried. But we didn't talk about it then either."

Boniczka fell silent again. For a long time. There was nothing to suggest he'd return to the subject that most interested them.

"And that night at the school you thought…" Nawrocki gently led him on.

"I thought I didn't want my daughter to be like my wife. Empty. I thought that sometimes death might be a solution. That if I were her, I wouldn't want to stay here either." Boniczka gazed at the palms of his hands. "But I couldn't kill her. I fastened the cord and went outside. I decided I'd go back in ten minutes, and if by then she hadn't made up her mind, I'd join her in pretending nothing had happened. As if I didn't know why she refused to wear shoes with heels, although she wasn't very tall."

The cassette ran to its end and the tape recorder stopped with a loud click. Nawrocki turned the cassette to the other side and pressed the red "record" button.

"When I came back, she wasn't alive. Before that she'd taken the shoes and put them neatly by the wall, next to mine. One was standing straight; the one without a heel had fallen on its side. I kept it as a memento."

"What about Sylwia?"

"I knew they were finishing repairs to the water main at the playschool and that next day they'd be covering it over. I threw her in and shovelled on some sand. No one worked it out. I often used to come and light a candle there."

Szacki couldn't get his head round it.

"Why didn't you bury her at the cemetery?" he asked his first question that evening.

"Because of my wife," replied Boniczka. "If they'd found her hanging at my workplace, there'd have been an inquiry, police interviews, lots of talk, reports of the rape in the papers. They'd have been sure to lock me up. My wife would never have survived that."

"But her child could have lived. Wouldn't that have been better?"

"Death is a neat solution. Often far better than life. Or at least that's what I think." Boniczka shrugged.

"Are you going to lock me up?" he asked after a pause.

Nawrocki glanced at Szacki. The two men left the room to confer in the corridor. They agreed they'd have to write out the clairvoyant's story as Boniczka's detailed account and give it to him to sign. On this basis they could instigate the rape case and lock up the guilty parties. And keep everything as secret as possible so the papers wouldn't write about the case.

"What shall we do with Boniczka?" the policeman asked the prosecutor.

"I'll put him on probation and charge him with desecrating a corpse."

There must have been an awful lot of dust in the corridor, because Nawrocki started sneezing like mad. Once he'd calmed down and wiped his nose, he looked at Szacki with watery eyes.

"Please let him go, Prosecutor," he said. "He's not guilty of anything. He's a victim, just like his wife and daughter. You'll only make matters worse."

Teodor Szacki straightened the knot in his tie. He was ashamed of what he was planning to say, but he had no alternative – that was his job.

"As you know well, Superintendent, every case is full of human tragedy, injustice, countless nuances, shades of meaning and doubts. And that's exactly why the state pays a salary to bastards like me. I know you're right, but my only concern is that a paragraph of the penal code has been infringed. I'm sorry."

IV

Luckily, when he got home, Helka was already asleep. He kissed her on the forehead and moved her away from the edge of the bed. It wasn't high, but he was always afraid she'd fall. She mumbled in her sleep and hugged her toy anteater tighter. The creature's long nose was bent out of shape by this sudden affection. Szacki knelt by the bed and looked at his daughter. She was breathing through her open mouth, her brow was sweating slightly, and her small body was emitting a warmth that had a pleasant fragrance of fresh bread.

A person stops being a child when he starts to stink, thought Szacki. When he starts to have bad breath, his sheets smell sour and his socks sweet. When he has to change his shirt every day and his pyjamas every other. Weronika was in the habit of sleeping in the same T-shirt for a week. He couldn't bear that, but he was embarrassed to tell her. Just as he tried not to notice the tops that had gone yellow under the arms. What could he tell her? That she ought to buy new ones? Then she'd reply that he should give her the money. Anyway, he himself was wearing yellowed underpants beneath his neatly creased pinstriped trousers. Could she possibly like that? Could Monika like that? Or any lover at all? How pointless. He knew this sort of reasoning was a trap, but he kept thinking more and more often that a stupid two hundred thousand would solve all his problems. He'd pay off his debts, take a year off, have a rest, see a bit of the world with the girls. And he'd be able to afford to stand Monika a coffee without feeling guilty for spending money meant for the most urgent domestic expenses.

He was glad Helka was asleep. She might have been able to see in his eyes the shadow of the story he'd had to listen to earlier. Did everything he experienced at work stay inside him? Did all those murders and rapes hover around him like a swarm of bees, stinging everyone he came near? He was afraid he was the carrier of all that hatred, that he spread germs of aggression, infecting his wife and daughter with the worst things in the world. It wasn't visible now, but one day the disease would show itself.

He found this thought so painful that he instantly left his daughter's bedside. He was taking a shower when Weronika came into the bathroom. She was only wearing knickers, but his eyelids were drooping despite the cold water pouring onto him. He hadn't the strength even to think about sex.

"What are you showering like that for? Have you been seeing someone?" she asked, as she brushed her teeth. She did it very energetically, making her breasts bounce comically. That didn't excite him either.

"I had a meeting in town with a lady sexologist. I didn't think a person could be so stretchy. From now on the phrase 'let's change position' will always remind me of gymnastics. Do you fancy vaulting the horse?"

"You idiot. Finish your shower and come to me."

They made love under the duvet, lazily, quietly and with satisfaction; calm with the calm of lovers who after fourteen years know perfectly where and how to touch each other. It was as fabulous as ever. With stress on the "as ever", thought Szacki, as they were lying side by side.

The digital clock showed 23:45:34. The figures showing the seconds kept changing steadily. They were driving him nuts, but he couldn't take his eyes off them. Why the fuck had he bought a clock that showed the seconds? Did he work at the air traffic control centre? On top of which the thing shone like neon – there was even a reddish glow on the wall. He'd have to buy something new. Wonder how much for.

Weronika cuddled up to him.

"What are you thinking about?" she said, blowing a smell of toothpaste and slightly tart saliva into his face.

"You."

"And really?"

"How great it'd be to win the lottery."

"So give luck a chance," she muttered, almost asleep.

"OK. Tomorrow's Saturday, I'll buy a few tickets with random numbers."

She opened one eye.

"Decided on the tenth of June 2005 at twenty-three fifty-one and thirteen seconds," she said. "Maybe you should write those very figures on the coupon, eh? Take some trouble over it."

Teodor Szacki twitched abruptly and sat up in bed. He no longer felt sleepy. His grey cells had started working at an accelerated rate. He'd just heard something very important, but what was it? He repeated the entire conversation to himself. What was the point? For God's sake what was the point?

"Have you gone mad or had a fit?" said Weronika, sitting up too.

"Go to sleep," he replied automatically. "I just remembered something, I have to look at my notes."

"Typical man," she said resignedly, and pulled the duvet over her head when he switched on the bedside lamp.

Soon he had found what he was looking for, written in his diary under 7th June. Telak's sequence of lucky numbers: 7, 8, 9, 17, 19, 22. Why exactly those numbers, and why was it that a few minutes ago not only had a bell rung in his head – sirens had started to wail? He quickly added them up: eighty-two. Eight plus two is ten. One plus zero is one. It made no sense – that wasn't the point.

Concentrate, he thought, rubbing his temples. Concentrate, focus, get thinking. When did something spark in your head? When Weronika said the date: 10th June 2005.

He sat up straight and suddenly felt himself go cold. And his throat was dry. He went into the kitchen, got a can of beer from the fridge and drank half of it in one go. Now he knew. It was Mrs Telak quoting her daughter's suicide note. "We'll meet again in Nangijala. Warsaw, 17th September 2003, 22:00" – twenty-two hundred hours. 17, 9, 22 – three of the numbers concurred with Telak's selection. Was it possible? Could someone be so round the twist as to choose the date of his daughter's death as his lucky numbers for the lottery? And even if he did, what about the rest: 7, 8 and 19? Maybe that was the year of her birth: 1987. Probably too early. Besides, it was illogical: just the year of birth, and just the day, month and hour of death. It would be logical to have the entire date encoded. Szacki stared at the figures, trying to put them in some sort of sequence. Finally he wrote down two dates and times:

17. 09. 1978, 22:00.

17. 09. 1987, 22:00.

And one question: on the exact anniversary – the twenty-fifth or sixteenth – of what had Kasia Telak decided to take her own life?

7

The annual Opole Festival of Polish song is as weak as usual. Cabaret Night is exceptionally embarrassing. Płock is celebrating the draw between the Kraków team, Wisła, and Warsaw's Legia in the final round of the First League. The Warsaw team will end the season in third place, the Płock team in fourth. Kraków is celebrating the seventy-fifth birthday of playwright Sławomir Mrożek with a large exhibition of his drawings and "a series of ridiculous events in the Planty Park". Meanwhile in Warsaw a series of ten unfortunate events takes place: 1. the "Enough Depravity" initiative to take tougher action against those convicted of paedophilia; 2. students illegally opposing the ban on the Equality Parade; 3. illegal civic disobedience opposing the ban; 4. the Law & Justice Party's Youth Forum opposing the promotion of civil partnerships; 5. the Society for Civic Liberties opposing any kind of work on a draft law on civil partnerships; 6. the Warsaw branch of the Catholic Society of Educators promoting education based on Christian values as a guarantee of a socially and morally healthy society; 7. the Warsaw branch of the Catholic Society of Educators saying Christians who respect the laws of God, i.e. the laws of nature, are first-class citizens; 8. the Society for Civic Liberties opposing movements in favour of legalizing gay adoption; 9. a privately organized group in support of action aimed at fighting discrimination against women within society; 10. "Ośka", the Information Centre for

Women's Circles' family picnic: "Warsaw — a city without hatred". Everyone does their protesting under a reasonably cloudless sky; there is hardly any rain, though it is cold again — the maximum temperature in the capital is barely sixteen degrees.

I

How I hate this place, thought Teodor Szacki, putting what must have been the fiftieth bag of shopping into the luckily capacious boot of his Citroën on the top level of the car park at the Carrefour on Głębocka Street. That shrine of sour faces and quite unjustified grievances; that plastic temple of offended sales assistants and dissatisfied waitresses, where every speaker emitted a different bloody awful pop song.

No trip he ever made to the supermarket went according to plan. First he had waited twenty minutes to get in, because some morons had had a minor crash at a junction, and of course they were standing by those Lanos of theirs waiting for the police, instead of just writing a statement and driving off, or at least moving onto the hard shoulder. Every driver in Poland knows that even if they've just smashed your indicator light you've got to summon the police, otherwise either the culprit will cheat you or the insurer will. So he was stuck.

Once he had found a parking place in a seedy corner of the jam-packed car park, a tramp immediately sprang out of nowhere offering to keep an eye on his car. Szacki blew a fuse.

"What do you mean, keep an eye on it? If three iron-pumping thugs come along to steal my car, what are you going to do about it? Lie under the wheels? Jump on them?"

He dug out a zloty for the tramp, because he was afraid he'd let the air out of his tires, scratch the door, steal the wipers or whatever else they do. Just in case, as a parting shot as he and

Helka left, he said he was a prosecutor, at which the tramp bowed low and ran off. So much for keeping an eye on the car.

He didn't have two zlotys for a trolley, so he tried changing a ten-zloty note at a newspaper kiosk – sorry, nowadays they're called "press emporia" – but the young lady didn't have any change. So he bought a fruit juice for Helka for one zloty fifty. She gave him the change. He didn't say a word.

He put in the coins and got his trolley, pulling it out of the line with some difficulty. Next to him stood a sweaty fat guy, watching him with hatred. Szacki realized the man wanted to take the same trolley. And now, although there were ten other lines of trolleys with no one anywhere near them, he saw that an attack had been made on HIS trolley, HIS master plan had been destroyed.

"You should have been quicker," quipped Szacki spitefully and went into the supermarket. He had a shopping list. He always read it a few times first, to work out the optimal route and not waste time running back and forth between sections. He crossed off each item in turn and took care not to buy anything unnecessary. He had only got as far as the bakery when he heard: "Would the owner of Citroën registration number WH25058 please return to his car immediately."

He left the trolley, took Helka by the hand and ran to the car park, sure his beloved Citroën had gone up in flames because the tank had exploded thanks to the eternally faulty autogas system.

It was parked in a disabled spot.

A small skinny guy in a black jacket that was too big for him marked Securitas was leaning on the bonnet. Pity it didn't say "Gestapo". Home-grown fascists. Szacki thought private individuals should be forbidden to wear any sort of uniforms.

"Permit me to make no comment," drawled the little Hitler.

"Yes, you bloody well have my permission," agreed Szacki, ignoring his daughter's presence.

He moved the car and went back into the shop, where his trolley had already gone. He suspected it was the revenge of the fat man from under whose nose he'd swiped it.

He tossed item after item into a new one, trying to avoid the importunate sales ladies with their bits of food cooked on an electric grill, thinking that the common denominator for the citizens of Warsaw was not their place of residence, employment or least of all birth – it was their better or worse concealed aggression. Not hatred, as even the most absurd form of hate was always in some way rational, thanks to the existence of the object of hatred. The All-Polish Youth nationalists hate gays, but if you're lucky enough to be a heterosexual, you can feel relatively safe in their company. The gays hate the Mayor of Warsaw, Lech Kaczyński, but as long as you're not Lech Kaczyński the problem is purely academic. Whereas the aggression was aimed at everyone and anything.

Most of the cases Prosecutor Szacki dealt with were actually the result of senseless aggression; anger that had materialized at a certain moment in the form of assault, rape, murder or battery. Where did it come from? From disappointment because life was so tough, boring and unfulfilling? From fear that any moment it might get even tougher? From envy because others had it better? He had often wondered, but he'd never been able to give himself a convincing answer to the question of where all that Polish rage came from.

The shopping took them two hours, until he was dropping with exhaustion. He felt that if it weren't for the trolley he'd keel over. He was ashamed of looking like all the other zombies struggling to push along their cheeses, soaps, meats, loo sprays and books by Dan Brown. He so desperately wanted to be different from them, feel like someone exceptional, disappear, forget, change, fall in love.

For starters he decided to buy ice cream in flavours he never ate: mango and Snickers (how can a scoop of ice cream cost two and a half zlotys – that's almost a dollar!). They were both disgusting, and he was sorry he hadn't had his favourites, lemon and strawberry.

He swapped with Helka, who luckily had chosen strawberry, and thought how great it is to have kids.

II

He was looking at Teodor Szacki, who was standing to one side, carefully observing the mourners. A handsome man, but he had looked better at his age. Because he had money. Money gives you some leeway and self-confidence. A strength that will never arise from good looks or a fine character.

Like the prosecutor, he hadn't come to the chapel – or rather "pre-funeral home" – at the cemetery in Wólka to say goodbye to Henryk Telak. He wanted to inspect the mourners, and above all Szacki. He took a few steps alongside a hideous concrete wall to get a better view of him. Was he an adversary who should be feared, or just another official, too weak to land himself a job as a solicitor or barrister?

He didn't look weak. He was taut as a string, surprisingly well dressed for a man on a public-sector wage. His classic black suit must have been made to measure. Or its owner had a perfect eye for the ready-made range. Frankly he doubted that, as the prosecutor's clothing was sure to carry labels saying Wólczanka and Intermoda, not Boss or Zegna. And the man had not been born who fitted the cut of the Polish firms – you only had to look at the second-rate politicians on TV. In addition, Szacki was quite tall, at least six foot, he guessed, and very lean. It was hard for men like that to find even jeans in the right size, let alone select a suit from a range meant mainly for small fat blokes. Personally he had his suits made to measure in Berlin; he had a tailor there whom he had known since the 1980s.

To go with the suit a white shirt with very subtle grey pinstripes and a plain graphite-grey tie. He thought cattily that his wife couldn't have chosen it for him – he didn't suspect the female lawyer from the City Council of having too much taste, especially as he'd seen how she dressed in photos. A pleasant woman, but someone should advise her against tapering skirts with a figure like that.

"He was a good husband, a loving father and an honest citizen," declaimed the young priest unemotionally. The words almost made him snort with laughter and he had to cough to hide his faux pas. A few heads turned his way, including Szacki's.

He looked him in the eye and held his gaze.

The prosecutor had a young face, though you couldn't have called his charms boyish. Subtly manly, rather. The softness of his features was shattered by his slightly furrowed brow and unpleasantly cold grey eyes. It wasn't the face of a man who often smiles. In July he'd reach the age of thirty-six, but many people would have given him less, if not for his thick, completely white hair. It contrasted with his black eyebrows, giving him a stern, slightly unsettling look. He was perfectly monochrome. Just black, grey and white, with no other colour to spoil the composition. Finally, without blinking, the prosecutor slowly averted his gaze, and it crossed his mind that this particular official didn't like to compromise.

The funeral-parlour employees, who despite their suits and gloves looked like dangerous ex-cons, vigorously lifted the coffin and carried it out of the pre-funeral home. Few people liked this place. It was impersonal, ice-cold and ugly with the ugliness typical of modern architecture. He did like it, because there was no stench of religion in there. Just communal death, no empty promises. That suited him. Once he used to think that like others he'd convert in his old age. He'd been wrong. He was prepared to believe in anything – he found everyday life full of surprises. But in God – never.

The mourners, not more than forty people, turned to face the passage down the middle of the room as they waited for the family to leave. Jadwiga Telak and her son came after the coffin, solemn, but not looking crushed by despair. Then came some relatives whom he didn't recognize. Not immediate family – Henryk Telak was an only child. Then a few friends, among them the Polgrafex employees and Igor, who glanced at him and nodded discreetly.

The procession ended with the people he found most interesting – the witnesses to Telak's death, and not just witnesses, because he was sure one of them was the murderer. Cezary Rudzki the therapist was walking alongside Barbara Jarczyk, and behind them came Hanna Kwiatkowska and Euzebiusz Kaim. From the other side of the passage Teodor Szacki was closely observing all four of them. As they passed him, the prosecutor joined the procession. He stood next to him, and shoulder to shoulder they left the pre-funeral home. He smiled. Who'd have thought we'd all meet beside Henryk Telak's coffin? Fate can be comical. Interesting to see if Prosecutor Teodor Szacki would find out what he already knew about the mourners. He didn't think so. He hoped not.

III

What a waste of time. But what had he been expecting from the funeral? That one of them would come in a red shirt marked "IT'S ME!"? Szacki knew it wasn't very polite, but after leaving the chapel he quickly said goodbye to the widow, cast a cold glance at the four suspects and ran off to the car park. As he walked down the concrete path, he could still feel the gaze of that older man, who hadn't taken his eyes off him throughout the entire ceremony. Probably some relative wondering who I am, he thought.

He got in the car and put the key in the ignition but didn't switch on the engine. Once again he had the feeling that something had escaped his notice. For a split second, there in the chapel, he had felt as if he were looking at something important. He could sense something very vague, gently tickling the back of his head. At what moment had that happened? Towards the end, just after the coffin was carried out. He was standing there, absorbed by the man watching him, who looked as if he were struggling not to smile. He must have been about seventy, but Szacki would be happy to look like that at his age – like Robert Redford's more handsome brother – and to be able to afford suits like that one. He was looking furtively at the man, people were coming out of the pews and walking slowly down the middle of – let's call it the nave. And that was when he saw something. Something important.

He closed his eyes and leaned his forehead against the steering wheel, trying to imagine that moment. The cold room, the solemn music that he didn't recognize, people dragging their feet. Rudzki alongside Jarczyk, Kwiatkowska and Kaim behind them. And that strange feeling, like déjà vu, a sudden discharge in his neurons. Why?

No, he had no idea.

He drove out of the car park, similar in size to the one outside the supermarket, turned into Wójcicki Street, and immediately stopped near Młociński Wood. He changed out of his funeral suit into jeans and a linen shirt, sprinkled mineral water on his hand and ruffled his hair a bit. He tried smiling roguishly into the side mirror. What a tragedy. Like a German pretending to find Polish humour funny. After pausing to think he took Helka's child seat out of the back and tossed it in the boot, then scooped up a heap of crumbs, the straw from a fruit-juice carton and a Milky Way wrapper. All with the thought that he might have to drive her home afterwards.

This time he arrived at Szpilka first. He sat down on the mezzanine, at a table by the wall. There were better places on small couches by the windows, through which you could watch life go by on Triple Cross Square, but he was afraid Monika would sit on the same couch next to him and he wouldn't know how to behave. And he had remembered that Weronika was meant to be taking Helka to Ujazdowski Park. He'd rather they didn't see him here. Monika came a little later, wearing tiny amber earrings, a tight black top with shoulder straps and a long flowery skirt. And sandals with heels and thongs that wound fancifully around her calves. She stopped in the café doorway, took off her sunglasses and blinked as she scanned the interior. When she noticed him on the mezzanine, she smiled and waved cheerfully. He thought she looked fresh and lovely. He automatically replied with a smile, far less forced than the one he'd practised in the side mirror, and thought how for years the only girl who'd been so pleased to see him was his daughter. No one else.

He stood up as she approached the table. She said hello and kissed him on the cheek.

"And now please explain to the high court," she said, frowning. "Why did the defendant choose the gloomiest table in the darkest corner of this otherwise brightly sunlit café, eh?"

He laughed.

"It was on impulse, I didn't know what I was doing. When I came to, I was already sitting there. I swear it's not my fault. The police framed me."

They sat down on a sofa by the window with a fine view of Saint Alexander's church. Along the pavement a dozen boys went past in black shirts marked "No camping", with a graphic showing two crossed-out little men having sex from behind. It must have been about the homosexuals. Suddenly they started chanting:

"Husband and wife, normal family life!"

Szacki thought they looked like a bunch of poufs themselves – a group of men in tight shirts getting each other worked up with stupid slogans – but he kept this observation to himself.

He lied that he'd eaten a big breakfast, for fear of a large bill. Finally he ordered a smoked-cheese sandwich, and she had spinach pierogi. Then two coffees. They chatted a bit about work and why it was so hopeless, and he amused her with a few funny stories about his colleagues at the prosecutor's office. Then he forced himself to pay her a compliment. He praised her shoes, and immediately rebuked himself mentally for looking like some sort of bloody fetishist. All because of that Russki, who's always regaling me with his fantasies, he told himself.

"Do you like them?" she asked, raising her skirt and turning her foot this way and that so he could take a good look at the sandals. He said yes, thinking she had very shapely feet, and that the whole scene was extremely sexy.

"It's just a pity you can't kick them off in a single go," she sighed. "The straps must have been invented by a man."

"What a clever guy. He knew what looks good."

"Thanks. I'm glad I've achieved the intended effect."

Just then the TV presenter Krzysztof Ibisz came into the café. He ran up to the mezzanine and looked round nervously. Szacki thought it embarrassing to recognize Ibisz – the novelist Jerzy Pilch or the former prime minister Tadeusz Mazowiecki would have been quite another matter – so he pretended not to notice him. He questioned Monika about her work. He wasn't really all that interested in stories about the editor from Gorzów who used any excuse to stare at her cleavage, as a result of which she had to keep correcting her articles several times and listening to his tirades about the pivotal point of the text. He found that he liked listening to her. He watched her gesticulating, adjusting her hair, licking her lips and playing with her coffee spoon – her mouth was just a minor element in the way the girl communicated; she seemed to speak with every muscle. He remembered that when a man stares at a woman's lips, it means he wants to kiss her, so he quickly looked up at her eyes. At once he remembered there were some rules about staring at the eyes too – you should only look long enough to show attention, but not too insistently. Where did he get all this nonsense from?

Suddenly she broke off.

"I'll tell you something," she said, pointing at him with her latte spoon and then digging the rest of the froth out of the tall glass. "But don't laugh. Either say no, after all, I don't know you at all, or yes – ultimately in a way it concerns you. I don't know myself."

"Do you want me to interrogate you?"

Once again he almost burned with embarrassment, and she laughed again.

"You see, I'd like to write a book. A novel."

"It happens in the best families."

"Ha, ha. It happens to every graduate and almost-graduate of Polish studies. But never mind. I'd like to write a novel about a prosecutor."

"A crime story?"

"No, an ordinary novel. But the hero would be a prosecutor. I had the idea a while ago, but when we met recently, I thought it really isn't such a bad one. What do you think?"

He had no idea what to say.

"And this prosecutor —"

"Ooh," she cut him short. "It's a long story."

He glanced discreetly at his mobile phone. Christ! He'd been sitting here for an hour and a half already. If their friendship was going to develop he'd have to murder someone every three days to justify these absences to Weronika in some way. He promised

Monika he'd be happy to hear the plot and equally happy to let himself be exploited. He'd tell her everything she wanted to know. But not today.

When the waitress brought the bill, he reached for his wallet, but she stopped him.

"Don't worry. It's very kind of you, but you paid last time and I'm a feminist, I work at an almost-private firm for almost-decent money, and I've got to corrupt you a bit so you'll be willing to cooperate."

He wanted to ask just what sort of cooperation she had in mind, but he decided against it.

He evidently wasn't the master of bold flirting.

"It's embarrassing," he said.

She put the money on the table.

"It's embarrassing that you're an educated man who chases bandits at God knows what cost, while I messed up my studies, write bad articles and earn more than you. Don't be so macho – it really doesn't matter."

"It matters enormously."

"How come?"

"If I'd known you were going to pay I'd have ordered soup and dessert too."

She admitted to living in the Żoliborz district, but she didn't want him to take her there. She was planning to go to the Empik bookshop first, to look for something interesting. She talked a great deal, and that suited him very well. He had once read that everything we most like at the start of a friendship will irritate us the most later on. Absolutely true. He used to adore watching Weronika turning all the flowerpots a fraction each evening so they'd get equal sunlight, but now it really annoyed him when he heard the daily scrape of the pots being turned on the terracotta tiles in the kitchen.

She'd only just vanished round the corner of Nowy Świat Street when his mobile rang. Kitten.

"Where are you?"

"In the car," he lied. "I'm driving from Wólka to Koszykowa Street, I've got to look something up at the library."

"So how long did that funeral go on for? Three hours?"

"It started late, it went on for ages, I wanted to see it all properly, you know what it's like."

"Of course I do. It happens to me three times a week. Nothing but funeral after funeral. Will you pick us up from Ujazdowski Park in two hours' time?"

"I don't know if I'll make it."

"Try. Your daughter mentioned that she'd like to be reminded what her father looks like."

"OK," he said, wondering why he'd only just had the idea of going to the library.

IV

He liked this place. While he was at college he'd always preferred coming here than to look for a spot in the eternally crowded university library. The main reading room was fabulous, like the ballroom in a classical palace. Two storeys high, it was decorated with pilasters and stucco, with light pouring in from the Koszykowa Street side through two rows of windows. There was something of the atmosphere of a church in here. Except that instead of the chill of stone walls and the odour of incense, there was a fragrance of oak parquet flooring and a nutty smell of old paper. The little tables that filled the room reminded him of church pews, and the small chairs next to them were just as uncomfortable as pews. But the unique atmosphere of this place came from the brass lamps with green glass shades that illuminated each table. On a November evening the reading room at the main city library was undoubtedly the most magical place in Warsaw.

He was looking forward to this mood as he parked down below, but the periodicals reading room turned out to be in an impersonal area on the fourth floor, a kingdom of laminated desks, fluorescent lamps and chairs upholstered in brown fabric.

In the computer he found catalogue numbers for the daily *Życie Warszawy* and the evening paper *Express Wieczorny*, filled out reserve slips for the binders dated September 1978 and September 1987, and waited. He spent a while watching the librarian filling in some forms. She had the archetypal look – long black hair with a centre parting, large, unfashionable glasses, a green, long-sleeved, polo-neck top and caricature-big breasts attached to a slender figure. She must have felt his gaze, because she interrupted her work and stared at him. He turned away.

He couldn't stop thinking about the meeting at Szpilka. He went back over every word, wondering what she'd been thinking and how she'd understood what he'd said. Hadn't he said something she might take wrongly? Hadn't he made too much fun of his colleagues at work? She might think he was a misanthrope and a braggart all at once. And was she actually pretty? She was sweet, it was true, very sweet even, but pretty? Her shoulders were a bit too broad, her breasts too small, her bum too low, and on top of that her legs were ever so slightly bowed.

Even if he was seeking out the imperfections in it, thinking about her body made him feel an immense urge for sex. He couldn't stop picturing the moment when, twisting slightly, with her skirt hitched halfway up her legs, she'd shown off her new shoes. He imagined her hitching her skirt even higher. Until it made him squirm. He closed his eyes and imagined it even more precisely. Not in the café, but at her place on the sofa.

I can't, he thought, I can't do that. I'm thirty-five, nearly thirty-six. I cannot go to the toilet at the main city library to wank, while thinking about some lassie with bandy legs.

But off he went.

When he came back, the newspapers were waiting for him.

He started with *Życie Warszawy* – "Warsaw Life" – from 1978, although he didn't think the case would go that far back. Henryk Telak was nineteen then, and his parents were already dead. The 17th of September fell on a Sunday. He leafed through the pages. The coldest summer of the decade was ending, the final phase of the harvest was proceeding efficiently, there was an aeroplane exhibition at Zwycięstwo Square to mark the thirty-fifth anniversary of the Polish People's Army. All very boring. Writer Zenon Kosidowski and eminent ophthalmologist Witold Starkiewicz had died, in the Tatra mountains a tourist had succumbed to a heart attack, and a mountaineer had fallen off a peak called Mnich. Could it possibly be to do with one of them? No. Curiously, *Życie Warszawy* had published a series of articles in the run-up to the sixtieth anniversary of Poland regaining independence after the First World War. Strange – he was sure that in Communist Poland 22nd July had been celebrated as Independence Day. Which wasn't so dumb – celebrating anything in mid-November makes no sense. It's always cold, pouring with rain, and no one even feels like watching a parade. He carefully read all the minor reports, especially from the capital, in search of information about a car crash or a killing. Instead of that he found reflections on the fact that "computers have made a rapid rise in popularity. At times their expansion even stirs anxiety." He automatically checked to see what was on TV on the evening of 17th September. Part one of the classic serial *The Doll* starring Jerzy Kamas and Małgorzata Braunek, and on Channel Two *A Soldier's Love* – a Yugoslav film production.

In the Ochota district a car ran two people over, one of them died. He meticulously wrote down the names of all the deceased. Including Professor Sylwester Kaliski, minister of science, higher education and technology, Polish United Workers' Party member and member of parliament in Communist Poland.

Sport. In the competition for ski-jumping on an artificial surface Tadeusz Tajner came sixth. A relative of the skiing champion Apoloniusz Tajner, perhaps? National soccer team trainer Jacek Gmoch's charges are preparing for their next match in the European soccer championship qualifying stages. They have already won against Iceland, and will now play Switzerland; Holland and East Germany are waiting their turn. The editor couldn't have known what Szacki knew in 2005 – that Poland had not played in the finals of that European championship or any since.

He went on looking, noting down the names in the death announcements for all the people who had died on 17th September. Most of them had died of old age, "after a long illness", or simply "departed". He thought it comforting that so few people were killed in accidents. It looked as if statistically he too had a chance of quietly reaching seventy. In the edition dated 20th September he finally found something interesting: "On 17th September Marian Kruk, aged fifty-two, and Zdzisław Kruk, aged twenty-six, died tragically". Two death notices of identical size and content, the only difference being the signature. In the first, "wife, mother and family" were bidding farewell to their "beloved husband and son", and in the second, "wife, daughter-in-law and family" to "beloved husband and father-in-law". So a father and son had died together. One accident, two deaths, a massive family tragedy. An earthquake within the system. He circled their names in red in his notebook. He'd have to check the circumstances of that incident.

He reached hopefully for the *Express Wieczorny* – "Evening Express" – expecting to find some juicy crime reports and gory descriptions of tragic accidents, but he was disappointed. The paper radiated nothing but dreadful boredom – he couldn't understand why its legend had endured for so many years. Maybe he was just unlucky and had hit upon some poor editions. The only information that grabbed his attention was the news that Andrzej Wajda had started filming *The Maids of Wilko*, with Daniel Olbrychski in the leading role. Once upon a time they made good films, he thought.

In *Życie Warszawy* dated 17th September 1987 – this time it was a Thursday – there was no mention whatsoever of the anniversary of the Soviet invasion of Poland. Just like nine years earlier, and every year. However, there was a lengthy piece about the anniversary of the Nazi bombing of the Royal Castle. And about Wojciech Jaruzelski, who was having talks with Erich Honecker during a working visit to East Germany. It won't last much longer, you bastards, thought Szacki vengefully. A year and a half and you'll all be put out to grass.

On television there was a British crime series, *Cover Her Face*, world championship gymnastics, a programme called *Vodka, Let Me Live* and the International Congress of University of the Third Age associations. It looked as if on 17th September 1987 only a few hours of communing with the telly would be enough to make you slit your wrists out of boredom. Part of central Warsaw had no gas. Failure in the heating supply. Szacki impassively ran his eyes over the headings. In the autumn a Gorbachev–Reagan summit meeting. Despite an extremely difficult harvest, the grain crop reached twenty-five million tons. A murderer wouldn't admit his guilt. He had been apprehended. It was a Warsaw murder. On 17th September.

"All Warsaw is talking about the tragedy that occurred yesterday in the city centre. Dozens of people witnessed the incident. At

4.15 Danuta M. was murdered at 125 Jerozolimskie Avenue in the sight of passers-by and people waiting at a bus stop. The murderer, fifty-three-year-old Ryszard W., stabbed her in the neck with a knife. The woman died on the spot, and members of the public apprehended the killer. The inquiry is being conducted by the Ochota District Office for Internal Affairs."

The District Office for Internal Affairs? What the hell is that? wondered Szacki as he made notes. The militia? The prosecutor's? A sort of camouflaged secret-police unit? The case was striking, but it smelled of illegal alcohol a mile away. Later he read that the culprit was drunk, so was the victim, and he'd stabbed her because she'd refused to go and get him cigarettes from a kiosk.

He went on looking.

The Polish film, *The Mother of Kings*, won the "Golden Lions" award at the Gdynia film festival. He almost whistled as he read the list of other prizewinners – nowadays any one of those films could win that festival hands down with no fear of competition. *The Magnate, On the Niemen, Blind Chance, The Faithful River, Inner Life, Train to Hollywood*. Nothing but classics, and all in the same year. Incredible.

In the *Express* dated 21st September he found a short note, just a few sentences: "The body of twenty-three-year-old Kamil S. was found by his nineteen-year-old sister in a city-centre flat on Mokotowska Street. 'The whole family was meant to be on a belated holiday,' we heard from Captain Stefan Mamcarz of the district Civic Militia. 'The boy stayed behind, and that was his undoing. The robbers expected the flat to be empty, and when they broke in and saw him there, they panicked and killed him.' The militia claim that the tragedy occurred on 17th September in the evening. An intensive search is under way to apprehend the criminals."

He made a note and tapped his disposable ballpoint on the historic newspaper, leaving some black spots on it. Again he felt a tickling in his brain. Either instinct was telling him this could have a connection with the case, or he had cancer. Except that he was looking for a dead girl, and this was a boy. Maybe it was to do with the sister who found the body. Telak's former girlfriend, perhaps? Or maybe this Kamil and Telak... No. All because of the homophobic panic – now he too thought he was seeing gays everywhere. But he'd have to check up on this case. It would be good to know the surname.

Three days further on he found two death notices. The first read: "On 17th September 1987 Kamil Sosnowski was taken from us, our beloved son and brother. Dearest Kamil, we will love you for ever, your Mummy, Daddy and sister." And the second was atypical: "On 17th September Kamil was murdered, our best mate and friend. Old pal, we'll never forget you. Zibi and everyone."

He didn't believe anything would come of it, but he decided he should ask Oleg to find the file relating to that case in the archive.

Mechanically he read the article he'd marked earlier with his pen. "Volume II of the *Universal Encyclopedia* is now available to the public. Issued upon fulfilling the following conditions: presentation at the waste-paper collection centre of a recyclable materials purchase booklet, subscription voucher, identity card and payment of 5,100 zlotys."

What nonsense. He couldn't remember the world of Communist Poland well, but it looked as if the film-maker Stanisław Bareja's satirical account of it was entirely true. Though on the other hand everything must have been simpler then. And funnier.

He took the binders back to the book trolley, bowed politely to the buxom librarian and ran down the stairs, quietly crooning the Michael Jackson hit, 'Liberian Girl', but changing it into "librarian girl". Only on the ground floor did he switch on his mobile phone and realize he'd spent three hours in the library. Bugger, he'd fucked up again. He swore out loud and called Weronika.

8

Monday, 13th June 2005

In America a jury has acquitted Michael Jackson on a charge of paedophilia. Nevertheless the King left the court building looking sad and dejected. In Belarus the militia have apprehended a gerontophile rapist. The youngest victim was sixty-one, the oldest eighty-seven. In Ukraine, councillors in Lviv have passed a resolution necessary for the opening of the "Eaglets" Polish war cemetery. In France, Polish actor Andrzej Seweryn has been awarded the *Légion d'honneur*. In Poland, boring news: nationalist politician Roman Giertych wants to take the Minister for Internal Affairs and Administration to court for not preventing the illegal Equality Parade. Conservative politician Jan Rokita of the Civic Platform party agrees with Law and Justice party leader Jarosław Kaczyński on the issue of vetting people in official posts to expose Communist-era collaboration and declares: "There is a chance for joint government." Left-wing former premier Leszek Miller has been thoroughly defeated in the primaries within the Łódź branch of the Democratic Left Alliance party, but even so he will be first on the candidate list. In Warsaw the police break up a gang of thieves which stole luxury cars by making the drivers get out to inspect non-existent damage. During the interrogations a gun with a silencer is seized, along with 5.5 pounds of amphetamines and an antique samurai sword. Beautiful weather in the capital city: twenty-two degrees, sunny, no rain.

I

Bright and early he arrived at Oleg's place on Wilcza Street. Unfortunately, no one had been murdered that weekend and Szacki was worried that if the policeman didn't provide him with new information about Telak he'd be forced to work on the drugs case.

They drank coffee out of plastic cups in the police station canteen. In his black fake-leather waistcoat thrown over a greenish T-shirt Kuzniecow looked like a black-market money changer from the old Thousandth Anniversary Stadium that was now home to a seedy bazaar. Szacki was in a grey suit, like a mafia accountant wanting to have a serious talk about business with him.

"I've got a voiceprint analysis for you," said Kuzniecow. "Unfortunately it's not an expert opinion, just an unofficial one. Leszek did it for me as a favour – normally you have to record comparative material in their special sound-analysis studio. They paid insane money for it – even the sound of electrons in the electrical wires has been silenced – and now they refuse to hear of any other recordings. They've got big-headed. But Leszek is all right. You know what, he spends most of his time tuning pianos. He has a fabulous sense of hearing, I'm surprised he bothers working for us."

Szacki bought a bottle of water to rinse out his mouth after the coffee, which tasted like a wet floor-cloth. Either they'd made chicory coffee, or else they hadn't cleaned the espresso machine for several years. Or maybe both.

"And what is Leszek's official opinion?"

"You have no idea what a nutcase he is – I once went to his house, I can't remember what for. He's got two rooms in a block in Ursynów, but the child sleeps with them, because the other room is for listening. A tiny table and nothing else – the walls and ceiling are entirely covered with egg cartons, the big square ones."

"Oleg, be merciful, I've got a heap of work to do, and I might have even more. The opinion."

Kuzniecow ordered another coffee.

"Just hold on, you won't regret it."

"I will," said Szacki resignedly.

"What do you think he listens to in there?"

"Not music, since you ask."

"His wife."

"What a good boy. Is that all?"

"No. He listens to his wife having orgasms."

Kuzniecow stopped talking and looked at him triumphantly. Szacki knew he should stab him with a well-aimed malicious remark to close the subject, but he couldn't restrain his curiosity.

"Very good, you win. You mean to say they fuck on those egg cartons?"

"Almost. He tells her to masturbate in that room and he records her moans. There can't be any interference."

Szacki was sorry he hadn't closed the subject.

"One last question: why on earth would he do that?"

"For money. He has a theory that women emit a very special noise while climaxing, which is partly beyond the auditory threshold. He wants to synthesize that sound, patent it and sell it to people for advertising. Get it? An ad goes out live on TV, eight out of ten prefer X etc., and you suddenly go wild with excitement, because that recording is built into the advert. Then you go to the shop, see that beer and at once you get a hard-on. And then what? Are you still going to buy the usual Warka beer? You may laugh, but there's something in it."

"I even know what. The tragedy of a child who has to sleep with his parents."

Kuzniecow nodded, no doubt wondering if he too could make a deal out of climaxing adverts, and took a notebook out of his waistcoat pocket.

"Leszek is ninety per cent sure the voice saying 'Daddy' is Kwiatkowska's. Warsaw accent, characteristic intonation, a bit similar to French – maybe the girl used to live in France – and a slightly voiceless 'r'. Only ninety per cent because the comparative material was everyday stuff. He definitely ruled out Mrs Telak, and Jarczyk too, though here he found more common features. He claims that both of them – Kwiatkowska and Jarczyk – must be at least second-generation residents of Warsaw, and from the City Centre. Their voices also have a similar timbre, quite high."

Szacki raised his eyebrows.

"You're joking. You can't persuade me you can tell by the accent if someone's from the City Centre or the Praga district."

"I was surprised too. Certainly not when you've only been living there for a few years, but if your grandparents already lived here, then you can. Not bad, eh?"

Szacki agreed automatically, wondering if, after living in the Praga district since birth, his daughter had already caught the proletarian pronunciation of the right bank of the Vistula.

They talked for a while longer about the inquiry, but Kuzniecow didn't have much to say. Only today would he finally be meeting with Telak's financial adviser. He'd also sent a man to find Telak's friends from technical college and the polytechnic and question them about his old love affairs. Finally they quarrelled when Szacki asked the policeman to find an investigation file from 1987 as soon as possible.

"No way," bristled Kuzniecow, eating a teacake and blancmange. "There's absolutely no bloody way."

"Oleg, please."

"Write a letter to the chief. You always were a pain in the arse, but in this inquiry you've surpassed yourself. Just you write down on a piece of paper everything you've demanded of me so far and you'll see for yourself. There's no way. Or submit an application to the City Police Headquarters archive. In three weeks it'll all be ready. I'm not going to deal with that."

Szacki adjusted his shirt cuffs. He realized Kuzniecow was right. But instinct was telling him he should check it out as soon as possible.

"It's the last time, I promise," he said.

Kuzniecow shrugged.

"You're lucky I've got a pal who just happens to work in the archive," he muttered in the end.

Why doesn't that surprise me? thought Szacki.

II

Janina Chorko was looking – luckily – as ugly as usual. This time she had skilfully emphasized her total lack of charm with the help of some black trousers ironed with a crease and a grey knitted top adorned with a monstrously large brooch made of leather. He could relax and look her in the eyes while they talked.

"Sometimes, Prosecutor," she drawled impassively, looking at him like a bump in the wallpaper, "I get the impression that you in turn are under the impression that you enjoy some sort of special regard in my eyes. That is a mistaken impression."

Szacki was happy. If she'd decided to be flirtatious again and given him a knowing look, he would have had to change jobs. What a relief.

"Wednesday," he said.

"Why is that?" she asked.

"For several reasons…" he began, but paused, because a bleep sounded, indicating the arrival of a text message. He'd forgotten to silence his phone.

"Please check what it says. Maybe someone has confessed," she grinned spitefully.

He read it. "I know this is stupid, but since yesterday I've got very fond of my new shoes. Guess why. Coffee? Mo."

"Private," he said, pretending not to notice the look on her face. "Firstly, I must have two more days to dig around in the Telak case, secondly, I must get ready for the Gliński trial, and thirdly, I've got a ton of paperwork."

"Everyone has, don't make me laugh."

"Fourthly, I don't think that case needs so many people working on it," he said, trying his best to make it sound as tactful as possible.

Chorko glanced out of the window, pouted her upper lip and made a puffing sound.

"I'll pretend I didn't hear that," she declared, without looking at him, "otherwise I'd have to acknowledge that you're questioning the way I run the office. Or else that you have doubts about your colleagues' competence. Surely that's not what you were thinking?"

He didn't reply.

She smiled.

"You have until Wednesday. And not an hour longer."

Barbara Jarczyk appeared in his room punctually at eleven. He blinked – once again something started itching in his head. Déjà vu. Barbara Jarczyk looked exactly the same as a week ago. Right down to the earrings. He thought perhaps she dressed differently each day, but kept to a weekly cycle.

He asked a few routine questions. Had anything happened? Had she remembered any facts that she hadn't told him earlier? Had she been in touch with Kaim, Kwiatkowska or the therapist Rudzki? She replied to all the questions with a curt "no". She merely mentioned that on Thursday someone from the police had been to see her on a trivial matter. She didn't understand the purpose of this visit.

"The police take all leads into consideration, it was probably just a routine check-up," he lied, realizing she didn't have to know about the voiceprint analysis. "Unfortunately you must come to terms with the fact that until the inquiry is closed such visits might occur even quite frequently."

She nodded. Unenthusiastically, but understandingly.

"Do you use sleeping pills?" he asked.

She frowned, probably wondering why he wanted to know.

"Sometimes," she replied after a pause. "Quite rarely nowadays, but I used to be virtually addicted. I had to take a pill every night."

"Addicted?"

"Not in the drug addiction sense. I had problems, I couldn't sleep, so the doctors gave me those pills. Finally, taking them became as natural as brushing my teeth at bedtime. I got scared when I realized that. That was one of the reasons why I ended up going to therapy."

"But do you still take a pill sometimes?"

"Not more than once every few days, once a week. Sometimes less often."

"Which drug are you using now?"

"Tranquiloxyl. It's a French drug."

"Is it strong?"

"Quite strong. On prescription. Nevertheless I've taken sleeping pills for a bit too long, so nowadays not just anything works on me."

"When did you last take Tranquiloxyl?"

She flushed.

"Yesterday," she replied. "I haven't been sleeping too well lately."

"Do you know why I'm asking?"

"To tell the truth, no."

He hesitated with the next question. Could it be that Telak

had stolen her pills? In that case she ought to have noticed they were missing.

"An empty bottle of Tranquiloxyl was found in Mr Telak's room at the monastery on Łazienkowska Street. The pathologist confirmed that shortly before he was murdered Mr Telak took a large number of them, but then vomited. The fingerprints on the bottle are Mr Telak's and yours. Can you explain that?"

For a change Mrs Jarczyk went pale. She gave him a terrified look. And didn't answer.

"Well?" he urged.

"I, I, oh my God, I've only just remembered now…" she stammered. "Surely you don't think I, oh my God…"

She burst into tears.

"I'm so very sorry," she said, searching her handbag for a handkerchief. Szacki would have liked to give her his, but to make matters worse he didn't have any. Finally she found one, wiped her eyes and blew her nose.

"I'm so very sorry," she repeated quietly, without once looking at him. "But how can I remember everything, what with the therapy and the murder, and that corpse and all the rest of it. The police and the prosecution. As a result I feel accused the whole time and I can't sleep. And I'm even afraid to call my own therapist, because who knows, maybe he's somehow mixed up in it all. And I simply forgot."

"Please tell me what you forgot," he said gently.

"On Friday evening, after supper, I ran into Mr Telak in the corridor. By accident – he was coming back from the bathroom, and I was just going to answer a call of nature. I think he said the place was a bit weird, and he felt shivers down his spine. I don't remember well, I was thinking about the therapy a lot and what it would be like, so I was a bit distracted. He said he was feeling very upset and did I have anything for sleeping. I said I could give him a pill."

Szacki raised his hand to interrupt her.

"And instead of giving him a pill or two, you gave him your whole supply of drugs that you were addicted to? I don't understand. Why?"

"I had two."

"Pills?"

"Bottles of them. I tossed one in my suitcase as I was leaving the house, and I had the other one in my make-up bag. I haven't taken it out of there since I went on a recent business trip to Hanover for the toy fair. I thought it would be silly to just hand out a pill when I had a whole bottle. We arranged that Mr Telak would give it back to me before we left."

"Were there lots of pills in it?"

"Half a bottle, maybe a bit less. Probably about twenty."

Szacki felt his phone vibrate in his pocket. Another text message. He'd replied to Monika earlier that he'd love to have a quick coffee at four, on condition she let him admire her new clothes. Interesting to see what she'd written back.

"And on Saturday weren't you afraid Mr Telak might make use of your pills to take his own life?"

She chewed her lip.

"I hadn't thought of that."

Szacki reached for the open case file and read: "And I thought perhaps someone did him a service, because there really can't be any worlds where Henryk could have been worse off than here."

"Those are your words," he said.

"But I don't remember them being in the statement," she countered, looking him in the eye.

"You're right, I was reading from my notes. Which doesn't change the fact that they're your words. Which prompts the question whether the entire scenario that you described didn't happen on Saturday. And whether by chance you didn't give Mr

Telak more pills than necessary in order – to put it delicately – to give him a choice."

"Of course I didn't!" she said, raising her voice. "That's a wicked insinuation."

He did not react.

"It prompts the question why during your previous interview you did not mention the late-night conversation with Mr Telak. It would have stuck in my memory."

She lowered her head and pressed her fingertips to her brow.

"I don't know. I can't explain it," she said quietly. "I really can't."

He took advantage of the fact that she was staring at the floor to glance discreetly at the phone display. "In that case I'm nipping off to change. C U @ 4 in Szp. Mo."

"Please believe me, I'm telling the truth now," she whispered. "Why should I lie?"

I'd like to know that myself, thought Szacki.

"This question might seem odd to you, but where did you grow up?"

She raised her head and looked at him in surprise.

"Here, in Warsaw, but my parents are from Łódź."

"Which district?"

"In the City Centre, not far from the police station on Wilcza Street. But I moved to the suburbs, to Grodzisk, in my early twenties. Ages ago."

He leaned slightly towards her. He didn't want her to avert her gaze as he asked the next question.

"Does the name Kamil Sosnowski mean anything to you?"

She didn't drop her eyes. She didn't blink. She didn't frown.

"No," she replied curtly. "Who's that?"

"An unlucky guy. It doesn't matter."

Hanna Kwiatkowska looked far more presentable than a week ago, nor was she quite so jittery. Perhaps her poor state hadn't been caused by neurosis, but the weekend therapy ending in the discovery of Henryk Telak's body. She seemed an energetic person, content with life, which made her more attractive. Szacki thought that objectively she was much prettier than Monika, though eight years older. Her answers to the non-essential questions that he asked to launch the conversation were brief and to the point. Once she even ventured to make a joke, but Szacki did not react. So she didn't try that again. It turned out Leszek was right, and Kwiatkowska had grown up near Konstytucja Square, though now she was living in Grochów, in the eastern part of Warsaw, not far from Szembek Square. Szacki felt like asking her if she felt exiled, like him, but he dropped the idea. However, he did ask her if she knew the name Kamil Sosnowski. She denied it after a moment's thought. She didn't want to know why that interested him.

"Do you know what voiceprint analysis is?" he asked.

She scratched her cheek.

"No, I don't," she replied. "But I would deduce from the name that it's something like fingerprint analysis, but to do with sounds. It must be a forensic technique involving recognizing voices. Am I right?"

"One hundred per cent. Why do I ask? Because in the course of our investigations we have succeeded in securing" – he mentally reproached himself for using Newspeak – "Henryk Telak's Dictaphone. I can let you into the fact that for him it was a sort of notebook and diary all in one. He recorded business meetings and personal reflections on it. What proved of most interest to us was something he recorded after the therapy on Saturday."

Kwiatkowska shook her head.

"I wouldn't want to hear what he recorded. It was dreadful enough for us, and far worse for him."

"I'll tell you briefly. Mr Telak was in a very bad way; he thought he was hearing voices; he reckoned he was having illusions, hallucinations. He decided to record them to check if they were real."

He broke off, closely watching Kwiatkowska's reactions. She didn't say anything, but her relaxed manner vanished. Her right eye blinked a few times. He asked if she would like to comment on that at all. She shook her head to say no, and adjusted her glasses. Again Szacki felt a tickling in his cerebral cortex. Either I'm no longer able to put two and two together, or I must go and see a neurologist, he thought.

"Listening to the tape, in the first instance we were shocked, because Telak had recorded a conversation with his daughter who died two years ago. The material was subjected to voiceprint analysis and the conclusions are unambiguous. The person who was standing outside the door of Telak's room pretending to be his dead daughter was you. Can you comment on that?"

Kwiatkowska had gone grey.

"This is some kind of joke," she gasped. "I don't believe it."

Prosecutor Teodor Szacki felt tired. He'd had enough of all this fibbing.

"Now look here," he said more firmly than he had intended. "I'm not giving you my hypothesis, just the facts. And the facts are that after a therapy session that was extraordinarily tough for Henryk Telak you pretended to be his dead daughter at his door, suggesting to him that he should come and join you – that is, his daughter – and shortly afterwards Mr Telak recorded a suicide letter to his wife and swallowed a bottle of sleeping pills! Please don't tell me what you believe, just comment on the facts, for God's sake, before I start thinking you decided to use the skewer because you had failed to induce Mr Telak to commit suicide, and simply lock you up."

He wasn't bluffing. After finding the recording and confirming that it was Kwiatkowska's voice, the schoolteacher had become the prime suspect. Just in case, in his desk drawer he had a ruling signed by Chorko to press charges on Kwiatkowska. He was ready to make her an official suspect in the inquiry, search her flat thoroughly, put her under police surveillance and send her for psychiatric tests. Two things were stopping him: instinct and the fear that he'd lose hands down in court at the very first hearing. Instead of hard proof he could only provide foggy circumstantial evidence and idiotic theories bordering on the esoteric.

The woman suddenly stood up and began to pace rapidly round the room.

"Well, this has to be a bad dream," she was saying to herself. "It can't be true, it can't."

She stopped and stared at Szacki.

"It's hard for me to believe you're not lying. But I do, because after all, what would you have to gain? Please record in writing that, aware of all criminal responsibility, or however you say it, I swear and insist with all my heart that I do not remember standing outside Henryk Telak's door and pretending to be his daughter. I swear it. You can have me tested by a lie detector, you can send me for psychiatric tests, I'll agree to anything."

If you don't now ask what exactly you are supposed to have said to Telak through the door, I'll press charges against you, thought Szacki and opened the drawer.

"But first of all," said Kwiatkowska, pointing her finger at the prosecutor, "I demand that you show me that recording. I want to know what I'm being accused of."

He took a CD out of the drawer and inserted it in an old boom box standing on the window sill. He played Kwiatkowska the "conversation with a ghost". After the first words he had to pause the recording, because the woman had an attack of hysteria. He gave her some water, lay her on the floor, shoved his rolled-up jacket under her head and sent away the colleagues who had come in, alarmed by the loud crying; he wondered if it was possible to fake it that well. Fifteen minutes later Kwiatkowska said she was feeling better and would like to listen to the recording right through.

She was pale, and her fists were clenched tight, but she wasn't crying any more.

"Over to you," he said, switching off the CD player.

"I recognize my own voice, but I feel as if someone's just about to leap out of the cupboard and shout 'Got you!', and you'll hand me the bunch of flowers you're hiding under the desk. I can't explain it, I don't know how it's possible; my only memory of that evening is that I brushed my teeth with my finger because I'd forgotten my toothbrush, and then I went to bed. I realize you might not believe me, but it's the strangest thing that has ever happened to me in all my life. I can hear my own words that I never uttered."

He noted it down and handed her the transcript. Before signing, she read it through twice, very carefully.

"I'm not going to press charges on you, though I could and no one would argue with me," he said. "But I'd like you to know that at this stage of the inquiry you are, let's say, under close surveillance. And so please do not discuss this with anyone and do not leave Warsaw. If I get the slightest hint of a suspicion that you are obstructing legal proceedings, you'll end up in custody that very day. Is that clear?"

The door had not yet closed behind Hanna Kwiatkowska when Teodor Szacki began to regret his decision. Trusting in instinct will be the end of you, he told himself. You should have locked her up and seen what happened next.

III

He gave his secretary instructions not to put through any calls, switched off the computer and sat back comfortably to listen via the intercom to the conversation going on in the next room. He was sorry they didn't have cameras installed at the office – he'd like to see the bear-like inspector interviewing Igor. If the cop suspected even a hundredth part of what Igor knew, what he was mixed up in, he certainly wouldn't have showed up here without an anti-terrorist squad. He felt like laughing at the thought that even if the cop had come up with such an idea, he would never have let it happen. One phone call would have been enough.

"Nice sword. Is it samurai?"

"A gift from one of our clients. It's an authentic eighteenth-century antique from Japan. If I were you I'd put it down, Inspector. Easy to do yourself an injury."

"I'm quite used to that. Yesterday I hurt myself cleaning fish. Last time I ever buy something that's not a fish finger. Do you know, some nursery school children in the States were once asked to draw fish and some of them drew rectangles? Not bad, eh?"

"Yes, indeed, fascinating. But in this particular case injuring yourself might mean losing a few fingers, or at least half the tendons in your hand. Please take a seat. You'll be more comfortable."

"I've spent so much time sitting down today I've got corns on my arse. Will it bother you if I keep walking about for a while? You've got a bigger office than the yards in plenty of Polish prisons."

"It's hard for me to tell, I've never had the pleasure."

"Don't praise the day until the sun goes down, as the ancient Chinese used to say. Or was it the Romans? I'm not sure. Anyway, let's get down to business."

"Gladly. I won't hide the fact that my agenda is pretty full."

"Please tell me about Henryk Telak's finances. I understand you were his accountant."

"Investment adviser. We are a consulting firm, we don't fill in tax returns."

"Pity, they say it's a lucrative business. You could buy a paper knife, it'd go nicely with the sword."

"We ran an investment account for Mr Telak, and he also deposited his life-insurance policy with us."

"Investment account, meaning?"

"We had power of attorney to manage the money accrued there to a set percentage quota. In this case fifty per cent of the total at the end of the previous half-year, but not more than the average of the last two years. Which means that the more we earned for Mr Telak, the more we could invest, but if we hadn't got it right and Mr Telak had lost, we wouldn't be able to reduce his account below, let's call it, the safety quota."

"Did you often lose?"

"Mr Telak never earned less than twenty per cent of his accrued resources annually. Of course after his death we stopped making new investments. What happens to his money next depends on his widow. She might close the account, she might withdraw part of the money, or she might entrust us to carry on dealing with her finances on the same or new terms."

"How much is there in the account at present?"

"Almost five hundred thousand zlotys in cash and six hundred thousand in assets."

"Sorry?"

"Altogether about one million one hundred thousand. Of course, this sum changes on a daily basis, depending on the share prices, currency rates and so on. Some investments are long term, so if Mrs Telak wanted to cash it all in as soon as possible and withdraw the money, it would probably be about a million."

"And the policy?"

"Half a million."

"It looks as if the widow won't have to ask for cheaper Polish substitutes at the pharmacy."

"Henryk Telak was our client, but also a good friend of mine for many years. And his wife too. I would ask you to choose your words more carefully."

"Did she know about the life-insurance policy and the investment account?"

"No."

"Are you sure?"

"She may have found out from Henryk."

"Has she already been to see you?"

"We saw each other at the funeral, but we didn't talk about money. She merely promised to drop in next week."

"That's a bit strange, don't you think?"

"No. As far as I know, Jadwiga isn't short of money for everyday expenses."

"I see. And you knew Henryk Telak for a long time?"

"We met while we were students at the polytechnic, I think it was the late 1970s, definitely before martial law. Then our paths diverged for some time. I got a bit of work through a friend at one of the foreign-trade offices, I was interested in economics, and he remained loyal to printing. We met again by chance after 1989."

"So this is your company?"

"I am one of the partners and also vice president."

"And did you deal with Mr Telak's finances for a long time?"

"Over ten years, since 1994."

"Can anyone just come in off the street to you?"

"They can, though there's no guarantee that we'll act for them. We're a small firm, but elite. We don't have many clients, and none of them is – how shall I put it? – working their way up.

They all came to us on recommendation. We're able to make a lot of money for them, but our fees are not among the lowest. Nevertheless, we have never known anyone to be dissatisfied with our services."

"You're not a secret sect, are you?"

"Meaning?"

"Initiation rites oozing with sex, hostesses dressed in nothing but two hundred-dollar bills, the rhythmic beating of the drums and banging in general…"

"I know nothing about anything like that."

"But maybe you know if Mr Telak had any enemies, people who envied him his status and money?"

"I know nothing about that."

"Do the names Cezary Rudzki, Euzebiusz Kaim, Barbara Jarczyk or Hanna Kwiatkowska mean anything to you?"

"I've seen Rudzki a couple of times on television, I think he appeared as an expert on some talk show. And my wife has his book about solving family problems. The other names mean nothing to me."

"What about Kamil Sosnowski?"

"No."

"Pity. Please don't be surprised by the next question, I'm not joking, I'm checking an important lead in the inquiry."

"Pity. I was getting fond of your jokes."

"In that case there's a prosecutor who'd say you were the first person ever to do so. Do you remember, either from your student days, or maybe Henryk Telak told you about even earlier times, the women he used to date? Did he have a great love? Did some great tragedy occur that affected both him and her, an alarming, traumatic experience?"

"I know nothing about that. The polytechnic was never any good for that sort of observation, there weren't many girls there, but I do remember that Henryk very rarely came along when we went out – forgive the expression – 'after pussy'. A couple of times he dated someone for a few months, though I wouldn't say it was anything serious. On the whole he was quite shy. In the final year of college, I guess it was 1984, he fell madly in love with Jadwiga. She didn't want him. He went about in a daze. It's a miracle he defended his thesis. But straight after that we parted ways, and then the next time we met, they were already married. They got married in 1988 or 1989."

"Was it a successful marriage?"

"We didn't see each other often enough for me to judge."

As soon as Kuzniecow had left the company headquarters, Igor went into his office. He wasn't wearing a jacket.

"What a bloody oik, enough to make me come out in a sweat. I felt a shudder run through me every time he opened his mouth. I hate people like that. Did you hear it all?"

He said yes.

"It looks as if we can't go on pretending. They're not just blundering about in the dark. I went cold when he asked about him. I never thought they'd get onto that."

The Chairman stood up and went over to the window. Indeed, it was an inconvenience, but compared with other threats he'd had to face in the past few years it was nothing to get upset about. He gazed at the concrete funfair that stretched out below and thought that if he had divine power, in a single instant he would reveal all the secrets hidden in the walls of this sad little city. All of them. Not just the major ones – he was their depositary too – that had to be kept for the sake of state security. But all the commercial frauds, disloyalties, marital infidelities, flirtatious lies, parents' half-truths and children's concealments. Just like that, at the click of his fingers, it would all be exposed. Would there be a single person left after that who would dare to repeat the words of the feeble little god they worshipped so blindly, "the truth will set you free"? He doubted it.

"You're right," he said, turning away from the window. "Time to start taking action. In my view Kuzniecow is harmless, but we need to know as much as possible about Prosecutor Szacki: where his wife works, where the daughter goes to school, who he's shafting on the side, who he meets for a beer and who he doesn't like at work. I think before the end of the week it'll be necessary to pay him a visit."

"How long have we got?"

"Until Wednesday morning. After that it might already be too late."

IV

Cezary Rudzki had recovered and returned to his stylish Hemingway look. A thin polo neck, fluffy-looking hair that had mostly gone white, beard, piercing pale-blue eyes and therapeutic smirk, kindly and mocking all at once. His entire appearance seemed to say that this man would definitely listen to you with interest and understanding, but he'd keep a healthy distance and restrain himself from invading your most personal territory. Yes, Cezary Rudzki could have appeared on billboards advertising psychoanalysis.

Szacki had started a conversation about hypnosis, and the therapist had been giving long wordy answers, until finally the prosecutor had had to ask him not to explain his theories to him in such detail, but just answer the questions.

"Are you able to hypnotize your patients?"

"Of course. I rarely make use of it, because in my view the therapeutic process should be fully conscious. But often the source of the condition is such a firmly denied memory that there is no other way of reaching it than by making the patient regress. I treat it as a last resort."

"Regress?" Szacki preferred to make sure he and Rudzki had the same thing in mind.

"Taking the patient back into the past. It's a delicate operation, demanding caution and tact. And courage, because the patient often brings up the memories that have set the most firmly in his mind or been the most strongly denied. It can be shocking. I once had a patient who had been abused in childhood by the carers at a children's home, a terribly badly scarred woman. But I didn't know about that. In a way, neither did she. During the regression, when she suddenly started telling me in the voice and words of a little girl about the details of the orgy she had been forced to take part in – just imagine, I vomited."

"Perhaps it's better we can't remember certain things."

"I think so too, though many therapists are of a different view. I think our brain knows what it's doing when it tells us to forget. Though of course there are deeds that we're not free to erase from memory. You know best about that."

Szacki frowned.

"What do you have in mind?"

"Deeds for which their perpetrators must suffer the penalty. Crimes, offences."

"And did you inform the police or the prosecutor's office about the carers at the children's home?"

"The patient was almost sixty."

"But if during hypnosis you came upon information about a recently committed crime and you knew that keeping it a secret would be better for your patient, what would you do?"

"I'd keep it a secret. I am guided by the patient's well-being, not society's."

"That's where we differ."

"So it would seem."

Szacki discreetly glanced at his watch; it was half-past three. He'd have to speed up the pace of the conversation if he didn't want to be late for his meeting with Monika.

"And could you hypnotize someone so that afterwards – regardless of their own will – they did something they wouldn't normally be capable of doing?"

This was one of his theories, which in spite of everything seemed to him more credible than the idea of Hanna Kwiatkowska committing murder. The charismatic therapist exploits his natural influence on people and uses hypnosis to settle his own scores by means of the patient's hands. All right, it's more fantastical than a TV crime series, but who said something like that couldn't happen? The reasoning had lots of weak points: first and foremost there was the lack of a motive, and apart from that it was hard to answer the question why Telak would have gone to have therapy with someone who had a score to settle with him. But Szacki felt instinctively that this case was not going to have an obvious solution and that he'd have to consider every theory, even the ones that at first sight looked the most idiotic.

"I don't know, I've never tried; I'm a doctor, not a conjuror, my dear Prosecutor." Rudzki was clearly hurt by the question. "But please don't believe what Dean Koontz describes in his trashy novels. Programming someone to make them do something against their own will and conscience would require not hypnosis, but plain old brainwashing. A lot of hypnotism sessions, probably combined with pharmacological back-up, aimed at rebuilding the patient's personality so that he might behave according to an imposed programme. But even then success is not guaranteed. In any book about hypnosis you will find the information that it is virtually impossible to force someone to act against his morality. To give you a well-known example: during classes at an academy the lecturer had to leave a patient who was deep in a hypnotic trance in the lecture room, so he put her in the care of a student. Of course the student immediately told her to undress, at which she woke up and hit him in the face. You see yourself, if it were that simple, hypnosis would be used by every firm to stop the employees from wanting to go out for a cigarette, gossip or play patience."

Teodor Szacki automatically agreed, wondering the whole time if he should tell Rudzki about Kwiatkowska pretending to be Telak's dead daughter. He had already spoken to Wróbel about it, so he didn't need a psychologist's opinion. But he could check something else. He asked Rudzki for total discretion and played him Telak's recording.

"Absolutely incredible," said the therapist, not looking at all shocked or horrified. Quite the opposite – he was flushed with excitement. "Do you know what that means? That the field can be stronger than anyone could have imagined. If the recording is from eleven p.m., four hours after the session ended, it's simply extraordinary."

He stood up and started pacing the room. Or rather skipping around in circles, as the size of the room did not allow for long walks or even a couple of energetic steps.

"Such a strong identification four hours after the session that it's hard to believe. You might suppose Miss Kwiatkowska's personality was in some way similar to that of Henryk's daughter, so that a link was made, but even so! Do you know what a potent force this attests to? I wouldn't be surprised if the theory of the field went beyond psychology and became the embryo of a new religion!"

Rudzki was getting more and more excited; meanwhile it was already three forty-five.

"Assuming she's not pretending," Szacki coldly put in.

"Sorry? I don't understand. What do you mean, 'pretending'?" The doctor stopped skipping about and looked at the prosecutor in amazement.

"Please don't forget that the conclusion of your therapeutic experiment was a body lying on the floor with his eye spilled down his cheek. Someone killed him and I won't conceal the fact – though I hope this will remain between us – that Hanna Kwiatkowska is my main suspect. Just take a look – it all fits. She plays the role of the daughter who committed suicide because of her father; her identification with her doesn't stop; she asks him to come to her, but he escapes; she can't bear that, so she seizes the skewer. It all fits."

Rudzki sat down.

"You're mad," he uttered. "Hanna had nothing to do with it. I'd stake my life on it. It's absurd."

Szacki shrugged and leaned back in his chair nonchalantly.

"Why do you think that? Do you know something I don't? Please tell me."

"No, of course not, you just don't understand. Murder overloads the system in a dreadful way, it's always against, never for. A constellation could be a source of suicide, but murder – never."

"Maybe she had another motive apart from the system."

The therapist was silent.

"I don't believe it," he said after a while.

"Definitely not? She came to see you for therapy; she told you about herself, her life, childhood, loves, hates. Don't you remember anything that could have been a motive?"

The therapist was silent.

"Yes, yes, yes," said Szacki and sighed. "Even so you won't tell me because you're guided by the patient's well-being, not society's. We've established that already. Never mind, even if people don't confide as readily in policemen and prosecutors as they do in analysts, sometimes we too manage to find things out. I hope you are aware that at present any contact with Miss Kwiatkowska could lead to your arrest? The court is not inclined to regard helping someone suspected of murder as part of keeping a medical secret."

Rudzki began to laugh quietly and shook his head.

"Dear God, you don't know how wrong you are."

"I'd love to find out."

"I've already told you everything."

"Sure. Did you know Kamil Sosnowski?"

"Sorry, what was the name?" Rudzki was doing his best to look as if he hadn't heard the question, but Szacki had interviewed too many people not to know when someone was trying to buy time. An old, simple trick providing a few seconds more to decide whether to tell the truth and to think up a lie.

"Kamil Sosnowski," he repeated instantly.

"No, I'm sorry. At first I thought you said Kosowski. I used to have a patient of that name."

Like hell you did, thought Szacki. You're trying to put me off the scent, you lying bastard.

"Kosowski? That's interesting. Did he get treated for depression after spending the entire season on the bench at FC Kaiserslautern?"

"I'm sorry, I don't understand."

"No, I'm sorry, I was having a little joke." He glanced at his watch. He was already late. "I've got one more request: I'd like to hear the tapes of Henryk Telak's individual therapy sessions. Could you get them to me by noon tomorrow?"

"But I have already told you the therapy wasn't recorded."

"That was when I didn't know you tell lies. Give me the tapes, or do I have to call the police so we can go and search your flat together?"

"Please be my guest. You can even rip up the parquet. If you find a single tape recording of Telak's therapy, I'll give you my year's income."

"Unfortunately I'm not allowed to accept even a ten-groshy coin from you. Under the law on prosecution."

Even if this information did worry Rudzki, he didn't let it show.

"In that case please answer one question. And I stress that this is a transcribed interview that can be used in evidence and you are obliged to speak the truth. Otherwise you might later be charged with bearing false witness."

"You already cautioned me earlier."

"I know, but I have noticed that you don't always hear what I'm saying. Did Henryk Telak tell you about the love affairs he had years ago, at college, or perhaps about a lover from the time when he was already married? About someone very important who might have died tragically, though not necessarily so? Or with whom Telak parted in dramatic circumstances?"

The man on the other side of the desk took off his glasses, wiped them with a piece of chamois taken from his jacket pocket and set them carefully on his nose. Szacki thought how lately he'd interviewed nothing but people wearing glasses. Jarczyk and Kwiatkowska had poor eyesight too.

"No, he never mentioned any woman of the kind," he said, looking Szacki in the eye, and the prosecutor was amazed, because the witness' expression was full of sorrow. "And I don't believe any such woman existed. Henryk Telak only loved his Jadzia and no one else. He didn't even love his daughter as much as her. He loved her so much that probably neither you nor – far more – I will ever experience such love. And perhaps we should thank God for that."

V

It was ten past four. Prosecutor Teodor Szacki quickly marched down Żurawia Street along a tree-shaded pavement. In the arcade of the building on the other side, people were sitting at the tables of the bars and cafés that had appeared here in recent years. One of them, the Italian Compagnia del Sole, would have been among his favourites if he could have allowed himself to go there more than once a year. He so rarely ate out in town that it was hard for him to say he had a favourite place, not counting the kebab shop on Wilcza Street. He knew all the local Turkish fast-food outlets, and in this particular sphere he was an expert. Bar Emil was in his view the best kebab shop in the City Centre. But he doubted if this information could make much of an impression on anyone who regularly spent forty zlotys on lunch.

He slowed down because he didn't want to arrive at Szpilka out of breath. He had just run across to the other side of the street opposite the Warsaw University ethnography faculty when Kuzniecow called.

"Be quick, I'm late for a meeting."

"Does your wife know about it?"

He thought that as long as Kuzniecow was working at the city police, he'd never dare commit a crime – Kuzniecow would be sure to catch him.

"I really am in a hurry."

"Telak's son and his mummy don't have to worry about the cost of an operation abroad. Our widow will inherit about a million in cash, and she'll get half a million from his insurance policy. Are you still standing?"

"No, I've rolled into a ball on the pavement. The guy was head of a prospering firm, he'd put money aside for years, someone was making good investments for him. It all makes sense. And as for the insurance, if a beggar like me is insured for a hundred thousand, what's he going to be worth? Let's say he paid a premium of 500 zlotys a month. Do you think that left him with nothing to tank up his Merc? Give over. Anything else?"

"There's no trace of Kamil Sosnowski and his murder in the City Police Headquarters archive, apart from a note of it in the registration book and the case compendium. The files have vanished into thin air."

"Maybe your pal doesn't know how to look?"

"My pal's been working there for seven years – there's never been a case he couldn't find in half an hour."

"What could that mean?"

"Nothing. Somebody must have borrowed it 'for a moment' once – for so much of a moment that it hasn't even been noted down – then they forgot, so the files are lying in some forgotten cupboard in Mostowski Palace. It happens. But if you're free this evening you can go and see the militiaman who handled the case – you're neighbours."

"Where does he live?"

"On Młot Street."

"Good, send me the details by text, I might drop in on him. And if I don't, you go tomorrow, or send one of your guys. I really shouldn't get involved in things like that. Sorry, Oleg, I've got to go. I'll call."

"Say hello to her from me."

"Say hello to my arse."

Twenty past four. He was just entering the café, imagining Monika getting ready to leave with a sour look on her face, when the phone rang again. This time it was Kitten. He sighed, answered it and went back outside towards Bracka Street.

"Where are you?"

"Out," he grunted, "I've been for something to eat, now I'm going back to work."

What a fine remark. One-third true, one-third half-true – he really had been to eat something earlier – and one-third a downright lie. What a bargain for a philosopher.

"Please, I beg you, pick up Helka from playschool. I've got to stay, I've got a meeting, there's a very important trial tomorrow, involving very big money. If I leave now I won't be able to get back again."

He held the phone at arm's length, covered it with his hand and cursed out loud. A nice buxom blonde, who was walking past pushing a stroller with twins, gave him a pitying look.

"What about your mum?"

"I called them, they went to Wyszków this morning to visit friends and they're still there. There's no way. Please, Teo, say you're not in the middle of interviewing a serial murderer…"

"OK, OK, what time do I have to pick her up by?"

"The playschool is open until half-past five, but please try…"

"I'll try," he interrupted her. "Don't worry. I've got to go. Big kiss."

"Bye, thanks."

Twenty-five past four. In a panic he ran into Szpilka, forgetting about putting on a show of cool. She wasn't downstairs. He looked on the mezzanine – not there either. She's gone. Great. So much for his flirtations with attractive young women. He should find himself a forty-year-old married woman who's bored with her old man and doesn't expect much from life any more, and drop in on her when her husband goes off to his air-conditioned office and the children have left for school. One good turn for another, a nice neat situation. But at least Helka wouldn't be the very last child to be collected from playschool. He knew all too well what that was like. You sit on the floor, play half-heartedly and jump up every time the main door opens. The teacher furiously reads her paper at the desk and looks at her watch now and then. When's that daddy coming, then? Oh dear, our dad hasn't exactly distinguished himself today.

He turned round and bumped into Monika.

"You're in a trance, Teodor," she laughed. "You keep running to and fro without noticing me. Surely you didn't think I'd sit inside on a day like this? Too few people would have seen me there." As she said this, she twirled on her toes in the same sandals he'd complimented on Saturday.

He thought he should retract everything he'd said about her figure. Her legs weren't bandy, her shoulders too broad, or her breasts too small. Everything about her looked absolutely perfect, and the credit couldn't only be due to her thin linen dress. Slit in all the places where it should be slit. He was reminded of the Russian fairy tale where they try to test the heroine's wisdom by telling her to come to the castle both dressed and undressed at the same time. The clever girl comes wearing nothing but a fishing net. Standing in the sunlight, Monika seemed to be dressed in not much more. Once they had sat down at a table, he could still discern the outline of her body and her white underwear.

"You really did get changed," he remarked idiotically.

"Do you hold it against me?"

"I'm just sorry I didn't bring a camera."

"No worries, I can put it on for you again one day."

"But without underwear," he automatically blurted, and almost fled on the instant. This isn't Weronika, you fool, it's a girl you've only known for a week. Control yourself.

"Hmm, I didn't know we were that well acquainted," she said with a laugh, plainly pleased, which shocked him almost as much as his own words had. He started to apologize, but she just laughed even louder and put her finger to his lips to make him stop.

"OK, it's a deal," she said, and moved back in her chair.

"What's a deal?" he asked unconsciously, still feeling her touch on his lips.

"Without underwear."

You've only yourself to blame, he thought.

VI

At a quarter to six he entered the playschool. Helka joyfully threw herself round his neck as if she hadn't seen him for ten months, not ten hours. She was the last child to be collected. Luckily the teacher, Miss Marta, didn't say anything, but just gave him a knowing look.

At home he let the little one switch on the telly. He felt too guilty to forbid her anything, and too distracted after the meeting at Szpilka to play with her. He and Monika had mainly talked about work again; she'd asked him about all sorts of details, claiming she needed them for her book. However, she was less interested in the technical details of a prosecutor's work and more in the emotions that go with it, and by drawing on confidences their meeting had become more intimate than he would have wished. On top of that there was a constant undercurrent of flirting.

"There's one thing I don't understand," she had said as they were getting up from the table. "You're a civil servant, you're thirty-five with a wife and a child, and white hair. Can you explain to me why I keep thinking about you and nothing else?"

He had replied that it surprised him too, almost as much as the fact that whatever spell she was under evidently worked in both directions. And had fled.

At home he had tried to call the retired Civic Militia captain Stefan Mamcarz, but his phone must have been out of order or disconnected, because all he got was a recurring message that the connection couldn't be made. Weronika came home a few minutes before seven, and he realized that Mamcarz offered the perfect excuse for him to get out of the house. He was afraid she'd read in his eyes everything that had happened that afternoon, every word heard and uttered.

Oleg was right. They were neighbours. He saw the hideous ten-storey block on Młot Street from his windows every day, unfortunately, and getting there only took him a couple of minutes. He tapped out "46" on the entryphone, but no one answered. He was going to give up, when a shaggy teenager with an intelligent and handsome, though rather spotty face and an eight- or nine-year-old fair-haired girl with the devil in her eyes came up to the entrance. Helka would definitely have loved her at first sight.

"His intercom doesn't work. I'll let you in," said the boy and tapped a code into the panel.

Szacki should have said thank you but he was tongue-tied. He always reacted like that when dealing with disabled people. The nice teenager uttered his remark incredibly slowly, dragging out his vowels infinitely. In his version the remark was so long that he said it in three stages, drawing breath along the way: "His intercom" – inhale – "doesn't work" – inhale – "I'll let you in." Poor kid, it must have been some speech-centre defect, rather than anything else. After all, his parents wouldn't have put him in charge of his little sister if he were seriously handicapped.

He pulled himself together and said thank you, trying to speak very slowly and clearly, but the boy looked at him as if he were mad, and the little girl ran through the open door onto the landing.

"Race you?" she asked, jumping up and down the whole time. Maybe she had ADHD. Szacki thought fate was really putting this family to the test, by giving them beautiful but ailing children. Instead of replying, her brother gave her a pitying look.

"You don't want to race because you're fat," she blurted as all three of them waited for the lift.

The boy smiled and addressed Szacki.

"Please" – inhale – "take no notice" – inhale. "She's still" – inhale – "little."

"I'm not little!" she squawked.

They all got in the lift. The boy looked at him inquiringly.

"Which floor is forty-six on?" asked Szacki.

"Fourth floor," said the teenager, pressing the button. The lift was old and dilapidated and it stank of piss. Unfortunately, soon he'd have reason to believe the stink was probably thanks to Captain Mamcarz or his friends.

"I'm not little," whispered the small blonde girl again spitefully, and kicked her brother.

"You are" – inhale – "a little" – inhale – "midget," he said, smiling the while, and tried to stroke her, which put the little girl into a fury.

"Get off!" She slapped his hand, which naturally made no impression on the teenager. "You'll get punished, you'll see! They won't let you eat fat, kiddywink."

Teodor Szacki found this discussion highly amusing, but unfortunately the lift stopped. The amiable siblings got out with him and disappeared behind the door of one of three flats on the same floor. As they parted the boy looked at him in amazement, then at the door he was standing outside. The prosecutor understood that look. The door had no lock and stood slightly ajar; there was a dreadful stench of piss coming from the other side of it, and two cockroaches were sitting quietly on the threshold. Captain Mamcarz clearly wasn't his neighbours' favourite person.

The bell didn't work, so he knocked hard. He wasn't expecting anyone to answer, but moments later there was a haggard man… woman… standing in the doorway – Szacki could only tell by the earrings that it was a woman in front of him. She could easily have played Mrs Morlock in *The Time Machine* without any make-up. She looked not quite sixty, but she could just as well have been forty. A square figure, a square peasant face and thick black hair most probably cut by herself. An evil expression in her eyes.

"Yes?" she asked. She had a pure, sweet, artificially polite voice, accustomed to asking favours.

"I'm looking for Stefan Mamcarz," he replied.

The woman moved back and opened the door to let Szacki in. A stale, filthy stench hit him in the face, making him feel sick, but he went inside. He knew he'd get used to it in a few minutes, just like the odour of corpses in the mortuary. But this knowledge was poor consolation.

The flat was a small dark studio with a kitchen annex, where there was a gas canister standing next to an out-of-order stove. Evidently his host's gas had long since been cut off. And the electricity. It was still light, but the stearin candles stuck in puddles of wax probably weren't intended merely to create an atmosphere over an evening glass of wine. Empty bottles of which stood neatly under the window, with the red-plastic tops in a neat row on the window sill.

"Someone to see you, Captain," she shouted into the interior, in a tone leaving no doubt about who wore the trousers in this dump.

A very small man with a tiny face got up from the couch. He was dressed in a striped shirt and an old jacket. He had a surprisingly pleasant, sad expression. He came up to Szacki.

"I don't know you," he said in alarm.

Szacki introduced himself – at which the man's alarm greatly increased – and briefly told him what brought him there. The retired captain nodded, sat down on the sofa bed and pointed Szacki to an armchair. He sat down, carefully concealing his disgust and trying not to stare at every spot where he saw a cockroach scuttling past. He couldn't stand the creatures. Spiders, snakes, slimy slugs, seafood – nothing aroused such revulsion in him as the small brown, unexpectedly speedy cockroach, which produced a horrid crunch when you trod on it, and which then died slowly in a pool of white sticky gunk. He was taking shallow breaths, trying not to smell the odour of the flat, but at the same time wanting to take deep breaths in order to get over his phobia of the insects. For a while he struggled with himself, then finally took a gulp of air and slowly let it out again. Better. Not much, but better.

Mamcarz was lost in thought. Mamcarz's woman – he doubted if she was his wife – offered Szacki a cup of coffee, but he refused. Even so he was sure she'd ask him for money when he left. He preferred simply to give a handout than pay for something that he probably wouldn't be able to swallow anyway.

"Do you remember that case at all?" he prompted Mamcarz.

"I do, Prosecutor. You don't forget a murder. Of course you know that."

Szacki nodded. It was true.

"I'm just trying to remember as many of the details as I can. It was almost twenty years ago, you see. I'm not sure which year it was, but it was definitely the seventeenth of September. A bigwig came to visit us from the USSR, and we were laughing behind his back that the Russkis only ever come on the seventeenth of September."

"1987."

"Maybe. Certainly before 1989. Just a moment. I must think."

"Hurry up, Stefan," snapped the woman, and then added in a sugary tone: "The prosecutor isn't going to sit here for ever."

Szacki summoned up his iciest facial expression.

"Please don't disturb the Captain," he said. "I'm giving you good advice."

The threat was vague, so she could take it as she wished. She muttered an obsequious apology and withdrew into the depths of the room. Despite which Mamcarz bucked up and started talking, glancing nervously towards his concubine, now hidden in the dark. Or maybe she actually was his wife. Szacki interrupted him.

"I'm truly sorry, Madam," he addressed the woman, "but would you mind leaving us on our own for a quarter of an hour? I beg your pardon, but this inquiry is extremely important for the prosecutor's office and the police."

The use in a single sentence of the words "inquiry", "prosecutor's office" and "police" did the job. In less than fifteen seconds the door had closed behind the woman. Mamcarz did not react. He was still thinking.

Teodor Szacki gazed out of the window to avoid noticing the insects frolicking on the carpet. He smiled to himself, because the balcony looked as if it had been stuck on from another flat. Nice and clean, its railing and balustrade were freshly painted blue, and there were petunias growing abundantly and neatly in green boxes. Along the sides, there were flowerpots filled with roses on wire stands. How was it possible? And was it his doing, or hers? He was curious, but he knew he wouldn't ask about it.

"I'm sorry, I haven't got much for you," replied Mamcarz eventually. "I was the first officer to arrive at the scene, I got to the flat on Mokotowska Street where there was just a decaying corpse, his sister in a catatonic state and two beat cops who kept telling her over and over not to worry. The body looked terrible. The boy was lying in the bath with his throat cut. He was bound and naked – his hands had been tied behind his back and then strapped to his tied-up legs. The flat had been turned upside down, and as we discovered later, when the victim's parents arrived, very thoroughly robbed, surprisingly thoroughly. All the valuables had gone."

"Why was that surprising?"

"Usually burglars act in a hurry. They take whatever's lying on the surface and whatever they can fit in their bags. No one wants to risk taking longer than they have to. Here the thieves had more time, thanks to the fact that they found someone at home."

Szacki asked him to explain.

"I think that when they broke into the flat and found the boy there, Kamil, they were surprised at first, then they quickly overpowered him and tied him up. Maybe they tortured him for fun. Though I think to start with they didn't want to kill him. They found out that the rest of the family weren't coming back sooner than the day after next. They had time. They may have sat there for quite a while, because they wondered what to do with the prisoner, who had got such a good look at them. During this time they looked into every drawer and took out every ring."

"Until finally they killed him?"

"Until finally they killed him."

"Did you consider any other possibility apart from assault and robbery?"

"No. Maybe to begin with, but we pretty quickly found out in the city that some shady character from that suburb, Gocław, was boasting that they'd tied this sucker up and cut his throat while they were doing a flat. But the trail went dead, apparently the shady guy wasn't local, he was just staying in Gocław. It all led to nowhere, there wasn't a splinter for us to hang the inquiry on. No tip-off, no clue, no fingerprints. In less than a month it got shelved. I remember being wildly angry. I can't have slept for a week."

Szacki thought the story of the investigation Mamcarz had conducted was strangely reminiscent of his own inquiry. He had had enough of these coincidences by now.

"What sort of flat was it?"

"Not large, but full of books. Quite intimidating, at least for me. I'm a simple guy, I felt awkward when I went to see them and they served me coffee in a fine elegant cup. I was afraid I'd break it if I stirred it, so I didn't add any milk or sugar. I remember that room full of books, Sosnowski's parents (they'd sent the daughter off to the family in the country) and the taste of bitter coffee. I had nothing to tell them except that we were 'temporarily suspending' the investigation, and that we were in no position to find the culprits. They looked at me as if I were one of the murderers. I left as soon as I'd drunk the coffee. I never saw them again."

"Do you know who they were?"

"By profession? No. I must have known at the time, I must have filled in the boxes in the witness-statement forms. But it can't have been crucial to the case, or I'd have remembered."

"Have you ever seen them again?"

"Never." Mamcarz got up and shambled into the corner to fetch a bottle of Golden Goblet sweet fruit wine. He filled two glasses and handed one to Szacki. The prosecutor took a sip, surprised that although he was almost thirty-six, it was the first time he'd ever drunk apple wine. He was expecting it to taste like Domestos, but in fact it was quite bearable. A bit like Russian sparkling wine without the bubbles. And sweeter. But he didn't fancy the idea of getting drunk on it.

"That is, I thought I saw Sosnowski on television once. At our friends' house," he added, noticing Szacki visually sweeping the room in search of a telly.

Szacki imagined Mamcarz with his girlfriend on his arm and a bottle of apple wine in his hand, marching along the back streets of the Praga district to drop in on their "friends". What a glamorous scene. He wondered if it was hard to overlook the moment when you turn onto the path that leads to drinking apple wine by candlelight in the company of an evil woman and a regiment of cockroaches. It probably was. It started with cheating on your wife.

"What was he doing on television?" he asked, strangely sure that once again he wouldn't learn anything specific.

"I have no idea. I saw him a while ago. If it was him, he's aged a lot. But I'm not sure."

Szacki asked Mamcarz a few more questions about the details, about people who might have known the Sosnowskis, and what might have happened to the files. In vain. The retired militia captain actually remembered very little. After yet another question that got no answer Szacki glanced with hatred at the bottle of apple wine, which over the years, along with its pals, had changed his personal source of information into someone whose brain structure resembled pumice. A semblance of solidity, but essentially full of holes. Only as Szacki was leaving, thinking how he'd probably have to burn his clothes in the courtyard dustbin before entering the house, Mamcarz said something that the prosecutor should have thought of earlier.

"You should ask your colleagues who dig around in secret-police files about Sosnowski," he said.

"Why?"

"He was a college boy from an intelligentsia home. There's a chance they kept a file on him. Even if they didn't gather much information, you might find some names or addresses. I know what it's like when you haven't a splinter to hang the inquiry on."

That must have been his favourite phrase.

Just as he expected, Mamcarz's concubine was waiting for him outside the door, smiling insincerely. He was upset by the thought that this woman was going back to the Captain, who had ultimately seemed to be a sympathetic, despondent man. But "if someone in the constellation seems to be good and someone else bad, it's almost always the other way around". Was it she who had planted the flowers and painted the railings?

Of course she asked him for a small favour. She was ready to spend a long time explaining her needs to him, but he waved a hand to stop her and reached into his pocket for some change. He gave her a ten-zloty note. She thanked him effusively, as the door –

behind which the siblings he had met downstairs had disappeared – opened, and out came a young couple. Their neighbour fled back into her den as fast as possible. The horrible thought crossed Szacki's mind that in Mamcarz's flat the cockroaches must run across the people's faces while they slept. He shuddered.

"The midget's to have her light out at ten, and you're not to spend the whole time playing games. We'll be late – if there's any need, I've got my mobile," a young man holding the handle of the open door was instructing the shaggy teenager.

The three of them got into the lift together. The couple gave Szacki the same sort of pitying look he himself would have bestowed on any visitor to Captain Mamcarz. He replied with an acid smile. They both looked about twenty-something, and Szacki thought they couldn't possibly have such big children. Or maybe they looked young because they were happy? Because they loved each other? Had sex often and kissed each other on the mouth a lot? Maybe he'd look younger too if it weren't for Weronika's worn-out Tatra Highlander slippers and pyjamas that had gone yellow under the arms. It was quite another matter that he wore just the same slippers. And to think he'd once said Tatra Highlander slippers were death for a man. He'd liked that joke a lot. One day he'd got them some of those peasant-style slippers from a souvenir shop on Krupówki Street in Zakopane – just for a laugh. And now they wore them every day. They were even comfortable.

Szacki averted his gaze from his fellow passengers. Reluctantly. The woman was very sexy, exactly his type. Not too skinny, but not fat, with nice womanly curves and full lips, wearing a red dress with small black flowers on it, with a low-cut neck that was enough to arouse the imagination without being vulgar. She looked like someone who laughed a lot.

The lift stopped, and Szacki felt like telling them they had fabulous kids, but he held back. Ever since the incriminating photographs had been found in the paedophile therapist's dustbin, such remarks were no longer considered innocent.

As he walked home he thought about the bantering siblings. He often wondered if they hadn't done Helka a wrong by not trying for another child. But perhaps it wasn't too late yet? There must have been six or seven years' difference between the teenager with the speech defect and his sister with ADHD. If he and Weronika were to decide on it now, there'd be eight years between Helka and her brother or sister.

And maybe then everything would become easy. Maybe then he wouldn't need change. Maybe, maybe, maybe.

All it took was to make a decision. For Teodor Szacki, a man who preferred everything to just happen to him rather than to be the result of his own decisions, that thought was on a par with deciding to climb Mount Aconcagua at the weekend.

He reached his block and glanced up at the illuminated kitchen window on the second floor. He didn't feel like going home, so he sat on a bench in the courtyard to enjoy the June evening. It was already after nine, but it was still warm and light, and there was a smell of the city cooling down. At moments like these he felt like the nightingale in Julian Tuwim's poem, who upsets his wife by coming home late for supper.

"My golden one, forgive me do, the night's so fine, I came on foot," he repeated the nightingale's excuse aloud and laughed.

He thought about what he'd heard from Captain Mamcarz. Once again all he had gained was information that didn't move him forwards. But the itching in his head was getting more and more irritating. He was sure by now he should have twigged what it was all about. He felt as if he had heard everything, but instead of joining the information together in a logical whole, he was twisting it all into nonsense, like a chimpanzee playing with a Rubik's cube.

A strange visit, slightly surreal because of the family with whom he'd shared the lift on his way in and out. He thought about the young couple – or at least young-looking – and sprang to his feet. The itching feeling had stopped, and in its place a thought had appeared, so clear and sharp it was painful.

Teodor Szacki started energetically pacing up and down outside his block, going round and round the green bench and the concrete bin, asking himself the same question a thousand times over, sometimes out loud and sometimes adding the word "fucking": is it possible? Is it really possible?

9

A new world record is set for the 100 metres. In Athens, Jamaican Asafa Powell runs this distance, equal to the length of Konstytucja Square, in 9.77 seconds. In Poland, as in twelve other European countries, the grand finale takes place of a police operation called "Ice-breaker", aimed against paedophiles, which began with surveillance of Internet chat rooms. One hundred and fifty houses and flats are searched and twenty people are arrested. The papers do not report whether anyone charged with the crime of paedophilia was on the Łowicz prison team that played a match against clerical students from the local seminary. Initially leading the game, the future priests ultimately lost to the crooks 1—2. Apart from that, members of a marksmen's society in Rawicz, including the mayor who has the backing of the Democratic Left Alliance party, held a competition to fire at a target bearing a portrait of John Paul II. They say they did it as a tribute to the Pope, but the opposition wants the mayor's head to roll. To keep the political balance, in Białystok a lecturer at the Higher School of Economics has lost his job for forcing the students to sign a letter in support of ultra-conservative politician Maciej Giertych to launch him as a candidate in the presidential elections. In Warsaw city guards appear patrolling the parks in the Powiśle district on roller skates. Maximum temperature in the city — twenty-seven degrees; no rain, no clouds. A perfect June day.

I

Prosecutor Teodor Szacki was furious when he finally ran out of the court building on Leszno Street. It was ages since he'd had a day like this, when everything went against his plans. That morning he'd quarrelled with Weronika, making her cry and incidentally Helka too, who witnessed the scene. Worst of all, he couldn't now remember what it was about. Moreover, he was sure that even as they were shouting at each other he couldn't remember what it had been about to begin with. He had got up quite early after a fitful night's sleep, planning to go to the swimming pool. He felt he should tire himself out properly and get all thought of the Telak case out of his head for a while. He'd woken his wife with a kiss and made coffee, but then he hadn't been able to find his swimming goggles, though he was sure last time he'd put them away in the underwear drawer. He'd rummaged in all the drawers, growling, while Weronika drank her coffee in bed and teased him, saying maybe he just hadn't been to the pool for such a long time that his goggles had dried up for lack of water and crumbled to dust. He'd retorted that as for keeping fit, he didn't have much reason to reproach himself. Then it had gone downhill. Who does what, who doesn't do what, who gives up what because of whom, who makes the sacrifices, who has the more important job, who takes more care of the child. The final remark hurt him, and he'd screamed back that didn't recall a father's main obligation being to take care of little girls, and that unfortunately he couldn't do everything for her, which she surely regretted. And left. It was too late to go to the pool, and in any case he had lost the urge to swim, plus he didn't have any goggles, and without them the chlorinated water made his eyes sting. The only good thing was that during the quarrel he hadn't thought about Telak.

At the office, he called a friend from college. He knew Marek had worked for some time at one of the suburban prosecutor's offices – it may have been in Nowy Dwór, Mazowiecki County

– and then been transferred at his own request to the investigative department at the Institute of National Remembrance, where Communist-era collaboration was investigated. Unfortunately, not only was Marek on holiday at a lake near Nidzica, he responded quite coldly, suggesting Szacki should stick to official channels.

"Sorry, old man, but since the Wildstein affair everything's changed," he said, with no hint of regret, referring to the famous leak to the press of an Institute file. "We're afraid to check anything on the side, because it could result in problems. They watch us like hawks, we daren't ask to check anything in the archives. Write an application, then call, and I'll do my best to make sure you don't have to wait too long for an answer."

It turned out "not too long" meant no less than a week. Szacki thanked him coldly and suggested at the end of the conversation that Marek shouldn't hesitate to call him next time he needed help with something. Fuck you, I'll get revenge on you, he thought as he heard the traditional assurances that one day they'd meet for a beer and talk about old times.

He tried calling Oleg, but he didn't answer his mobile, and all they could tell him at the police station was that he'd been held up by important family matters and would only be in after twelve.

He lit his first cigarette, though it wasn't yet nine.

On impulse he called Monika. She was ecstatic, and ardently assured him she'd been up for hours, though he could tell he'd woken her. He was so preoccupied with the Telak murder that he didn't even try to flirt. In a rather official tone – as she told him later – he asked her if she had any friends or press contacts at the Institute for National Remembrance archives. Incredible, but she did. Her ex-boyfriend from high-school days had graduated in history and then ended up among miles of files at the secret-police archive. Szacki couldn't believe his own luck, until she said that last time she'd seen the man he'd just had a child with Down's syndrome and he might have changed his job for something better paid. But she promised to call him. He had to leave to get to court on time for the start of the Gliński trial, at nine thirty, so he regretfully ended the conversation.

He was in the courtroom at nine fifteen. At ten the court clerk arrived and announced that the prison van bringing the defendant had broken down on Modlińska Street, so there was a recess until noon. He ate an egg in tartare sauce, drank a cup of coffee, smoked a second cigarette and read the newspaper, including the business news. Boring, boring and more boring – the only interesting thing was a debate about the pearls of Communist-era architecture. In the architects' views, they should be treated like monuments and put under conservation orders. The owners of the Central Committee building and the Palace of Culture were in a panic – if they had to fight for permission for every hole in the wall, no one would rent so much as a studio flat from them, and the buildings would turn into empty shells. Szacki thought sourly that if the Palace of Culture had been blown up straight after 1989, there'd be no problem, and Warsaw might have had a central landmark worth its salt by now. Fuck knows, in this Third World city you couldn't be sure of anything.

At noon a recess until one was announced. Oleg turned up at work, but Szacki didn't want to talk to him about the conclusions he had reached on the phone. He just asked him not to intrude upon Rudzki and Co., and to dig further into Telak's past, because that was sure to be the key to the whole case. Kuzniecow had no desire to talk about the inquiry, but did confess that he was late for work because every other Tuesday in the month he and Natalia had a traditional "morning romp".

At one the case almost began, the defendant was finally brought in, but there was no barrister, who had "nipped out to the office for a moment" and got stuck in a traffic jam, for which he was deeply sorry. With stoical calm the judge declared a recess until two. Almost shaking with rage, Szacki invested in a copy of *Newsweek* to keep him occupied. He flicked through the weekly and felt like phoning the publisher to ask for the four and a half zlotys back that he'd spent on *A Portrait of the Modern Polish Prostitute* – attractive, educated and hard-working.

At two he finally read out the indictment. Gliński pleaded not guilty. Nothing more happened in the trial, because for a Warsaw court it was quite late now, and the defence counsel threw up half a ton of formal motions that Szacki forgot as soon as they'd been put forward, but which were enough to postpone the trial for six weeks. He stood up and left without waiting for "Your Honour" to leave the courtroom. He only just stopped himself from slamming the door.

When he found a parking ticket under his windscreen wiper he just shrugged. He lit his third cigarette and thought: frankly, to hell with his rules – he was a free man and he'd smoke as much as he liked.

He was incapable of concentrating on his work. He kept thinking about the Telak murder, or, more often, about Monika. He had trouble restraining himself from calling her just in order to hear her voice. He used Google to try and find information about her, but there was nothing but articles from *Rzeczpospolita* and an old site where her name appeared as a member of the student's union in the Polish department. No pictures, unfortunately. Would it be rude of him to ask her to send him her photo by email? He felt as if even considering that idea was embarrassing, but he couldn't stop himself. A moment of shame seemed to him a small price to pay for a photograph of Monika, especially in the dress she'd been wearing the other day. He could make it the wallpaper on his computer – after all, no one used the computer except him, and Weronika never came by his office.

His visions were very graphic, and he started to wonder if, were he now to go and masturbate in the toilet at the district prosecutor's office, it would mean he should go and get specialist help. He hesitated for not more than a few seconds. He got up and put on his jacket to hide his erection.

Just then she called.

"Hi, what are you doing?" she asked.

"Thinking about you," he replied truthfully.

"You're lying, but that's nice. Have you got email there, or doesn't the state budget run to the Internet?"

He gave her his address and asked what she wanted to send him.

"A dreadful virus that will accuse you all of subversive activity and send you on a five-day seminar to Łódź. Eight hours of compulsory lectures a day by Miller, Jaskiernia and Kalisz, finishing with Pęczak pole-dancing," she said, referring to a very unappealing group of left-wing politicians. "Don't you want a surprise?"

He explained that he didn't like surprises.

"Everyone does," she said gently, "but that's not why I called. I talked to Grześ this morning – just imagine, he still likes me – and he promised he'd be happy to help. He called just now and said he'd found something there and that he'd prefer to meet up with you. I didn't want to give him your mobile number, so I'm going to give you his. You can call at the taxpayer's expense. In other words, mine."

He started to thank her, but she said the editorial meeting had just begun so she had to go, and hung up before he'd had a chance to invite her for another coffee.

So he quickly made an appointment with "Grześ" and went to the toilet.

In full "Grześ" was called Grzegorz Podolski, and he looked like a nice guy, though he gave the impression of being biologically incapable of getting past adolescence. He was tall, disproportionately skinny and stooping, his arms and legs were too long, and on top of that he was slightly spotty and clean-shaven. He was dressed in an extremely old-fashioned way, like the hero of an East German youth film from the 1970s. Gym shoes, trousers made of brown stuff, a greenish shirt with short sleeves and braces. Szacki didn't know that this old-school style cost Podolski a large part of his archivist's salary.

"Do you know what Department 'C' was?" Podolski asked him once they'd exchanged formalities.

He didn't.

"It was the nervous system of the SB – the Communist secret police – you could say, the neurons connecting every functionary, department and unit. On official documents the name 'Central Archive of the Ministry of Internal Affairs' appeared, but within the firm no one ever called it anything but 'C'. I've been interested in it for years, and I have to tell you, if the Reds had had the sort of computers we have nowadays, they could have reduced us to dust at a single mouse click. And that's nothing: I think the card-index system they had in those days for registering and compiling information was miles better than the famous ultra-modern computer system at the National Insurance Agency."

Szacki shrugged indifferently.

"Impressive, but it's no news that bureaucracy is a vital element of any totalitarian regime."

"Exactly," said Podolski, for whom it really must have been a fascinating topic. "Without bureaucracy, without cataloguing information, without keeping the documents in order no such system could be maintained. That's why the Germans did so well – because they had order, there were receipts for everything. But it cuts both ways. On the one hand, thanks to bureaucracy a totalitarian system can function, but on the other, it leaves behind a lot of paper for those who are going to appraise that system. For us, in this case. I'll give you an example…"

Szacki tried to interrupt him with a gentle wave, but Podolski didn't even notice.

"Do you know the story of Lesław Maleszka? Everyone must know it. Maleszka was a well-known member of the opposition; of course he had his number on the list of internees, like everyone they kept under surveillance or kept operational files on, etc. Of course, not any old secret policeman or militiaman could just take a look at the documents on secret agent 'Zbyszek', as Maleszka was dubbed – it was all secret and of special importance. But just imagine – in the operational budget's completely unclassified reports there's a note saying how much was paid to 'Zbyszek' for informing, and there's the same number for Maleszka. Makes no sense? Oh no – it's just that the papers had to be in order. One person – one number. That's why it riles me so much when every little sneak starts whining that the wicked Reds falsified his file to incriminate him. All the functionaries had heaps of work to do filling in forms. Only someone with no idea about it could claim they spent their evenings faking dodgy receipts. The SB were bad, sometimes stupid, but they weren't retarded. Just imagine, every person they were interested in – even in the most trivial way – was instantly registered under the next ordinal number in the general information index. On condition they hadn't been registered there earlier, which of course had to be checked using some special cards. Once they'd been registered, every time something happened to them, supplementary cards had to be filled in that ended up in the individual files and indexes."

"What for?" asked Szacki automatically when the archivist stopped for a moment to take a breath. Though in fact he didn't want to know the answer to that question.

"What do you mean, what for? So that when you go on holiday to Łeba on the coast and the secret policemen watching the local 'enemy' there find out you ate flounder with him off a paper tray, at once they'll want to know who you are. They'll submit a question to 'C'. There someone will check if you're in the index, what your number is and if your case is 'open' and under the management of one of the regional commands, for example, or is in the archive. And provide the relevant information as far as possible – because you might be or have been a very valuable secret agent whose files do of course exist, but gaining access to the information contained in them is limited by numerous…"

Szacki was utterly uninterested. He switched off and sank into erotic fantasies.

They had already talked for an hour. In this time he had learned, among other things, what the differences were between registration forms EO-4 and EO-13-S, and he only remembered the second of these because he associated it with Canon EOS cameras. He'd like to get himself one of those one day. Maybe on hire purchase? He'd have to have a chat with Weronika about it – after all, they should have a digital camera. Everyone had one by now. He was bored with this discussion of secret-police card indexes and forms. He felt like shaking Podolski and shouting: "Man, I've got to lock up a murderer and you're screwing me around with bloody card indexes!"

"I'm very sorry, Mr Podolski," he politely interrupted his argument on the fact that practice doesn't always follow theory, files wandered, were detained, added to other cases "for a while", and sometimes he, archivist Grzegorz Podolski, felt as if it would be easier to find the Ark of the Covenant and the Holy Grail in a single day than a bloody secret-police file.

"But we do find them all the time," he said, raising a finger, "so they shouldn't be under any illusions."

Szacki didn't even try to imagine who "they" were in Podolski's mind.

"I'm very sorry," he cut in more decisively, "and thank you very much for telling me all this, but what about Kamil Sosnowski's file? Is it there? Or not? What happened to prevent you from telling me over the phone?"

Podolski behaved like someone who has been suddenly hit in the face. He buried his head in his arms, folded his hands on his chest and turned down the corners of his mouth. But at least he shut up.

"It's not there," he said after a pause.

Szacki sighed and started rubbing his temples with his left thumb and index finger. He felt a headache coming on.

"Thank you for taking the trouble. Your knowledge is impressive and I'd love to talk to you some more, but please understand me, I have a lot of work to do." What he'd have loved most would have been to kick the boring Podolski out of the door, but he restrained himself, because a friendly expert from the Institute for National Remembrance archive could still come in handy.

"There's no file," said Podolski, plainly wanting to torture him with this fact. "But that doesn't mean there's no information. I realize you're bored, but I will tell you that the main thing is knowing which catalogue to look in. Monika told me your subject was young, not much over twenty, so it's fairly hard to imagine he'd be a secret agent or a candidate secret agent – then he'd be inventoried under the symbol 'I' for PSIs, candidate PSIs, LCs and CF owners…"

"Sorry?" The abbreviations meant nothing to Szacki.

"Personal Sources of Information, Local Contacts and Conspiracy Flats. I thought it was obvious." Podolski gave him a superior look. "In any case, at once I started looking in the 'II' index, where the investigation operational files were catalogued."

Szacki took the manly decision to throw him out. He stood up.

"And I found him. Your subject, Kamil Sosnowski, was thoroughly investigated by the Warsaw SB. He was registered in the general information index under catalogue number 17875/II. The file was started in 1985, two years before his death. He was twenty years old then. He must have been fairly active in student organizations, or his parents were in the opposition – they rarely kept files on such very young people."

Szacki sat down.

"Did you manage to find out anything else?"

"From the inventory you can only tell how the files have roamed – when someone took them out and when they returned them. Nothing more."

"And did these ones roam?"

Grzegorz Podolski folded one skinny leg in unfashionable trousers over the other and leaned back in his chair.

"Well?" prompted Szacki.

"From the case compendium it appears that in July 1988 they were removed by Department 'D'."

"Meaning? Is that another sort of archive?"

"No, it's not. I don't know anything about them. That is, I know a bit, I can guess a bit. I don't want to talk about it."

"Why not?"

"Because I don't want to. I don't know, I'm not an expert, I'm just an archivist. I can give you details of a person who deals with all that. He's a real SB-hound, he's not afraid of anything. Unmarried, no children, his parents are dead, some say he has cancer. Someone like that can take risks."

Podolski uttered the final sentence with evident envy, which Szacki found strange.

"Would you prefer to be alone and dying so you could track down secret policemen?" he exclaimed.

"No, of course not. But if you'd seen what's in those files... If you knew as much as I do, had seen the photos, read the reports, leafed through the receipts. And the whole time knowing that most likely no one will ever see it, the truth will never come to light, it will all be swept under the carpet in the name of peace and quiet for whatever regime happens to be in power... Wildstein did take out that list of names, but what did that add? Have you seen the film *Fight Club*? Or maybe you've read Palahniuk's book?"

Szacki hadn't seen or read it. He felt ashamed, because he remembered the title as pretty well-known.

"In it ordinary people band together to blow up this world of hypocrisy, lies and financial gain. Sometimes I dream of how brilliant it would be to set up an organization like that, take over the Institute archives, scan everything in a week and post it on a server in a truly democratic country. If only it could happen."

"Not all secrets should come to light. Sometimes the price of fighting injustice is too high," said Szacki cautiously.

Podolski snorted with laughter and stood up, getting ready to leave. He handed the prosecutor a card with the name of the "SB-hound". Karol Wenzel.

"Fucking hell," he said, standing in the doorway. "Can a prosecutor of the Polish Republic really have said those words? In that case I'm emigrating to join my brother in London. Well, fucking hell. How could you? Not even reading all those biased editorials in *Gazeta Wyborcza* should have killed the desire within the Prosecution Service to establish the truth at any cost. That's what you're for – not to look at the balance sheet of losses and injustices, but to establish the truth. Fucking hell, I simply do not believe it."

He shook his head and left before Szacki had a chance to say anything in reply. He should have called Karol Wenzel at once, but instead of that he checked the emails, curious to see if Monika had sent his surprise yet.

She had. A picture from the seaside, taken in the same dress she'd been wearing the other day. It must have been taken a year ago – she was very tanned, with shorter hair. She was wading barefoot in shallow water and the whole bottom of the dress was soaked. She was smiling flirtatiously towards the camera. To a man? Szacki felt a pang of jealousy. Irrational jealousy, considering the fact that he had a child and a wife, with whom lately he had been sleeping pretty regularly, not with her.

He looked at the picture for a while longer, came to the conclusion that maybe she wasn't wearing a bathing costume underneath, and went to the bathroom. Not bad, not bad. He couldn't remember the last time he'd had sex twice in one day.

III

The conversation with Karol Wenzel went completely differently from how he'd imagined. He had expected he'd just be telling an older man to come and see him as soon as possible, but the voice at the other end of the line was young, and its owner had no intention of showing up at the prosecutor's office.

"Please don't crease me up," said Wenzel emphatically, exaggeratedly rolling the letter "r". "On the list of places where I wouldn't want to talk to you, your office is in the top five. Well, maybe the top ten."

Szacki asked why.

"What do you think?"

"If you say you're afraid of bugs, I'll know that years of contact with secret-police files have driven you into... a sort of paranoia." Szacki was sorry he couldn't simply define his interlocutor's mental state.

"I have no desire to explain the obvious to you," bristled Wenzel. "But out of the goodness of my heart I'll advise you that as you have reached a point in your inquiry – whatever it may be about – where you want to talk to me, I would recommend caution. No interviews at the prosecutor's office, just over a private phone, maximum discretion with regard to colleagues, superiors and the police."

Teodor Szacki suddenly felt the phone receiver get very heavy. Why? Why was this happening to him right now? Why could there not be one single ordinary element in this inquiry? A decent corpse, suspects from the underworld, normal witnesses who come to be interviewed by the prosecutor with fear in their hearts. Why this zoo? Why was each successive witness more eccentric than the one before? He had thought after the feline Dr Jeremiasz Wróbel nothing could surprise him, but here if you please: first a crazy denouncer of collaborators and now a nutcase seized with persecution mania.

"Hello? Are you there?"

"Yes, sorry, I've had a tough day today. I'm very tired, I'm sorry," he said, to say something.

"Has someone already been asking questions about you?"

"Sorry?"

"Has someone pestered your family or friends, asking about you, on some trivial pretext? From the police, perhaps, the Internal Security Agency or the Office for State Protection? So has anything like that happened?"

Szacki denied it.

"Then maybe it's not that bad yet. But we'll see tomorrow. Be sure to drop by without fail after ten. I'll be waiting."

Szacki agreed automatically. He didn't want to argue. He wanted to read the message from Monika.

"A year ago at the seaside. It was fabulously sunny, like being in Greece. The other day I saw you liked that dress, so *voilà*: you can have it for good. And if you'd like to see some of my other clothes for real (there aren't many of them today, I admit), let's meet this afternoon in town."

IV

They met for a while in Ujazdowski Park. It was the first place that entered his head, he didn't know why. He grew up in this district, and if his childhood photos were to be believed, he first used to visit this park in a big pram, then in a pushchair, then holding his mother's hand, and finally he came here on his own with girls. The older he was, the tinier the beautiful city park became. Once it had seemed to be full of paths leading to nowhere, mysterious back alleys and undiscovered places, but now, as he entered the gate, Szacki could plainly see every nook and cranny of it.

He arrived early to have a bit of a walk. The old playground and its battered steel ladders with peeling paint had been replaced with modern toys – a rope pyramid, and a complicated adventure playground with little bridges, slides and swings. All on a foundation made of strange soft slabs, so the falls were less painful. Only the sandpit was in the same place as ever.

He remembered how every time he'd been here with his mother he'd stood hesitantly with his toys in his hand, watching the children who were already playing together. He'd start to tremble, because he knew what was going to happen next. His mother would gently push him towards the other children, saying: "Go and play with your mates. Ask if they want to make friends with you." So off he went, as if to his beheading, sure he was just about to be rejected and ridiculed. And although nothing like that ever happened, every time he passed the gate into the park with his mother he was choked by the same fear. Until later in life, when at a party, he'd go up to a group of people he didn't know, and the first sentence to appear in his mind was: "Hello, I'm Teodor – can I make friends with you?"

Someone covered his eyes.

"A penny for your thoughts, Prosecutor."

"Nothing interesting, I was just dreaming about sex with those children in the sandpit."

She laughed and removed her hands. He looked at her and felt completely defenceless. He stepped back a pace. She noticed his reaction.

"Are you afraid of me?"

"Like any femme fatale. I wanted to see how you're looking today," he lied.

"And?" she asked, standing in contrapposto. She was wearing an orange shirt with the sleeves rolled up, white trousers and flip-flops. She looked like the allegory of summer. Her freshness and energy were quite unbearable, and Szacki thought he should run away, or else he wouldn't be capable of resisting them and would turn the life he'd toiled away at building all these years into a heap of steaming rubble.

"Extraordinary," he said, sincerely at last. "Perhaps even too extraordinary for me."

They walked, chatting about unimportant things. Szacki got pleasure from listening to her voice, so he encouraged her to talk as much as possible. He teased her a little with his big-city superiority when he found out she was born in the town of Pabianice. She told him about her family, that her father had died recently, about her younger brother, her older childless sister stuck in a toxic relationship, and her mother, who in her old age had decided to go back to Pabianice. Her stories kept breaking off and lacked any conclusion, so Szacki couldn't always keep up with them, but it didn't bother him.

They walked around the pond, where some children were throwing balls of bread at some indifferent overfed ducks, hopped across the stepping stones in the fake stream, the source of which was a rusty metal pipe – all too visible – and reached a small hillock crowned with an undefined something. It was a modern sculpture, a bit like a Vienna doughnut but without the wrinkles. It was covered in declarations of love, and Szacki remembered how once he had carved his own initials here, and those of his "sweetheart" in year eight at primary school.

He leaned against the statue and she sat in its hollow. Below, the Łazienkowska Highway roared by in its gully, on the other side they had Ujazdowski Castle, and on the left swaggered – what else could it do – the church crossed with a fortress, where a few days ago he had been kneeling beside the body of Henryk Telak.

They didn't say anything, but he knew that if he didn't kiss her now – despite all later explanations and attempts to rationalize – he would never cease to regret it. So for fear of being ridiculed, he leaned over and kissed her awkwardly. She had narrower, harder lips than Weronika, she didn't open her mouth as far and generally wasn't a champion kisser. Either she stood without moving, or she swivelled her head and stuck her tongue in his mouth abruptly. He almost snorted with laughter. She tasted great – a bit like cigarettes, a bit like mango, a bit like watermelon.

She quickly pulled away.

"I'm sorry," she said.

"What's that?"

"I know you've got a family. I know you're going to break my heart. I know I shouldn't, but I couldn't stop myself. I'm sorry."

He thought she was right. He wanted to say it wasn't true, but he couldn't. At least that was that.

"Come on," she said more cheerfully, and grabbed his hand. "You can see me to the bus stop."

They went down the hillock – once he had thought it so big – and walked along a path past Finnish cottages standing behind the fence, proof of the fact that stopgaps last longest. At first they didn't talk, but suddenly she pinched his side hard. He was afraid it would leave a mark.

"Hey, Mr Prosecutor, we've just been kissing in a romantic setting, no need to be so glum, eh? I liked it – what about you?"

"It was fantastic," he lied.

"I'll tell you more: I really did like it. I could even get to love it, though till now I've always thought kissing was just the boring bit before sex," she laughed loudly. It sounded fake. "I shouldn't tell you, but as we've almost become lovers now, maybe I can." More laughter. "Looks like you're going to be promoted soon."

"What makes you think that?" he asked, meaning the bit about becoming lovers.

"The Internal Security Agency was asking me about you today. Anyway, they must have been checking up on you for some time if they know we're seeing each other. The cretins, they asked such stupid things I almost died laughing. I don't know what significance it can have for state security, but…"

He wasn't listening. Could it be possible that Wenzel was right? Had he touched on untouchable matters? But it was nonsense, just a coincidence. He pulled himself together and abruptly started questioning Monika about the details. She was surprised, but she answered. Soon he knew there were two of them, they were quite young – under thirty – dressed like the FBI agents in TV serials. They had showed her their identity cards. Matter-of-fact, they had asked short, precise questions. Some of them, for example whether he squandered money, whether he talked about the criminal underworld, seemed justified. Others, about his political views, habits and addictions, less so. In spite of himself he felt more and more unnerved. He couldn't calm down. If they'd found her, they could even more easily get to his family.

Romance had suddenly evaporated from his mind. They had already left the park – Monika increasingly surprised by his importunate questions – when he remembered this was a date. He suggested she should weigh herself on the antique scale at the entrance.

It was an entertainment – one of his favourites as a child. First the old man in charge of the scale measured his height, then sat him in the seat, fiddled with various weights for a while, until finally he gave a mighty pull on a worn-out lever and handed him a small card, on which was stamped – just stamped, with no ink – the date and his weight. Funny, he'd had so many of those little cards and they'd all got lost somewhere. Or maybe they'd been kept at his parents' house?

"You're joking," she said indignantly. "So you can make sure how small I am, and how heavy too? There's no way."

He laughed, but he felt sorry.

V

At home, he had fabulous sex again. The more often he saw Monika, the more he fantasized about her, the better he got on with Weronika. He had no idea why that was happening.

He lay beside his sleeping wife and thought things through.

Firstly, he shouldn't accept that it had actually been the Internal Security Agency that had questioned Monika, but find out from Wenzel who was after him and why. Check it himself at the Internal Security Agency and ultimately submit a crime report. He wasn't too keen on this last idea, because of Weronika. There were sure to be some leaks as usual, and his wife might find out about his affair – quasi-affair for now – from the papers.

Secondly, was Kamil Sosnowski, the mysterious corpse from the late 1980s, of whom all trace had vanished, his missing person? The person Jeremiasz Wróbel had told him to find? The phantom whom Henryk Telak had been staring at so fearfully throughout the therapy? He had no idea what it could mean. From the theory of Constellation Therapy it emerged that the missing person should be a woman, Telak's first great love – he'd never come to terms with losing her. And he felt guilty about her death. Then his sense of guilt and loss were the reason why his daughter – identifying with the dead woman and at the same time wanting to relieve her father's suffering – had committed suicide. And now? It was hard even to make any guesses, as all he knew about Sosnowski was that he had been murdered during a break-in. Nothing more. Could Telak have been the murderer, one of the burglars? Extremely doubtful. Highly improbable. Questions, questions, nothing but questions.

Thirdly, was he in love with that girl with the small breasts? Maybe not. But if not, why couldn't he get her out of his head? Why was she his last thought before sleeping and his first on waking? He snorted with laughter. Christ Almighty, like something out of an old-fashioned romantic novel! Either every love affair was like bad emotional scribbling, or he was only capable of experiencing love in a juvenile way. Not surprising, considering the last time he'd fallen in love had in fact been as a juvenile, with his present wife. Maybe it was time to fall in love as a man? The idea occurred to him that perhaps he should test out this new sort of falling in love on his wife, but he quickly dropped it. The world was so big. And you only had one life.

So he went to have a pee before sleep, carefully picking up his mobile from the bedside table. Lately he'd always kept it on silent at home, fearing the question: "Who is it this time?" – and his own lies.

The message was short: "What have you done to me? I'm about to go crazy. M." He sent a safe answer: "Me? Just you stop putting drugs in my coffee", and went happily to bed.

He cuddled up to Weronika and instantly fell asleep.

10

Wednesday, 15th June 2005

The Japanese have built a machine that will drill through the earth's crust. The Spanish have arrested sixteen people on suspicion of Islamic terrorism. The Dutch have set fire to a mosque. "I'm impressed by the development of events both within Poland and concerning Poland, and the highly varied arguments that are reaching me," Włodzimierz Cimoszewicz tells the Polish Press Agency; he isn't excluding the idea that he will in fact compete in the presidential elections. In her turn, Government Plenipotentiary for Male and Female Equality Magdalena Środa is not impressed by the Polish textbooks in which Mummy flies about with a duster and does the cooking, while Daddy is a businessman graciously coming home for dinner. She announces a feminist crusade. And Warsaw's mayor, Lech Kaczyński, who recently argued that sexual orientation cannot be the subject of a public demonstration, agrees with the nationalist group All-Polish Youth's homophobic crusade, the "Normality Parade". After being the stronger team for 120 minutes at Grodzisk Wielkopolski, Legia only manage a draw with Groclin 1—1, and then in lamentable style lose on penalties the chance to get through to the Polish Cup final. In Warsaw it is either sunny and almost thirty degrees, or the sky is so dark that the street lamps come on, and there are violent storms. A thirty-five-year-old woman is killed by a bolt of lightning.

I

He scowled as he parked the Citroën by the pharmacy on the corner of Żeromski and Makuszyński Streets in the Bielany district. The curbs in this city were too high even for the hydraulic suspension of his big French cruiser. He soon found the low building where Wenzel lived and ran up to the second floor. Before pressing the bell next to the surprisingly armour-plated door, he crossed his fingers and glanced upwards. If he didn't get anything this time that would let him solve the Telak case, that was the end of it.

Karol Wenzel opened the door, at once surprising him in two ways: behind the door solid bars had been fitted, providing another barrier between the flat and the corridor, and Wenzel himself looked like the last person you would suspect of being employed at the Institute for National Remembrance. He looked more like a manager at a thriving advertising agency. He was quite small, probably not much taller, if at all, than Tom Cruise, but there was nothing else to fault him. Barefoot, dressed in shorts and a white polo shirt, he looked as if he consisted only and exclusively of muscles. Not in an exaggerated way, like a bodybuilder, but like someone who spends every spare moment doing sports. He was tanned and clean-shaven, with thick black hair cut short. He must have been Szacki's age, but alongside the historian the prosecutor looked like his uncle.

"Aren't you going to ask if anyone followed me?" asked Szacki more cuttingly than he'd intended, thinking at the same time that if he stood on his toes, Wenzel could pass under his arm.

"They know where I live," replied Wenzel curtly.

Every detail of the interior seemed to shout: here lives a bachelor. The whole flat couldn't have been more than a hundred square feet, and must once have consisted of a main room and a kitchen. Now the rooms were joined into one. Two windows looked onto the same western side. Between them another one had been painted on the wall, with mountains beyond it. Szacki wasn't sure, but it may have been the ridge of the High Tatra Mountains with the peaks of Kozi Wierch and Zamarła Turnia, seen from the direction of Gąsienicowy Tarn. He hadn't admired that view for ages. Life was passing by, and all he ever knew was work, wife, work, child, wife, work. But that was going to change. It was already changing.

One entire wall of the flat was taken up by shelves full of books and files – this alone bore witness to the resident's profession. The rest of it – a desk combined with a folding sofa, a TV, computer, hi-fi, speakers in each corner, posters from all the *Star Wars* films on the walls and a designer espresso machine in pride of place in the kitchen – were toys for a big boy who lives alone.

"Want a coffee, Teo?" asked Wenzel, pointing at the espresso machine.

Szacki said yes. He thought his host could at least for the sake of formality ask before calling him by his first name, even though they were more or less contemporaries working in the same profession. As Wenzel was fussing over the espresso machine, Szacki wondered if he should start by telling the case history, or by saying that they'd already found him. He chose the first option.

He gave a precise account of the therapy, described the potential killers: Rudzki, Jarczyk, Kaim and Kwiatkowska, and summarized his conversation with Wróbel, who had told him to look for the person missing. He talked about Telak's lucky numbers, about the newspapers and the strange murder of Kamil Sosnowski, all trace of which had vanished in the police archives. About his conversation with Captain Mamcarz and the file cleaned out by Department "D", which Podolski didn't want to talk about.

Wenzel was quiet for a while, then burst into noisy laughter.

"As far as I can see you already know the whole story," he said. "You just have to put the facts together."

"Please, leave out the riddles."

"This Sosnowski, in the bath with his throat cut and his hands and legs tied together. You must know who else was tied up like that in the 1980s, only a few years earlier. Everyone knows."

"Oh God."

"Close."

"Father Jerzy Popiełuszko."

"Exactly." The shocking murder of the priest by the secret police was world famous.

"Are you trying to say Sosnowski was murdered by the secret police? Why?"

Wenzel shrugged.

"Either to subdue his parents, or they made a mistake. Things like that did happen. I'll tell you briefly whose corns you've trodden on, so you know what we're talking about. I'm sure you've got a rough idea of their operational chart – Department III for the opposition, Department IV for the Church, subject surveillance, moulding personal sources of information, central card index, filing system and so on?"

Szacki said he did.

"People think it was a sort of militia bureaucracy, and that all those SB-men, like the lieutenant played by Kowalewski in *Monitored Conversations* were just dim-witted functionaries who gathered non-essential information. Incidentally, I can't stand Bareja. And I don't like Chęciński for *Conversations* either," he said, referring to the film-makers who had sent up the Communist era.

"Because?"

"Because it's all lies. Lies that are nice and convenient for those sons of bitches. And that will continue to be for all time. Lies that make people believe Communist Poland was this wacky country, where life may not have been easy, but at least it was funny and we all had a jolly good time."

"Wasn't it a bit like that?" Personally Szacki adored Bareja's films.

The historian sighed and looked at him as if planning to throw him out.

"Ask Kamil Sosnowski. Do you really think he was the only victim? Why doesn't anyone bloody well want to understand what the People's Republic of Poland was really like? It was a totalitarian system relying on the repression and persecution of its citizens, using all sorts of means, where those with the most to say – however pathetic it sounded – belonged to the apparatus of terror, in other words the omnipresent services, keeping an eye on almost everybody and ready to react at any moment. Fuck it all," – Wenzel was plainly furious – "can't you see that they want you to keep believing in films like *Teddy Bear* and *Brunet Will Call*? It's not surprising. There's nothing there about prisons, accidents and disappearances. There's no Division III, no blackmail or traitors. There's no Department 'D'."

"I'm sorry," said Szacki humbly. "I was seventeen in 1989."

"And I was eighteen. So what? Does that let you off knowing history? Allow you to reduce your childhood and your parents' lives to a silly satire full of jokes about sausages? Congratulations. Go and buy a pound of frankfurters and put them on Jacek Kuroń's grave. Let him have a laugh." The late Solidarity leader had spent plenty of time in prison for his brave stance against the Communist regime.

"I'm extremely sorry," muttered Szacki, "but I don't work at the Institute for National Remembrance. I don't find out about secret-police crimes every day. And if I come to find out, instead of receiving information I get fucked. If you want me to leave, just tell me. If you don't, then explain what you know. But leave the rest of it out."

Wenzel frowned and ruffled his hair.

"'D', or disinformation and disintegration. It was the most well-camouflaged structure within the Ministry of Internal Affairs – they called themselves 'a conspiracy within a conspiracy'. It existed both centrally and regionally, as section 'D'. Those were the guys who did the dirty work. Their activities involved spreading rumours, setting the opposition against each other and slander. Blackmail, kidnapping, beating people up, also murder. I know you've never heard of it, but their existence is logical. Can you believe in an apparatus of terror that stops at just gathering reports and statements from its collaborators? Well, quite."

Teodor Szacki had never thought about it. Bah, he'd never heard of anyone who would consider it. But he had to admit it all sounded credible. He asked what the SB hitmen – who in spite of everything must surely have come into play as a last resort – could want of a young student.

"As I've already said: his parents or a mistake. What did his parents do?"

"That's strange too," muttered Szacki. "I have no idea. It was an intelligentsia family, they may have been lawyers or doctors. I haven't managed to find them yet, they've vanished. I do have some fanciful suspicions, but most probably they took the younger daughter and went abroad with her. That's the best thing they could have done in the circumstances."

"Surely. In any case you have to know that the people working for the Reds weren't cretins. An open attack, as in the case of Father Popiełuszko, meant a scandal, a trial, a storm in the West. But if someone's mother were suddenly murdered during a robbery – that's how Aniela Piesiewicz died, the mother of the Solidarity lawyer – well, accidents can happen. If someone's child went missing or had an unfortunate accident, someone's wife got killed in a fire at their flat – what bad luck. But the people who were meant to interpret the message certainly understood it. Do you know when Krzysztof Piesiewicz's mother was murdered?"

"Well?"

"On the twenty-second of July, the anniversary of the official founding of the Polish People's Republic. Do you think that's a coincidence? Some aspects of these murders – such as the way someone was tied up, or an important date – were like the Red killers' signature. When did they kill this Sosnowski of yours?"

"The seventeenth of September."

"Well, exactly – the Soviet invasion. Any more questions?"

Szacki felt his mouth go dry. He asked for a glass of water.

"Twice you've repeated that it couldn't be a coincidence. Did that really used to happen?"

"Yes. Unfortunately. Don't forget, the officers didn't go 'on the job'. Sometimes common criminals were hired through various intermediaries so they wouldn't dirty their own hands. And a thug's a thug. He could have read the address wrong, or got the flats mixed up, or the officers identified the case wrongly and sent him where they shouldn't. We have documented examples of such cases. Shocking. All the more shocking considering the fact that the people fighting, and their families too, knew they were taking a risk. And the others had nothing to do with it – they just led nice, peaceful lives. But it also means that in the totalitarian era no one could live in peace. And that abandoning the fight, sticking your head in the sand did not justify or protect you."

Teodor Szacki was mentally arranging the information he had gained. He could suppose Sosnowski had been murdered by the SB. Maybe because of his parents' activities, which he had no idea about. The date of his murder was lucky for Telak. Why? Was he somehow mixed up in the murder? Or maybe he had profited from that death? The prosecutor asked Wenzel about that.

"Where did this Telak work?"

"He was the director of a printing firm with the musical name of Polgrafex. Quite a prosperous company – we found out he put aside a large sum and was insured for not much less."

Wenzel started to laugh.

"Do you know who owns Polgrafex?"

Szacki said no.

"Polish Gambling Enterprises. They may be known to you for having a virtual monopoly on running casinos in Poland. Or for the fact that no prosecutor or tax inspector is capable of getting at their arses. Or for the fact that they're riddled with former functionaries. If you've been wondering whether Telak was mixed up in the Communist secret services, you can stop. He must have been. The question is, was he also mixed up in the boy's murder. And if that's why he's now been murdered. But I can't help you there. I can try to check if he was an SB agent in the 1980s, but if he worked in 'D' I'm sure it'll all have been beautifully cleaned up."

"Destroyed?"

"You're joking – things like that are never destroyed. They're lying in a safe in some villa in Konstancin." The smart suburb had a reputation as home to the richest profiteers from the old regime.

Szacki asked if he could smoke. He could, but outside. He went onto a narrow balcony. It was muggy and there was absolutely no wind, so everything seemed sticky. The sky was filling with inky clouds, and he hoped there would be a proper storm at last. Everyone was longing for it. He felt calm now. With every thought, the next piece jumped into place, and two colours were already complete in his Rubik's cube. Truth to tell, lots of the joined-together pieces were his assumptions, not circumstantial evidence, not to mention hard proof and facts, but even so he felt as if this case wasn't going to be shelved, marked "perpetrator unknown". There was something else he had to ask Wenzel.

"They've been asking about me already," he said when he returned to the sofa.

Wenzel smacked his lips.

"That was foreseeable. I think they'll have had their eye on you ever since they found out you'd be conducting the inquiry. Now they want to get close, so they can strike like lightning if anything happens."

"How much do they know?"

"Best to suppose they know everything. Even if you're wrong, it's insignificant."

Szacki nodded. Christ Almighty, he still couldn't believe it was really happening.

"Who are 'they'?" he asked.

"Good question. I know a lot about them, but it's still not much. Have you read *The Odessa File* by Frederick Forsyth?"

He said yes.

"So you know that 'Odessa' was a society of former SS officers, who after the war set up a secret organization in support of their former comrades-in-arms. Money, jobs, business, help with hiding, laying false trails, new identities, sometimes rubbing out people who guessed too much. Or people who were too keen on exposing the truth. And although I know many people might find this analogy dramatic, we've got our own, let's call it 'OdeSB' too. Maybe even far better functioning than 'Odessa'. Our officers didn't have to run away to Argentina, they've never really been hunted, and various timid inquiries have been nipped in the bud. We didn't even manage to lock up the people who gave the orders for Popiełuszko's murder, not to mention the hundreds – who knows, if not thousands – of lesser cases. Just think: a superbly organized network, lots of information including dirt on almost everyone, files pulled out at the right moment, big money – both from the pre-war past and from the jump to state ownership when the Communists took over, as well as sixteen years of successfully run business activity since 1989. You know what word is used to define that sort of organization."

"Mafia."

"Exactly. Probably the only one that can compare with the best Italian models. And that is your 'they'. So if you're thinking of getting at them in any way, back off right now. Think about it in the morning, and in the evening you'll be crying over your daughter's body. As you won't be able to solve your case without that, put it on the shelf. Life's too short."

"What about you?"

"I'm one of a few people who deal with SB crimes; in fact even within that circle they think I'm a crazy fucking SB-hunter. No one supports me and my research is ignored. I'm not surprised. The Institute for National Remembrance is number one on the list of organizations infiltrated by 'OdeSB'. Probably even more than – with all respect – the Prosecution Service. Of course, they know about everything I do, but they don't regard me as a threat. Besides, I'm terminally ill – although it's hard to see it now – I've got another two years, not more. I know a lot, but I realize I won't publish it in my lifetime. Maybe one day, when they've all died out, some historian will make use of what I've put together."

"You're exaggerating," said Szacki. "This isn't Sicily. Surely we're talking about a few fellows who rent an office under some cover in Warsaw and play at big, scary secret policemen there because they've got a few files out of the index. I'm going to do my job."

Wenzel winced.

"Exaggerating? Correct me if I'm wrong, but did some special 'C-bomb' go off in 1989 that made all those fucking bastard Commie apparatchiks, thugs on Soviet leashes, SB agents, personal sources of information, secret collaborators and all that totalitarian rabble suddenly vanish into thin air? I'll tell you something: they'll bribe you or frighten you. Maybe even today, as soon as they find out you've been talking to me. Just in case."

"You don't know me."

"I know the guys who've been here before you. All just as invincible. They all said I didn't know them. I have never heard of any them or the cases they were conducting again. I don't bear any grudges. It's just life – when you've got a lot to gain or a lot to lose personally, it's easy to change your mind."

II

At work he started by making an appointment with Dr Jeremiasz Wróbel for the next day. A crazy idea had occurred to him for a trial experiment, but to conduct it, first he'd have to work out the details with the doctor. It was funny, but Wróbel, who had irritated him so much with his superior air and his schoolboy jokes during their conversation, had gone down in his memory as a likeable, trustworthy man. He'd be happy to meet him again.

Then he called Kuzniecow. For once the policeman picked up the phone, but he was as down in the mouth as usual.

"In theory a little, in practice a zero so big you could fit the entire turnover of Mayor Piskorski's team inside in ten-zloty notes," he replied, when asked about progress in his research into Telak's past. The former mayor was notorious for his extravagant use of the city budget. "We found his pals from school, who only remembered that he was there. We found his pals from college, who remembered just the same. We found his pals from the Warsaw Graphics Company, where he ended up after college. Most of them didn't remember him at all, just one foreman recalled that he was a quick learner and wanted to experiment with new technologies. Which in those days probably meant ink-jet printers, I've really got no idea."

"Drop Telak," said Szacki after a moment's hesitation. "We won't find anything there. It looks as if we've been digging in the past of people we shouldn't."

"Excellent." Oleg didn't hide his resentment. "But if you want us to look for someone else's high-school pals now, find yourself another district police station for the job or ask City Police HQ to help you."

"Don't worry. It's just small things. And they might be the last check-ups in this inquiry. Listen" – he broke off and looked around the room; he was mindful of Podolski's and Wenzel's stories – "or rather don't, because this isn't a conversation for the phone. We have to talk in person."

"OK, I've got to go out for a bit anyway, I can drop in at Krucza Street."

"No, that's not a good idea. Let's meet on the steps outside the Ministry of Agriculture. In fifteen minutes."

Kuzniecow sighed theatrically, whispered "OK" in a depressed tone and hung up.

Szacki spent the next quarter of an hour noting down what Wenzel had told him and drawing up his own hypotheses. He wondered what exactly he wanted from Kuzniecow and how much he should actually tell him. Was he thinking like a paranoiac already? It looked like it. Of course he'd tell him everything and together they'd wonder how to proceed. After all, that's what they always did. He tore a page from his notebook and divided it in two. On one half he wrote out the names of the people featured in the case, and on the other code words corresponding to people connected with the 1987 murder. Could they be linked in some way? Apart from most probably Telak, were there any common elements? Now he was convinced there was at least one. But he didn't rule out the idea that this was a false trail. Or that the person linking the two stories would not be the one he was now thinking about. Fortunately he had an idea how to find out.

As usual, he was halfway out of the door when the phone rang.

"Is that Prosecutor Teodor Szacki?" asked an older man in a kindly tone. Szacki didn't recognize the voice.

"Speaking. Who's that?"

"I'm an old friend of Henryk Telak – we used to work together for the same firm. I think we should have a chat. I'll be waiting for you in half an hour at the Italian restaurant on Żurawia Street, the one between Krucza and Bracka Streets. I hope you haven't eaten yet – it would be my pleasure to invite you for lunch."

Wenzel was right. Today already.

III

He ordered water and waited. He felt like a cup of coffee, but he'd already drunk two and that day the pressure – both atmospheric and otherwise – was high. Even so he wouldn't deny himself a small espresso after the meal, so drinking extra coffee now would have been foolish. He knew that, but even so he was suffering. Funny how a minor habit can change into an obsession.

Prosecutor Teodor Szacki arrived punctually. In a suit the colour of diluted silver, standing straight, self-confident. Straight away, without looking around the room he came up to his table and sat down on the other side. He didn't offer him his hand. He'd have made a good officer. The prosecutor did not speak, and he was silent too. Finally he decided to break the silence – he didn't have quite enough time to play staring games all day.

"I don't know if you're familiar with this place, but a visit to the chef is more effective than waiting for the menu. You can take a look at what he's doing, have a chat and make your choice. And above all assemble your own salad."

Szacki nodded. They stood up. He – yet another habit that had changed into an obsession – took a bit of rocket and mozzarella, the prosecutor chose grilled artichokes and aubergine, romaine lettuce, and a few sun-dried tomatoes. For the main course – still without speaking to each other – they chose tortellini with ricotta and mushrooms and cannelloni stuffed with spinach in Gorgonzola sauce. Maybe only in Krakowska Avenue was the pasta better than here.

"Are you going to try and buy me, or frighten me?" asked Szacki once they were back at the table.

First point to the prosecutor. If he'd spent such a long time saying nothing because he was wondering how to open the conversation, it was worth it. He hadn't expected a beginning like that. Now he'd have to pull back a bit, and that immediately put him in the worse position. The rocket seemed to taste more bitter than usual.

"I see you like to dress smartly," he said, pointing to his suit.

"I prefer the word 'elegantly'."

He smiled.

"Elegance starts at ten thousand. You are smart."

"So it's the bribe. To tell the truth, for some time I've been curious to know how much you were going to offer me. So please spare yourself the introductions and name your price. We'll see where we stand before they've brought the pasta."

A second point. Either he was playing with him, or he really meant it about the money. Could it be quite so simple? He already knew so much about Prosecutor Szacki that he'd forgotten he was a badly paid civil servant, just as greedy for cash as all the rest. He felt disappointed, but indeed, they could get the whole matter settled before the pasta. He glanced at a man sitting a few tables away. The man nodded, letting him know the prosecutor wasn't carrying a bug or any other recording device.

"Five hundred thousand. For fifty you can take your family

on a round-the-world trip. Or maybe you'd prefer to go with your lover – in fact I don't know how your affair will develop following yesterday's tender kiss. For the rest you can buy your daughter a small flat that can gain in value while it waits for her."

Szacki wiped his mouth on his napkin.

"Are you going to knock something off that sum for the financial advice?" he jibed. "Or does your donation come with conditions about how I'm allowed to spend the money?"

A third point. He had said too much and got a slap on the wrist. High time to take control of the conversation.

"Five hundred thousand, and of course we'll help you to substantiate the income on paper. It's a serious offer, so please spare yourself the little jokes."

"I'll give you my answer a week on Thursday."

Mistake.

"No, you'll give me your answer now. This is not a conversation about a job, but the offer of an enormous bribe. You must make your decision without consulting your friends, wife, lover, parents or whoever else there is. You have until, let's say, the end of our farewell espresso."

Szacki nodded. The waiter brought the pasta and they got on with eating. They ordered another glass of water each; despite the air conditioning their shirts were sticking to their backs. The sky was black, and somewhere in the distance there was thunder and lightning, though still not a drop of rain had fallen.

"And if I don't?"

"I'll be sorry. Mainly because you're an excellent prosecutor and apparently a very likeable fellow, but you have accidentally touched upon a world you shouldn't touch. I think you'd find the money useful, it'd make life easier. In any case, let's look the truth in the eye – this case is going to end up on the shelf anyway."

"In which case why don't you just wait it out in peace?"

"To put it mildly, my priority is my own peace and that of my comrades. We do not feel threatened, please don't flatter yourself. We're just afraid that if you unwittingly stir things up, it'll cost us more bother, more thousands, more deeds that – despite popular opinion – we have always regarded as a necessary evil."

"So there is a threat. How shoddy."

"I realize that better than you, please believe me. I respect you too greatly to tell you what we know about your family, friends, acquaintances, work colleagues, witnesses, suspects and so on. I just wouldn't want you to get any mistaken belief about our weakness. Because guided by this belief, you might do something that couldn't be called off, couldn't be talked over at a table in a nice restaurant."

Teodor Szacki didn't answer; without a word he finished his course, and then asked:

"Aren't you afraid I'm recording this conversation?"

He almost spat a delicious piece of tortellini back onto his plate. He'd been expecting just about anything, but not such puppy-dog impertinence, like something from a spy film made by a group of primary-school amateurs. He felt embarrassed by the need to answer.

"I know you're not recording it. That's obvious. The question is whether or not I am recording this conversation. Whether my colleague at the City Police Headquarters forensics lab won't edit it so perfectly that his other colleague who's going to analyse it on the instructions of the Regional Prosecutor won't recognize that it's a montage. And your colleagues on Krakowskie Przedmieście will rack their brains wondering how you could have had the cheek to try and extort a half-million bribe."

"That's a bluff."

"In that case please inspect me."

"Another bluff."

He sighed and pushed away his empty plate. The sauce was so good he felt like wiping the plate with his fingers. Sheer poetry. He wondered if it wasn't time for a show of strength. The waiter came up, from whom he ordered two small black coffees and a helping of tiramisu. Szacki didn't want dessert. Another mistake; this way he showed he was afraid. In other words that they'd only have to squeeze him a bit more, and it'd all be over.

He looked around. Despite it being lunchtime, the restaurant was fairly empty; most of the customers were at tables outside, almost invisible from here. In their part of the room there were two businessmen in expensive but ugly suits, talking about something they could see on a laptop screen; a couple of thirty-year-olds having pizza, probably foreigners – when they raised their voices he recognized some English phrases; a chap on his own in a linen shirt, completely absorbed in reading the paper.

The waiter brought the coffee. He sprinkled two teaspoons of cane sugar into the little cup and stirred it thoroughly. The result was a syrupy drink the consistency of fudge that's been left in a car on a very hot day. He took a small sip.

"A bluff, you say. Please listen carefully. Right now I could take out the gun I have on me and shoot you. Just like that. There would be a bit of a fuss about it, it would cause a bit of confusion – something in the press, a well-publicized inquiry. They'd say it was the Mafia, settling scores, that you'd trodden on someone's corns. It'd turn out you weren't as squeaky clean as everybody thought. A strange recording would turn up. Finally, upstairs they'd come to the conclusion that it may be better not to dig around in all that. Of course I would never do anything like that – it would be extreme stupidity. But in theory I could."

Szacki drank his coffee in one gulp, took the napkin off his knees and laid it on the edge of the table.

"That's the most idiotic bluff I've ever heard in my life," he said wearily. "I'm sorry you're round the fucking twist. If you like I'll be glad to help you find a specialist – I've been talking to some psychologists lately. In any case, I've got to fly. Thank you for lunch, I hope we never meet again."

Teodor Szacki pushed back his chair.

From the holster under his arm he took a small pistol with a built-in silencer, and put it to Szacki's heart.

"Sit down," he whispered.

Szacki went pale, but apart from that he kept his cool. He slowly moved his chair towards the table.

"I don't know how mad you are," he said calmly. "But maybe not mad enough to rub me out in front of witnesses."

"And what," said the man, smiling gently, "if there aren't any witnesses here? What if there's no one here but my people?"

As if to order, the foreign couple, the guy in the linen shirt and the two businessmen raised their heads and waved merrily at Szacki. The prosecutor looked round at the bar. The waiter was waving at him just like the rest.

He released the safety catch and pressed the gun hard into the prosecutor's chest. He knew it would leave a mark on his white shirt and a smell of grease. Good, let him remember.

"Do you have any other questions? Do you want to tell me I'm bluffing again? Or maybe stress how badly fucked-up I am?"

"No," replied Szacki.

"Excellent," he said, put the pistol in its holster and stood up. "I'm not expecting a declaration. I know that would be humiliating for you. But I believe this was our final conversation."

He left, signalling to the man in the linen shirt to settle the bill. As he walked to the car, the wind began to blow hard and large drops fell on the dusty city, heralding a cloudburst. Lightning struck very near by.

IV

He was wet with sweat and rain as he knelt down and vomited into the toilet at the Warsaw City Centre District Prosecutor's Office. He couldn't stop the convulsions. He'd already thrown up the coffee, cannelloni and grilled artichokes, his breakfast too; stinging bile was pouring from his throat, and he couldn't stop the convulsions. His head was spinning and he was seeing stars. Finally he managed to restrain his stomach. He took off his puke-stained tie and threw it in the waste bin next to the urinals. A few more deep breaths. He stood up on shaky legs, went back to his room and locked the door. He had to think.

He picked up the receiver to call Oleg, but replaced it without dialling the number. Firstly, he couldn't tell anyone about this. No one. The conversation in the Italian eatery had never taken place, there had never been an "OdeSB", no one had ever wiped the tip of a barrel against his shirt, on which he could still see a faint brown mark. He was still going to work out how to get those bloody bastards in the arse, he was still going to rip them to shreds, but not a word to anyone for now. Anyone who came in contact with him was now in danger. Whoever found out something might suffer an unfortunate accident. A word too much could mean his loved ones would be in danger every time they stepped into the road even when the pedestrian light was green. Weronika, Helka, Monika too. Indeed, Monika – he'd have to end this embarrassing affair as soon as possible to take the blackmail tool out of their hands.

He called her. He said he'd like to meet briefly. He adopted his most official tone. She laughed, saying she felt about to be accused of genocide. He didn't pick up this lead. It turned out she wasn't in the city, but at home, writing an article, and she wasn't going anywhere until she'd finished.

"Maybe I'll drop in for coffee," he suggested, not believing he'd do it. Of all possible ways to break off their relationship this one – dropping in for coffee – was undoubtedly the worst.

Of course she was delighted. How could it be otherwise? He asked for the address and couldn't help snorting with laughter when she told him the name of the street.

"What are you laughing at?"

"Andersen? Anyone can tell you're not from Warsaw instantly."

"How?"

"Because you said you live in Żoliborz."

"All right, if you like, it's in Bielany."

"Bielany? Girl, Andersen Street is in the provinces, it's the Chomiczówka flat blocks."

"Administratively it's the Bielany ward. And I have to tell you you're not being very nice."

"What if I bring you a packet of coffee?"

"I might forgive you. I'll think about it."

It was coming up to six. He was stuck in the traffic at Bankowy Square, listening to the radio. The wipers were on full, lightning was striking in the very centre of town, and it felt as if every second flash was hitting the car's antenna. There was a small bag of cakes sitting on the passenger seat. He had recently vomited, and now he felt as if he could eat them all and put away a plate of pork knuckles too. Next to the cakes there was some mint-flavoured mouthwash he'd bought on his way to the car. He'd used it once at the car park, opened the door and spat it onto the wet tarmac. The people at the bus stop had given him a surprised look.

Six o'clock. He turned up the radio and switched from Antyradio to the ZET channel to listen to the news.

"We're starting with a tragedy in Warsaw," said the presenter cheerily, and Szacki wondered if ZET paid lower taxes in return for employing handicapped people, and whether it had the status of a sheltered workplace for the disabled. "In a city-centre area surrounded by high-rise blocks and trees, lightning killed a woman who was on her way to fetch her seven-year-old daughter from playschool. Our reporter is on the spot in the North Praga district."

Teodor Szacki felt he had ceased to exist. He was nothing but hearing, despair and the hope that it wasn't her. He drove into a bus bay and switched off the engine.

"The thunderclap was immense. I've never heard anything like it in all my life," an excited old man was saying. "My wife and I were standing at the window, watching the lightning, we both love to do that. We saw the lady running along, she seemed to be hopping from tree to tree, trying not to get wetter than necessary, but even so she was soaked through." He could see this scene in his imagination. He could see Weronika, in jeans, flip-flops, a wet shirt clinging to her body, her hair dark with water, raindrops on her glasses.

"Suddenly there was thunder and lightning all at once, I thought it was the end of me, the entire courtyard lit up, I was dazzled, I don't think she even screamed. When I got my sight back, I saw her lying there."

Reporter: "That was Władysław Kowalski, who lives on Szymanowski Street. An ambulance came immediately, but unfortunately resuscitation attempts failed to save the woman. Her daughter is at present in the care of police psychologists. This is Marek Kartaszewski for Radio ZET, from the Praga district, Warsaw."

Presenter: "We'll go back to that story in the news at seven, when our guest will be a professor from the Warsaw Polytechnic who's an expert on lightning strikes. Marshal of the Sejm Włodzimierz Cimoszewicz announced today at a press conference…"

Szacki wasn't listening. For the fifth time he called Weronika's number and for the fifth time he got her voicemail. Half-conscious, he called directory enquiries, got the number for Helka's playschool on Szymanowski Street and called. It was busy. He called both numbers by turns. The first wasn't answering and the second was busy. He was just about to call Oleg, when he heard a ringing tone. He didn't know which number it was.

"Hello, Playschool."

"Good afternoon, Teodor Szacki calling. My daughter's at your school in group four. I'd like to know if my wife has already picked her up."

He was sure the woman would answer: "What? Don't you know what's happened?" He could almost hear those words, and he felt like hanging up to put off the moment when he knew for sure that his wife was lying dead on the tarmac in a Praga courtyard, he was a widower and his dearest darling daughter had lost her mother.

He imagined himself living alone with Helka, the two of them coming home to an empty flat. After something like this would the mysterious SB-man still go on threatening him? Would Monika want to meet with him? Would Helka grow fond of her? He was furious with himself for these idiotic thoughts.

"Just a moment, I'll go and check," said the playschool lady and put the phone down.

He thought she must surely have gone to fetch a policeman. She was afraid to tell him herself.

Someone picked up the receiver.

"Hi, Teo," he heard a man's voice and felt like starting to howl. Tears were streaming down his face. "Konrad Chojnacki, now North Praga, formerly City Police. We worked together a year ago on the scrap merchant case, remember?"

"Fuck it all, just tell me," he croaked.

"Tell you what?"

"The truth, dammit, and what —" He started sobbing into the phone. He couldn't gasp out another word. He wanted to hear it at last.

"My God, Teo, what's wrong? Wait, I'll get the wife."

The wife? Whose wife? What was he talking about? He heard some whispering in the background.

"Mr Szacki?" It was the same lady's voice as before. "Helka's not here any more, her mother collected her half an hour ago."

He couldn't understand a word of it.

"What about the lightning?" he asked, still crying.

"Oh yes, it's a dreadful story. Konrad told me. Dear God, when I think it could have been at our playschool, that one of our children's mothers could have been killed, it makes me want to weep. Such a tragedy. But I'll hand you back to Konrad."

Szacki hung up. He didn't want to talk to his old pal now, who had turned up in the worst place at the worst moment. He leaned his head on the steering wheel and wept for all he was worth, this time out of relief. The phone rang.

"Hello, why are you trying to get hold of me so badly? Is something wrong? We were in a shop, I didn't hear the phone."

He took a deep breath. He felt like confessing all to her, but he lied instead.

"You know, sometimes I deal with matters I can't even tell you about."

"What a job. I'd prefer not to tell you about some of my trials too."

"Unfortunately, today I've got to stay late and I can't very well explain."

"How late?"

"I don't know. I'll be at City Police Headquarters. I'll send you a text when I can."

"Well, tough, Helka will be upset. Just remember to eat something normal, and don't live on nothing but cola and chocolate bars. You'll get a fat tum, and I don't like guys with pot bellies. OK?"

He solemnly promised to eat lettuce, told her he loved her and that at the weekend he'd make it up to Helka somehow. After which he turned on the engine and sailed into the stream of cars heading for Żoliborz.

The high-rise in Chomiczówka was big and ugly – like all the blocks in Chomiczówka – but the flat was very nice, though the ceilings were low. And surprisingly big for one person, about two hundred square feet. He was holding a glass of white wine with ice and letting himself be led around. There was a book-cluttered sitting room with an antediluvian television set and a soft sofa in the leading role, and in two smaller rooms Monika had established a bedroom and a dressing room/junk room. It was evidently a rented flat – the kitchen fittings, wardrobes and bookshelves said: "Hello there, made in the 1970s when there was no Ikea yet." The hall was decorated – how else? – in pine panelling.

There were photos everywhere – stuck on the walls, pinned up, hanging in clip frames. Postcards, photos from journeys, photos from parties, photos from the papers. But most of them were personal: Monika as a child with an inflatable elephant, Monika on a camel, Monika asleep on the floor, with someone's (her own?) knickers on her head, Monika on skis, Monika by the sea, Monika naked reading a book on the grass. There was also the picture she'd sent him, in the white dress at the seaside. He saw how young and fresh she was in the photos, and felt bloody old. Like an uncle visiting his niece. What was he doing here? Earlier, still in the car, he'd taken off his jacket, undone his top shirt button and rolled up his sleeves. But compared with Monika – barefoot, in denim shorts and a shirt with a reproduction of Edward Hopper's *Nighthawks* on it, he looked like a civil servant. He smiled at this thought.

After all, he was a civil servant, so what should he look like? "I wondered whether to take half these photos down when I found out you were coming. I even started, but I gave it a rest and went shopping. Do you like pasta and spinach?"

"Why?"

"It's nearly dinner time so I thought we could eat something before coffee."

She was awfully tense. She didn't look him in the eye, her voice faltered, and the ice lumps rattled in her glass. She wouldn't stop pacing, almost hopping around him. Now she ran into the kitchen.

"Why did you want to take down the photos?" he called after her.

"I look bad in some of them. I'm too thin or too fat, or too childish, or something else isn't right. Anyway, you can see for yourself."

"I see a great-looking girl in a thousand scenes. Never mind if you've got an awful hairstyle in this one. Aren't you too young to have had an Afro?"

She came running.

"Well, exactly. I should take that one down at least."

She ran back into the kitchen. He wanted to kiss her, but he'd prefer it to happen of its own accord, like yesterday. To occur naturally. Besides, he had come to tell her it was over, hadn't he? He sighed. Better get it behind him quickly. He went into the kitchen. She took a thread of spaghetti out of the pan and tried it.

"Another minute. You can get the plates out of the cupboard over the fridge."

He put his glass on the tabletop and fetched out two deep plates with a blue border. They reminded him of the canteens at the old workers' holiday camps. The kitchen, though long, was hopelessly narrow. He turned round with the plates and for the first time that evening gazed into her eyes. She immediately looked away, but in that moment he found her beautiful. He thought how he'd like to wake up beside her, at least once.

Feeling embarrassed, he picked up his glass and went into the sitting room to poke around in the bookshelf. This whole situation seemed comical. What was he doing? He'd agreed to meet a pretty girl for coffee a few days ago, and instead of just screwing her, forgetting her and seeing to his wife, as everyone else did, he was gazing into her eyes and dreaming of breakfast together. Unbelievable.

At the thought of Weronika and Helka he felt a stab of regret. A sense of guilt? Not necessarily. More like sadness. Everything in his life had already happened. He would never be young again, he would never fall in love with the feelings of a twenty-year-old, he'd never be so deeply in love that nothing else mattered. So many emotions were always going to be repeats now. Whatever happened, he'd always be a guy – just a middle-aged one for now, then an older and older man – who's been through a lot, with an ex-wife and a daughter, with a flaw that's obvious to any woman. Maybe some woman would want him for shallow reasons, because he still looked quite good, because he was slim, had a permanent job, and you could talk to him. Maybe he'd accept someone, because in the end it was easier to live in a twosome than on your own. But would anyone ever go crazy with love for him? He doubted it. Would he? He just smiled bitterly and felt like crying. His age, his wife, his daughter – at once it all felt like a sentence, an incurable illness. A diabetic can't eat pastries; someone with high blood pressure can't run up mountains; Teodor Szacki couldn't fall in love.

She put her hands over his eyes.

"A penny for your thoughts," she whispered.

He just shook his head.

She snuggled against his back.

"It's so unfair," he said at last.

"Hey, don't go over the top," she said with artificial cheerfulness. "A little is more than nothing."

"A little doesn't interest me."

"More isn't always possible."

"Maybe never."

"Did you come here to tell me that?"

He hesitated for a moment. He felt like lying as usual. Since when had it come to him so easily?

"Yes. And it's not just to do with…" he broke off.

"Your family?"

"Yes. Something else has happened, I can't tell you the details, I've got tangled up in a murky affair, I don't want to drag you into it."

She stiffened, but didn't let go of him.

"Do you take me for a fool? Why don't you tell the truth, that you got me to fall in love with you for fun, that it was a mistake and now you've got to get back to your wife? Why all the fibbing? Next you'll be telling me you're a government agent."

"In a way that's true," he said, smiling. "And I swear I'm not lying. I'm afraid they might use you to get at me. And as for making you fall in love – believe me, it's completely different."

She snuggled up to him even closer.

"But will you stay today? You owe me that at least."

He had imagined this scene earlier in every possible way, but he hadn't envisaged this scenario. He followed her through the hall into the bedroom, and suddenly he had a terrible urge to laugh. You're waddling, he thought. You're waddling like a satyr with bandy hairy legs. You're waddling like a constantly horny bonobo chimp with a red behind. You're waddling like an old dog on the scent of a bitch. You're waddling like a middle-aged fool. Right now there's nothing human about you.

When she opened the bedroom door ahead of him and smiled flirtatiously, he had to bite the inside of his cheek hard to stop himself from bursting out laughing.

They were very gentle, exploring each other like school-children, not like mature people who had decided to go to bed together. Unbuttoning her shorts, watching her lying on the bed as she raised her buttocks to pull them off and then pulled her T-shirt with the Hopper reproduction over her head – all he felt was cold curiosity. And soon after, as he lay naked beside her and stroked her body, he ceased to feel anything.

He was horrified. He knew she was very lovely. Young. Attractive. Different. Above all, different. He had seen how men looked round at her. He had imagined every part of her body a hundred times. But now, when this body was lying in front of him, hoping for sex, he had become totally indifferent to it. He was horrified, because he had suddenly realized he wouldn't be able to perform as a man. His body didn't want her body, and was utterly indifferent to all the efforts his brain was making. His body refused to be unfaithful. And if it weren't for the thought that nothing was going to come of it, maybe it all would have gone differently. But that very worst of all the thoughts that can occur to a man was making him go stiff – unfortunately not in the key areas. He was half filled with panic, half with embarrassment. There was no room left for desire.

He wanted to vanish.

Finally she forced him to look at her. Amazingly, she smiled.

"Hey, silly boy," she said. "You know I could just lie here next to you for weeks on end and I'd be the happiest woman in the world?"

"I'm sick," he moaned in despair. "Fetch me a razor blade. I don't want to go on living."

She laughed.

"You're silly and tense as a schoolboy. Cuddle up to me and we'll sleep a few hours. I've been dreaming for days of waking up beside you. I'll never understand it."

He didn't get it. He wanted to die. She made him lie on his side, nestled her back against him and fell asleep almost instantly. Amazing, but, as he was wondering if she were already fast enough asleep for him to make his getaway, he too soon drifted off.

He woke up a few hours later, sweaty because of the sultry night. In the first instant he didn't know where he was. He felt alarmed. But only in the first instant.

It had been – well – maybe not fantastic, but decent. At the key moment he remembered the story of a school friend who, when he finally got the girl he'd been fantasizing about for years, came to school next day and, still wistful, admitted over a cigarette: "You know what? I had more fun with her when I was whacking off in the bog."

He had to bite his lip again.

The car clock showed a few minutes past five, and the sun was already quite high as he parked outside his house on the other side of the city. He quietly went inside, got undressed in the hall and shoved his underwear to the bottom of the linen basket so Weronika wouldn't smell the scent of another woman. In their sitting room cum bedroom there was a computer game lying on the table, tied with a thin ribbon – the latest part of *Splinter Cell*. And a note saying: "For my sheriff. W". He smiled bitterly.

11

Friday, 17th June 2005

The health-protection agencies in all the European Union countries are planning to withdraw food products that contain paprika, turmeric and palm oil. Carcinogenic food colourings have been banned. Research shows that Russians do not notice severe censorship in the state media. Doctors at a conference in Toruń conclude that Polish women are less sexually active than German or French women. Thirty per cent of women suffer from frigidity. The Institute for National Remembrance's team triumph in a shooting contest for security-firm employees. Extreme nationalist politician Andrzej Lepper is suggesting that Prime Minister Marek Belka, head of the National Bank Leszek Balcerowicz and Marshal of the Sejm Włodzimierz Cimoszewicz all collaborated with the SB. Meanwhile, the last mentioned is having fun with President Kwaśniewski and his wife at Lech Wałęsa's name-day party. The incumbent president gave his predecessor a bottle of red wine. In Warsaw the standard-bearers of "normality" — League of Polish Families party leader Roman Giertych, All-Polish Youth and the skinheads from the National Radical Camp — march in their parade. They shout: "Paedophiles and pederasts are Union enthusiasts." Citizens can visit the capital's museums and galleries at night, and in the metro they can hear the children of refugees announcing the names of the stations in garbled Polish. Maximum temperature — eighteen degrees; cloudy, a little rain

I

How Szacki managed to get through Thursday was a mystery to him. He had woken up – or rather been woken – with a headache and a temperature of almost thirty-nine degrees. When he had dragged himself out of bed to be sick, he had almost fainted on the way to the toilet, and had had to sit down on the floor in the hall until the black spots before his eyes had gone. He had called work to say he'd be late, taken two aspirins and gone back to bed where – he was sure of it – he hadn't fallen asleep but passed out.

He had woken up at two p.m., taken a shower and gone to the prosecutor's office. On the way up to the second floor he had had to stop every few steps to catch his breath. He told himself nothing was wrong with him, it was just his body's reaction to a concentrated dose of the emotions he usually experienced over the course of several years, not a single day. But it didn't make him feel any better.

Once at his desk, he finally switched on his mobile phone. He ignored the text messages from Monika and listened to the voicemails from Oleg, who had left several, each more furious than the last, screaming that if Szacki didn't call him back immediately he'd put out a warrant for him.

He called back and found out what he had suspected ever since his visit to Captain Mamcarz. So in theory he shouldn't have been surprised, but even so a shiver ran down his spine. Always, whenever the truth about a crime came to light, it wasn't satisfaction that he felt, just sickening sorrow. Once again it turned out a human being had not died by accident; that someone's memories and hopes had been extinguished in the brief moment it took for the sharp end of a skewer to pierce his eye and penetrate the thin layer of skull in that spot. Does the person feel anything at a moment like that? Does the consciousness last for much longer? The doctors say he died instantly. But who can really know that? What would he have felt if that SB bastard had pulled the trigger the other day?

He drove away the thought, which made his breathing go shallow again, quickly wrote out a to-do list and called Kuzniecow to prepare the necessary site for the trial experiment. Then in turn he contacted Cezary Rudzki, Euzebiusz Kaim, Hanna Kwiatkowska, Barbara Jarczyk and Jadwiga Telak. This time it went smoothly. They all answered the phone. Curious how when things aren't going well, nothing works, but when they start to fall into place, suddenly everything goes the right way. "If only that were the truth," he said aloud, nervously tapping his fingers. "If only."

He gave his boss a laconic account of what he was planning to do, without mentioning the previous day's events and without waiting for her surprise to turn into fury, then left for the appointment he had made with Jeremiasz Wróbel. He still had a few questions for the feline doctor.

He was playing for the highest stakes. If he succeeded, the inquiry would be closed by Tuesday. If not, they'd have to put it on the shelf. Of course, another way would be to track down "OdeSB", but that, unfortunately, he couldn't do.

He felt sick again.

II

But that was yesterday. Now it was coming up to eleven on Friday. He was sitting in the Citroën, parked outside the arts centre on Łazienkowska Street, trying to understand why the pump regulating the hydraulic fluid pressure in his French monster's bloodstream kept turning itself on. Whenever he switched off the radio there was a regular hiss, recurring at several-second intervals – it was truly irritating. He turned off the engine to stop hearing the nerve-jangling noise.

It was one of those wet summer days when, instead of falling from the sky, the moisture rises in the air and clings to everything. The world outside the car windows was misty and fuzzy, as raindrops ran down the glass now and then, blurring its contours even more. Teodor Szacki sighed, reached for his umbrella and very cautiously got out of the car, trying not to dirty his pale-grey trousers against the bottom edge of the door. Dodging puddles, he crossed the street, stopped outside the brick chimera of a church and – to his own surprise – crossed himself. Once upon a time, as a child, he'd had the custom acquired in the family home of making the sign of the cross every time he went past a church. In adolescence he'd started feeling ashamed of what seemed to him a blatant show of religious feeling, and he only occasionally thought of this childhood habit when he passed a Catholic shrine. Why couldn't he stop himself from doing it now? He had no idea.

He examined the ugly gloomy building from under his umbrella. Damn this bloody church, damn Henryk Telak and the murder that meant his life would never be the same again. He wanted to have the case off his hands as soon as possible, whatever the outcome. I'm getting like the others, he thought sourly. Just a little longer and I'll be sitting at my desk, staring longingly at the clock and wondering if anyone will notice if I nip off at a quarter to four.

"Documents, please," boomed Kuzniecow's voice close to his ear.

"Get lost," he growled in reply. He wasn't in the mood for jokes.

Together they went into the church annex, via the same entrance as almost two weeks earlier, when in the small religious education classroom Henryk Telak's body had been lying on the floor, and the cherry-and-grey stain on his cheek had made Szacki think of a Formula One racing car. This time the room was empty, not counting a few chairs and Father Mieczysław Paczek, whose face in the livid light of the fluorescent lamps seemed even softer than before.

Szacki chatted to the priest. Meanwhile, Kuzniecow and a technician from Wilcza Street set up a camera on a tripod and arranged some extra spotlights in the dark room, so they could record the trial experiment.

At a quarter to twelve everything was ready, and only the main characters in the drama were missing, who were due to appear at noon precisely. Father Paczek reluctantly went back to his room, and the technician reluctantly left his toys behind, not encouraged by Kuzniecow's assurances that he was better at handling electronic equipment than women.

On small ugly chairs with metal legs and brown covers the cop and the prosecutor sat next to each other in silence. Lost in thought, Teodor Szacki started laughing quietly.

"What is it?" asked Kuzniecow.

"You'll laugh, but I was thinking about what Helka will look like in fifteen years from now. Do you think she'll still look like me?"

"Fate could never be so cruel."

"Very funny. I wonder how children can be so unlike their parents."

"Maybe because first they're themselves, and only then someone's children?"

"Maybe."

III

They turned up punctually, almost simultaneously, as if they'd all come on the same bus. Jadwiga Telak was as sad as usual, in beige linen trousers, a polo neck of a similar colour and elegant shoes with heels. Her hair was tied in a plait, and for the first time during the inquiry she looked like an attractive, well-preserved forty-something of elegant, proud beauty – rather than her sister who was fifteen years older. Cezary Rudzki had fully recovered. Once again he was the king of Polish therapists – thick grey hair, white moustache, a piercing look in his clear eyes and a simpering smile encouraging you to confess, "what are you really feeling as you talk about this?" Good jeans, a sports shirt buttoned up to the neck. A dark-blue tweed jacket tightly hugged his broad shoulders. Without a word they sat down next to each other on the ugly chairs. They waited. The prosecutor could sense the atmosphere was solemn.

Hanna Kwiatkowska did not disturb it. She lacked her typical quivering, perhaps because she seemed extremely exhausted; her make-up failed to conceal the dark shadows under her eyes. Her hair was still mousy, her suit still wasn't in any way different from tens of thousands of other suits parading about the capital city, but the low neckline of her blouse and the height of her stilettos made Szacki wonder if he hadn't judged her a bit hastily, in labelling her an asexual covert nun. At the same time as Kwiatkowska, Barbara Jarczyk entered the room – once again she looked exactly the same as the first time Szacki had seen her, and may even have been wearing the same clothes. She smiled at the prosecutor, who thought she must once have been very pretty, and now – if it weren't for the mascara – she'd have deserved to be called handsome. Euzebiusz Kaim arrived last, a minute after twelve. As usual, he radiated self-confidence and class. Even the SB bastard would have regarded his outfit as elegant – not just smart. His shoes and trousers alone must have cost as much as Szacki's entire suit. His heavy white shirt with rolled-up sleeves looked as if it had come straight from Brad Pitt's wardrobe.

Once they were all sitting down, Szacki asked if anyone wanted to use the toilet. They didn't.

The prosecutor took a deep breath and started to talk.

"I have assembled you here to conduct a trial experiment that will help me and Superintendent Kuzniecow to understand better what happened in this room two weeks ago. Of course I am familiar with all your accounts, and with the theory of constellations – many thanks to Mr Rudzki for explaining it – but in spite of all that, I feel it essential to conduct an experiment of this kind. Forgive me for forcing you to come to this place again, which is sure to prompt negative feelings in you. I realize that being here must be painful, and I promise I'll do my best to make sure the whole thing takes as short a time as possible."

He recited the speech he'd prepared in advance, conscious of how wooden it sounded, but he couldn't give a damn about its style. The point was to put them off their guard, make them believe it was just about a simple repetition of the therapy from two weeks ago. He tried not to look at Oleg, who was standing in the corner of the room, absorbed in chewing his fingernails.

Rudzki stood up.

"Am I to position the patients in the same way as they were standing then?" he asked.

"There's no need," replied Szacki calmly. "I'll do it, and then I'll be better able to understand how the mechanics of it function."

"I am not convinced —" began Rudzki in a superior tone.

"But I am," the prosecutor interrupted him brutally. "This is a trial experiment being conducted by the prosecution in connection with an inquiry into a case of the most serious crime, not a lecture for first-year students. That wasn't a polite request, but information about what I'm going to do, so please let me do my job."

Szacki went a bit too far with the bluntness, but he had to put the doctor in his place at the off, otherwise he'd start questioning every move he made. And the prosecutor couldn't allow that.

The therapist shrugged and scowled disapprovingly, but shut up. Szacki went up to him, took him by the arm and positioned him in the middle of the room. With his mocking smile, Cezary Rudzki can't have suspected that the spot where he was standing – just like for all the others – was not accidental, but the result of the very long conversation Szacki had had the day before with Dr Jeremiasz Wróbel.

He took Barbara Jarczyk by the arm and arranged her next to Rudzki. Now they were standing shoulder to shoulder, facing the door. The mocking smirk had left the therapist's face, and he was staring anxiously at the prosecutor. Szacki permitted himself a glance in his direction.

Next he arranged Hanna Kwiatkowska opposite Rudzki and Jarczyk, so that she was facing them. He positioned Kaim to one side, slightly out of the line-up, and told him to look at a point more or less halfway between Kwiatkowska, and Jarczyk and Rudzki. Near this point he arranged Jadwiga Telak, who looked at him in surprise when he took her by the arm. She probably wasn't expecting to have to take part in this. But she stood politely near point X, turned to face it, far enough to the side for Kwiatkowska, Jarczyk and Rudzki to be able to see each other easily.

Rudzki was as pale as the wall. By now he must have known where Szacki was heading. But he was still hoping it was an accident, and that the prosecutor was fumbling in the dark, just hoping to chance upon something.

"Doctor Rudzki," said Szacki. "Please tell everyone what the most important question is during a constellation. Or at least one of the most important. The kind you'd ask yourself if someone showed you a line-up like this one."

In the empty room every utterance sounded unnaturally loud, on top of which it was followed by a low echo, and so the silence that fell after Szacki's question was all the more intense.

"It's hard for me to say," replied Rudzki at last, shrugging. "It looks quite random, I can't see any order. You must understand that —"

"In that case I'll tell you, as you don't want to say," Szacki cut him short again. "The question is: who's not here? Who is missing? And indeed, it now looks as if you're all staring at someone who isn't there. Instead of that person there's an empty space. But we can easily solve that problem, by putting Superintendent Kuzniecow in that place."

Szacki went up to the policeman and took him by the arm, at which he blew a gentle kiss in his direction. Szacki made himself a mental promise to murder the cop afterwards, and led him to point X, right in the middle between Kwiatkowska, and Jarczyk and Rudzki, very close to Jadwiga Telak. He positioned him so that he and Jadwiga were looking at each other. The woman gulped and motioned as if wanting to withdraw.

"Please stay in place," barked Szacki.

"Please let me see her at once," cried Jarczyk, trying to lean so that she could look at Kwiatkowska. "Please let me see her at once, do you hear me?" Her voice was quivering, and she was on the edge of tears.

"You're playing a dangerous game, Prosecutor," hissed Rudzki, at the same time putting his arm around Jarczyk. The woman huddled up to him. "You don't know what forces you're toying with. I'm glad this entire 'experiment' is being recorded, I hope you know what I have in mind as I say those words. And please hurry up."

"Yes, you really should hurry up," muttered Kuzniecow, gulping. "I don't believe in fairy tales, but if I don't move from this spot instantly, I'll faint. I feel truly awful, as if the life were leaking out of me."

Szacki nodded. Victory was close. Kuzniecow took a deep breath; opposite him Jadwiga Telak had tears pouring from her eyes. She was following Szacki's instructions and standing on the spot, but she was leaning her body in an unnatural way, trying to get as far as possible from Kuzniecow. However, she had not averted her gaze. Jarczyk was trying hard to control her sobbing in the arms of Rudzki, who was staring fearfully at the prosecutor. Now he could no longer have any doubts what Szacki was intending. Kwiatkowska had not stopped staring at Kuzniecow's broad back for a moment, and was smiling gently. Kaim stood quietly with his arms crossed on his chest.

"Well, yes, but are we now playing Mr Telak's family, with the inspector as Henryk Telak?" asked Kaim. "To tell the truth, I don't fully understand who is who."

Szacki took off his jacket and hung it over a chair. Fuck elegance, he was sweating like a pig. He took in a deep breath. This was the key moment. If they kept calm once he had said who they were playing, if they had foreseen it and knew how to behave, that was the end, and he'd have nothing left to do but bid them a polite farewell and write a decision to suspend the case. If he surprised them and they broke – one of them would leave the unwelcoming religious classroom in handcuffs.

"Superintendent Kuzniecow is indeed the key figure in this constellation," he said. "But he's not Henryk Telak. In a way, quite the opposite – he's the man who died because of Henryk Telak."

Jadwiga Telak groaned, but Szacki ignored that and went on talking.

"You," he said, pointing at Kaim, "are this man's best friend, his confidant, confessor and mainstay. You," he addressed Jarczyk and Rudzki, "are his parents. You," he quickly turned to face Kwiatkowska, "are his sister, who in dramatic circumstances discovered her brother's death. And you," he looked sadly at Mrs Telak, "are this man's greatest, truest, sincerest love, and his name was…" He pointed at her, wanting her to carry on.

"Kamil," whispered Jadwiga Telak, and tumbled to her knees, gazing adoringly into Kuzniecow's face, who also had tears running down his cheeks. "Kamil, Kamil, Kamil, my darling, how I miss you, how much I do. It was all meant to be different…"

"Show me my daughter," yelled Jarczyk. "I can't see my daughter, he can't keep my daughter hidden from my sight – he's not alive, he's been dead for so many years. I beg you, please show me my daughter, I want to see her."

Szacki moved Kuzniecow back a few paces so that he wasn't standing between Jarczyk and Kwiatkowska. Without a word, Kwiatkowska, smiling sadly throughout, followed the policeman with her gaze; Mrs Telak held an arm out towards him, as if wanting to detain him; Jarczyk calmed down, and gazed at her daughter. Only Rudzki stared with hatred at the prosecutor, standing to one side.

"I demand that you stop this immediately," he said coldly.

"I don't think in the present situation you can demand anything of me," replied Szacki calmly.

"You don't realize what this means for these women. Your experiment could leave a permanent mark on their psyches."

"My experiment?" Szacki felt his blood pressure rise abruptly, and found it hard to control himself. "My experiment? It has just turned out that for the past two weeks of the inquiry you people have been lying to the police and the prosecution. It's not my job to worry about the psyche, especially yours, but to bring people who break the law to justice. Besides, we haven't yet discovered the answer to the most important question: which of you committed the murder of Henryk Telak in this room on the night of the 4th to the 5th of June this year? And I assure you I will not stop 'my experiment' until I'm sure one of the people present is going to be led away by the police."

"We didn't want to kill him," said Hanna Kwiatkowska, speaking for the first time since entering the room.

Prosecutor Teodor Szacki slowly let the air out of his lungs.

"So what did you want to do?"

"We wanted him to realize what he'd done and commit suicide."

"Shut up, girl, you haven't a clue what you're saying!" screamed Rudzki.

"Oh, stop it, Dad. You have to know when you've lost. Can't you see they know everything? I've had enough of these endless plans, all these lies. For years and years I lived as if I were in a coma, until I finally came to terms with Kamil's death – you have no idea how much it cost me. And when at last I was starting to live normally, you appeared with your 'truth', your 'justice' and your 'compensation'. I never liked your bloody plan for revenge from the start, but you were all so convinced, so sure, so convincing." She waved her hand in a gesture of weariness. Szacki had never heard so much bitterness in anyone's voice. "And you, and Euzebiusz, and even Mum. Oh my God, when I think what we've done... Please, Dad. At least do the decent thing now. If we go any deeper into these lies, there really will be 'permanent marks' on our psyches. And believe me, they won't be caused by the prosecutor's doings."

She sat down resignedly on the floor and buried her face in her hands. Rudzki stared at her sorrowfully and silently; he looked crushed. Yet he said nothing. They were all silent. The stillness and silence were perfect; for a moment Szacki had the strange impression that he wasn't taking part in a real event, but was looking at a three-dimensional photograph. He watched Rudzki, who in his turn stared back at him with his mouth clenched shut and waited. The therapist had to start talking, though God knows how much he didn't want to. He had to, because he had no alternative. As they stood without dropping their gaze, both men were fully aware of that.

Finally Rudzki gave a deep sigh and started to talk.

"Hanna is right, we didn't want to kill him. That is, we wanted him to die, but we didn't want to kill him. It's hard to explain. Anyway, perhaps I should speak for myself – it was I who wanted him to die, and I forced the others to take part in it."

Without a word Szacki raised an eyebrow. They had all seen too many American films. Murder is not like firing wads of paper in the classroom. You can't just get up and take the blame on yourself, so your pals will be pleased and the teacher lady won't suss it out.

"How exactly was it meant to look?" he asked.

"What? I don't understand. How was the suicide meant to look?"

Szacki shook his head.

"How was it meant to look from the beginning, ever since you hit upon the idea of driving Henryk Telak to suicide. I realize such things are not prepared in a weekend."

"The hardest bit was the beginning, in other words getting close to Telak. I ordered leaflets at his company for a lecture on life after the death of a child, to catch his interest. Then I made a scene at Polgrafex saying they hadn't done things the way I wanted, which wasn't true, of course. I demanded to see the director. I succeeded in steering the conversation so that he started talking about himself. I suggested meeting at my office. He was defensive, but I persuaded him. He came. He kept coming for half a year. Do you know how much it cost me, week in, week out, to get through a whole hour with that bastard who murdered my son? To conduct his bloody 'therapy'? I sat in my chair and the whole time I kept wondering whether to just hit him with something heavy and get it over and done with. I kept imagining it non-stop. Constantly."

"I understand we can put the word 'therapy' in quotation marks," put in Szacki. "The aim of your sessions was not any kind of cure, was it?"

"Henryk was in a terrible state after those meetings," said Jadwiga Telak quietly, staring intently at Kuzniecow throughout. "I thought it was worse after every session. I told him to stop going, but he told me it had to be like that, that was how it worked, and that before an improvement the crisis always worsens."

"Did you know who Cezary Rudzki was?"

"No. Not at that point."

"And when did you find out?"

"Not long before the constellation. Cezary came to see me and introduced himself... He brought back all the ghosts from the past. Really. He told me what Henryk had done and what they wanted to do. He said they'd leave him alone if that was what I wanted."

She fell silent and chewed her lip.

"Was that what you wanted?"

She shook her head.

"You're right, the aim of the therapy was not therapy at all," said Rudzki, quickly picking up his thread, evidently in order to draw Szacki's attention away from Mrs Telak too. "At first I wanted to find out if it was definitely him who had caused me to lose my son. I had fairly complete information, but I wanted to confirm it. The bastard admitted it at the very first session. Of course he skirted around it somehow, maybe he was afraid I'd go to the police, but his confession was unambiguous. Then... Never mind the details, but my aim was to arouse the greatest possible sense of guilt in Telak for the death of his daughter, and to persuade him that if he departed too, it might save his son. Which was in fact true."

"And did you talk to him again about Kamil, about your son?"

"No. We probably could have, if I'd pressed him, but I was afraid I wouldn't be able to. I concentrated on his parents, on his present family; several times I threw something in to increase his sense of guilt. I was quietly counting on succeeding in manipulating him like that so he'd commit suicide without a constellation, but the bastard clung to life tightly. He kept asking when he'd be better. As God is my witness, those were hard moments for me.

"Finally I prepared the constellation. I spent a long time writing the scenario, various versions, depending on how Telak might behave. I analysed the session that had led to the suicide of Hellinger's patient in Leipzig dozens of times, and sought out the strongest emotions, the words that would prompt them. I had to do the whole thing as a dry run – practising that on people would have been impossible and cruel. Barbara and I came to the conclusion that it'd be easiest for that coward to swallow some pills, and that he wasn't likely to go for hanging or cutting his wrists. That's why after breaking off the therapy at the worst moment for him we offered him some pills, bloody strong ones."

"We were walking down the corridor," Jarczyk suddenly cut in, ignoring her husband's reproachful look, "I was barely alive, he was grey in the face, hunched, devastated, with his head drooping. For a moment I felt sorry for him, I wanted to give up and tell him not to lose heart. But then I remembered Kamil, my first-born child. I gathered my strength and said I was sorry about his children, and that in his place I'd prefer to die than live with it. He admitted he was thinking about that too – that in fact he was only wondering how to do it. I replied that I would take pills, and that in my case it would be easy, because I took strong sleeping pills anyway. I'd only have to take a few more. I told him it was a beautiful death. To fall asleep peacefully and simply never wake up. He took the bottle from me."

Jarczyk fell silent and glanced fearfully at her husband, who ran a hand through his grey hair – it occurred to Szacki that he did exactly the same himself when he was tired – and went on describing the sophisticated murder plan.

"I wouldn't be saying this if not for that bloody Dictaphone of his and his mania for recording everything, but as it has been revealed anyway, I must. The idea of Hanna imitating Telak's dead daughter was a bit theatrical," – Kwiatkowska gave her father a look that left no doubt that 'a bit' was not the right phrase – "but I realized it would be the straw that broke the camel's back. I knew after something like that Telak would run to the bathroom, take the pills and that would be it. Vengeance taken."

Teodor Szacki listened with outward calm. He had enough self-control not to show his disgust. Once again he felt sick. The aversion he felt for Rudzki was almost physical. What a cowardly old fool, he thought. If he wanted to get revenge, he could have shot him and buried the body, and counted on succeeding. It usually works. But not him – he had to drag his wife into it, then his daughter, making himself resemble Telak in the process, and he dragged in Kaim too. What for? To blur the responsibility? To burden them with the blame? Hell knows.

"You can congratulate yourselves," he said sarcastically. "Henryk Telak recorded a farewell letter to his wife, in which he said he was planning to commit suicide for the good of Bartek, and then he went back to his room and took the pills. The whole bottle. You almost succeeded."

Cezary Rudzki looked shocked.

"What? I don't understand… But in that case why…"

"Because immediately afterwards he changed his mind, vomited, packed and left his room. Maybe he chickened out, or maybe he was simply putting it off for a few hours to say goodbye to his family. We'll never know. Anyway, it doesn't matter. What matters is that at about one a.m. Henryk Telak finishes packing his case, puts on his coat and quietly leaves. He walks down the corridor, goes into the classroom, where only a few hours ago the therapy took place, and…" He pointed an encouraging hand at Rudzki, and felt his stomach turn, as the stain the shape of a racing car appeared before his eyes again.

The therapist had become subdued. The jacket that had hugged his proudly erect figure had suddenly become too big, his hair had gone dull, and his gaze had lost its haughty expression and wandered to one side.

"I'll tell you what happened next," he said quietly, "if you'll answer a couple of my questions first. I want to know how you know."

"Please don't make me laugh," bristled Szacki. "This is a trial experiment, not a detective novel. I'm not going to tell you exactly how the inquiry proceeded. If only because it's a laborious procedure involving hundreds of elements, not one brilliant investigator."

"You're lying, Prosecutor," said the therapist, smiling gently. "I'm not making a request, but setting a condition. Do you want to know what happened next? Then please answer my question. Or I'll start insisting I can't remember."

Szacki hesitated, but only for a short while. He knew that if they dug their heels in now, it would be impossible to prove their guilt in court. He'd even have a problem with the legal classification of their twisted revenge.

"Four elements," he said at last. "Four elements that I should have linked up much earlier. Curiously, two of them are entirely accidental, they could have appeared at any point. The first element is the constellation therapy, which for you has proved a double-edged sword. You could manipulate everyone, but not Telak."

"Who did you consult?" put in Rudzki.

"Jeremiasz Wróbel."

"He's a fine specialist, though I wouldn't invite him to give a lecture at a seminary."

Szacki didn't smile.

"Throughout the therapy Telak was stubbornly staring at someone. Who was it? I had no idea. I was misled by the principle that, if they haven't been allowed to depart, former partners are represented by the children. And that a child from the next relationship symbolizes the lost partner. I was sure Henryk Telak had a former lover whom he had lost in dramatic circumstances. I suspected that he might have felt guilty about her death. With Dr Wróbel's help I established that this was extremely likely. And that in an unconscious way Kasia Telak identified so strongly with his lost love that she followed her into death. And Bartek was heading the same way, to remove his father's guilt and fulfil his wish of joining his beloved sister. But all the police's efforts to dig into Telak's past brought no result. No trace of any lover or any great love was found. It looks as if the only woman in Henryk Telak's life was you –" he pointed at the widow. "It would have been a blind alley, if not for Henryk Telak's wallet – leaving it behind was a big mistake on your part. And this is the second element. The most interesting thing in it were the lottery coupons on which he regularly repeated the same set of figures. It meant nothing to me, until I discovered the date and time of Kasia Telak's death. Then I realized that the numbers on the coupon were a date – to be precise, the seventeenth of September 1978, or the seventeenth of September 1987, and the time was ten p.m. That same day, at that same time, on the twenty-fifth or sixteenth anniversary the girl committed suicide. I started looking through the newspapers and among many others I found information about the murder of Kamil Sosnowski. In theory, there was nothing to connect the cases, but at some point I started wondering if the missing link could be a man. Did that mean Henryk Telak was gay? Or maybe all that time I'd been focusing on the wrong half of the Telak marriage? What if the missing link in the constellation was the dead lover of Mrs Telak? Henryk's rival? His death would have been one of the luckiest moments in Telak's life. Lucky enough to use the date for his lottery numbers.

"At this stage I reckoned there was a sort of twisted meaning to it all, and the whole therapy did indeed have a causative power. Hellinger claims that a person wishing to remain faithful to a deceased partner goes after them – into death, into illness. That would make sense, except in this case Mrs Telak was replaced by her daughter. In addition, the ABC of constellations is the principle that if a woman loved some man very much in the past, she often sees him in her son. Which in turn explained Bartek's illness. Your son had a weak heart too, didn't he?"

Rudzki nodded.

"I myself can't say how it's possible," continued Szacki, "but I came to believe in a fantastic hypothesis: Henryk Telak was in some way – perhaps as directly as possible – mixed up in the death of his wife's lover in the late 1980s. During the therapy he discovers that the crime he committed led to his daughter's suicide and is connected with his son's fatal illness. In some inexplicable way, thanks to the 'knowing field', his wife senses that too. Her emotions, including hatred and a desire for revenge, are so strong that her representative in the therapy, Barbara Jarczyk, picks them up, and commits the murder. It's neat, but I didn't even have circumstantial evidence to link Telak and Sosnowski, or Mrs Telak with the victim from the past. The police were unable to locate his family, and the files from the old inquiry are missing – end of the line. Besides, something kept bothering me, all those little cracks. The mistakes you made in your art during the constellation, the pills, the recording on the Dictaphone. Too many coincidences. And here we reach the third element – my daughter."

Kuzniecow gave him an anxious glance. Pretending not to notice, Szacki went on.

"Of course, she has nothing to do with this case, she's just very like me and not at all like her mother – next to her she looks adopted. It's amazing how very dissimilar children can be from their parents. I was thinking about it one day, and I was also thinking how very different your son –" he indicated Mrs Telak again – "looks compared with you or your husband. Sometimes it's just tiny gestures, using similar phrases, a manner of intonation, things that aren't noticeable in a conscious way that bear witness to kinship. And suddenly it leaped out – I had both your interviews before my eyes." He nodded towards Kwiatkowska and Jarczyk. "Two completely different people, different types of appearance, different – now I think perhaps deliberately exaggerated – ways of talking. Yet the identical sight defect – a slight astigmatism – and a one hundred-per-cent identical way of adjusting your spectacles. Leaning your heads to the left, frowning and blinking, straightening the frames with both hands, and ending by pressing them to your nose with your thumb.

"As we're on the subject of my daughter," said the prosecutor, smiling at the thought of his little princess, "fathers and daughters are linked by an exceptional, special bond. That also set me thinking, when during our one conversation you leaped on me to defend Miss Kwiatkowska. In the first instant I thought you were lovers, only later did I understand. As often happens when some things go wrong, everything does. When some things start to fall into place, everything else does too. At the same time, it turned out Henryk Telak was mixed up in Kamil Sosnowski's murder, though he didn't do it with his own hands – perhaps that case will be passed on for a separate hearing, and you'll be interviewed again." Szacki was lying through his teeth – he knew nothing would be 'passed on for a separate hearing', and even if it was, the matter would be hushed up within a week. The whole time he took great care not to say or let any of the others say anything that could mean he'd have to launch an inquiry into the murder case from the past.

"The police checked the civil-registry files. Barbara Jarczyk, born in 1945, and Włodzimierz Sosnowski, born in 1944, got married young, in 1964, when she was only just nineteen. A year later their son Kamil was born. The same year Euzebiusz Kaim was born too, his later friend at primary school, high school and college. The boys were five when Hanna Sosnowska was born. When Kamil died tragically in September 1987, his family went abroad – is that right?"

Rudzki shrugged.

"What else could we do in that situation?"

"They probably came back in the mid-1990s, because that's when the next entries appear in the civil registry. Barbara and Włodzimierz Sosnowski got divorced. She went back to her maiden name. He became Cezary Rudzki – the officials had no problem acceding to his request because Mr Sosnowski had published under that pseudonym before 1989 and had also used that name in France. Hanna Sosnowska married Marcin Kwiatkowski, but her marriage didn't last long; they divorced in 1998, but she kept her husband's name. I don't know if all this name-shuffling resulted from the fact that you were already planning your revenge then, or whether it was an accident that later turned out to be an unexpected gift."

"The latter," said Rudzki.

"As I suspected. As for Mr Kaim, in the first instant, when I read the death notice from 1987 signed 'Zibi', I didn't twig at all that it could come from the name 'Euzebiusz' – after all, 'Zibi' was the nickname of Zbigniew Boniek, the football player, and sometimes it's short for Zygmunt. Only later, when I hit upon the idea that you were all tied together, did I remember the name 'Zibi'. The police easily checked where you were at school and college, and with whom. Your friends confirmed that you and Kamil were practically joined at the hip. Am I right?"

Kaim smiled and made a gesture as if removing the hat from his head.

"I hang my hat up to you," he said.

"The phrase is 'take my hat off to you', birdbrain," muttered Kwiatkowska.

Prosecutor Teodor Szacki didn't feel like saying more. He knew one of the people present would leave the gloomy room in handcuffs. He'd have to press charges on the others too, but for the mental harassment of Telak and for obstructing the inquiry rather than for collaborating in murder. After all, only one of them had run into Telak that night, only one of them had killed him. The rest, even if they had desired his death and wanted to cause it, did not take a direct part in it. But there was another reason why Szacki didn't feel like saying more – yet again, his human conscience had clashed painfully with his civil servant's conscience. He thought of Kamil Sosnowski's corpse – the bloody body in the bathtub, with his hands and feet tied from behind. He thought of the body of Kasia Telak, stuffed full of pills. He thought of Bartek Telak, rapidly heading towards the end of his life. He believed the girl would not have died or the boy fallen ill if it weren't for the terrible deed their father had once let happen, cynically and with calculation, in order to win their mother. How had it happened? Then, in the 1980s? He couldn't ask about that. Not now. He wasn't even free to mention it.

"Can we sit down now?" asked Kaim.

"No," replied Szacki. "Because we still don't know the answer to the most important question. And Mr Rudzki hasn't finished his statement." At the last moment he bit his tongue because he almost said "his story".

"I'd prefer to do it sitting down," said the therapist, and looked at Szacki in a way that made the prosecutor frown. Something wasn't right. Something definitely wasn't right. He felt he might be losing his grip on it all, that Rudzki was planning a dodge he couldn't control, but it would be preserved on tape and he'd never be able to hush any of it up. Concentrate, Teodor, he kept telling himself. He agreed to let them sit down, in order to gain time. Soon they were sitting in a semicircle, so that the camera could see all of them. But Szacki was imperceptibly starting to tremble, because he still didn't know what was wrong.

"The whole idea was mine," Rudzki began. "It was I, through a totally incredible accident, who found out why my son had been killed and by whom. At first I tried to come to terms with it, to rationalize it – after all, I am a trained psychologist, the time I've spent supervising patients adds up to years by now. But I couldn't – I couldn't. Then I simply wanted to kill him – go and shoot him and forget about it. But that would have been too simple. My son was tortured for two days, and that bastard was going to die in a split second? Impossible.

"I thought about it at length, at great length. How to do it to make him suffer. Suffer so much that he'd finally decide on his own death, being unable to take the pain any more. So I thought up the therapy. I knew it might not work, that Telak wouldn't commit suicide, and would go home as if nothing had happened. And I agreed to that. I agreed, because I knew that after the therapy he would go on suffering like that for ever.

"That night I couldn't get to sleep. I walked up and down my room and wondered: has he done it? Has he swallowed the pills yet? Has he gone to sleep yet? Is he dead yet? Finally I went out into the corridor and crept up to his door. It was quiet. I was revelling in that silence, when I heard a rush of running water, and Telak came out of the bathroom at the far end of the corridor. He was pale, but unarguably alive. He frowned when he saw me, and asked what I was doing at his door. I lied, saying I was worried about him. He didn't comment, but just said he was breaking off the therapy and getting as far as bloody well possible from this whole fucking shambles – I'm sorry, but I'm quoting him.

"And he went into the room for his suitcase. I didn't know what to do. Not only was he still alive, he didn't even look like someone dying of pain and guilt. It had all flowed off that bastard like water off a duck's back. I went into the kitchen to have a drink of water and calm down, and I saw that skewer... beyond that I can hardly remember a thing, my brain refuses to admit those images. I went to the classroom, and he was there. I think I tried to explain to him why I was doing this and who I really am, but when I saw that hateful face, that cynical glint in his eye, that mocking sneer... I just struck out. Oh God, forgive me for doing it. Forgive me for not feeling guilty. Forgive me, Jadwiga, for murdering the father of your children, regardless of who he was."

With a dramatic gesture, Cezary Rudzki – or rather Włodzimierz Sosnowski – hid his face in his hands. Now the room should have been filled with a silence thick enough to cut and impale on a skewer, but it was the middle of the city. An old Fiat 126 was rattling its way down Łazienkowska Street, a clapped-out Ikarus bus came to a noisy halt at the bus stop near the church, the Vistula Highway roared monotonously, someone's heels clattered, and a child cried as its mother told it off – but even so Teodor Szacki could hear everything clicking into place in his head. The human conscience and the prosecutor's conscience, he thought, then hesitated, but only for a millisecond, before nodding to Kuzniecow, who stood up and switched off the camera. Then he went out and soon returned with two policemen in uniform, who led Rudzki away.

Without handcuffs, in spite of everything.

12

Monday, 18th July 2005

International Courts and Prosecution Day. Abroad, a court in Belgrade sentences the notorious Milorad "Legija" Ulemek to forty years in prison for assassinating the Prime Minister of Serbia, Zoran Djindjić, in 2003. Saddam Hussein is formally charged at last, for the time being with the extermination of a Shi'ite village in 1982. Roman Polanski testifies from Paris to a London court in a case against *Vanity Fair*, which wrote that straight after the tragic death of his wife, Sharon Tate, he had tried to seduce a Swedish beauty queen. In Poland a court in Wrocław bans a publishing company from printing *Mein Kampf*, and the Prosecution Service in Białystok charges left-wing politician Aleksandra Jakubowska with falsifying a draft media law. In Warsaw the prosecutor demands a life sentence for a former shop assistant accused of a mysterious murder at a shop called "Ultimo". Her lawyer calls for an acquittal. Apart from that, on Stawki Street a plaque is unveiled in honour of the Home Army soldiers who liberated nearly fifty Jews during the first few hours of the Warsaw Uprising, and the Zachęta Gallery decides to advertise itself via sweets that will be sold in grocery shops. The Palace of Culture and Science is getting ready for a big fête on 22nd July, when it will be fifty years old. Twenty-five degrees, no rain and actually cloudless.

I

It was a few minutes after three p.m. Prosecutor Teodor Szacki was sitting in his office, revelling in the silence, which had fallen the moment his colleague had rushed off to take her child to an allergy expert. He had made no comment. Her departure meant he didn't have to go on listening to Katie Melua oozing out of her computer ("I hope it won't disturb you if it's just on very quietly?") and the conversations she had with her mother on the phone ("So tell them that for eight hundred zlotys you can carve the letters on Daddy's stone yourself. Tell them that. Crooks, bodysnatchers, grave robbers").

Exactly a month ago Cezary Rudzki had been taken away by the police from the monastery on Łazienkowska Street. A few days later Szacki had interrogated him in the "inquiry against Cezary Rudzki". The therapist had repeated word for word what he had said in front of the camera in the classroom, and the prosecutor had written it all down precisely, pretending to accept it all as the honest truth. However, he did have to ask why Rudzki was so convinced of Telak's guilt. What did he know about the background to his son's murder?

"As I said earlier, it was an accident, one of the thousands of inexplicable coincidences that we run into every day," said Rudzki, dressed in beige prison uniform in the interview room at the remand centre on Rakowiecka Street. He looked a hundred years old, and not even a hint of his proud posture and piercing gaze was left. "I was giving therapy to a man suffering from bone cancer, in the terminal stage, and three months later he died. The man was poor, from the lower social orders, and I took him on for free as a favour for a friend at the Oncology Institute. He wanted to confess to someone. He was a criminal, a petty one really, petty and careful enough never to have ended up behind bars. He really only had one sin on his conscience – he had taken part in the murder of my son. He may not have laid hands on him directly, but he and the murderer had broken into our flat together, he had witnessed the torture and the killing. He shook with fear, he claimed they'd only been paid to frighten him and rough him up, but in the end his 'boss' had decided they had to rub Kamil out 'just in case'. It was a shock. I came completely unstuck before this bandit, and told him who I was – we cried together for hours. He promised to help me find his 'contractor'. He gave me an exact description of him, and all the circumstances of their meetings, all their conversations. He said it might have been about a woman, because one time the contractor had let it escape that 'now he'd be able to get her'. At once I thought of Jadwiga – Kamil was madly in love with her, though she was a few years older than him. I found her and also took Telak's photo. The man recognized him one hundred and twenty per cent."

Teodor Szacki wrote down the suspect's lies word for word, without so much as batting an eyelid. Rudzki signed the statement, also without the slightest wince. They both knew the danger to their families if the truth were revealed – and above all if an inquiry were initiated. However, when it was all over Szacki told the old therapist what he knew about Henryk Telak's work in the Communist security services, about the "department of death" and about the still-operative SB organization. And asked for the truth.

The patient with bone cancer was real, so was his guilt and his confession. The accidentally overheard remark about how "now he'd be able to get her" was also true. But the instruction was different. They were supposed to terrify and rough up the boy "as firmly as possible" – which was tantamount to an order to kill – so that his father would desist from activities that could damage state security. They were persuaded that it was a matter of the highest importance, that they'd be heroes, that perhaps they'd be secretly decorated. They didn't give a shit about being decorated. For carrying out the job they got a pile of cash and a guarantee of impunity, and could also plunder from the flat anything that took their fancy. At the start, when no specifics were mentioned, they had met with three officers, including Telak. Then Telak had seen them twice more on his own. He had given them all the details, the exact date and time, and instructed them how they were to tie him up and hurt him.

On completing the job, when they came for their money, he'd been very upset. He said there had been a mistake in the reconnaissance. He gave them more than they were initially going to receive, and warned them that if they didn't disappear for two years without trace, someone else would find them the way they had found the boy. So they had vanished.

Szacki told him what he had heard from Karol Wenzel: the activities of Department "D" were so top-secret that mistakes really did occur in the reconnaissance and in sending people out on operations. The hired thugs also made mistakes. That was probably how Telak could justify within the firm the fact that an innocent man had been murdered. Oh dear, an accident at work.

The prosecutor and the therapist shook hands in parting and embraced sincerely. They both owed each other something. Above all, silence.

Two weeks after the interrogation at the remand centre, Cezary Rudzki died. He had felt ill and been taken to an isolation cell, where he felt even worse. He died before the ambulance arrived. A massive heart attack. Teodor Szacki would even have believed it was an accident, if not for the fact that next day a courier brought him a bottle of twenty-four-year-old whisky. He poured the whole lot down the sink and threw the bottle in the waste bin by the pedestrian crossing near the prosecutor's office. He'd been expecting it. He had believed that SB bastard when he'd said he and his colleagues only stepped in if there was no alternative. And he believed they preferred peace. But a man in prison is not a guarantee of that kind of peace. He gets too bored, he talks too much, it's all too likely that one day he might think his freedom is worth a bit of a risk. Could Szacki feel safe himself? As long as he did nothing stupid, he probably could. He didn't go to the funeral.

That same day he had called Monika. Though he mentally cursed himself for his own stupidity, someone was guiding his hand as it dialled the number, and someone else spoke the words for him, suggesting they meet. Since then he had met with the journalist on several occasions, and although each time Szacki drove to see her, convinced it was their final meeting, and that this time he had to break off the affair because it made no sense, he had less and less control over it. He was afraid of what would happen next, but also curious about it.

He switched off the computer and realized there really was nothing to do. Chorko was on leave, people had left the city for their summer holidays, and Warsaw had temporarily stopped being the capital of crime. The indictment against Kaim, Jarczyk, Kwiatkowska and Mrs Telak was almost complete. He had shifted the burden of guilt onto Rudzki, which allowed him to charge the rest with nothing but withholding information from the organs of the judiciary. He also hid the fact that on the night of the murder the therapist and his patients had stood over the corpse and wondered what to do. According to the official version of Telak's murder, Kwiatkowska, Jarczyk and Kaim had only found out when Barbara Jarczyk found the body on Sunday morning. He rarely admired criminals, but when he discovered that Rudzki had forbidden them to talk about it and told them all to behave at breakfast as if they didn't know a thing – so they'd come out as well as possible later during their interviews – he almost bowed his head. In the hands of a murderer, knowledge of the human psyche is the most powerful weapon.

He had always thought the penal code existed so that anyone who broke it could be punished with full severity by the state – so that others would clearly see what was the outcome of crime. Now here he was falsifying the case of Henryk Telak's murder to the advantage of the people mixed up in the inquiry. And he was disgusted with himself, because he knew this wasn't going to make up for his greatest fault – giving up. Because he had no intention of doing anything that might strike at "OdeSB".

He picked up the receiver. He wanted to talk to Weronika and Helka, who since Saturday had been sunbathing at Olecko in the Mazurian lakes, and he preferred to do it now than for his wife to call at the exact time when he'd be at Monika's.

He was halfway through dialling the number when someone came into his office. It was Jadwiga Telak.

II

Sad as usual, elegant as usual, in the first instant colourless as usual, but soon making a dazzling impression.

As she took a cigarette out of her handbag he almost snorted with laughter. How did it go? And of all the lousy offices of all the underpaid prosecutors in this rotten city, she had to come into mine. He took an ashtray out of the drawer and lit up himself. That's my second, he thought out of habit, though since his encounter in the Italian restaurant he had stopped rationing the smokes. He didn't speak, he just waited.

"You know, don't you?" she said.

He nodded. Not from early on, but when they'd all met a month ago in the classroom at the architectural monstrosity on Łazienkowska Street, he knew. Because he trusted Wróbel when he claimed that none of the participants in a constellation would be inclined to commit murder, because such an act would destroy the order. And the constellation works because the participants strive towards order. Because she was the one who had the most to gain from her husband's death – in terms of life, emotionally and financially. Because during the murder she said she'd been watching a film on television that – as he later checked – was on the day before. Because she said she had listened to her son playing racing cars in his room, when Bartek was banging away at *Call of Duty*. The sounds of machine guns, exploding grenades and the groans of dying soldiers could not be confused with the roar of engines. Just circumstantial evidence. A bit of intuition. The memorable remark: "If someone in the constellation seems to be good and someone else bad, it's almost always the other way around." And the itching in his head when Cezary Rudzki took the blame on himself.

"I thought now that the case is closed, you are owed some explanation."

He said nothing more. He didn't feel like it.

"I don't know if you have ever been in love. Really and truly. If you have, you're a lucky man. If not, I envy you like the devil, because you have the greatest adventure of your life ahead of you – perhaps. Do you know what I'm talking about? It's like with books. It was great to read *The Master and Margarita* at grammar school, but I'm green with envy to think there are adults who still have that ahead of them. I sometimes wonder: what would it be like to read Bulgakov for the first time now? Never mind. Anyway, if you want to reply: 'I don't know', it means you haven't loved yet."

Curious, he thought, that's just how I'd answer, if I felt like talking. He shrugged.

"I have loved. I was twenty-five when I met and fell in love, reciprocally, with Kamil Sosnowski. He was three years younger. It makes me want to laugh when I think I couldn't sleep because of the age difference. I was afraid those three years would spoil it all. The whole time I was afraid something else would spoil it, that it was impossible, that such things didn't happen. There's no point in my describing it to you – that state of mind is indescribable. But you should know that almost twenty years have gone by, and I can still describe every moment of our friendship just as it happened and repeat every remark we uttered, word for word. I can remember what books we read and what films we watched. Every last little detail."

She lit another cigarette. Szacki no longer felt like smoking.

"Do you know, he was waiting for me that day? We had arranged to meet for supper. He was going to whip up some food, and I was going to get hold of something to drink and a 'Warsaw Delight'. Do you remember those? Chocolatey stuff with broken wafers inside, a bit like a big fairy cake crossed with a Wedel's Medley. Our magic pudding. Other people have special songs, we had our 'Delight'.

"When I ran over to his place, deliriously happy, they were already there. I knocked and knocked, but no one opened the door. I stood there for an hour, maybe two, but no one came. I went home and called every half hour. I knew something must have happened and he'd had to leave with his parents and sister, but I still kept calling and going round there. When I called for the umpteenth time, Hanna answered. You can imagine the rest for yourself. At least try. The worst thing was knowing he'd been there all the time, and that they were there, bullying him. If only it had entered my stupid head to call the militia… everything might have been different."

Szacki lit up after all. What else did he have to do? Somehow he couldn't get worked up about this melodrama.

"In a way I died with him. Henryk was at my side the whole time. Tender, sympathetic, understanding, ready to forgive anything. He didn't interest me, but he was there. I got used to him. I married him. I soon fell pregnant. Kasia was born and I started living for her. Then Bartek. Sometimes it was better, sometimes worse. That's family life. It ended with Kasia's death. I'm ashamed, but if I could resurrect just one person, it would be Kamil. And then his father appeared, damn him, with his truth and his justice. I wish that day had never dawned."

She lit another cigarette, and the small room was filled with smoke. Combined with the oppressive heat, it was getting unbearable.

"I don't know why I went to Łazienkowska Street that evening. I can't explain it. But I went. I came in as he was packing. He confessed to me what he'd found out during the constellation. He was badly shaken, crying and saying he'd almost committed suicide. I thought that was the best thing he could have done, and I asked if he shouldn't complete the therapy, for Bartek's sake. He refused to. I ran out of his room and went into the kitchen for a drink of water, because I thought I was going to be sick. You know what happened after that."

Not long ago, in spite of everything, he would have wanted to take her to court. Now he didn't care. So much so that he didn't even feel like responding. She went on staring at him in silence, nodded her head and stood up.

"I'd like to know, were your motives for the deed purely emotional?" he finally asked.

She just smiled and left.

Prosecutor Teodor Szacki got up from his chair, took off his jacket, opened the window wide and tipped the dog-ends from the ashtray into the bin. He opened the drawer to put the ashtray away, and his gaze fell on a piece of paper where he'd written out an extract from a newspaper interview with Bert Hellinger, probably from *Gazeta Wyborcza*.

I'm always being asked to condemn the perpetrators of all sorts of crimes, but I know the only way to cope with the presence of evil is to admit that they are people too, in spite of everything. We should find a place in our hearts for them as well. For our own good. That doesn't free them of responsibility for their acts in the least. But if we exclude someone, we deny them the right to belong, we put ourselves in the place of God, we decide who is to live and who not. And that is quite extraordinary.

III

On the way to Monika's place in Chomiczówka he stopped at Wilson Square to buy two cream puffs at Blikle's patisserie – those were their favourite cakes. As he stood in the queue, he thought about Jadwiga Telak and her Warsaw Delight, and felt very, very tired. Tired by this case, tired by his work, tired by the lover who didn't really entirely interest him. There was something missing again, but what?

Justice, he thought, and was startled by this idea. It sounded as if someone next to him had said it aloud. He looked round, but the Żoliborz old-age pensioners were standing meekly in line, examining the cold counter full of pastries and the shelves full of cakes in mute concentration. Justice, meaning what? He hoped the voice would answer him. But this time he didn't hear words – instead an image appeared. The image of the metal cylinder from which he had extracted the twenty-four-year-old whisky. He thought of Karol Wenzel, who lived on the way to Monika's. Maybe he should pay him a call? Maybe there was a way to deal with the senders of exclusive Scotch? What was the harm in checking? Surely a chat with a slightly nutty historian was too little for them to rub him out?

He bought the cream puffs, called Wenzel, who happened to be at home, and drove up to the house on Żeromski Street.

As he was getting out, he took the cakes with him; he felt silly turning up empty-handed. He was walking towards the stairwell between the garages and a dustbin, when a little girl Helka's age came flying out of a side alley on a scooter, almost ramming into him. He jumped out of the way, but the handlebars caught on the packet of cakes. The paper tore open, and one of the cakes fell out and smashed on the tarmac. The little girl, really very like his daughter, stopped, and when she saw the cake lying on the wrinkled tarmac, the corners of her mouth turned down in dismay.

"I'm terribly sorry, little one," he said quickly. "I didn't see you coming, I was miles away and I whacked you with my cakes. Are you all right?"

She nodded, but there were tears in her eyes.

"Phew, that's a relief. I was afraid one of my cream puffs might have hurt you. Do you know, cream puffs can get really cross? They suddenly go for you, just like weasels. That's why I keep them in this packet. But perhaps this one's not dangerous – what do you think?" He leaned tentatively over the cream puff and prodded it with a finger.

The little girl laughed. He took the surviving cake out of the torn packet and handed it to her.

"Have it to say sorry," he said. "But eat it carefully so it doesn't get cross."

The little girl looked round uncertainly, said thank you, took the cream puff and rode away, finding it hard to keep her balance. She really was very like Helka. Did he really want to go and see Karol Wenzel, dig up the case and risk the lives of his loved ones? He remembered what the historian had said during their conversation: "So if you're thinking of getting at them in any way, back off right now. Think about it in the morning, and in the evening you'll be crying over your daughter's body."

And he froze.

He hadn't told him he had a daughter.

He thought about little Helka Szacka, about the smell of fresh bread and about a skull opening with a hideous squelch on the dissection table.

Only seconds earlier he'd been sure this story had to have a continuation.

He was wrong.

Author's note

My sincere thanks to the prosecutors who told me about their difficult and, unfortunately, underappreciated work. I hope they do not bear me any grudges for the things I have invented or twisted to make reality fit the needs of fiction. My thanks too to Dorota Kowalska of *Newsweek* for her article 'In the Service of Crime', without which this book would have been completely different. To those interested in constellation therapy I recommend Bert Hellinger's *Ordnungen der Liebe* (*The Orders of Love*) (Carl-Auer-Systeme Verlag, Heidelberg 2001), and to anyone wanting to know more about the secret services in Communist Poland, Henryk Głębocki's excellent *Policja tajna przy robocie* (*The Secret Police at Work*) (Arcana, Kraków 2005).